BRUSH WITH DEATH

AN ART LOVER'S MYSTERY

Hailey Lind

A SIGNET BOOK

SIGNET
Published by New American Library, a division of
Penguin Group (USA) Inc., 375 Hudson Street,
New York, New York 10014, USA
Penguin Group (Canada), 90 Eglinton Avenue East, Suite 700, Toronto,
Ontario M4P 2Y3, Canada (a division of Pearson Penguin Canada Inc.)
Penguin Books Ltd., 80 Strand, London WC2R 0RL, England
Penguin Ireland, 25 St. Stephen's Green, Dublin 2,
Ireland (a division of Penguin Books Ltd.)
Penguin Group (Australia), 250 Camberwell Road, Camberwell, Victoria 3124,
Australia (a division of Pearson Australia Group Pty. Ltd.)
Penguin Books India Pvt. Ltd., 11 Community Centre, Panchsheel Park,
New Delhi - 110 017, India
Penguin Group (NZ), 67 Apollo Drive, Rosedale, North Shore 0745,
Auckland, New Zealand (a division of Pearson New Zealand Ltd.)
Penguin Books (South Africa) (Pty.) Ltd., 24 Sturdee Avenue,
Rosebank, Johannesburg 2196, South Africa

Penguin Books Ltd., Registered Offices:
80 Strand, London WC2R 0RL, England

First published by Signet, an imprint of New American Library,
a division of Penguin Group (USA) Inc.

First Printing, July 2007
10 9 8 7 6 5 4 3 2 1

Acknowledgments

Thanks are due to so many people! To the women and men of the FBI for answering a multitude of strange and suspicious questions about art crime, criminal enterprise, and firearms; to Chapel of the Chimes and in particular Allison Rodman, whose warmth adds to that of this beautiful and peaceful place; to Susan Baker and Bee Enos, RNs willing to discuss all sorts of ways to kill people and not think less of the one inquiring. Special thanks to Shay for Pete's malapropisms and the mud slide, and so much else. To Kendall, for her smile and her sweet friendship through the years. To Camille Minichino, Margaret Dumas, Simon Wood, Ann Parker, and all the Sisters (and Brothers) in Crime. To our extended family for a truly boisterous welcome in Seattle, and Sherri at the lounge at the Sixth Avenue Inn—a patient and wondrous waitress. To Chris Casnelli, Scott Casper, Anita Fellman, Steve Lofgren, Sandra Pryor, Anna Cabrera, Mary Grae, Suzanne Chan, Pamela Groves, Jan Strout, and the entire Mira Vista Social Club (including honorary members) for unflagging friendship. To Kristin Lindstrom, agent extraordinaire, and Kerry Donovan, editor nonpareil. To Bob and Jane Lawes, Susan

Lawes, Sergio Klor de Alva, and Malcolm Martin for—
well, everything. And finally, to all the independent book
merchants who keep books and those who read and write
them alive, armed only with stubborn tenacity, a passion
for reading, and a whole lot of humor!

Chapter 1

He who possesses most must be most afraid of loss.

—Leonardo da Vinci (1452–1519),
Italian painter and inventor

He who hungers most must be most afraid of a buffet.

—Georges LeFleur (1932–   ), art forger extraordinaire

The sweet-faced boy, one arm curled around his cocker spaniel puppy, paid no attention to the swaying and bobbing of the sagging helium balloons near the doorway. Fluffy brown teddy bears, shiny toy trucks, and wooden alphabet blocks lay at his feet, but Louis Spencer didn't notice them. He never would.

Louis Jonathan Spencer, "Our Sweet Angel," had died in 1937 at the age of six.

"I can't believe his family still leaves toys for him after all these years," I whispered.

"They don't."

The young woman finished measuring the doorway with a heavy carpenter's tape and jotted the dimensions on a pad of paper. With a delicate frown of concentration, she clicked her ballpoint pen closed, stuck it under the hinge of her clipboard, and stowed the items in a large canvas carryall.

Picking up a complicated-looking camera the size of her head, she squatted and began snapping photos of the many offerings to the memory of Louis Spencer.

"The crypt's not even endowed," she continued. "That's why it's falling apart."

The camera's insistent strobe light flashed through the night's darkness, lending the pyramid-shaped stone-and-concrete crypt an incongruous disco effect. In the sporadic illumination I caught glimpses of the interior beyond the rusty wrought-iron gate. A broken stained glass window in the shape of a cross with a rose in the center bowed under its own weight, and had been protected from further disintegration by an overlay of cheap chicken wire. Despite the damage and makeshift repair, I could easily imagine sunlight cascading in through the window, filling the crypt's interior with the soft brilliance of fine jewels.

Near the door an intricate floor mosaic was covered with a thin layer of mud and leaves, while bald patches in the abstract pattern revealed that dozens of the exquisite blue and metallic gold ceramic tiles had long since been lost or destroyed. The marble figure of little Louis Spencer, embracing his beloved dog, was missing two fingers and bloomed with a bad case of greenish white lichen. My own fingers itched to restore the water-stained canvas of angels that sagged from the steep ceiling.

"I'm Cindy Tanaka," the young woman said as she dismantled her camera and packed it, piece by piece, into a large black leather bag. "I'm writing my dissertation at Cal on the phenomenon of public grieving. Louis Spencer's crypt has become a place for strangers to make offerings to a little boy who died before most of them were even born. What are you doing here at this hour?"

"My name's Annie Kincaid," I said. "I'm restoring some paintings at the Chapel of the Chimes next door."

"That right?" Cindy's cool, dark eyes swept over me. Her pencil-slim figure was clad in pressed khaki chinos, a crisp white blouse, and spotless striped espadrilles, and her straight black hair was swept off her smooth forehead with a wide pink band. My not-so-lithe figure was dressed in its usual business attire: a paint-stained black T-shirt, faded denim overalls, and scruffy running shoes worn without socks. My curly brown hair was piled in a messy knot on top of my head, anchored by an artist's paintbrush. My chic friend Samantha, a jewelry designer, had complimented my use of the brush as "fashion-forward," but the truth was I could never find bobby pins when I needed them.

"Nice to meet you." As I held out my right hand, I noticed the tips of my fingers were stained a virulent shade from the vermilion I had been using while painting angels' robes, and my thumb was smeared with the burnt umber glaze I used for antiquing.

Cindy shook my multihued hand with her firm, clean one. We gazed into the crypt, our flashlights illuminating slices of the inky interior.

"What's with the Egyptian motif? I noticed another pyramid nearby, as well."

"It was popular in the twenties and thirties, when a lot of the Great Pyramid excavations were going on. I'm trying to decipher some of the hieroglyphs, but I think they're mainly decorative," Cindy mused. "It's funny, there's something special about this crypt. People bring things here all the time. A lot of them sit for a while, meditating or praying or talking to themselves. Sometimes they let me take their pictures."

"Is it open to visitors?" I asked, nodding at the bouquets of flowers and small toys strewn about the floor.

"No, they throw those things through the bars. Bayview Cemetery keeps the crypts locked. There's no telling what would happen if they didn't. Speaking of which, how did you get past the front gates?"

"I'm working nights, so I've got a master key," I said, playing my flashlight's beam across the interior of little Louis' sepulcher. "I was taking a break when I noticed your light up here on the hill and got curious. But what are—"

I squeaked, jumped, and dropped the light.

"Something wrong?" Cindy asked, frowning.

"Sorry, I thought I saw something move." My heart pounded as I bent to retrieve the light from the lap of a drooping Raggedy Ann doll. I pointed the beam through the gate but everything was still. "Guess it's just my imagination."

"Cemeteries at night," Cindy said with a shrug as she crouched down to zip up the camera bag. "A lot of people get jumpy. It was probably just a rat."

"That's a comforting thought," I murmured.

"Don't worry, it's locked up tight," she said, with a hint of condescension. She grabbed the gate and rattled it to prove her point. "Believe me, no one could possibly—"

Something leapt out from behind the bronze urn next to the sepulcher. I caught a glimpse of a distorted green face and shrank against the cold stone wall as a tall figure barreled toward us. Throwing one shoulder against the wrought-iron gate, the ghoul burst through, knocking Cindy flat on the ground, and tore down the curved access road, its long, dark cape flapping in the breeze. Swearing a blue streak, Cindy scrambled to her feet and gave chase, all five feet, one hundred pounds of her. Graceful as a gazelle, she took off like a cross-country runner, leaping over grave markers and zigzagging around monuments until she was nearly abreast of the fleeing creature. Scampering onto the roof of a burial chamber burrowed into a hillside, Cindy hurled herself onto the ghoul's back, sending them both sprawling into the shallow drainage ditch at the side of the road.

I sprinted toward the dark forms as they thrashed and rolled and emitted muffled shrieks. Cindy seemed to be holding her own, but when I was still twenty yards away the ghoul broke free and half ran, half hobbled toward the main gates, shielding its face with the cape.

"Cindy! Are you all right?" I cried as I helped her to her feet.

"Go after him!"

"Are you *insane*?"

"We can't let him get away!"

"I don't think—"

"*Dammit!*" Cindy swore as we watched the ghoul disappear into a grove of fragrant eucalyptus trees at the edge of the cemetery. She was covered in mud and grass stains, and her pink headband had fallen out. A green rubber Halloween mask of an elongated, howling face dangled from two fingers. "*Shit!* Why didn't you follow him?"

"Because he was hiding in a *crypt*!"

"Did you at least get a good look at him?" she asked, her lips pressed together in dissatisfaction.

I closed my eyes. "Tall. Thin. Green."

"I know that," she said waspishly, shaking the Halloween mask at me.

"I think he had white hair," I offered, recalling a glimpse of stringy hair on the neck of the retreating figure.

"Are you sure it wasn't a wig?"

"I guess I wasn't, um, focusing," I said. My artist's eye usually took note of anatomical details, but during midnight encounters with graveyard ghouls all bets were off. I looked at Cindy warily. What kind of a person tackled a ghoul in a cemetery?

"I'd like to know what he was up to," Cindy muttered, brushing dirt from her blouse.

"You said people liked to hang out here," I replied, rescuing her pink headband from the ditch and shaking off some leaves. "Isn't that what you're writing your dissertation on?"

"Respectable people hang out at crypts in the daytime. At night you're looking at a whole different breed. We're talking druggies or Satan worshippers."

Ick, I thought.

"Still," she continued. "Junkies and Dark Lord types don't wear cheesy Halloween masks and capes."

"What's that?" I asked as my flashlight beam illuminated a rectangular object the size of a shoe box lying in the grass a few feet away.

"I *thought* that guy dropped something," Cindy said, picking it up.

It was a dull gray metal box, rusted in spots, with a small, keyed latch. The sole embellishment was a simple cross with a rose in the center, echoing the design of the stained glass window in Louis Spencer's crypt.

"Is it—um—an urn or something?" I quelled a desire to flee as I envisioned a tornado of ashes bursting out of the box and devouring us.

"I doubt it. I've never seen an urn like this."

We stared at the box for a moment.

"Let's go back and check out the crypt," Cindy said with a determined look on her face. She started marching up the hill toward Louis Spencer's final resting place.

I reluctantly fell in step. For the past few weeks I had been restoring two murals in the Chapel of the Chimes Columbarium, adjacent to Bayview Cemetery. As I learned only after I accepted the job, a columbarium is similar to a mausoleum but holds urns of cremated remains, known in the business as "cremains." Designed in the early twentieth century by the renowned architect Julia Morgan, Oakland's Chapel of the Chimes was a glorious Romanesque-Gothic building decorated with fabulous mosaics, colorful murals, and elaborate carvings.

One of the commission's stipulations was that I paint at night to minimize the disruption to the columbarium's visitors. Disconcerted at the idea of working in the midst of grieving families, I had been happy to oblige. But adjusting to the swing shift had been more of a challenge than I'd anticipated, and halfway through the evening I often fought waves of drowsiness. Twenty minutes ago I had taken a break from the neck-breaking work to get some fresh air. I had not bargained on encountering Cindy— much less a masked ghoul—and at the moment wanted nothing more than to return to the restoration. Paint, unlike so many other things in my life, was eminently predictable.

"I hate to be a party pooper, Cindy, but I need to get back to work," I said as we skirted a lush pond dotted with water lilies and edged with aromatic hyacinths. "I don't want to leave you out here by yourself, though. Why don't you investigate the crypt tomorrow, during business hours?"

"What if he comes back tonight to finish the job?"

"That's what I'm afraid of."

"Aren't you the least bit curious about what that guy was doing in Louis Spencer's crypt?" Cindy asked, not slowing her pace one bit.

"Not if he was communing with the dead, I'm not."

"He wasn't communing with the dead, he was *stealing* from the dead."

"That makes me feel so much better."

She ignored me as we picked our way up the grassy hill and through the maze of headstones. Some of the markers were large and ostentatious, featuring sculpted angels and complex family lineages, while others were all the more poignant for their simplicity. When I began working here I had sought out the grave of the columbarium's architect, Julia Morgan. Morgan had been one of the best-known professional women of her day, and the first ever to be admitted to the École des Beaux-Arts in Paris. Morgan designed hundreds of buildings in the Bay Area, and spent more than twenty years working on the spectacular Hearst Castle on the California coast. In death, Morgan's name had been simply chiseled into an unpretentious block of granite along with other family members' names. I had sketched the plain memorial, hoping some of her talent and tenacity might rub off on me.

"I'll just wait out here," I told Cindy when we arrived at Louis Spencer's pyramid. I was not unduly skittish around the dead—so long as they were ensconced in urns or graves—but I wasn't as sanguine about the living. Especially when they wore masks and hung out in cemeteries robbing graves.

Cindy stood at the open gate, crossed her slender arms over her chest, and lifted one eyebrow in what I presumed was a supercool form of "double-dog dare ya." Apparently we'd time-warped back to the fifth grade.

"I'll stand guard if you want to poke around," I said, sticking to my guns. "But I am *not* going in there."

"Suit yourself."

The gate screeched as she swung it wide, and from my position of relative safety I peered inside as Cindy's flashlight beam swept the interior. On either side of the mosaic floor were two dusty Carrara marble benches flanked by massive bronze urns. Denuded branches bore witness to the long-dead floral sprays that had once filled the urns with symbols of life. Bright Egyptian funerary designs had been frescoed on the crumbling plaster walls. At the rear of the crypt was the lichen-covered sculpture of the boy and his dog resting atop Louis Spencer's sepulcher of dove-gray marble. Behind the tomb, weeping stone angels in scalloped wall niches watched over the boy, the drooping stained glass window between them. From the ceiling hung an ornate, and very dusty, bronze chandelier.

Louis Spencer had been a much-loved boy.

Cindy inspected the marble benches, the bronze urns, the weeping angels, and the sepulcher.

"No drug paraphernalia, no candles, no animal sacrifices," she muttered.

"Animal sacrifices?" I repeated, aghast.

"Wait a minute—*hell-o,* Betty . . ."

"Hello who?" I rasped, hoping she hadn't spotted something that had once been alive.

"I found some tools."

Curiosity got the better of me, and I slipped inside. On the floor between the sepulcher and the rear wall were a shiny new crowbar, a mallet, a hammer, and a chisel. Scuff marks in the dust and the tattered remnants of once-splendid cobwebs indicated the tools had been placed there recently. I shone my flashlight on the sepulcher. A marble panel on one end was crooked and showed fresh gouge marks, as though it had been removed and replaced.

"It looks like the box came from the sepulcher," I said. "See this panel here?"

The graduate student inspected the pry marks. "I think you're right. Let's open it."

"Absolutely not. I draw the line at opening graves. Besides, I don't want to be trapped in here if that guy comes back, do you?"

"I guess you're right," Cindy conceded. "But I don't want to leave the box here, either."

She tucked the metal box under one arm and we hurried out of the crypt. I slung the leather photography bag over my shoulder, Cindy grabbed her canvas carryall, and we wasted no time jogging down the hill to the main gates. Actually, the perky graduate student jogged, while I sort of stumbled, feeling the effects of my earlier sprint. Cindy unlocked the pedestrian gate and held it for me.

"What do you suppose is in the box?" I asked as I shut and locked the gate behind me.

"Beats me," she said with a shrug, popping the trunk of a yellow Volkswagen Cabriolet parked at the curb. "It's locked. We'd have to break into it to find out."

Our gaze held for a moment.

"That wouldn't be right," I said, superstitious enough to fear a curse from beyond the grave but rational enough to hide my fear behind ethics.

Cindy nodded. "Well, whatever it is belonged to little Louis. It's probably just an old G.I. Joe or something."

"G.I. Joes weren't made until after World War Two," I said, recalling last summer's "Toys Toys Toys!" exhibit at the Brock Museum in San Francisco. "More likely it's a Shirley Temple doll."

"Even for a boy?"

"Lead soldiers, maybe."

"A petrified gum ball, or whatever." Cindy wrapped the metal box in a bright orange beach towel emblazoned with the grinning face of Garfield the Cat, and nestled it between her camera bag and a cardboard file box. "I'll bring it to the cemetery office in the morning. They'll probably want to call the police."

I reached into my pocket and extracted one of the business cards I was so proud of.

TRUE/FAUX STUDIOS
ANNIE KINCAID, PROPRIETOR
FAUX FINISHES, MURALS, TROMPE L'OEIL
"NOT FOR THE FEINT OF ART ALONE"

"True/Faux Studios, huh?" Cindy said, pronouncing the name correctly.

"I'm restoring some paintings at the columbarium," I said. "Chasing goblins through graveyards is just a sideline."

"Really?" Her dark eyes assessed me. "Can I ask you a question about art?"

Artists—especially those who did restoration work—often felt a bit like a doctor at a cocktail party: complete strangers did not hesitate to demand instant, free appraisals. The sad truth was that most artists were not well schooled in art history, much less in the chemistry of paint, and seldom knew anything more esoteric than how to maintain a red sable paintbrush. (Rinse thoroughly with mineral spirits, wash with mild soap and water, apply brush conditioner, and never, *ever* lend it to your young nephews, even if they swear "to be supercareful this time, honest.")

"Shoot," I said.

"What do you know about a painting titled *La Fornarina*?"

"Raphael's *La Fornarina*? It's one of his most famous pieces, a portrait of his mistress, though some believe she was one of his patron's lovers. A couple of experts attribute it to his student, Giulio Romano, and not to Raphael at all."

I knew *La Fornarina* well, though not because of my academic training. In 1966, my illustrious scalawag of a grandfather, Georges François LeFleur, had been arrested for forging the Raphael masterpiece while working in Florence as an *angeli del fango*, or mud angel, on an otherwise selfless mission to save the city's art treasures from the flooding Arno River. Georges' last-minute escape from the clutches of the Italian Ministry of Culture—a swashbuckling tale involving a bighearted hooker, a sinister mime, and a hot-wired Ferrari—had established my grandfather as a player in the world of art forgery. As a child, it had been my favorite bedtime story.

"Interesting," Cindy said with a dainty frown. "But I was wondering if the *Fornarina* hanging in the columbarium— the one labeled a copy—might be genuine."

I laughed.

"I'm serious."

"*La Fornarina* is one of Italy's national treasures," I replied. "It hangs in the Barberini Palace in Rome, under tight security. I haven't seen the columbarium's copy, but there's no way it could be genuine. Not possible."

"How can you be so sure? People screw up all the time."

"That's true, but—"

"What about da Vinci's *Madonna of the Yarnwinder,* which was swiped off the wall of a Scottish castle during an estate tour a couple of years ago? Or those Qing Dynasty vases at Cambridge's Fitzwilliam Museum, which were left on a windowsill and smashed by a visitor tripping over his shoelaces?"

"Mistakes happen. . . ." I trailed off. Art security could be shockingly inadequate, but it was ludicrous to think *La Fornarina*—or any Old Master painting—was hanging in our local columbarium. In fact, it was strange that Cindy even knew what *La Fornarina* was. Most people's knowledge went only as far as *La Giaconda*—the Mona Lisa— and even then they would never assume what they saw was genuine outside of the protective, legitimizing casing of the Louvre.

On the other hand, she seemed to have a rare knowledge of the art world. How many people were familiar with the details of the shattered Qing Dynasty vases?

"Cindy, are you an art historian?"

"No, someone I know told me it might be real, and asked me to check it out. I did a little research on it, but I don't really know what I'm looking at."

"I really doubt—"

"What could it hurt to look at it?"

I shrugged. Why not?

Cindy reached into the trunk and extracted the clipboard from her tote, flipped up several sheets of paper, and pulled out a folded map of the columbarium's convoluted floor plan. Resting one foot on the car's bumper, she smoothed the map over the makeshift table of her elevated knee and pointed to an area highlighted in hot pink. "It's in the Alcove of the Allegories, past the Hall of the Cherubim, through the Corridor of the Saints, next to the Alcove of Tranquility."

Her cell phone rang out harshly in the night, and she pulled it from her pants pocket. Surprised at the sound of a giggle, I looked up from the map to see Cindy's serious face transformed into that of an ingénue. She turned her head away and murmured, giggled again, and hung up.

"I'm late. I was supposed to meet someone fifteen minutes ago. Why don't you take a look at the painting and we'll talk tomorrow?"

"Okay, but I guarantee you the Chapel of the Chimes does not have a multimillion-dollar masterpiece hanging on its walls. This place can scarcely afford *my* artwork, much less the great Raphael's."

She slammed the trunk shut. "Want me to see you into the building before I go?"

I had thirty pounds, several inches, and more than a few years on this young woman, yet she was offering me protection. I decided I liked Cindy Tanaka, despite her propensity for running after graveyard ghouls.

"Thanks, I'm fine."

"I'll call you tomorrow, then." She climbed into the Cabriolet, started up the engine, and disappeared down Piedmont Avenue.

Time to return to my work in the house of the dead.

Chapter 2

The painting is not on a surface, but on a plane which is imagined. . . . It is not physically there at all. It is an illusion, a piece of magic.

—Philip Guston (1913–1980), Canadian painter

If art is but illusion, why is art forgery a crime?

—Georges LeFleur

"Did you get lost *again*?"

Perched on ten-foot scaffolding in front of a half-circular lunette mural, my assistant Mary Grae held three paintbrushes in one hand and a smeared paint palette in the other, and cradled a cell phone to her ear with her shoulder. She interrupted her phone conversation to shout at me as I walked through the Chapel of the Madonna's carved stone Gothic archway.

"You said you'd be right back! I was *totally* freaking out!"

"Keep it down, Mare," I said, cringing as her voice bounced off the tiled floor and stained glass ceiling. For some reason—I'm sure a physicist could explain it, though I'd probably get bored halfway through—sound was magnified within the columbarium's alcoves but became lost or distorted around corners. Thus the tinkling of the garden fountains could be heard throughout the cloisters, but Mary and I had once gotten separated and couldn't find each other even though it turned out we were in chambers only a few yards apart.

Mary snapped her cell phone shut, set down her paint and brushes, and scampered down the scaffolding, landing light as a cat. "You left me here surrounded by *dead* people!"

"They're not dead people," I corrected. "They're ashes. A bone fragment or two at the most."

"Eeeeew. But they *used* to be people, right? And they're dead now, right?"

Busted on a technicality. The rooms of the columbarium were lined with thousands of small compartments that, to an apartment-dweller like me, resembled nothing so much as glass-fronted mailboxes. Each compartment held urns or decorative containers—some were ornamented ceramic vases, others were bronze cast in the shape of a book, as in "the story of one's life"—that stored the cremains. Here and there larger and more richly decorated "feature niches," glassed in on two sides, created windows between the alcoves.

The labyrinthine floor plan of the Chapel of the Chimes Columbarium had been designed to create a series of intimate spaces, each unique and elaborately adorned, to allow family and friends to visit their lost loved ones and reminisce in solitude. Alcoves and passageways branched off into more alcoves and passageways, some opening onto cloistered hallways or courtyard gardens, others leading to dead ends. When I first started working here I spent twenty minutes at the beginning of each painting session wandering around, turning this way and that, ducking down one blind alley after another until stumbling, seemingly at random, upon the Chapel of the Madonna, where Mary and I were restoring two water-damaged lunettes. I now had the route memorized, and only took a wrong turn when distracted.

"This place is creepy," Mary said, pawing through her backpack until she found a foil-wrapped burrito.

"This place is beautiful. It's also a great commission. And you shouldn't eat in here."

"That manager guy, Troy Whoozits, said I could."

"His name's Roy, not Troy, and he only said that because he thinks you're cute."

She shrugged. "He's kinda creepy too."

"No, he's not," I said, wondering why I was arguing. The columbarium's manager, Roy Cogswell, *was* kind of creepy. "Let's take your burrito into the garden, okay?"

Our footsteps tapped down the tiled halls until we reached a courtyard garden complete with a gurgling fountain, miniature palm trees, and a birdcage with two sleeping canaries. Three stories above us stars twinkled through the retractable glass roof. On nice days you could sit by the fountain, listen to the birds sing, enjoy a pleasant breeze from above, and imagine yourself in a sunny courtyard in the south of Spain.

Until you remembered all those "cremains."

Sinking onto a marble bench, Mary unwrapped her whole-wheat vegetarian burrito and took a healthy bite. My assistant's outfit tonight consisted of a short black skirt over ripped black jeans, a black lace camisole topped by a ripped see-through gauze tunic, a black-and-silver studded leather belt with silver chains, and black fingerless gloves. The sole exception to Mary's monochromatic look was her long blond hair, which hung loose down her back, and her bright blue eyes, outlined with a thick line of kohl.

Mary was nearly six feet tall, wore heavy motorcycle boots, and could kick some serious butt. Yet this Goth girl was afraid of cemeteries.

"I have *got* to get over this," she mumbled around a mouthful of beans and cheese. "It's so embarrassing. My friends think it's totally fly I'm working here, but it scares the snot out of me."

" 'Fly'?"

"It means 'off the hook,' or 'cool' in Old Fogey."

Only eight years separated my assistant and me, but the cultural divide was huge. I had spent a good part of my formative years learning art forgery from my grandfather in Paris, Brussels, and Rome. I could rattle off recipes for crackle glazes and sixteenth-century egg tempera, recite the dates that various pigments and canvas linens had been introduced in Florence versus Amsterdam, and expound ad nauseam on the relative merits of seccatives, turpentine, and rabbit-skin glue.

Mary, in contrast, had grown up in America's heartland. She spent her childhood piercing her body in odd places, dying her hair colors never seen in nature, and experimenting with innovative ways to outrage her staid elders. The day Mary turned eighteen she hitchhiked to San Francisco, where her native shrewdness helped her to survive on the streets until she joined a band and moved in with the drummer. I often called upon Mary to translate contemporary slang and modern mores.

"I only need you for a few more nights. Then you can go back to avoiding cemeteries and mausoleums," I said. "Don't be so hard on yourself. Americans are the most talented people in the world at pretending death doesn't exist."

"Thanks, but I'm Goth, Annie. I have to conquer this," she sighed. "It's not, ya know, *consistent*. Dried mango?"

I took a piece and munched. Consistency was low on my list of Things to Fret About. I spent my time worrying about staving off creditors, figuring out how to input numbers into my new cell phone, and wondering if exposure to toxic lead white oil paint would turn me into one of those artists who thought smearing cow dung on parking meters was "public art."

"So how are you going to conquer your fear?" I asked.

"I've been giving that some thought. I know there's nothing out there, not really. I just need to prove it to myself. So I decided to spend a few nights in the cemetery."

"You're going to *what*?"

"I said—"

"I heard you. Are you nuts?"

"What could possibly go wrong? There's nobody *real* there, right?"

Nobody but grave-robbing ghouls, I thought with a shudder. It was on the tip of my tongue to tell Mary about tonight's encounter, but given her current state of mind I feared the chance of confronting a green-faced goblin would make her all the more gung ho.

"It's against the rules to be in the cemetery at night. Besides, they lock the gates at sundown. How would you get in?" I didn't mention that my master key to the columbarium also opened the cemetery gates.

Mary rolled her eyes, shoved the last bite of burrito into her mouth, and gazed at me as if I were the dimmest bulb in the chandelier. "*Hell-o-o?* Climb over the wall?"

I am a woman of considerable imagination, but scaling a ten-foot wall to spend a night in a cemetery would never have occurred to me, and not just because I was decidedly less athletic than my twenty-four-year-old assistant. I had spent a memorable, miserable seventeenth birthday in a Parisian jail, and most of my adult life had been focused on distancing myself from my grandfather Georges LeFleur's world of felonious forgers. I was still recovering from an incident last Thanksgiving when, through almost no fault of my own, I had been busted for smuggling drugs. I gave the police a wide berth these days.

"Mary, the cemetery people don't want strangers traipsing around the grounds at night. You never know what could happen."

"You're such a wuss, Annie."

"I am not a wuss!"

"Yes, you are. But that's one of the things I love about you."

"Mary, I'm serious—"

"Fear not, dear friend and employer," she said, gathering the foil wrapper and napkins to sort for the recycling bin. "I'll bring Dante with me." Dante was Mary's very large, very scary-looking boyfriend.

"Promise?"

"Promise."

"All right. But for the record, I think it's a bad idea."

"So noted, Ms. Law-and-Order."

Now, that made me smile. "Be sure to bring a sleeping bag. It gets cold in Oakland at night."

"I'll put it on the list, right after vino and smokes," Mary said.

"Garlic and a crucifix."

"A squirt gun filled with holy water."

"A revolver with silver bullets. And don't forget the wooden stakes."

"Would a paintbrush work?"

"Just don't use the Russian sable. A hog's hair brush ought to be good enough for your average ghoul."

We laughed and retraced our steps to the Chapel of the Madonna, picked up our palettes, and settled in to work.

The half-moon "lunettes" we were restoring were painted in the manner of the early Renaissance, featuring a bevy of angels surrounding a flock of wooly lambs. In the background a da Vinci–style landscape with a curving river, a rise of sandy bluffs, and a faraway medieval town were crowned by an azure sky with wispy clouds and soaring birds.

The murals had been painted on canvas and attached with strong wallpaper adhesive. Water leaking through the plaster had detached the canvas in spots, trapping the moisture and creating an ideal environment for mold and decay. Mary and I had begun by laboriously removing the canvas from the walls, taking care not to stretch the weave. We dug out the damaged plaster, applied a stucco patch, and sealed the area with a water-impermeable shellac primer. Next we removed the adhesive from the backs of the murals. This was the trickiest step, and I was relieved to discover that the lunettes had been applied with "milk glue," which was not uncommon in old installations. The casein in milk curds is made into glue and used in many household paints. Although the milk glue rendered the canvas vulnerable to decay, it was easy to strip off with water and a mild soap.

Parts of the canvas of both murals were unsalvageable, and so, using a sharp-edged razor, we had cut along the natural divisions of the painting so that when we patched the holes with new canvas and repainted, the seams would be invisible. In areas where the paint had bubbled up or flaked off but the canvas remained intact, we scraped off all shreds of the old paint. We next glued the lunettes back onto the walls, allowing the heavy-duty wallpaper paste to dry thoroughly. The prep work completed, Mary and I started applying the underpainting. Only then could we move on to the fun part: filling in the areas where the original paint and gold gilt were stained, faded, or had flaked off altogether.

While we painted I told Mary the romantic legend of *La Fornarina*. She insisted on referring to the woman in the painting as "Fornie," but otherwise was enraptured by the tale. I was about to recite an excerpt from Honore de Balzac's nineteenth-century poem about the love affair between Raphael and his model when Dante called to announce he was out front to drive Mary back to San

Francisco. She packed up her supplies and bid me a cheerful good-bye. I was a little sleepy but wanted to put the finishing touches on the background before calling it a night. Dabbing the tip of my paintbrush in a blend of lead white, oxide of chromium, and sap-green oil paints, I concentrated on applying the tiniest highlights to the background trees.

One of the challenges every artist faced was resisting the lure to do too much. Whenever I was tempted to overpaint, I remembered the cautionary tale of my college friend Gerald the Mad Sculptor. Gerald had worked two jobs for six months to afford a five-foot-tall, two-foot-wide block of black marble for his first major sculpture. Excited at finally being able to sculpt, he had holed up in his studio and commenced carving. By the time he put down his chisel a month later the black marble was only eighteen inches high and as big around as his stringy thigh.

In art, as in life, it was important to know when to quit.

After filling in a few shadows and highlights, I covered my palette with plastic wrap to keep the paint from drying out or skimming over. Then I rinsed my brushes in solvent, wiped my palette brush clean, and recapped the paint tubes and jars of mineral spirits. Time to check out *La Fornarina*. I studied the floor map Cindy Tanaka had given me to locate the Alcove of the Allegories, then shoved the map into the bib pocket of my overalls and headed to the bathroom to wash my paintbrushes. I walked down the Romanesque cloister along the east side of the building, made my way down three small flights of tiled stairs to the tiered gardens patterned on the Alhambra, and passed through successive alcoves known as the Chapels of Slumber, Serenity, and Spirit.

Following the twists and turns of the mazelike corridors, I pondered Cindy Tanaka's odd request. *La Fornarina,* Italian for "the little baker girl," was not just *a* Raphael—one of the greatest painters of the Italian Renaissance—it was arguably *the* Raphael. By far the most personal of Raphael's exquisite portraits, *La Fornarina* depicted a young woman with almond-shaped eyes, alabaster skin, a forthright expression, and a seductive smile. Clad in a bejeweled turban and a gauzy cloth that she hugged to her rounded belly, the nearly nude woman gazed boldly at the viewer, her right hand touching her left breast. Art historians tripped over their bow ties to insist that the gesture owed more to classical Roman sculptural conventions than to lewd intent, as if Raphael's desire for his subject would lessen the painting's beauty. *Because no great artist ever painted with lewd intent,* I thought.

It was inconceivable that the original *La Fornarina* was hanging in the columbarium, labeled a copy. Famous paintings might be disguised as reproductions to fool customs officials, but in general it was the other way around: a fake was painted to conceal the fact that an original had been sold or stolen, to commit insurance fraud, or to dupe greedy or gullible collectors. Only when a painting was assessed for insurance purposes or for sale might its origins be discovered, and, if the forger were sufficiently talented, the truth might never be revealed. The best forgeries—the kind by artists such as my grandfather—were themselves works of art. One of the art world's dirty little secrets was that museums regularly bought and exhibited forgeries; indeed, experts estimated that as many as forty percent of museum paintings could be fakes. San Francisco's own Brock Museum displayed my grandfather's copy of the great Caravaggio masterpiece, *The Magi.*

But the odds of a genuine Raphael hanging in Oakland's Chapel of the Chimes Columbarium were roughly akin to the odds of da Vinci's *Last Supper* decorating the men's room of the 12th Street Greyhound Station. What could possibly have given Cindy such an idea?

Turning the corner into the California room, I spotted the tiny bathroom door at the end of a narrow corridor. After washing out my brushes and using the bathroom, I would follow the Hall of the Cherubim to the Corridor of the Saints and take a look at the copy of *La Fornarina*. Then I could go home and climb into be—

"Annie."

Letting out a shriek, I leapt in the air before collapsing onto a low garden wall opposite a statue of the angel Gabriel. I ducked my head between my knees and concentrated on breathing as black spots danced before my eyes.

"How I've missed you," said a deep, amused voice.

I tilted my head to peer up at the man I knew as Michael X. Johnson. The last time I had seen him he was being dragged off to jail. Apparently he had managed to talk his way out of a well-deserved prison sentence.

No surprise there.

Michael and I met a year ago, yet I had no idea what his real name was, where he lived, how old he was, or what he looked like naked—though my imagination had taken a good run at that one. I *did* know he was a no-good thieving scoundrel, and one hell of a fine kisser.

"Go away," I said, my voice muffled by my denim-clad legs. "I hate you."

He laughed and collected the scattered paintbrushes I had dropped.

I sat up and glowered at him. "Why can't you call on the telephone, like a normal person? Why do you have to pop out of thin air and scare the you-know-what out of me?"

"And miss your reaction?" Handing me the brushes, he sank onto the bench and stretched out his long legs. Michael's devilish grin revealed straight white teeth and made his eyes crinkle adorably. His broad shoulders were clad in an aged brown leather bomber jacket, his snowy white shirt was open at the throat, and a pair of faded Levi's hugged his narrow hips and muscled thighs. Wavy dark brown hair brushed the top of his collar. As if this were not enough, his long-lashed eyes were as green as the beer at a North Beach pub on St. Paddy's Day.

Each time I saw Michael he was sexier than the time before. *How was that possible?* I wondered, irritated by his abundance of masculine pulchritude. Must be a trompe l'oeil—a trick of the eye.

"I only scream when you're around," I grumbled.

"Oh, I doubt that. How've you been, Annie?" he asked, his eyes roaming over my overalls with a hint of lust and a glint of amusement.

Why did I always look so awful when Michael dropped in? Maybe I'd sinned in a previous life and the Fates were feeling vengeful. That would explain a lot.

"I'm fine. What are you doing here in the middle of the night? Are you after the—"

I caught myself. The columbarium had many valuable artifacts, such as the carved Roman birdbaths, the tables inlaid with precious stones, antique religious texts, and a superb collection of American portrait miniatures. But these relics would not attract Michael X. Johnson, art thief extraordinaire. He specialized in big-ticket items, art so expensive it would give Bill Gates sticker shock. Could Cindy Tanaka's wild suggestion be true? Why else would Michael be snooping around a columbarium in the middle of the night?

Relax, Annie, I chided myself. It was a coincidence, nothing more.

"Am I looking for the what?"

"Nothing."

"Annie, I do believe you're fibbing."

"Go away." I glared at him.

"I just got here."

"Go away anyway."

"Okay," he said, standing up.

"Wait!"

"I thought you wanted me to go."

"I'll see you out," I said, unwilling to allow him to roam the columbarium unescorted. Not that throwing him out would slow him down. He'd broken in once, he could do it again.

Michael smiled. "Feeling better?"

"Right as rain," I said and stood, only a little wobbly. "I just have to use the bathroom."

"Of course."

"On second thought, it can wait." In my mind's eye I saw Michael locking me in the toilet while he stole whatever he'd come for, leaving me to face the authorities without even a decent lie at my disposal. Talk about getting caught with your pants down. "Come with me."

"I'd follow you anywhere, my love."

I snorted.

"Aren't you curious as to why I'm here?" he asked.

"I know why you're here."

"I don't think you do."

"Maybe I don't care."

"Are you sure?"

Our eyes held for a moment and I tried not to recall the touch of his lips. My heart remembered and sped up, the traitorous thing.

"Okay, pal, time for you to run along." I grabbed his arm and pulled him down the hallway to the Chapel of Brotherhood. From there it would be a quick jog over to the Gregorian Garden, through the Cloister of Contentment, past the Garden of Enchantment, then a quick left and a right to the Main Cloister and the exit. I hoped.

"Interesting place," he commented, gazing about as we

walked. "Quite lovely, in fact. A bit of a maze, though, isn't it? Do you ever get lost?"

"Nope."

"Really." The suppressed humor in his voice made my blood boil.

"My mind is like a global positioning system," I bragged, though this was not even remotely true.

"So I guess that means we've been going in circles on purpose?"

"We haven't been going in—" I halted as we emerged in the Gregorian Garden for the second time. "What I mean is, this isn't the same place. It just looks like it."

"Ah," he said with a nod.

I stomped off, Michael in tow. He launched into a long-winded tale about encountering a ghost while attempting to steal—"to liberate," he insisted—a Gainsborough painting from a castle on the coast of Ireland. "It was a knight, complete with armor. I don't know how they fought in those things. This guy could scarcely walk. Then again, he *was* dead. . . ."

I listened with half an ear as I tried to remember where the exit was. As Michael droned on, we snaked through the twists and turns of the narrow hallways, went up and down stairs, and arrived once again at the Gregorian Garden.

"I'm enjoying our stroll," Michael murmured as I stopped short, confused but unwilling to admit it to Mr. I'm-So-Cool-Even-Ghosts-Don't-Scare-Me. "But could I make a suggestion?"

"What."

"I believe the exit's that way." He pointed in the opposite direction.

"I knew that." I yanked him by the elbow in the direction he had suggested.

"Excuse me?"

"Keep walking."

"It's always so special spending quality time with you, Annie."

I ignored him.

"I ran into your assistant as she was leaving. Such an interesting fashion sense, that one. She's a Goth, isn't she? Anyway," he continued, "she said something about someone called Fornie, and—"

"Oh, for the love of—" I cut myself off, afraid that swearing in the presence of religious icons and human remains would double my no doubt lengthy sentence in purgatory. "I can't *believe* she told you—"

"Relax, Annie. Haven't you heard? I'm no longer in the business."

I snorted.

"Seriously."

I snorted again, and spotted the Main Cloister through the Gothic arches ahead of us.

"Why do you never believe me?"

"Because you're a liar. And a cheat."

"Not anymore. At least, not as much. I've gone legit."

"Oh, please." I unlocked the carved walnut front door and pushed Michael into the cool spring night. "A leopard doesn't change its spots. How did you get in here, anyway?"

Michael nodded at the alarm box above the door. "Pretty rinky-dink system."

"That thing? That's just for show," I fabricated as I led him down the circular flagstone drive. Michael had no doubt disarmed his first burglar alarm the day he mastered potty training. The columbarium's ancient system would slow him down for a minute or two, tops. "I turn on the state-of-the-art system and release the guard dogs when I leave. We call them the Hounds from Hell."

"You're a terrible liar, Annie," Michael said as we reached the sidewalk.

"I happen to be an excellent liar," I said, miffed. If I did one thing well, it was lie. I'd had a lifetime of practice. "You're just a suspicious person. Must be the crooked company you keep."

"How *is* your grandfather?"

"Fine, thanks. Leave him alone." Georges and Michael had worked together on a number of projects over the years—a world-class art forger and a world-class art thief made for a profitable alliance—and I tried not to think about the prison sentences they would receive if the authorities ever caught up with the dynamic duo. "Listen, Michael. If anything goes missing from this place, anything at all, I'm coming after you. I swear I will."

Michael cocked his head, his green eyes searching my face. "What would I want from a columbarium, Annie? I already have a fireplace full of ashes."

"That's sick. Where's your car?"

The last time I'd hung out with Michael he'd been driving an elegant champagne Lexus. The time before that it had been a snazzy red Jeep. I wondered what it would be this time. A '59 Thunderbird? A brand-new Corvette? A monstrous Humvee?

He gestured at a dented, ten-year-old white Ford pickup truck.

"You're driving a *truck*?" I loved my own truck because it was handy for hauling ladders and tubs of paint, inexpensive to run, and even cheaper to insure. Michael didn't need the cargo space and could afford to drive the best. Had he fallen on hard times? More likely he was working on a scam I wouldn't figure out until the cops came a-knocking.

"I like trucks," said Michael. "Bolsters my image as a manly man."

"How did you know where to find me, anyway?"

"I dropped by your studio today. Mary said the columbarium was not to be missed."

"There's a public tour the first Saturday of each month."

"She thought you might give me a private tour."

"She thought wrong." I leaned against the fender and crossed my arms over my chest. "I find it hard to believe Mary was such a chatterbox."

Michael chuckled. "I suspect she entertains romantic notions about the two of us."

"Yeah, well, Mary's dating a Samoan wrestler named Dante who's never even read *The Divine Comedy*."

"I suppose you've read it in the original?"

"I would if my name were Dante."

"I'm afraid you've lost me," he said with a slow smile and a quizzical look. "I don't see the connection between a Samoan wrestler and *The Divine Comedy*."

"I'm just saying Mary's view of romance is different from mine."

"I imagine most definitions of romance are different from yours, sweetheart," Michael said, grinning now. "Speaking of romance, I dropped by your studio after meeting with your boyfriend."

"Josh? What business do you have with Josh?"

"Who's Josh?"

"You said you had a meeting with my boyfriend, Josh."

"I met with Frank DeBenton, of DeBenton Secure Transport. Remember him? I have to say I'm surprised at you, two-timing good ol' Frank."

"Frank's my landlord, not my boyfriend."

"Oh? You two seemed rather, shall we say, *cozy* the last time I saw you. So, tell me about this Josh person. Wait a minute—don't tell me he's Mr. Muscles?"

Last fall I had made the mistake of mentioning Josh, stud

muffin extraordinaire, to Michael. It seemed he had remembered.

"Josh is a kind, *decent* person."

"Bored already, huh? Well, these things happen."

"You know what? Just go away," I said, irked at Michael's unerring instinct for pushing my buttons. Josh was out of town for a few weeks, and without his sweet smile and beautiful body clouding my mental processes I was rethinking our relationship. He was a great guy, but I was starting to wonder if I represented Josh's Walk on the Wild Side. Worse yet, I feared he might be my Walk on the Mild Side.

However, I wasn't about to admit that to a no-good thieving scoundrel. "You are the least qualified person in the world to give romantic advice."

"Cold, but true." Michael handed me a business card, kissed me lightly on the lips, and opened the truck door. "*À bientôt, chérie.* Don't forget to unleash the pooches of perdition before you leave."

I watched the taillights disappear into the darkness and glanced at the card in my paint-stained hand.

MICHAEL X. JOHNSON, ESQ.
FINE ART SECURITY ANALYSIS
& DISCREET RETRIEVAL SERVICES
"WE SKULK SO YOU DON'T HAVE TO"
WWW.ARTRETRIEVAL.COM

No way, I thought. No. Freaking. Way.

Chapter 3

Raffaelo was a very amorous person, delighting much in women, and ever ready to serve them.

—Giorgio Vasari (1511–1574), Italian art historian

Raffaelo was a very popular man.

—Georges LeFleur

My mind was still reeling at the thought of Michael X. Johnson, International Art Thief, working on the side of the angels when I pulled into the gravel parking lot behind my apartment near downtown Oakland. My art studio and the majority of my clients were in San Francisco, which meant that most mornings I faced the Commute From Hell across the Oakland Bay Bridge. For the past two weeks I had been reveling in the novelty of a breezy commute to the columbarium, a mere five-minute drive from where I lived near Lake Merritt.

Home was the former maid's quarters of a nineteenth-century Victorian that had been divided into apartments: one on the first floor, two on the second, and mine on the third, tucked under the eaves. Small but spacious, my four rooms were flooded with cheerful sunlight during the day, thanks to the dormer windows that dotted each wall, while at night the slanting roofline created a warm and cozy ambience, especially when I lit the candles on the mantel and hearth of my nonfunctioning fireplace. I loved my airy little retreat, high above the street and surrounded by mulberry trees. Best of all, the rent couldn't be beat. The old Victorian was owned by a pair of aging hippies who lived in a dome house in the Santa Cruz Mountains and with whom I had struck a tacit bargain: I didn't ask for repairs, they didn't raise the rent.

In deference to my slumbering neighbors, also single professional women, I crept up the squeaky stairs, let myself into my apartment, then slipped down the hall to the bathroom and ran a hot shower. As I stood under the steaming water I tried to figure out what the hell Michael was up to this time. Twenty minutes later the hot water ran out, and I was still clueless.

I pulled on an old T-shirt, climbed into bed, and flipped through the two and a half channels I received with the rabbit ears antenna on the television I had rescued from the curb on Big Waste Pickup Day. It was well after three in the morning and I was hoping for a rerun of *Casablanca* or even *Three's Company,* but all I could find was an infomercial for a hair thickener. A thirty-something woman wearing a distressing amount of baby-blue eye shadow tearfully recounted the horrors of having to wear a turban to hide her thinning hair.

The turban reminded me of *La Fornarina.* After my close encounter with Michael at the columbarium I'd lacked the courage to prowl about for the copy Cindy Tanaka thought was genuine, especially since I suspected it was a fool's errand. Raphael's signature masterpiece was worth a fortune, but more importantly it was a fundamental part of Italy's cultural heritage. The legendary love that had inspired the painting was one of the most romantic stories in the history of art, which was saying a lot. There was no way it could have ended up at the Chapel of the Chimes without someone in the art world knowing about it.

And why was I entertaining the notion that Cindy knew what she was talking about? She was writing a dissertation on public mourning rituals, I reminded myself, not art history. Still, Cindy had done some homework on the oddities of the art world. Clearly she felt there was reason to wonder, and the graduate student did not strike me as a person given to wild speculation. Who was this "someone" who asked her to check out *La Fornarina*? I blamed sleep-deprivation for not following up on that little tidbit.

What really gave me pause was Michael's sudden appearance. Could it have anything to do with the rumor of a genuine Raphael hanging, virtually unprotected, at the columbarium?

Tomorrow I would swing by the columbarium and take a look at the painting so that I could assure Cindy—and myself—that it was indeed the copy it claimed to be.

I flipped the channel to yet another infomercial, this one for hay baling equipment. A clean-cut man with a deep tan and squinty eyes explained, oh so sincerely, that big round balers and small round balers were necessary for the success of today's modern rancher. I wondered if there were any ranches left in the crowded Bay Area. The last time I'd seen a round bale of hay was in the French countryside, when my grandfather took me on a tour of the magical Loire Valley.

The telephone shrilled and I snatched up the receiver, my heart in my throat. "Hello?"

"Chérie! Comment ça va, toi?"

I must have telepathic powers. Born and raised in Brooklyn, master art forger Georges François LeFleur had long ago given his heart to *la belle France*. He now spoke his mother tongue with an accent as heavy as a traditional

French cream sauce, a fact of which he claimed to be unaware.

"Everything's fine, Grandfather. How are you? Where are you?"

"*Alors,* zees I must not say, *chérie.* One never knows when ze Interpol may be listening, *n'est-ce pas?*"

"Why would Interpol be listening, *Grandpère?*"

"Zey air such clowns. Zey sink zey can catch your *grandpapa.*"

"What do you mean? Who is after you, Grandfather? I mean, other than the usual suspects?"

Last year, ignoring my heartfelt pleas, Grandfather had published a memoir of his long career in the art underworld. *Reflections of a World-Class Art Forger* had become a runaway international best seller, and Georges had been on the lam ever since. All a prosecutor would have to do to secure a conviction for art forgery against the old reprobate would be to quote from his damned book. Indeed, were Grandfather ever brought to trial, I suspected he would insist upon reading it to the jury himself, so proud was he of what he considered—not without cause—to be a life of extraordinary artistic accomplishment.

"Ah, zees man. I *'ate* 'im."

"Who do you hate, Grandfather?"

"Doughnut Somezing. Doughnut Spumoni."

" 'Doughnut Spumoni'? Are you sure that's his name? Sounds like a dessert."

"*Bof!* 'Ow should I know? *Quel connard!*"

"Grandfather!"

"*Pardon.*"

"So, who is this guy?"

"A leetle Italian bureaucrat."

"Why is a little Italian bureaucrat after you?"

"Pairhips because he envies me."

"Perhaps. Any other reason? 'Fess up, old man."

"Zere was zat leetle incident in Firenze."

A shiver ran down my spine. "Did this incident have anything to do with *La Fornarina*?"

"*La Fornarina* was years ago. 'E could not prove a zing."

"So you know nothing about a fake Raphael floating around?"

"*Mais non!*"

"Are you sure?"

"Ah, *ma petite,* 'as your old *grandpapa* ever lied to you?"

I bit back a rude retort. Georges had lied to me plenty, and had taught me to be an artful forger and an artful fibber as well. His modus operandi, though, was to bluster in French, change the subject, or pretend a solar flare had zapped his phone. I tried to take comfort from the fact that this time his denial was in English and he was still on the line. "What's going on, Grandfather?"

"Zis man 'as published a list of my *plusieurs réussites.*"

"Your many accomplishments? You mean your forgeries?"

"*Exactement!*"

"That's not good."

"It ees worse! 'E 'as included two by *Jazz Hart*!"

"That *is* worse."

Jazz Hart was a thirty-something British forger who churned out fakes that relied more on the gullibility and greed of art dealers and collectors than on technical skill. He'd forged *The White Horse*—which Gauguin had painted in 1898—with polymer paints, which were not invented until the 1950s. Georges' generation of art criminals dismissed Hart as a third-rate hack.

"As eef I would 'ave anyzing to do wiz such vile reproductions! I *speet* on 'im. I will *not* be associated wiz zat contemptible *poseur*! *Jamais!*"

"Georges, think about this, please," I said, my stomach

clenching. "If you deny you painted the ones by Hart, you're as good as admitting you forged the others."

"But 'ow can I keep silent? 'E is challenging my genius!"

"Just let it roll off you."

"Roll off me?"

"Sure, you know—like water off a duck's back."

"You are suggesting I be a duck? A *duck*? *Quel canard!*"

"I'm *suggesting* you stay out of prison, old man." For several seconds I heard nothing but faint static. "Georges? Are you there?"

"This Spumoni authenticator is as good as you are, *chérie*." Grandfather's voice was low, his accent slipped, and I realized we'd gotten to the purpose of his call. "He appears to know me."

That gave me pause. Few realized what a challenge it was for even expert authenticators to tell a genuine painting from a top-notch forgery. As long as a skilled forger used an aged canvas and paints chemically indistinguishable from those of the original painting, science was of limited assistance. Often the final judgment came down to intuition, the almost magical ability to appreciate an artist's unique style. I had been born with a rare gift for what Georges called "aesthetic profiling" and Interpol called "fake busting," and my ability had been honed by a lifetime of study. If Doughnut Spumoni had a similar talent, my grandfather could be in serious trouble.

One of the ironies of the art forgery business was that, by definition, the best forgers were anonymous. Anyone with a paintbrush could paint a lousy fake; only an elite few had the talent and training to paint a convincing one. The professional fake buster's secret weapon was the skilled forger's understandable desire to have his or her artistry recognized and admired. A peculiar relationship thus tended to spring up between forger and fake buster: the latter was among the few to truly "get" the forger's skill, yet was dedicated to exposing it. Doughnut Spumoni—or whatever his name really was—might be my grandfather's biggest fan, but he would stop at nothing to out Georges. For an artist like my grandfather, being unable to paint was tantamount to being unable to breathe.

"Listen, Grandfather," I said. "Why don't you let me look into this? In the meantime, promise me you'll keep your mouth shut and stay underground for a week or two."

I heard some halfhearted sputtering. Georges was in his seventies but saw himself as a much younger man. He did not easily ask for, nor accept, my help.

"*S'il te plaît, Grandpère. Laisses-moi t'aider.*"

"*Bon.* I thought you might have contacts in the legitimate art world. It is good you live such an artless life, *non*?"

Fat lot he knew.

The next morning I stood before the columbarium's *La Fornarina* and realized that Cindy Tanaka was right. The painting was not what it seemed.

It wasn't, as I had feared after last night's phone call, one of my grandfather's forgeries. Nor was it a genuine Raphael. But it also wasn't what the brass tag affixed to the frame claimed: A COPY OF RAFFAELO'S *LA FORNARINA*, 1871, BY CRISPIN ENGELS. The "painting" before me was instead a computer-generated copy, available over the Internet for $179.99 plus shipping. I hated these cheap digital reproductions with the kind of visceral passion I reserved for imminent threats to my livelihood.

But why would Cindy imagine it to be genuine? For that matter, why would a computer-generated knockoff be labeled a nineteenth-century reproduction?

Intrigued, I retraced my steps from the dead-end Alcove of the Allegories through apse after apse to the Hall of the

Cherubim, passed through the Corridor of Saints, and headed toward the main office, where I found the columbarium's director, Roy Cogswell, signing some papers at the reception desk.

"Annie." He greeted me politely and glanced at his watch. "What are you doing here so early?"

Blue-eyed and sandy-haired, with the gangly physique of an aging basketball player, Roy Cogswell was not the type one expected to find running a funerary business. Still, his somber, almost somnambulant way of speaking, his habit of folding his hands in front of him, and his measured response to any comment suggested the impact of three decades spent in the service of the bereaved. Apparently, one learned not to make any sudden moves around the grief-stricken.

"I stopped by to take a look at something. Do you have a minute?"

"I'm afraid I don't," he said. "I have a meeting. Boring financial matters. Speaking of which, how goes the assessment of our miniatures collection?"

"So far it's not too encouraging, but I'm still working on it," I hedged. My friend Samantha's former assistant, Rachel, worked in appraisals at Mayfield's Auction House, and I'd shown her the miniatures collection last week. According to Rachel, the collection was historically interesting but not very valuable, in part because of the portraits' diminutive size and primitive style but mostly because in art, as in so much of life, market value was relative to desire. There just wasn't a demand for miniatures these days.

These appealing "likenesses in little"—some by artists whom I recognized, such as John Singleton Copley and Charles Wilson Peale—had been popular in the mideighteenth and nineteenth centuries. Before the invention of photography by Louis Daguerre, a former painter, miniature portraits were the cheapest and easiest way to capture a loved one's image. The tradition had been brought to the American colonies from England and Italy, where Rosalba Carriera had pioneered the technique of crosshatching or stippling watercolors or gouache on ivory, rather than on less durable vellum. At that time, miniature painting was one of the few arenas in which women artists competed successfully with men.

Just a few inches tall, the ovals were small enough to slip in a pocket, and were sometimes set into lockets to be kept near the wearer's heart, or framed in cases of fine leather, worked gold, or etched silver. Locks of the subject's hair, braided or arranged in a "plaid" pattern, were often fixed beneath a thin layer of glass on the back of the portrait. To me the most intriguing aspect of the miniatures was their personal significance. The portraits were treasured remembrances of cherished husbands gone off to war, perhaps never to return; of dewy brides destined to die young in childbirth; of beloved children who fell victim to any of a thousand terrors, including what we today airily dismiss as "childhood diseases"; of revered mothers and fathers—in short, they were reminders of loved ones whose visages would otherwise live on only in the fading memories of those who survived, or glimpsed in the faces of their descendants.

Rachel had estimated the columbarium's collection would sell for perhaps five hundred to a few thousand dollars apiece. Not exactly the windfall the columbarium needed to pay for its long-overdue earthquake retrofit.

One other possibility, Rachel suggested, was that full-sized early American portraits often showed women wearing a miniature. If we could match the columbarium's miniatures with such paintings their value would skyrocket. To determine this would require extensive research, and Rachel would do only so much without being paid. I wasn't much good at research. Or computers. Not to mention I had a million other things on my To Do list.

But something about Chapel of the Chimes tugged at my heart. It was unique, a testament to turn-of-the-century Oakland's wealth and ambition to be taken seriously as a cultural center. Architect Julia Morgan's mosaic-encrusted Gothic design was stunning, and even the newer section, whose crisp lines and soaring heights harkened more to Frank Lloyd Wright, was soothing and reflective. As final resting places went, the columbarium was a gem.

"Well, keep me posted," Cogswell continued. A spark lit up his blue eyes. "Or perhaps I might drop by later. Are you and Mary painting tonight?"

"It might be more convenient if I swing by your office tomorrow morning," I replied. Mary would not be able to conceal her impatience with the columbarium's smitten director, and I feared the diffident Roy would be slow to recover from her sharp tongue.

Roy nodded and shuffled into a small conference room, where I glimpsed the columbarium's accountant, Manny Ramirez, chatting with two gray-suited men.

"I'll be surprised if we're open past June," a dour woman announced in clipped tones as she stared at me over the rims of her rhinestone reading glasses. Roy Cogswell's intimidating administrative assistant, known to all and sundry as "Miss Ivy," liked nothing better than to ambush anyone foolish enough to pause on their way past the redwood counter and subject them to lengthy doomsday monologues. The employees referred to this as "Miss Ivy's office arrest." I used to think it was funny.

"Mmm," I responded, trying not to encourage her.

"Building's falling down about our heads as it is," she continued, smoothing her leopard-print miniskirt over her thin thighs. Miss Ivy was fifteen years my senior, worked in a mortuary, and never cracked a smile, but she dressed like a Las Vegas hooker on her day off. It was disconcerting, to say the least. "I'm sure you've seen the state of the glass ceiling tiles. Been that way since the eighty-nine earthquake. Can't afford to fix 'em. Mark my words, it's only a matter of time until they close this place down. If you could see what I've seen—"

"Is the situation really that dire?" I interrupted. "I would think there's no shortage of demand."

"Oh, sure, people die every *day*," she said, as if announcing late-breaking news. "But what with those so-called environmentalists kicking up a fuss about the smoke from the crematorium, and advocating those 'green burials' that don't even use caskets, no better than the heathen Hottentots, well, I ask you, how are we supposed to turn a profit? Now, it seems to me—"

"Miss Ivy, do you know anything about the columbarium's artwork?"

"Do I *look* like a tour guide?"

"No, but I thought you might—"

"I'll tell you one thing, the management would do well to focus less on aesthetics and more on the day-to-day operations of—"

"Such a shame. *Such* a shame," I babbled, backing out the door. "I think I'm coming down with something. Must be that plague that's going around. Gotta go!"

I beat a retreat and ran to my truck, looking askance at the sky. An unseasonable drizzle had started to fall. It wasn't supposed to rain after early April in this part of California. That was part of the deal: we paid exorbitant rents and lived with overcrowded freeways in exchange for sunny, beautiful weather almost year-round.

Motoring down Piedmont Avenue, I doubled back through a complicated maze to reach the hidden on-ramp to

580. Oakland had numerous freeway exits but only a handful of poorly marked entrances. Normally during off-hours I could whiz from Oakland to San Francisco in under fifteen minutes, but not today. Screeching to a halt half a mile from the toll plaza, I switched on Alice's morning show for a traffic update.

"Here's a good one. An ostrich is loose in the westbound lanes of the Bay Bridge, and traffic is at a complete standstill. I'm talkin' zee-ro miles per hour. But fear not, our heroes from Cal Trans are working with officers from Animal Control to capture the critter. So roll up your window, don't try to pet Big Bird, and remember it could be worse. You could be livin' in LA."

I tried to catch a glimpse of what promised to be an entertaining sight, but saw only a sea of red taillights. At least a free-ranging ostrich was more benign than the time last fall when a flatbed truck transporting brimming Port-o-Potties tipped over, closing the Bay Bridge until spacesuit-clad Haz Mat workers cleaned things up. For weeks afterward, I'd sworn the bridge smelled funky.

Armed with a commuter mug of Peet's French Roast coffee and three crumpled dollar bills for the toll, I watched the rain and used the delay to think. Had Michael absconded with the columbarium's nineteenth-century copy and hung the mass-produced version in its place? A good hundred-plus-year-old copy might be worth several thousand dollars, a great one tens of thousands. But it seemed out of character for him. Art theft was a business for Michael, which was why from time to time he teamed up with my grandfather for high-risk but highly lucrative forgery-and-switch schemes. Michael was unlikely to consider a Crispin Engels worth stealing. On the other hand, the columbarium's pitiful security system meant the downside of theft—arrest—was negligible. Still, Michael had a genuine love of art; it was hard to imagine him unleashing $179.99 digital prints upon the world.

I checked my cell phone for the umpteenth time, closed my eyes, and sent Cindy Tanaka telepathic messages to call me. What did she know about *La Fornarina*—or rather, what did she think she knew? It was one thing for an untrained eye to be fooled by a nineteenth-century copy, which would look genuinely old; quite another to assume an obvious digital reproduction might be real. Still, it was hard to imagine her making up the tale out of whole cloth. The more I thought about it, the more I wanted to know who had sent her—and by extension, me—on such a wild-goose chase, and why.

I also wondered how the cemetery personnel had responded when Cindy told them about last night's break-in at Louis Spencer's crypt. Who would rob a crypt—while dressed as a ghoul, no less? What was in that metal box? I had hoped to ask Roy Cogswell about the break-in, but he might not have heard anything, anyway. The cemetery and the columbarium were owned by the same corporation, but had separate management.

My mind's eye conjured the image of petite Cindy Tanaka leaping onto the back of the man in the Halloween mask. On this drizzly spring morning the ghoulish encounter seemed even odder than it had last night. Perhaps Cindy was not all she seemed.

Ostrich rescued—safe but sporting a bad case of road rash—and on its way to a new life on a ranch in Pacifica, traffic began to move. I inched toward the tollbooth and handed over my three dollars. Once past the metering lights, traffic picked up speed and I zipped across the bay, exited at Ninth, and drove along surface streets toward the district known as Cow Hollow. A long time ago farm animals grazed these hills, but these days Cow Hollow's location near Russian

Hill, the Presidio, and the Marina made it one of San Francisco's pricier neighborhoods. In a city where even ramshackle dwellings commanded upwards of a million dollars, that was no small thing.

I nosed my pickup into the driveway of a scaffold-encrusted Edwardian mansion. Alongside the three-quarter-ton Chevy and Ford trucks near and dear to the hearts of contractors everywhere, my dusty Toyota looked like a four-cylinder newborn. But its collection of dents, and the magnetic TRUE/FAUX STUDIOS signs stuck to its doors, gave me a little street cred.

Job sites are dusty, noisy, chaotic, masculine places. Those of the female persuasion who venture into this domain either leave in a great big hurry or cultivate a tolerance for country music played at earsplitting levels, the endless fascination with foul-smelling bodily functions, and monosyllabic jokes whose punch lines invariably referenced "hooters," "jugs," and/or "tits." My boyfriend, Josh, was the general contractor on this job, and the rough-and-tumble crew overlooked his easygoing and nonsexist vegan ways because he was a talented carpenter who knew the construction business upside down and inside out. It didn't hurt that Josh also had a sixth-degree black belt in karate.

I'm no interior designer—those licensed professionals must be able to gush over each season's new fabrics, to swoon over furniture choices, and to enjoy shopping with a fervor that bordered on lunacy. But with my eye for color and form I found myself helping a growing number of my faux finishing clients who shied away from a "designed" look for their homes but needed assistance wading through the endless variety of styles for everything from bidets to duvets, faucets to window treatments. Best of all, artistic consulting paid better, and required less actual work, than faux-finishing.

The owner of this house, Aaron Garner, was lacking in both taste and a wife, and so had hired me as the job's artistic consultant. A hearty sort whose likeness one expected to see on a bottle of expensive gin, Aaron Garner styled his gingery hair in an elaborate swooping comb-over in the fond but misguided belief that it hid his creeping male pattern baldness. I had first met the wealthy philanthropist last winter when I was volunteering with the "Save Oakland's Fox Theater" campaign. Garner had offered to match any pledge to our cause, and when the community responded with enthusiasm, he'd paid every cent with good humor. Garner discovered I shared his love of art and history, and commissioned me to paint a portrait of his son. I had recommended Josh when Garner was looking for a contractor to preside over the high-end remodel of his Cow Hollow mansion.

Last week Garner had put me in charge of the renovation for a couple of weeks while Josh accompanied him to Aspen, where Garner was breaking ground on a new vacation home. Some of the macho construction crew chafed at taking orders from me, but in general they came to accept my supervision when they realized I was an artist, not a competitor.

Plus, every so often I brought them fresh coffee and baked goods. I knew which side my doughnut was glazed on.

As for me, putting up with fart and booger jokes was a small price to pay for a generous and steady paycheck. Stuffing my clipboard and papers in a vinyl tote to keep them from getting wet, I climbed out of the truck. As I made my way up the walk to the front of the house, I spied a man the size of a small grizzly bear at the top of the entry stairs, framed by dust billowing from the open front door behind him.

"How's it going, Norm?"

Norm had dirty blond hair, a complexion that reddened easily, pale gray eyes, and nicotine-stained teeth. He was dressed in a worn pair of dirty jeans and a faded navy T-shirt emblazoned WHO'S YOUR DADDY?

"You're late," Norm growled over the high-pitched whine of an electric saw. "I'm s'posta fax those fireplace details to Italy by eleven. And the Spanish guys out back are goin' nuts about somethin', but I can't understand a goddamned word they're sayin'."

"They're not Spanish, they're Mexican. I'll see if I can figure it out."

Last January Norm had handed me a gift certificate for a three-month, intensive Spanish language course at the University of San Francisco. He claimed to have been moved by the holiday spirit, but a few discreet inquiries—I took his lead carpenter out for beer and nachos on Chestnut Street and grilled him mercilessly—yielded the information that Norm had intended to take the class himself but chickened out. He had given me the certificate so he could write its cost off his taxes as a business expense. Since I had just been through an adventure where speaking Spanish might have saved me considerable grief, I was willing to be a pawn in Norm's IRS dodge.

Norm grunted and ducked back into the disemboweled house. I nodded at the electrician and exchanged a few words with the men pouring the concrete slab in the garage before picking my way down the house's narrow side alley to the backyard.

"*Buenos días,*" I said to the men in the garden. "*Que pasa?*"

Two dark-eyed workmen, one in a Raiders cap, the other sporting a 49ers windbreaker, leaned on their shovels and launched into rapid-fire Spanish. I must have looked as befuddled as I felt because the crew's leader, Ricardo, slowed down and began supplementing his words with gestures. He led me over to a pile of marble stepping stones the crew had found in the weeds and, holding one up, used a blue bandana to brush off mud and grass. I crouched down and peered closely. A string of carved letters was barely legible, and the top portion of the stone had broken off. Ricardo held up another piece, this one with deeper engraving: . . . MEMORY . . . ETH ANNE . . . VING MOTHER. These marble "stepping stones" looked a lot like old gravestones. I understood only a portion of what Ricardo was saying, but the meaning of *mortuaria* wasn't hard to guess.

A shiver went up my spine. Why would anyone use gravestones as garden decorations? Had Aaron Garner's home been built atop an old graveyard?

And what was it with me and cemeteries lately?

Chapter 4

The first man to compare the cheeks of a young woman to a rose was obviously a poet; the first to repeat it was possibly an idiot.

—Salvador Dali (1904–1989), Spanish painter

To be a fool for love is the essence of being human. To be a lousy poet is unforgivable.

—Georges LeFleur

"*Goddammit,*" a gruff voice swore behind me. "Annie, I gotta get these fireplace doohickies finalized. Damned rain's screwing up the schedule as it is. Can we get a move on?"

"Hey, Norm, have you seen these?"

He leaned in to examine the broken stone Ricardo was holding. "I'll be damned," Norm said, his pale eyes lighting up. "I've heard about this. My dad told me that when they moved the graveyards years ago they used the unclaimed headstones to build other stuff. The city parks are full of 'em, I guess."

I frowned. That seemed to be taking California's "reduce, reuse, recycle" motto a bit too far. "Which cemeteries were moved?"

"Whole bunch of 'em," Norm replied, turning over another stone and brushing off the grime to read the engraving. Norm was a proud sixth-generation San Franciscan and, according to Josh, waited impatiently for the Big One to strike and send the yuppie interlopers scurrying back East.

"I grew up off Turk, in a neighborhood built on an old Catholic graveyard," Norm mused. "But they had places for everybody—Jews, Chinese, even them Mason guys. Didja know the pet cemetery near the Presidio used to be an Indian graveyard?"

"Someone turned a Native American burial ground into a *pet* cemetery?" I glanced at Ricardo, who looked as appalled as I.

Norm shrugged. "Hell, they're *dead*. What do they care? Okay, back to work, men. *A trabajo, amigos. Capisce?*"

"That's Italian, Norm."

"What?"

"*Capisce* is Italian. You mean *comprende*."

"Yeah, whatever."

"Norm? Since the gravestones weren't moved, dare I ask what happened to the bodies?"

"Paved over 'em would be my guess. Don't make sense to move the bodies but not the headstones."

Ricardo and the man in the Raiders cap made the sign of the cross. I would have, too, but I always forgot which shoulder to touch first.

Norm's story sounded like the opening scene of a lousy horror movie, and I hoped it was another of his tall tales of old San Francisco. Only last week the cantankerous carpenter had tried to convince me the abandoned federal prison on Alcatraz Island was haunted.

In my broken Spanish I asked Ricardo to clean the stones and set them aside. Maybe a local history group would be willing to take them. I would have to make a few calls.

Yet another item for the To Do list.

I spent the rest of the morning going over trim details with Norm, confirming the lighting plan with the electrician, and detailing the bathroom tile patterns with the stonemasons. At one o'clock the project's architect, Ethan Mayall, arrived. Ethan was a prim, tucked-in young man who wore his hair short, his shirtsleeves long, and his John Lennon glasses perched upon his long, straight nose. He was the kind of guy whom everyone assumed was gay, but wasn't. The type who would marry a raving witch who dressed him in suspenders and cut up his meat for him.

For the next forty-five minutes I stood hunched over a roll of blueprints spread out on the temporary plywood kitchen counter, mediating between Ethan, who had vision but scant knowledge of the hands-on aspects of construction, and Norm, a skilled carpenter with the aesthetic sensibility of a sewer rat. I did my best, but if Josh didn't return from Aspen soon I feared we were in for bloodshed, à la *West Side Story*. I imagined a rumble on the quiet streets of Cow Hollow between Ethan and his gang of tweedy architects, brandishing hand calculators and straightedges, and Norm and the rugged carpenters, armed with levels and awls.

I just hoped that didn't make me Maria.

It was nearly two o'clock by the time I headed across San Francisco to my art studio in the once-affordable neighborhood known as China Basin. I breathed a sigh of pure satisfaction as I pulled up in front of the DeBenton Building, a converted chair factory with old redbrick walls, huge multipaned windows, and wide-plank wood floors. In the past few years the building's tenants had formed a close-knit, creative community. On the ground floor was an artisan bakery; the corporate offices of DeBenton Secure Transport; three potters who shared a kiln; and a birdhouse maker who never seemed to sell anything. In the upstairs studios were my good friend Samantha Jagger, a brilliant jewelry maker; a weaver who made itchy, tentlike dresses out of hemp; a freelance photographer; a novelist who liked to talk about writing more than he liked to write; and a clutch of architects and computer graphics people. As far as I was concerned the architects and computer folks didn't count as artists, but since they paid more in rent than all the rest of us combined I kept my mouth shut.

The artisan bakery turned out mediocre bread but filled the air with delicious aromas, and my stomach growled as I climbed the wooden outdoor stairs to the second floor, yanked open the sticky exterior door, and proceeded down the hall to my studio, number 206. I walked in to find Mary snoring on the red velvet sofa while Pete, a big man with kind brown eyes, cleaned out the espresso machine in the studio's tiny kitchenette.

"Annie! How are you?" Pete called out as he dried his large hands on a towel embroidered with a garish Santa Claus. "How does it go in the moratorium?"

"It's a *mausoleum,* Pete," I said with a smile. Pete had emigrated from Bosnia at the age of fourteen, and his enthusiasm for new words, combined with his lack of formal education, created an entertaining take on American English. The other evening he had offered me a cup of "decapitated" coffee. "Where in the world did that ugly towel come from?"

"My mother, she makes it and sends it to you."

Oops. Once more I reminded myself to engage my brain before engaging my mouth. "Oh! How sweet of her. It's just lovely!"

He beamed. "My mother, she is so gladdened about the restoration you achieved she begs you to join us to dinner on Sunday!"

Last month Pete had asked me to restore a cherished

family portrait that had suffered extensive smoke and water damage during the family's difficult journey from Bosnia. I had been happy to do so, but refused to accept payment from a friend. Ever since, I had been dodging rapid-fire dinner invitations. I didn't want to hurt Pete's feelings by rejecting his family's hospitality, but the memory of his signature hot dish, which he brought to every potluck and Mary had dubbed "the Cabbage Rolls of Death," made me hesitant. But Pete was undaunted, and his persistence was wearing me down.

"I have wanted you to taste our cousin—I mean our cuisine—from the gecko, and now is our chance!" Pete continued.

"You mean 'from the get-go,' not 'from the gecko,'" I corrected him, praying I was right. Bowing to the inevitable, I crossed my fingers that Mama Pete's cooking had nothing in common with her bachelor son's. "Dinner on Sunday sounds lovely, Pete. Thank you."

Mary awoke with a loud snort, sat up, and squinted at us. "New guitar player," she explained with a jaw-cracking yawn as she stretched her long arms over her head with cat-like grace. Living with a constantly shifting circle of bandmates in a run-down Victorian flat, my assistant didn't get a lot of rest.

"Why don't you crash on the futon in my apartment until we finish working at the columbarium?" I suggested.

"Thanks," she said with another yawn. "But I'm gonna sleep in the cemetery, 'member?"

Pete frowned. "Have you heard this plan? This does not sound wise to me, Annie. She portends to sleep without a man."

"I thought Dante was joining you," I said to Mary.

"Wrestling tournament in Reno." She shrugged. "Evangeline's coming instead."

"*I* offered to accompany her," Pete said. "But she won't have me."

"Don't worry, Mary will be fine," I assured him. "Evangeline's rather formidable."

Pete's Old World gallantry was offended, but I heard him repeating "formidable" to himself as he returned to his task at the sink. "Cappuccino?" he called out.

"Thanks," I said.

"Double for me," Mary piped up.

"Annie," Pete said, his booming voice drowning out the spitting of my cranky garage-sale espresso machine. "I stopped by today because my mother, she believes there may be Ibrahimbegovics in the cemetery where you are working."

"Sounds like some kind of toxic waste," Mary mumbled.

"Play nice, Mare," I warned as I started sorting mail at my desk.

"They are my family, the Ibrahimbegovics. Perhaps even Hadzipetrovics. My mother, she is so gladdened to think this."

"I didn't know you had family buried around here, Pete," I said.

"Oh yes, the brothers Ibrahimbegovics left our town of Varcar Vakuf in 1862 and came to California in search of gold. Of course, in 1924 Varcar Vakuf was officially renamed Mrkonjic-Grad in honor of the 'old king' Petar Karadjordjevic and to venerate his Chetnik exploits under the hajduk name Petar Mrkonjic, during the 1875 uprising on the border between Bosnia and Lika, in Crni Potoci. The king's Chetnik exploits did not last long, nor were they esteemedly glorious, but—"

"Oh my Gaaaaaaawd," Mary groaned as she fell back onto the sofa and clutched a tasseled purple satin pillow over her head. "Make him stop, make him stop!"

When he started in on Bosnian history Pete was inclined

to run off at the mouth, but since I had the same tendency when discussing art, I was more tolerant than Mary. Besides, I had a serious caffeine addiction and the man whipped up a wicked espresso. It would take a lot more than a little boring conversation to turn me against my supplier.

"I'm afraid I don't know much about Bayview Cemetery's history," I said to Pete. "Why don't you tell your mother to talk to one of the docents? They give tours and everything. Wait a minute, I may have something you could show her."

I dug a crumpled Bayview Cemetery brochure out of my backpack and flipped through it. I noticed that leading the list of the cemetery's more illustrious "residents" was Josiah Garner, Aaron Garner's great-grandfather. According to the brochure, Josiah settled in the East Bay during the gold rush and made a fortune in construction. Business boomed after the 1906 earthquake, when nervous San Franciscans pulled up stakes and fled to the comparative safety of the East Bay. Garner's ostentatious tomb was built into one of the hills, not far from little Louis Spencer's final resting place.

Once again I was reminded of a certain graduate student. I checked the studio's message machine. Josh had called twice, "just to check in," his voice sweet and familiar. Nothing from Cindy. I cursed myself for not getting her number last night. Handing Pete the brochure in exchange for a frothy cappuccino, I powered up my computer and Googled Cindy Tanaka—157,000 hits. *This will take forever,* I thought as I sipped. There must be a better way.

"What department would someone studying 'public mourning' be in?" I asked no one in particular. "Sociology, maybe? Anthropology? Religion?"

Mary and Pete looked blank.

"It could be an interdisciplinary degree, I suppose," I muttered.

"It's almost like she doesn't need us," Mary said to Pete, who nodded solemnly and sank onto the chair facing the red velvet sofa, coffee in hand.

Apart from the seating area, my disheveled desk, and the kitchenette, the studio was given over to art. Three huge windows along the back wall and two skylights high above suffused the studio with light, even on the grayest of days. Four easels held canvases in varying degrees of completion; mismatched bookshelves were filled with supplies ranging from mineral spirits to broken tiles; and the huge worktables were piled with half-finished projects, including one hundred linear feet of fluted curtain rods and five hundred rod rings that Mary and I were painting, gilding, and distressing for a showroom at the San Francisco Design Center.

I reminded myself that the curtain rods were due the day after tomorrow as I started calling departments at the University of California at Berkeley, known locally as "Cal." On the third try I reached a secretary in the Anthropology Department who recognized Cindy's name. She explained that there were 142 graduate students in the department and she couldn't be expected to know where they all were, now, could she, but agreed to leave a message in Cindy's mail cubby. She also volunteered that Cindy's dissertation adviser, Dr. Gossen, would be available during office hours tomorrow from eleven to one.

I hung up, turned back to the computer, and brought up an image of *La Fornarina*. She gazed at me serenely but refused to share her secrets. I searched for fake Raphaels but found only a reference to the legend of the great master himself perpetrating a fraud on an innkeeper by dashing off a tabletop trompe l'oeil (literally, a trick of the eye) of a napkin holding several coins to pay his tab. The story might well be apocryphal, but many revered Old Masters had indulged in a spot of forgery when it suited their purposes. Michelangelo in particular was fond of fakery, and had recently—five hundred years after his death—been accused of forging an ancient Roman statue. Given our modern standards, the attribution sent the statue's value sky-high since a work by the incomparable Renaissance artist was far more desirable than yet another anonymous Roman relic.

Next I checked the art crime registries and museum security networks for chatter about *La Fornarina*. Italian authorities had stored the painting during World War I, but ever since it had been on display in the Galleria Nazionale d'Arte Antica at the Barberini Palace, seldom allowed out on tour. Crispin Engels' 1879 copy had been catalogued in the same storage facility, along with numerous reproductions by lesser artists. Except for a brief mention of my grandfather's 1966 scam, there was nothing about known forgeries of *La Fornarina*. But as an eminent New York museum curator once told me, we only notice the bad forgeries; the good ones go undetected.

I was about to log off when my eye caught a reference to an Italian fake buster named Donato Sandino. "Donato, you sly devil," I muttered. "Are you by any chance 'Doughnut Spumoni'?"

I kept reading. After outing Grandfather's forgery of *La Fornarina* in 1966, Donato Sandino had accepted a position in the Italian Ministry of Culture. According to an article in *Curator's Monthly,* in the early 1980s Sandino and "an unnamed American woman" had raised questions about the authenticity of the Barberini's most famous Raphael. Shortly afterward the inquiry had been dropped, and Sandino left the employ of the Italian government to become the director of the prestigious Dietrich Laboratories in Germany. Dietrich Labs had a well-deserved reputation for uncovering art fakes of all kinds. And now Donato Sandino was after my grandfather.

It had never occurred to me to ask Georges what had happened to his 1966 forgery. Could the Barberini Palace's Raphael have been stolen and replaced by Grandfather's copy? Assuming it was possible, why would the original wind up in Oakland, hanging unprotected in a columbarium and labeled a nineteenth-century copy? And assuming *that* was possible, who would have replaced it with a computer-generated copy? And where was Crispin Engels' painting?

I rubbed my forehead, fending off a headache.

Speaking of headaches . . . six months ago Michael X. Johnson had been driven away from a crime scene in the back of a police car, and I hadn't heard a peep from him since. I had assumed he was languishing in prison somewhere, and had even worried about him. Clearly that concern had been misplaced.

"By the way," I said to Mary, "I thought we agreed that you would never reveal my personal information to the enemy, aka Michael Johnson."

"This you know I never would do," Pete said. "I honor and esteem you, Annie. You are to me the most transfigurent of women."

"Thank you, Pete," I replied. "I aspire to transfigurence. But I was talking to Mary."

Mary put a pillow over her head and pretended to be asleep. Her snore sounded a lot like a Bronx cheer.

I pulled out Michael's business card and typed in the URL. The Web site opened with exploding multicolor graphics, a blaring musical score of Beethoven's Fifth set to a hip-hop beat, and a string of black-clad women high-kicking across the top of the screen. With a jolt I recognized the women as *Whistler's Mother.* Directly below the octogenarian chorus line, in a screaming eighty-point font, a fuchsia sentence took shape against a black background: *What's in your grandmother's attic?*

Whistler's mothers cha-cha'd off the left side of the screen, and a more sober Web page loaded. A Biography section described Michael X. Johnson as "an internationally recognized art expert" with "decades of experience in all aspects of the professional art world," whose "extensive hands-on knowledge of the world's finest art collections" put him on a first-name basis with "the leading curators and collectors in Europe, the United States, and Asia."

From a "profound love of art and artistry," the Letter from the Expert page explained, the "fabulously successful and recently retired" Michael X. Johnson had launched this Web site to provide "low cost!" assessments of art and artifacts, and invited viewers to send in photographs of their art objects for a professional evaluation. *Don't be fooled by greedy art dealers and collectors,* the Web site warned. *Go straight to the source! Let my wealth of experience and intimate knowledge of the mysterious world of art work for you!*

I stared at the screen, impressed and appalled. Michael X. Johnson knew everything there was to know about art theft and the art of seduction. He knew nothing about authenticating art and artifacts. What in the world was he up to this time?

The Contact Me! page listed an e-mail address and a post office box in Cupertino, which I recalled was somewhere in the South Bay, but no street address or phone number. After a few minutes of silent debate I sent Michael an e-mail to call me ASAP. I wanted to find out what he might know about Grandfather and Donato Sandino. In addition, his mere presence lent a whisper of credence to Cindy's tale of an errant multimillion-dollar painting.

I logged off the computer and started working my way through a stack of bills. Paying my debts was usually enough to send me into a downward spiral of fiscal shame, but Aaron Garner's checks had fattened my bank account, as had a long-overdue payment for a mural in an upscale home in Piedmont. And for the next four Saturdays I had a paying gig teaching a faux-finishing course to do-it-yourselfers at the Home Improv store in the City. For the first time in a long, long while I had some financial breathing room.

I breathed deeply, enjoying the sensation and figuring it wouldn't last.

The studio door banged against the wall as Evangeline Simpson strode in, a thin cardboard box held aloft in each hand. Last fall Evangeline's sculptor boss had gotten mixed up with some unsavory characters and nearly ended his days as a human sculpture exhibit, and since then she'd been working at a pizzeria in the Mission. She had the strong, square body of an East German shot-putter, and today was clad in a motorcyclist outfit of silver-studded leather pants and matching black jacket.

Evangeline and Mary had hit it off from the gecko.

"Pizza!" she called out in her upstate New York honk. "I got one Veggie and one Super Meat Lover's. No anchovies, Annie, sorry. Too stinky."

Happy to abandon my paperwork, I joined the impromptu pizza party around the old steamer trunk that I'd found on the curb next to my "new" television. As I lay sprawled on the floor with Pete, Mary, and Evangeline, it occurred to me that I should always keep such company. My jumbo-sized companions made me feel downright petite. Then I remembered the elfin Cindy Tanaka and the fact that I couldn't inch my favorite jeans past my increasingly dimpled thighs, and decided against a third slice of pizza.

"Annie, tell Evangeline about the painting. About Fornie," Mary said, and took a huge bite of pizza redolent of cheese and garlic and loaded with luscious vegetables.

"*La Fornarina* means 'little baker girl' in Italian," I said, delighted at being asked to pontificate. Generally my audi-

ence had to be held captive in some fashion. "It's a portrait
Raphael painted shortly before he died on his thirty-seventh
birthday. Some think the subject was Margherita Luti, the
daughter of an Italian baker. Rumor has it that Raphael was
so obsessed with Margherita that he was unable to complete
the frescos at his patron's Roman estate until she was
brought to the villa."

"That's *so* awesome," Mary sighed.

"It created quite a scandal because Raphael was already
engaged to the niece of a Vatican cardinal. The painter de-
layed the nuptials for six years, dragging his feet until his
betrothed finally died."

"Bummer for her," said Evangeline, stifling a belch.

"Others believe *La Fornarina* was another woman,
whose portrait had been commissioned by Raphael's power-
ful patron, Agostino Chigi, at whose villa Raphael and
Margherita lived. Chigi married *his* longtime mistress,
Francesca Ardeasca, in a ceremony conducted by the pope
in 1519. Still other art historians argue that Raphael didn't
paint *La Fornarina* at all, and that it should be attributed to
his student, Giulio Romano."

"But, Annie," said Pete. "If she is lovely, this painting,
what does it matter who the woman was or who painted
her?"

"Because if Raphael didn't paint *La Fornarina,* then it's
just a nice Renaissance painting," I insisted. "It isn't a genuine Raphael."

"Can't argue with that logic," Mary said. "Annie, tell them
the best part."

"There is more?" Pete asked as Mary handed him a slice
heaped with what appeared to be half a pound of cured meat,
glistening with oil and dripping with mozzarella. Now that I
was sated, just looking at all that cholesterol made me wish
for a bowl of oat bran.

"There's some speculation that Raphael and Margherita were secretly married," I continued. "*La Fornarina* has an expensive pearl bauble on her turban, a jewel that was much too pricey for the daughter of a mere baker. It would, however, be an appropriate wedding gift from the great Raphael. And here's the best part. 'Margherita' means 'pearl' in Italian."

"Hol' on. I thought a margarita wuz a drink," Evangeline interrupted. "We had a coupla bitchin' pitchers of margaritas with our fish taco platters at Chevy's last week." She and Mary whooped and high-fived. Pete looked impressed.

"The drink was named after a woman, who was named after a pearl. Or a daisy. Same word in Spanish and Italian. Do you guys want to hear the story or not?"

"Yes, please, Annie," Mary said with a wink.

"Yes, please, Annie," Evangeline echoed with a giggle.

In the past few months Mary and Evangeline had become fast friends, and in the process regressed a dozen years in maturity.

"Okay, then," I continued, mollified. "There are other clues supporting the secret marriage theory. For one thing, Raphael signed the painting on the woman's blue armband, indicating a possible attachment to her. During the romantic age of the late 1800s, the story caught the public imagination. The artist Jean-Auguste-Dominique Ingres painted five different portraits of Raphael and *La Fornarina*. The French writer Balzac wrote about the love affair. And Pablo Picasso did a series of erotic drawings of Raphael and his lover caught *in flagrante* by the pope."

"Imagine being busted by the pope while you're doing it," Mary said. "Now, that's what I call a buzz kill."

"What are the other clues?" Pete asked, intrigued.

"A few years ago art restorers at the Galleria Nazionale discovered myrtle and quince bushes—the traditional symbols

of love, fidelity, and fecundity—in the painting's background, and, most importantly, a small ring on *La Fornarina's* left hand. The bushes and the ring had been
deliberately painted over, either by Raphael or by one of his
students. After Raphael's death, the woman believed to be
La Fornarina entered a convent where she was known as '*la
vedova Margherita,*' which means 'the widow Margherita.' "

"That's so romantic," Mary breathed.

"I still don' geddit," Evangeline said.

"Which part?"

"Who painted *Da Fornicator*?"

"It's not important," I sighed. I checked my watch, got to
my feet, and brushed pizza crumbs from my overalls. "It's
just a pretty story."

"C'mon, Evangeline," said Mary. "I'll explain it to you
on the way to Oakland. Did you bring your stuff for the
overnight?"

"I really wish you would reconsider, guys," I said, thinking of last night's grave robber. True, the ghoul in the green
mask had been scared off by a woman who weighed less
than the average Great Dane, but what if he returned with reinforcements? "I heard there's been some trouble at the
cemetery recently."

"Don't worry, I've got my can of mace," Mary said. "And
if we get busted I promise I won't mention your name."

I glared at her. I was jittery about any interaction with the
police, and had recently learned that if someone knew a
painting was stolen and didn't alert the authorities, that
someone could be prosecuted, in some instances more seriously than the thief. Even worse, there was a statute of lim-
itations on criminal acts, but not on criminal knowledge.

This was the sort of thing that kept me up nights.

The happy campers wrapped up the leftover pizza,
grabbed Mary's sleeping bag and tote, and lumbered out of

the studio. As I stood in the door watching Evangeline's leather-clad form bump into the wall twice as she made her way down the hall, I wondered how she and Mary would secure their gear, plus their two ample bodies, on Evangeline's BMW motorcycle for the trip across the bridge to Oakland. I decided I didn't really want to know.

"I have always found this Evangeline to be a very handful woman," Pete murmured. His soft brown eyes were shining and there was a goofy half smile on his face.

Well, well, I thought. "I think you mean 'handsome,' Pete. But you're right about one thing. Evangeline *is* quite a handful."

Chapter 5

The job of the artist is always to deepen the mystery.

—Francis Bacon (1909–1992), British painter

The job of the art forger is to render the mystery impenetrable. Especially to Interpol.

—Georges LeFleur

At the end of my first year in business I had been shocked to discover that the IRS expected me to pay hefty self-employment taxes even though True/Faux Studios had lost money. As my unsympathetic tax accountant commented: "You gotta pay your taxes. Business is ninety percent paperwork whether you're selling art, paper clips, or pigs' snouts."

Kind of took the glamour out of the old day job.

Then again, being self-employed allowed me to deduct the cost of art supplies as a business expense, which was a boon for an artaholic like me. More than once I had assuaged my woes with a ream of expensive Belgian linen canvas or a pot of powdered pigment. And though I wouldn't be caught dead wearing fur, I was known to salivate over brushes of sable and rabbit hair.

I spent the next few hours blasting partway through the mountain of paperwork that is the reality of running a business: keeping the books and paying estimated quarterly taxes to the IRS and the State Board of Equalization; filling out reams of forms for Mary's biweekly check; making sure my insurance policies and business licenses and resale numbers were current; updating inventory and supplies so we didn't run out of boiled linseed oil in the middle of faux-finishing a ballroom; developing a Web site for increasingly computer-dependent designers and the public; and every now and then taking clients to task for "failing to fulfill their contractual obligations"—i.e., not paying me.

Given my family history one might think I would know that a love of art did not always accompany a sterling character, but I still took it as a personal insult when clients—usually the wealthiest ones—tried to stiff me.

My cell phone rang and I leapt on it, hoping for Cindy or Michael. It was Josh. I gave him the rundown on Aaron Garner's renovation, and he made me laugh as he described the moneyed inhabitants of Aspen. We lingered for a while on the phone. Josh was sweet and steady, and I pondered why I doubted my relationship with one of the few men I knew who had no unclear, possibly nefarious motives in wanting to be with me.

After hanging up, I spent a few minutes tidying up the studio, gathered my things, switched off the lights, and headed downstairs. Maybe tonight I'd catch up on my sleep deficit. Great. Thirty-two years old, single, and I was looking forward to a quiet evening at home and an early bedtime.

Maybe I should get a cat.

As I descended I noticed the lights blazing in the office of DeBenton Secure Transport. Peeking in the window, I saw Frank DeBenton sitting behind a massive desk, his neatly combed head bent low over paperwork, and felt a perverse satisfaction that my landlord worked even longer hours than I.

I opened the office door and poked my head in. "Heya, Frank."

His dark eyes swept over me, and I felt the little *zing* I had been getting lately around Frank. He sat back in his chair and gave me a slow smile.

Double zing.

Dammit!

"We've missed you around here, Annie," Frank said in his deep, deliberate voice. "The alarm hasn't tripped once since you began working in the East Bay. And hardly anyone uses the fire escape anymore."

Last fall I had gotten a reputation for setting off the building's shrill alarm, even though I had done it only once. Come to think of it, I had only used the fire escape once, too.

But as my mother used to tell me, once was enough to ruin a girl's reputation.

"Very funny," I said, plopping into one of the two cushy red leather chairs my landlord kept for clients and visitors.

"Aren't you working at the columbarium tonight?"

"The paint needs to dry." I knew from painful experience that if we jumped the gun the still-volatile underpaint would mingle with the new overglazes to create an all-around muddy disaster. The only remedy would be to start over from scratch.

"Mmm." A man of few words, Frank.

"May I ask a question?"

"You just did."

"You're a *riot,* Frank."

My landlord was looking especially handsome tonight. Last fall Frank and I had taken tentative steps towards developing a personal relationship, but just as we were about to head off to have Thanksgiving dinner with my parents, Josh had shown up and Frank had backed off. *It was probably just as well,* I thought. He was smart and funny, but he was a real straight arrow. Which explained why my mother was planning the wedding and I was doing my level best to ignore those pesky *zings.* Frank was a security man who hung out with law-and-order types. I was an insecurity woman who ran around with wanted-by-the-FBI types. I feared Frank might have to turn me over to the cops one day, or testify against me in court, and it was difficult to build a relationship when one person was looking for an escape route. Literally.

Not to mention I already had a boyfriend. Good ol' Josh.

Frank grinned.

Zing.

"Fire away," he said.

"Are you familiar with Raphael's *La Fornarina,* which is supposed to be in the Galleria Nazionale at the Barberini Palace . . . ?" I trailed off as Frank sat back in his chair and laced his fingers over his flat stomach in his customary "We Need to Talk" posture. It never ceased to amaze me how his warm brown eyes could turn so cold, so quickly.

"Go on."

"You okay, Frank?"

"Jim dandy. Continue."

"You're cozy with art security types. I was wondering if you'd heard anything about the Barberini's *La Fornarina.*"

"Like what?"

"Like whether it's been sold."

He shook his head.

"Removed from the museum for restoration?"

Another head shake.

"Replaced by a forgery?"

"You're the forgery expert, Annie." Frank's voice became quiet and measured, a sure sign he was agitated. "I transport fine art, but *La Fornarina* has never been under my care. Cut to the chase and tell me what you're fishing for."

"There's a version of the painting in the Chapel of the Chimes Columbarium, and it's been brought to my attention that—"

Frank interrupted. "Are you saying you saw a painting you believe to be a genuine Raphael?"

"Not in so many words."

"What *did* you see?"

"A cheap copy. One of those created by paint jets and a computer, you know the kind."

Frank nodded.

"But it was labeled a copy from the nineteenth century."

"Let me get this straight," Frank said, running a large tanned hand over his face. "You saw a computer-generated copy of Raphael's *La Fornarina* that was labeled a nineteenth-century copy, and this prompted you to imagine Raphael's original wasn't in the Barberini Palace?"

"When you phrase it like that it sounds kind of silly."

"Is there any way to phrase it that *doesn't* sound silly?"

"I know it's a wild idea, Frank, but my gut's telling me something is wrong. Another scholar swears the one she saw in the columbarium was the original. Maybe it was switched with the computer copy. I know there's nothing substantial to go on at this point, but I would feel a lot better if I knew the original Raphael was safe. And, um, an original."

"Who's this 'other scholar'?"

"She's a, uh . . . Okay, she's an anthropologist. But you know as well as I that academic training only goes so far in this field. I don't have an MFA either."

"Yes, but you're a former art forger. Which brings me to my next point. You're far more qualified than I to determine the authenticity of a Raphael masterpiece," Frank said, his head tilted to one side. "Not to mention you have more contacts in the art underworld. So why are you asking me?"

"Because I don't have any *official* contacts. Nor do I have the time or money to hop a plane to Rome to check it out for myself. I was hoping you might give your buddies on the FBI art squad a call."

The art squad was the FBI's answer to Interpol. Over the years the European law enforcement agency had worked to foil international art crime. In the U.S. of A., stolen art had traditionally been the jurisdiction of local law enforcement agencies, which meant that if the Guggenheim lost a priceless work of art it called in the NYPD. But urban police departments, overwhelmed with street crime, drugs, and random violence, rarely had the time, interest, or expertise to track down stolen masterpieces. A few years ago the FBI launched a specialized unit dedicated to tracking art and art criminals. Not only did the formation of the new squad recognize the historical and cultural value of art, but it was also a response to trends in crime in the new millennia. Stolen and forged art were now the third most profitable international crime, and were often used to launder drug money and as collateral for arms deals.

Frank was on good terms with the FBI art squad. I feared I was on file with the FBI art squad.

"I'll make a few inquiries," he said.

"Thank you."

"You're welcome."

"One more thing. Have you ever heard of Donato Sandino?"

"Of course. He's a fake buster. Probably *the* fake buster. For the last decade or so he's been the director of the Dietrich Labs in Germany. I'm surprised you've never run into him."

"Well, you know me. I keep my nose out of fakes and into faux." I repeated the phrase to myself. I liked it.

"Smart woman. Why the sudden interest in Sandino?"

"I was just wondering what he's been up to lately."

"He's rumored to be chasing a forger he calls 'the Bandit.' I don't suppose you know him?"

"Who?"

"The Bandit."

"The Bandit?"

"Because if you did happen to know the Bandit," Frank said with a ghost of a smile, "you might want to warn said Bandit he'd better beat it out of Bavaria."

" 'Fraid I don't know who you're talking about, Frank, but thanks for the heads-up." I kept my face straight while my mind raced. Had straight-and-narrow Frank DeBenton just tipped me off to warn my grandfather about Sandino? Maybe I should make a phone call or twenty to Bavaria. I rose to leave.

"Now I have a question for you," Frank said.

I sat back down. "Shoot."

"How well do you know a man who goes by the alias Michael X. Johnson?"

"Doesn't, um, ring a bell. . . ."

"Johnson came by yesterday to discuss what he calls the 'discreet retrieval' of stolen art and artifacts. As I suspect you know, he is uniquely qualified for the position."

"Oh?"

"Indeed."

"What makes you think—"

"Annie, please."

I looked away. Frank's scorn was harder to deal with than it used to be.

"Remember my friend Kevin, the FBI agent? If I'm not mistaken, you met Kevin last fall at a cocktail party in Hillsborough. Your escort that evening was a man who called himself 'Raphael,' aka Michael X. Johnson. Ring a bell now?"

Damn. "How's Kevin doing?"

"He's recovered nicely from the bullet wound," Frank said. "His ego took more of a beating. Answer my question."

"Now that you mention it," I said, "Michael's an old family friend. I had no idea what he was up to that night."

"Are you telling me your father, the eminent art scholar Dr. Harold Kincaid, consorts with art thieves?"

"The family's tie to Michael sort of skipped a generation," I said. "But, Frank, Michael has nothing to do with—"

"Annie," Frank said, a hint of sadness in his voice. "I doubt you can appreciate how much I regret having to say this, but . . ."

My heart sped up.

". . . if you continue your relationship with this man I will not be able to employ you. In any capacity. In fact, if you continue your relationship with this man, it would be better if we did not associate. At all."

A few months ago Frank and I had worked out our mutual difficulties regarding the studio rent—I had trouble paying, he had trouble collecting—by striking a deal: I functioned as his on-call art restorer and expert, and he reduced the rent. Since Frank not only owned the building but also ran an art transportation service, it seemed like the perfect fit. I had not counted on Michael X. Johnson complicating my life.

Yet again.

"What are you saying?" My voice caught in my throat.

"I cannot have a tenant—much less a friend—who is in cahoots with an art thief, even one who claims to have gone straight."

"But I'm not in cahoots with anyone! I'm one hundred percent cahoots-free!"

"Be that as it may," Frank said as he opened a manila folder on the desk in front of him. He continued without looking up. "I can't afford even the appearance of impropriety. My clients would pull their accounts so fast I'd be bankrupt in six months."

"Surely you're exaggerating. It's none of your clients' business with whom one of your tenants 'consorts'—and may I add that Michael X. Johnson has never been convicted of art theft?" I did not mention that I knew for a fact Michael was guilty as sin.

"I can't take that chance."

"Are you throwing me out of the building?" I rasped. I loved my studio. I *needed* my studio.

"Of course not," Frank said, his face softening. "I'm not an ogre, remember? But please—for both our sakes, do not continue your relationship with Johnson. He's bad news, Annie. *Very* bad news."

He closed the folder, picked up the telephone, and started dialing.

I had been dismissed. *Guess I better tell Mom to cancel the caterer,* I grumbled as I shuffled out to my truck. On the way home I rewrote the conversation with Frank in my head and dazzled my landlord with my biting, clever replies. I stopped at the Safeway on Grand Avenue to pick up something for dinner and found myself vacillating between buying a fifth of Stoli and splurging on a pint of New York Super Fudge Chunk.

I got both.

The next morning I awoke with an upset stomach and a pounding head. Rats. Time to lay off the booze and chocolate. If I weren't careful I'd turn into a fat, drunken, studioless artist.

I glanced at the clock: ten thirty. Double rats. I had intended to get up early and accomplish a million and one things, but working the swing shift had played havoc with my biorhythms. Make that a fat, drunken, studio-less, *unemployed* artist.

My late rising wasn't entirely the fault of the Stoli ice cream floats and strange work schedule. I had spent almost an hour on a fruitless round of international phone calls, and wound up leaving a trail of messages for Grandfather from Sussex to Sicily. After that, Frank's assumption that my past associations would drive away his current clients had kept me tossing and turning half the night. I hadn't been arrested since my seventeenth birthday—I didn't count the two brief detainments for civil disobedience because, after all, protest marches were one of my few regular forms of exercise—but that one teensy accusation of forgery had made me an outcast. And as much as I denied it, the rejection of the legitimate art world rankled. I was happy with my faux-finishing business, but I missed the world of rarified galleries and fine museums. If nothing else, it would be nice to be able to take in an exhibit without feeling as though I had to avoid the security cameras.

On the other hand, if the preposterous story about *La Fornarina* was true, and I could help to return the masterpiece to the Barberini Palace, I might be able to redeem myself. It was a long shot, but what would it hurt to nose around a little? As my friends liked to remind me, I was the queen of long shots. Invigorated, I pulled on my overalls and a long-sleeved black T-shirt, made a thermos of Peet's coffee, and packed a lunch of Sukhi's samosas from the local farmers' market. First stop: Roy Cogswell's office. At the very least, he might be able to enlighten me as to why the Chapel of the Chimes displayed a computerized reproduction of *La Fornarina* labeled a nineteenth-century copy by Crispin Engels. Genuine Raphael or no, that was strange.

One thought occurred to me: if the original had been hanging in the columbarium all these years, its very

anonymity had been its safekeeping. Just in case the staff
had unknowingly replaced the real *La Fornarina* with a digital copy while they sent the precious masterpiece out to be
cleaned, for example, it was best to be circumspect when
asking around. The last thing I wanted to do was give someone the idea of selling the painting to the highest bidder on
the black market.

I entered the columbarium through the front door, but
halted in my tracks when I spied Cogswell near the conference room chatting with Billy Mudd, a contractor I knew
only too well. In this land of crunchy granola environmentalists, Mudd's business cards introduced him as BILLY THE
EVIL DEVELOPER. I had to give the man points for honesty.

Last year Mudd and I had squared off at a town meeting
over his plans to replace the Fox Theater, an aging art deco
palace, with a concrete parking garage. The forces of historical preservation and all-around righteousness—bolstered
by Aaron Garner's deep pockets—had prevailed, and Mudd
had held it against me ever since. A few months ago he had
driven me off a posh Alamo job site by hinting to the owner
that I'd had a few run-ins with the law.

If only he knew.

Hoping the men were too engrossed in conversation to
notice me, I backed into a narrow apse and glanced out a
leaded window overlooking the vast graveyard. Frederick
Law Olmsted, the famous landscape architect who created
New York City's Central Park, had also designed the beautiful Bayview Cemetery, its rolling hills offering a serene
venue with breathtaking views of downtown Oakland, the
bay, San Francisco, and the Golden Gate Bridge. A handful
of dog walkers, several joggers, and a gaggle of young
moms pushing strollers took advantage of the cemetery's
willingness to act as a de facto park.

The view reminded me of a new friend who ate lunch in

the cemetery most days, and who might be a source of information about the goings-on at the columbarium. Breezing past the reception counter, I nodded at Miss Ivy, ignored her glower, and poked my head into Manny Ramirez's office.

"Hey, Manny. How's tricks?"

"Annie! The murals are looking great!" he said with a big smile. Manny's ergonomic desk chair protested as he leaned back, one outsized hand fiddling with a marble pen set he'd received for being chosen Alameda County's Accountant of the Year two years running. In his early thirties, Manny wore his shock of shiny black hair combed forward across his broad forehead in a style originated by Julius Caesar and revived by George Clooney. Thick-rimmed, retro-style glasses perched on a large nose that presided over a wide mouth. Manny wasn't fat, just extralarge, as if his parents had ordered him from the Super-Sized Infants menu. "Looks like you're making excellent progress."

"We are. We reattached the canvases to the walls last week," I said. "Now it's time for the fun part—painting and gilding."

"That's super. I can't wait to see how everything turns out."

"You and me both. Listen, I wanted to pick your brain about something. Join me for lunch on the hill?"

He glanced at a grease-stained brown paper bag sitting atop a utilitarian metal bookshelf. "Let me see . . . lunch alfresco with a lovely, talented artist? Does this mean I have to split the bologna-on-rye that I fixed this morning with my own two hands?"

"I'll trade you half a bologna-on-rye for some samosas from the farmers' market," I offered. "I'll even spring for a soda to wash 'em down."

"Best offer I've had all week," Manny said as he pulled on a light blue windbreaker.

I retrieved my shoulder bag from my truck, bought Manny a can of orange soda from the vending machine in the employee lunch room, and found him waiting for me at the cemetery gates. Making up for yesterday's rain, today was sunny and mild, the sky a brilliant, cloudless blue. We chatted about the plans for Manny's upcoming wedding as we climbed the winding road, passing the memorial to Civil War veterans, with its stack of real cannonballs that the National Park Service replenished whenever vandals made off with a few. A large tan Buick crept past us, the faces of its elderly occupants marked by age and loss. Two men in dark blue jumpsuits operated a machine that dug a grave for an interment. The muted roar of lawn mowers and whine of weed whackers revealed the presence of the fleet of gardeners at work in the distance.

At last we arrived, slightly winded, at the Locklear Family Memorial, which had been built on a scale commonly reserved for public monuments. In addition to the twenty-foot-tall central cylinder bearing the bas-relief likenesses of assorted Locklear kin—a homely bunch, judging by their squinty eyes and drooping jowls—the memorial boasted a circular stone bench that was a favorite graveyard haunt for locals in the know. It was Manny's favorite lunch spot.

From our hillside perch we enjoyed a crystal clear view of downtown Oakland and, across the bay, San Francisco's distinctive skyline marked by the pyramidal Transamerica Building. My gaze drifted down the hill to the bobbing helium balloons that indicated Louis Spencer's crypt below us. I still hadn't heard from Cindy Tanaka. Probably just busy at school, I told myself. I wondered what the police had learned about the grave robbery, and decided to inquire at the cemetery office after lunch.

I handed Manny his soda, poured myself a cup of Peet's

coffee from the thermos, and set out the samosas, peach chutney, and hot lime pickle. One of the best things about working nights and sleeping late was having lunch for breakfast. I wasn't a scrambled-eggs-and-pancakes kind of gal.

"I wanted to ask you about some of the art at the columbarium," I began, breaking open a crusty samosa, a savory Indian pastry stuffed with potatoes, vegetables, and spices.

"Miss Ivy said you were asking around," Manny mumbled through a mouthful of bologna sandwich, which he had insisted on finishing before partaking of the samosas. "I'm a numbers cruncher, remember? I'm not so good with history. You know who you should talk to? Old Mrs. Henderson. She was secretary to the director for fifty-one years, been here longer than Cogswell."

"No kidding?"

"Can you imagine working here for that long? That's dedication."

"Or lack of options."

"You're too young to be so cynical," Manny laughed. "By all reports, Mrs. Henderson loved this place."

"Maybe she has family buried here," I suggested, struggling with the concept of doing anything for fifty-one years. I had a wee problem with commitment. "Do you know where I can find her?"

"She's at a retirement home off Piedmont Avenue. Evergreen Something-or-other. You should look her up."

"Maybe I will. Tell me, Manny. What do you know about the painting in the Chapel of the Allegories, *La Fornarina*?"

"I know that she's sexy as hell," he said with a wolfish grin. "What about it? It's a copy from the 1800s. Henderson loved it, had it hanging in her office for years. When she left she made a big deal about getting the Alcove of the Allegories ready for it. Even finagled a grant to renovate it."

That cheap digital reproduction hadn't been hanging any-where until recently, I thought.

"What kind of grant?"

"The columbarium enjoys the support of a handful of bene-factors who provide targeted grants for special projects. Hen-derson was a real whiz at grant writing, as is Miss Ivy, believe it or not. Aaron Garner—the rich guy with the weird hair?—paid for the restoration of the Fornarina alcove. As a matter of fact, he's funding the alcove you're working on, too."

"Really? I'm working for Garner in the City. I didn't re-alize he was funding the mural restoration as well."

"I don't know what we would do without him. He's de-voted to the place."

My cell phone shrilled out the Mistah F.A.B. hip-hop tune Mary had downloaded when I wasn't looking. That was two weeks ago, and I still hadn't figured out how to change it back.

Amused, Manny watched me root around in my bag for the phone. "You're a rap music fan, are ya?"

"Not so's you'd notice," I muttered, flipping the phone open just as Verizon bounced the call to voice mail. I recog-nized the number: Mary. I'd call her back later. "My assis-tant did it."

"Mary?"

"Mary."

"Ah."

"Sorry about that. How did the columbarium come to own a copy of *La Fornarina*?"

He shrugged. "It's been here forever. The architect, Julia Morgan, may have purchased it in Europe when she bought a lot of other things."

"Tell me about that."

"When Chapel of the Chimes was nearing completion in the twenties, Lawrence Moore, the director of the columbar-

ium and crematorium, sent Morgan and her artist friend—
Doris Something-or-other—on a buying trip to select art and
artifacts. Morgan picked up the Roman fountain in the Gregorian Garden on that trip, as well as the Medici lapis-and-
malachite table in the Main Cloister."

"Those are amazing pieces," I said, recalling the ancient
fountain's gorgeous mosaic and the shimmering stones of
the Medici table. "Manny, is the columbarium in financial
trouble?"

"I can't discuss privileged information with you, Annie,
you know that," Manny said as he doused a samosa with
chutney and lime pickle. "These are yummy, by the way."

"Have another."

He nodded. "I can tell you this, though. There's been talk
that the columbarium may need to sell off some of the more
valuable artwork to pay for the earthquake retrofit."

"Which pieces are they thinking of selling?"

He shrugged. "Well, there's the miniatures collection.
But I think Roy's already spoken with you about that. I
wouldn't worry about *La Fornarina,* though. It was assessed
a few years ago and isn't worth much."

"Who did the assessment?"

"I don't recall offhand. I could look it up if you'd like."

"If you don't mind."

"Sure. Any special reason?"

"I know a few people in the field, that's all." My non-
answer seemed to satisfy the accountant, who started
munching another samosa. "I saw Roy Cogswell talking
with Billy Mudd earlier. The management isn't thinking of
selling some of its land to Mudd, is it?"

"They couldn't, even if they wanted to."

"Why not?"

"Because the cemetery doesn't own the land, the residents do."

"What residents?"

With a sweep of his arm Manny gestured to the hills below us.

"You mean the *dead* people?"

He nodded. "We call them the residents."

"That's . . . different."

"Can you think of a better alternative?"

I thought of several. None was better.

"How can dead people own real estate?"

Manny laughed. "It's not as creepy as it sounds. It works like this—living people purchase the plots of land in the cemetery, or the boxes or niches in the columbarium. It's a real estate transaction, same as buying a house or a condo. Legal deeds, the whole shebang. Upon the owner's death, the title to the land reverts to a trust in perpetuity. The trust is structured so that the land can't be sold without a vote of the board and the residents."

"The dead people."

"That's right."

"So that would make a vote unlikely."

"Yep," Manny said with finality. He checked his watch and began stuffing the remnants of his meal into a crumpled brown bag. "All this talk of death has put me off my lunch, Annie. Remind me of that the next time you ask me out."

"A columbarium accountant who eats in a cemetery every day should have a stronger stomach," I said, noting that in addition to his sandwich, Manny had managed to choke down three samosas and taken a huge bite out of a fourth.

"I'm a deeply sensitive soul," he said with a wink. "Back to the salt mines. Coming with me, or are you going to stay awhile?"

"I think I'll soak up a few rays, while they last. Hey— good luck deciding on your reception hall."

"Thanks, but it's not up to me. Never underestimate the

power of a future mother-in-law. Soda's my treat next time," Manny said and started to amble down the road.

I watched as he stopped to chat with one of the gardeners; then I shoved the thermos and sack of leftover samosas into my shoulder bag and picked my way down the hill and around the tombstones to Louis Spencer's crypt. I was several yards away when I spotted a hunched old man wearing a mangy overcoat and a black beret placing a nosegay of violets on the pyramid's steps. The man scuttled away as I approached.

Except for the violets everything was as it had been the other night. The iron gate was still ajar, the balloons and toys and flowers remained, the sad-looking Raggedy Ann stared at me unblinkingly. No yellow police tape warned intruders away, no black fingerprint dust marred the surface of the white marble statues. Then again, it had been a simple grave robbery. It seemed doubtful the busy Oakland Police Department would be pulling out all the stops to find ghoulish fingerprints.

I glanced around to make sure no one was watching, pulled the gate open, and slipped inside. In the light of day the crypt felt more poignant than sinister, and the splashes of light filtering through the cross-and-rose stained glass window highlighted the evidence of decay and neglect.

I peeked behind the sepulcher. The ghoul's tools were still there.

Shutting the gate behind me, I proceeded down the hill to the cemetery offices that were housed in the old caretaker's cottage. Inside, an elderly couple sat at a desk conferring with a pale, curly-haired young man in an ill-fitting blue blazer. Three women in colorful, embroidered saris perched on a brown Naugahyde sofa and paged through a catalogue of caskets. A young couple murmured in German as they perused a map of the graves.

Death and mourning I could deal with. What appalled me was the Tim O'Neill painting hanging over the large stone fireplace. I assumed it was genuine, though I couldn't be sure. My talent for aesthetic profiling was most accurate when I felt an affinity for an artist, and O'Neill's work left me not just cold, but frozen. A self-proclaimed "painter of radiance," O'Neill mass-marketed digital reproductions of his soft-focus paintings of flower-filled villages and romantic ocean views. At a thousand dollars a pop, he was making a fortune. It wasn't bad enough that cemetery visitors were coping with the loss of a loved one; they also had to deal with O'Neill's cheesiness?

Get a grip, Annie, I thought. *Everyone has a right to an opinion—and O'Neill's more popular than you'll ever be. Plus, unlike you, he hasn't broken any actual laws.*

Other than the law of good taste.

I approached the long reception counter and nodded at the plump, fiftyish woman whose name tag indicated she was HELENA—HEAD DOCENT.

"Good afternoon and welcome," she said with a subdued smile. Helena's straight blond hair was cut in a pageboy. A single strand of pearls encircled her neck and a coral sweater-set complemented her salmon-toned lipstick. I tried to calculate the odds that there would be a time in my life when my lipstick matched my clothes. The smart money was on "fat chance."

"This may sound odd," I began, "but did anyone report a grave robbery the night before last?"

Helena's smile congealed like day-old egg yolk. Out of the corner of my eye I saw the curly-haired man glance at us, but everyone else seemed preoccupied with thoughts of death.

"Come with me, please," Helena said frostily, and I followed her down a narrow hall to a small conference room.

She slammed the door. "Who are you?" she demanded as she took a seat at the head of an oval table of dark polished cherry. "What on earth are you talking about?"

"I'm Annie Kincaid. I'm restoring some murals in the columbarium." I sank into an upholstered chair. "The other night I met Cindy Tanaka, and—"

"Who?"

"Cindy Tanaka. She's a graduate student doing a research project involving Louis Spencer's crypt?"

"I have no idea what you're talking about."

"She's researching public manifestations of death, or something like that, and—"

"Never heard of her."

"Perhaps someone else might know more about—"

"I assure you, Ms. Kincaid, *nothing* happens in this cemetery that I don't know about. I'll grant you that, from time to time, teenagers vandalize the unendowed section, or meet in groups to howl at the moon, or whatever it is they do when they should be at home in bed, but there have been *no* incidents of grave robbing. Why, the very idea . . ." She pursed her orangey lips and glared.

I became aware of the aroma of samosas and coffee emanating from my shoulder bag and filling the small, stuffy room. What with the smell, my ratty overalls, and my paint-stained T-shirt, I feared I wasn't putting my best foot forward. I tried again.

"You've never heard of a Berkeley graduate student named Cindy Tanaka doing work on public mourning?"

"I assure you, I have not."

"She was taking pictures of Louis Spencer's crypt."

Helena's lacquered pageboy swung as she shook her head.

"But she had a key to the gates."

"Impossible."

"Look, Helena, I'm not making this up," I said, frustrated. "I met Cindy here, in the cemetery, the night before last. And there was a, uh, incident."

"What kind of incident?"

"A man in a green mask tried to remove a metal box from Louis Spencer's sepulcher."

"*What?* Are you sure?"

"Positive."

"This is terrible," Helena said and stood up. "I'll look into it immediately."

The head docent scurried out of the conference room. Unsure whether or not to follow, I lingered for a moment before retracing my steps, leaving my business card on the counter in the reception area and heading out to the street.

As I emerged I saw Billy Mudd leaning against my truck. What fun.

Chapter 6

The vulgar will see nothing but chaos, disorder, and incorrectness.

— James Ensor (1860–1949), Belgian painter

The truly vulgar will see nothing but economic opportunity.

— Georges LeFleur

I had heard of love at first sight, though I remained skeptical. I had never heard of loathe at first sight, but thanks to Billy Mudd I believed in it wholeheartedly.

With spiky hair bleached bone-white by the sun and skin bronzed to a precancerous ruddiness, Billy resembled the stereotypical California surfer dude. Blond brows and lashes highlighted his cobalt-blue eyes, which strafed the world with icy disdain. A few years older than I, Billy acted much younger, and was far buffer than I could ever hope to be. His relaxed aura, combined with the über-masculine air common to construction workers, was undeniably sexual, though in a way I found repellant. If the Aryan Brotherhood had a surfing and carpentry division, Billy would be its Führer.

"Well, if it isn't Annie Kincaid," Billy sneered, his cold

eyes sweeping over me. "I *thought* that was you slinking around."

"What's up, Billy?" I said, tossing my things into the truck's cab. "Plotting to raze something of historical or artistic import?"

He laughed. "Roy tells me you're doing some restoration work at the columbarium."

"Yup."

"No interest in the cemetery, then?"

"What kind of interest?"

"Word on the street is that you've been messing around the graves."

"What street would that be? *Rue du Morgue?*"

He curled his lip, no doubt confused by the reference.

"I don't know what you're talking about, Billy," I snapped. "I ate my lunch at the Locklear Memorial. I didn't break any rules, did I?"

"No need to get defensive."

"You started it."

Billy snickered. "Do yourself a favor, Kincaid. Keep your nosy nose out of the cemetery."

"My 'nosy nose'? Did you make that up all by yourself, Billy?"

"Don't push me, toots."

"Let me ask you something, *toots,*" I said. "Are you cooking up some kind of development deal? Because I have it from a reliable source that the cemetery's land can't be sold."

"Why don't you stick to mucking around with paints and brushes, and let me worry about real estate." He glanced at the heavy Rolex encircling his wrist like a diamond-encrusted shackle. "Just remember, your buddy Aaron Garner won't always be around to save your butt."

"I'll take my chances."

"See you later," Billy said.

"Not if I see you first."

Maturity isn't my strong suit.

I watched Billy's shapely backside saunter over to the big Chevy truck parked across the street. As he climbed in and roared off, I realized with a jolt that in a weird way Evil Billy had been responsible for my meeting Aaron Garner in the first place, and for now being able to pay my bills.

I hated that kind of karmic bitchiness.

I sat in my truck for a few minutes, humming along to an old Temptations tune and wondering what the story was with Cindy Tanaka. Not only had she not called me about *La Fornarina,* but she had not informed the cemetery's management of her research, nor had she turned over the metal box from Louis Spencer's crypt. That seemed like bad form all around. I tapped the steering wheel, wondering what my next step should be. The cheap digital clock superglued to my cracked vinyl dashboard told me it was half past noon. I needed a few things from an art supply store in North Berkeley. Might as well combine that errand with a visit to Cindy's thesis adviser.

I took Telegraph Avenue north to Berkeley, the flagship of the mighty University of California system. After looping up and down Oxford, Hearst, and Bancroft streets, I snuck into a permit-only parking lot, gambling that my visit with Dr. Gossen would be over before the parking cops made their rounds.

I was just wondering where the Anthropology Department was when Pink Man whizzed past and I asked him for directions. Named for his habit of wearing a bright pink leotard, hood, and cape, Pink Man zoomed about Berkeley on a unicycle, flapping his arms to get onlookers to laugh or to clap, or in some other way to acknowledge that life was absurd.

It was a Zen thing. I thought. Or maybe he was just nuts.

I followed Pink Man's cape as he wove deftly through the hordes of book-toting students, across Sproul Plaza—the site of massive demonstrations during the Free Speech Movement of the 1960s—around the Barrows Building, past Hearst Memorial Gymnasium, and up the hill to Kroeber Hall. Waving good-bye to my colorful escort, I consulted the directory in the marble foyer and took the stairs to the second floor.

My sophomore year in college I had briefly flirted with abandoning art for anthropology when the professor of a required course explained the importance of eating local cuisine. One of my special talents was the ability to eat just about anything, and in truly astonishing quantities, so I figured I was a natural for fieldwork. Fried grasshoppers and whale blubber? No problem. The secret was in the seasoning. The flirtation came to an abrupt halt with the unit on genealogical charts: patrilineal, matrilineal, affinal, fictive . . . I don't do charts. I returned to art—my first love, my *true* love—and had never again strayed.

Halfway down the long, windowless hall was a clutch of administrative offices and a door marked DEPARTMENT OF ANTHROPOLOGY—ADMINISTRATIVE ASSISTANT. A crowded bulletin board advertised an upcoming graduate student colloquium, a presidential lecture series, and next semester's course offerings. Intrigued, I read a call for proposals for grant monies to fund a year of fieldwork among the Maya near Chichén Itzá. I liked Mexico, especially the Yucatán Peninsula. No whale blubber there, and no one to accuse me of forgery.

Too bad I had a business to run. Maybe in my next lifetime.

A pear-shaped woman with short brown hair and large round glasses was playing a game of Minesweep in the main office. "Caught me!" she laughed, looking up from the computer. "I gave up smoking two weeks ago and whenever I feel the urge to go outside for a puff, I play this stupid game instead."

"How's it going?"

"Let's just say I'm the department Minesweeper champion, and if you know graduate students, you know that's quite an accomplishment."

"I've never gotten past the intermediate level," I confessed. "I keep blowing myself up."

"Beats emphysema or lung cancer. Two weeks smoke-free! So what can I do for you?"

"I think we spoke on the phone. I'm trying to get in touch with Cindy Tanaka?"

"Still haven't seen her." She craned her neck to peruse a bank of cubbyholes on the far wall. "Looks like she hasn't picked up her mail or messages, either. That's odd."

"Is she usually more reliable?"

"We set our watches by her. Cindy lives and breathes anthropology. I keep telling her she should get out more, have some fun—which is unusual, come to think of it. Anthropologists are famous for socializing."

"But not Cindy?"

"Not recently. She's kept to herself a lot. I hope she's not sick."

"You said her thesis adviser has office hours now?"

"Randall Gossen. Down the hall, room 257."

Dr. Gossen—"Call me Randy," he said jovially when I introduced myself—was a small man in his forties, with shaggy brown hair, a graying goatee, and thick tortoiseshell glasses. He wore the tenured male academic's unofficial uniform of rumpled khakis, green-and-tan-checked cotton shirt, and brown corduroy sports jacket, none of which complemented his pasty complexion. Clearly the professor did not waste any time basking in California's legendary sunshine.

"I'm glad you came," he said as I took a seat in a beige plastic chair in front of his messy gray desk. He shoved a stack of journals aside, placed his hands palms-down on the green blotter, and leaned toward me. "I was shocked when Ms. Tanaka didn't show up for her talk at the department's lunchtime colloquium yesterday. Absolutely gobsmacked. Have you heard from her?"

"I'm afraid not. I'm looking for her myself. She was supposed to be somewhere yesterday and never arrived."

"I don't have to tell you I'm concerned," Randy said, pushing his glasses up the bridge of his long nose. "She's not answering her phone, either. This isn't like her, not like her at all. Have you been by her apartment?"

"Actually, I was hoping to get Cindy's address from you."

Gossen fixed me with a strange look. "I thought you said you were her friend."

"We met the other night. I wouldn't say we're friends so much as friendly."

He shook his disheveled head and the glasses slid back down his nose. "Can't help you, then. I'll tell you what I told that other guy. It's against federal privacy laws to disclose students' personal information. Sorry."

"What other guy?"

"This is all highly irregular. . . ."

"I understand," I said, biting my tongue in frustration. Fortunately, my father was a professor so I knew how to get the breed talking. "Perhaps you could tell me about Cindy's research? That's not classified, is it?"

"No, not at all. Her research focuses on the phenomenon of public grieving, with particular emphasis on the shrinelike constructions that emerge spontaneously at the sites of traffic accidents, drive-by shootings, natural disasters, that sort of thing. It's quite a big suitcase of ideas to unpack, as we say around here. Lots of teddy bears and balloons, but they're significant when you consider the larger picture of—"

The telephone rang.

"Excuse me," the professor said and picked up the receiver. "Randy Gossen. Yes, I am. No, in fact a friend of hers is here right now, asking about her." He glanced at me and I thought he might have paled slightly. " 'Annie Kincaid.' You don't? Brown hair and eyes, medium . . . ? I see. Yes, I certainly will." He hung up and scowled.

I smiled uncertainly.

"How did you say you knew Cindy?" he demanded.

"We met the other night, in the graveyard—"

"What were you doing in a graveyard?"

"Talking to Cindy. I was working nearby, and saw a light at the crypt, and—"

"That was Ms. Tanaka's roommate on the phone. She's on a research trip and is worried because Cindy hasn't answered the phone for the past few days. She also says Cindy's been harassed by a person or persons unknown. I think perhaps I should call the authorities—" He leaned back in his chair, bumped a metal shelf behind him, and dislodged a globe. It fell to the floor and rolled over to my feet.

I scooped it up. "Dr. Gossen, I assure you I haven't been harassing Cindy Tanaka, or anyone else for that matter," I said, deciding Frank DeBenton didn't count. "I met Cindy at the cemetery the other night, she told me she was doing research on public grieving, and—"

"May I have my world back, please?"

He held out his hands and I passed him the globe. He cradled it against his thin chest and stuck out his goateed chin.

"Dr. Gossen," I persisted. "If I were harassing Cindy, why would I come to see you?"

His mulish expression remained unchanged, but at least he did not reach for the phone.

"One more question," I said. "Does Cindy have any training in art, or art history?"

"She's an anthropologist." Dr. Gossen frowned. "There's some crossover in the realm of the funerary arts, but she's not an art historian. That's a whole other chestnut. Now, don't contact me again and stay away from Cindy."

I grabbed my bag and beat a retreat before the professor changed his mind and brought the wrath of the campus cops down upon my head. The drab hallway was crowded with chatty students streaming into classrooms, and I searched in vain for Cindy's face. Hearing no cries of "Stop that artist!" from Dr. Gossen, I decided to risk one last inquiry into the whereabouts of the mysterious Cindy Tanaka and ducked back into the main office.

"Hello again," I greeted the Minesweep player. "Dr. Gossen said to ask you for Cindy Tanaka's address so I could mail her a fellowship application." I lied with the ease of a maestro. It was one of the many disreputable things I did well.

"Randy okay'd it?"

"He's in his office, we just spoke. Give him a call if you'd feel more comfortable."

"That's all right," she said, her fingers flying across the keyboard. "Randy's nice enough—you wouldn't *believe* how pompous some of these professors can be—but he does get huffy when he's working. Here you go." She jotted Cindy's address on a pink Post-it note and handed it to me.

I thanked her, hurried out of the building, and made my way through the throngs of boisterous undergraduates taking advantage of a break in the rain to play Hacky Sack and toss Frisbees on the plaza. I presumed the graduate students were squirreled away in claustrophobic library carrels or working at their computers with fiendish devotion. All things considered, it was for the best that I hadn't pursued a career in anthropology. Why spend your days in a library when you could spend your nights in a columbarium?

Cindy Tanaka had struck me as a responsible scholar. But she had not picked up her mail or messages, had not called when she had said she would, and had not turned the box over to the cemetery management. Was she really being stalked and thus was keeping a low profile? Or had she opened the metal box and found something worth more than a PhD in anthropology? For all I knew she'd gotten sick of the grind and dropped out to go dance in the streets of Rio. So why did I think her disappearance had something to do with *La Fornarina*?

The mournful chiming of the campus campanile reminded me of the hour. I dashed to my truck and hopped in just as a cute campus cop with a gleam in his eye pulled up in his putt-putt cart. Waving as I roared out of the lot, I ditched the errand to the art supply store and headed south on Martin Luther King Boulevard.

According to the address on the pink Post-it, Cindy's apartment was in Oakland, near the old Neldam's Danish Bakery, in the shadow of the 980 overpass. This part of town was generously referred to as "transitional," which meant it was a mix of upwardly mobile students, downwardly mobile retirees, and more or less stable working families. Folks in this neighborhood minded their own business and did their best to avoid the rampant drug dealing and petty street crime. I knew the area because a "green builder" I had worked for was rehabbing some run-down buildings with the idea of creating an urban commune, complete with solar and wind power.

I took a right onto Thirtieth and pulled up in front of a two-story stucco 1940s duplex. Cheerful marigolds bordered a sun-parched lawn, and ancient rosebushes flanked the front steps. A cracked concrete path led to the front door. I knocked. No response. I rang the doorbell. Still nothing.

A little girl skidded up on a pink, long-handled bicycle. An old-fashioned wooden clothespin attached a playing card to the bike's frame so that it rubbed against the spokes as the wheel turned, making a pleasant clicking sound. She wore red cotton shorts and a white T-shirt, and her hair was plaited into dozens of beaded braids that fell to her slim shoulders.

"Hi," the little girl said, her face serious.

"Hi there."

"I'm Shawna. What are you doing?"

"I'm looking for a friend of mine. Do you know the women who live here?"

She nodded. "They go to school up to Berkeley."

"Have you seen them around today?"

She shook her head. "Everybody just walk in. They leave the door open."

I gave the doorknob a tentative twist. It turned, so I stuck my head inside and called out, "Hellooooo?"

The drab but clean foyer was crowded with a ten-speed bicycle and a shoe rack holding six pairs of sneakers and es-padrilles. Straight ahead was a door with K. SMYERS printed on an index card. To the right a flight of carpeted stairs led to the second floor.

"Jus' go on up," Shawna said. "I tol' you, they don' mind."

She rode off, her hair beads and the playing card clacking.

I didn't usually take etiquette advice from children, but since I was here I figured what the heck. "Cindy? Anybody home? Hello?"

At the top of the stairs another door sported another card labeled B. NGUYEN/C. TANAKA. I knocked again, again no reply. I tried the knob.

The door opened onto a bright living room furnished with a large television set, a CD player and speakers, a tall rack filled with CDs, a maroon futon sofa, a bamboo papasan chair, and a bookshelf crammed with texts. Beyond the living room was a combination kitchen/dining room with a light green Formica-topped table and four chairs. The living room walls were hung with inexpensive framed prints from local museum exhibitions. A neat stack of sky-blue bath towels were piled on the futon sofa next to a white plastic basket of clean clothes. The apartment was neat as a pin. It was also empty.

I jumped as a black cat with green headlamp eyes rubbed against my legs and mewed.

"Hello, sweetheart," I crooned, picking up the friendly feline and scratching her behind the ears. A red metal heart attached to her pink collar said her name was Lurleen.

Lurleen purred, leapt from my arms, and strolled into the kitchen, looking over her shoulder at me. A plastic dish was half-full of dry cat food, but I didn't see any water, so I filled a large bowl from the dish rack next to the sink and set it on the floor. As I watched the cat delicately lap the water, I felt an unexpected warmth. Maybe I *should* get a cat.

A door off the living room stood ajar. Lurleen dashed into the room, then returned and rubbed against my legs some more. I scooped her up.

"What's up, sweetie? Is that your room?" I pushed the door open.

The rank smell of stale vomit hit me in the gut like a sucker punch. The bedroom was lined with shelves full of textbooks, precisely labeled binders, and boxes of minicassette tapes, and was spare and tidy except for an empty bottle of Jägermeister and some vials of pills lying on the bedside table.

Cindy lay on her stomach, one arm dangling off the side of the bed so that her fingers lightly touched the floor.

Lurleen leapt from my arms and bolted from the room.

"Cindy?" I whispered. "Are you okay?"

As though in slow motion, I reached out my hand and brushed the hair from her face. Her eyes were closed, but a trickle of vomit trailed from her open mouth and pooled on the sheets. I touched her arm. It was cold and rigid.

I yanked my hand away and jumped backward, tripped, and fell on my butt. Black spots danced before my eyes. I heard someone choking and making unintelligible guttural sounds, and it took a few seconds to realize it was me. Staggering to my feet, I made it out of the room and stumbled down the stairs to the front stoop, where I sank onto the top step. Lurleen climbed into my lap with a feline air of entitlement. I stroked her sleek black fur, took great gulps of fresh air, and tried to clear my mind and get my emotions in check.

I *hated* finding dead bodies. I *really* hated the fact that finding dead bodies had become an all-too-common occurrence in my life.

There was a clicking sound. Shawna sat on her bike on the sidewalk.

"Hey, Lurleen," she said. "You okay, lady?"

"Yeah." I managed a shaky smile. "But the lady upstairs isn't so good. Have you seen anybody go in there lately?"

She shook her head. "She sick?"

"She, uh—well, she needs a doctor. Would you do me a favor, Shawna?"

"'Kay."

"Run home and call 911? Tell the operator you need an ambulance." I'd read in a library brochure called *Safety Is No Accident!* to call from a landline so the address would show up on the 911 operator's computer.

"Mama said to do that only in a 'mergency."

"This is an emergency, Shawna."

"'Kay." The girl's eyes widened, and with a push of a sandal-clad foot she headed off on her bike.

I called 911 on my cell phone just in case, wondered at the beauty and grace of cats, and tried to pull myself together.

It took only a few minutes for the emergency vehicles to arrive. A squad car was the first to pull up, followed by paramedics and a fire truck. I moved out of the way as uniformed personnel swarmed up the stairs. A potbellied, mustached cop listened to my story with a weary but compassionate air. We both fell silent as the EMTs came downstairs, shaking their heads. The cop thumbed his shoulder mike and requested that detectives be dispatched. I saw black spots again and sat down suddenly, leaning against the metal rail.

Disembodied voices spoke of a bottle of booze and vials of pills. Lurleen had abandoned me when the newcomers arrived, and I already missed her. I tried humming to block out the voices, but the only song I could think of was "Oops, I Did It Again."

A middle-aged paramedic with a kind, no-nonsense manner squatted in front of me and said she needed to check me over. I smiled at her. I liked paramedics. They helped people and never threatened to take them to jail. The woman wore her hair in a short, practical bob that Mary called a "mancut." She gave me something sweet to drink, and I started to feel less spacey.

Twenty minutes later an unmarked car pulled up and two suit-clad detectives got out. They chatted with the uniformed cops, who pointed at me. I braced myself.

"I'm Detective Hucles," a tall, soft-spoken detective said. I noticed his partner interviewing Shawna and a woman I assumed was her mother. "You found the body?"

"Yes."

"Name and address?"

I told him.

"You a friend?"

"Yes."

"How long have you been here?"

"I drove up about, I don't know—maybe forty minutes ago? I went upstairs and found Cindy. Came back downstairs and asked Shawna, the little girl, to go home and call 911."

"You have a key to the apartment?"

"No, the door was open."

"Wide open?"

"Um, no. I meant it was unlocked."

"So you just walked on in?"

"Shawna said I could."

The detective smiled. "See anyone when you got here?"

"Just the little girl. And Lurleen."

"Who's Lurleen?"

"The cat."

As if on cue, Lurleen strolled over, and I scooped her up. Her rusty purr put me at ease.

"Ah. You feeling okay?"

"I'm all right."

"Okay, then. You touch the body?"

"I moved her hair aside. And touched her arm." My skin crawled at the memory of Cindy's cold flesh.

"That's all?"

"Yes."

"Name of the deceased?"

"Cindy Tanaka. She is—was—a graduate student at Berkeley. Anthropology. A Dr. Gossen is her professor."

"Looks like she had a roommate."

"She's out of town."

"Name?"

"I don't know—I think it's on the card next to the door."

"Contact number?"

I shook my head.

"Know when she's getting back?"

"No. I've never met her. I didn't know Cindy all that well, either."

"Any reason Ms. Tanaka would want to kill herself?"

"You think she killed herself?"

"The medical examiner will make the final determination, but so far there are no signs of foul play."

"I can't imagine her doing such a thing."

"You said you didn't know her that well," he said with a shrug. "It's often hard to figure these things out."

The other detective walked up, and the two huddled. Detective Hucles turned back to me. "I'd like the EMTs to check you out again. Then you can go."

"I'm fine."

"Humor me. The first time you see a dead body can be quite a shock." He gave me an encouraging smile, and I thought, *If only the nice detective knew.* . . . He signaled the paramedic with the man-cut, who checked my vital signs again and confirmed I was safe to drive.

Shawna and her mother approached.

"Nice to meet you, lady," said Shawna.

"Are you all right?" Shawna's mother asked, her voice gentle. "What a terrible thing."

"Thanks, I'm okay. It was nice to meet you, too, Shawna."

"We'd be glad to care for Lurleen until Brianna, Cindy's roommate, gets back," Shawna's mother said. "That is, unless you'd planned to take her."

"I'd better not. I don't know anything about cats," I said and regretfully passed Lurleen to Shawna.

Detective Hucles glanced up from his notebook and handed me a business card. "You think of anything else, give me a call. We have any questions, we'll call you. Take care, now."

*   *   *

I drove straight to the cemetery. Someone there must know Cindy. She had a key to the gates, after all. A grave-robbing ghoul, wild speculation about a mistaken master-piece, and now the death of a vibrant young woman . . . how did all this fit together? *Did* it fit together?

The minute I walked into the stone cottage that housed the cemetery offices I felt assaulted by the huge Tim O'Neill painting. The downside of my sensitivity to art was that it was almost physically painful to be around something I found distasteful. At the moment my nerves were so jangled that the painting brought tears to my eyes, and the walls seemed to close in on me.

The only employee in the room was the curly-haired man, who sat at a desk talking to two young men.

"Excuse me, do you know someone named Cindy Tanaka?" I interrupted.

He shook his head, his pale eyes expressionless.

"Is Helena around?" I persisted.

He shook his head again and turned back to his clients.

I spun on my heel to leave. Big mistake. I swayed, and my knees started to buckle.

A strong hand grasped my elbow. "Why don't you have a seat for a moment?" a man's sympathetic voice suggested.

The kind-eyed stranger led me to the Naugahyde sofa and sat beside me. The gray pinstripes in his subdued, well-cut suit complemented the spray of silver at his temples. He gave me a sad smile, and white teeth flashed in a distin-guished, tanned face whose wrinkles suggested he'd seen his share of sorrows. I imagined working in the funeral business took its toll.

"You're pale," he said. "May I get you some juice?"

"No, thanks."

He took my hand in his fine-boned one. "Has someone passed?"

I nodded, and realized I'd come to the right place to mourn. "I'm sorry," I mumbled. "I hardly even knew her. I don't know why I'm reacting like this."

"Death is always a shock," he said. "No matter how much you're around it. Every once in a while a case really gets to me, and I wish I could have done more."

I stared at him. "More how?"

"Often I think that had I been called in earlier things might have turned out differently."

Turned out differently? What was this guy talking about? Dead was dead, and no funeral director in the world could change that.

The eyes that had seemed so warm and reassuring a few minutes before now took on a sinister cast. What kind of a pervert was this guy? Did he have some kind of Dr. Frankenstein complex?

"Just what do you do to them?" I demanded.

"To whom? My patients?"

"You call them your *patients*?"

The man looked bewildered. "My dear, I'm a physician."

"You don't work here?"

"You thought—oh my." He gave a hearty laugh. "No, though I do hang around often enough. My wife, Helena, is the head docent. I'm a gastroenterologist."

"A gastroenterologist?"

"A guts n' butts man, as we say in the biz."

I decided gastroenterology was even scarier than proctology.

"I was here looking for my wife. Did you know that Russell over there"—he nodded toward the curly-haired man at the desk—"is something of a cemetery savant? He wrote this." He handed me a picture book from the coffee table. Its cover read *Bay Area Cemeteries*.

I presumed the good doctor was trying to distract me, but

I appreciated his efforts. Intrigued, I flipped through the glossy photos. There was a section on modern cemeteries, but most of the book was devoted to the funerary history of the San Francisco Bay Area.

"You're that artist working next door? Annie something?" I looked up to see the curly-haired cemetery employee, Russell, standing in front of us. "What are you doing here?"

"She's looking for Helena," the doctor said. "I was just showing her your book."

"You wrote this?" I asked Russell, impressed. "It's really something."

"He certainly did," the doctor replied. "Russell knows everything there is to know about the area's cemeteries."

"It's self-published," Russell mumbled, blushing, and I realized he was more shy than unfriendly.

"What an accomplishment," I complimented him. "And what a fascinating topic. I've been working on a construction site in the City, and we found some gravestones being used as stepping stones in the garden."

Like a snake in the sun, Russell came to life. He started talking. A lot.

". . . and then between 1902 and 1917 they moved the cemeteries to Colma, and some of the remains came to Oakland. Did you know that Colma has more dead residents than live ones? It's a city built for cemeteries."

Helena's husband stood up. "Well, you seem to be in good hands now . . . Annie, is it? It was a pleasure to meet you."

"Thank you for your kindness, Dr. . . . ?"

"Dick. Call me Dick."

I nodded, though I would never understand why someone with the respectable name of Richard would prefer to be called a penis. I watched Dick walk down the corridor and go out the side door.

". . . get together Saturday, I could tell you more."

"I'm teaching a course on faux-finishing at the Home Improv in San Francisco this weekend. Maybe another time," I dodged. "Russell, is there anyone else who might know about a graduate student doing some research in the cemetery?"

"Helena's the one to talk to. She knows everything that goes on here."

"Okay, thanks." Without Dick's presence, the cemetery office felt stifling and I was anxious to leave. I wrote my cell number on a business card and handed it to Russell. "Would you ask Helena to call me when she comes in? I'll be working next door all evening."

"I'll tell her," he said, taking the card with fingers that were clammy and cold.

I ducked out the door and headed to my truck. Through the cottage's front window I saw Curly Top Russell watching me, his expression flat, almost reptilian. I tried to be charitable, but the guy gave me the creeps. Among other things, someone should tell him permanents weren't a good look for a man. And if *I* noticed someone's hair was bad, it must be *really* bad.

My visit with Dick and Russell had distracted me from the afternoon's events, but now gloom settled over me. I unearthed a sketch pad and bag of pencils from behind my truck's bench seat and hiked the hills of the cemetery in search of stone angels and inner peace.

One of the drawbacks of making art for a living was that I seldom had time to sketch or paint just for the sheer pleasure of it. I found a sweet-faced, melancholy angel resting her head in her hand, took a seat on a patch of lawn, and started to draw.

Unlike painting, which encourages the mingling of light and shadow, sketching requires the artist to impose arbitrary lines, dividing the world into separate and distinct planes. In nature there are few real lines, only swaths of color. Painting and drawing are thus two different artistic processes, two ways of interpreting the world. After a day like today I felt a need to impose order on my unruly reality, so I sat with the sounds of the trees and the birds and the faraway city, and focused on creating the length of lines, the breadth of curves, and the relative values of darks and lights. By the time I tossed my sketch pad into the truck and headed into the columbarium, I was relaxed and able to focus on the restoration.

The last of the columbarium's staff was pulling out of the employee parking lot as I let myself into the Main Cloister. I was absorbed in thoughts of tonight's restoration work, relishing the opportunity to commune with the long-dead anonymous artisans who had adorned this beautiful building so many years ago.

Someone grabbed my arm and yanked me into the empty Middle Chapel.

"Manny!" I yelled when my eyes had adjusted to the chapel's dim light. "What are you doing? You almost gave me a heart attack!"

"I'm sorry, Annie, but I need to speak with you in private," the accountant said, his big brown eyes worried.

"Well, here I am. What's up?"

"Something strange is going on. I can't find the name of the person who appraised *La Fornarina* last year."

"Don't worry about it. I'm sure it'll turn up."

"No, you don't understand. The whole *file* is missing."

"It was probably just misplaced," I said, shaking off a frisson of fear. "These things happen."

"Not in my office they don't. It's my *job* to keep meticulous records for insurance and tax purposes, Annie. I've never lost a file. *Never.*"

"Well, surely—"

"Have you spoken with Mrs. Henderson yet?" he interrupted. "The retired secretary?"

I shook my head.

"I wonder if she might know something," Manny muttered, more to himself than to me. "I found her address, by the way. Will you ask her about the file?"

I nodded and took a slip of paper from him.

"There's something else. A friend of yours came by yesterday and dropped off something with Miss Ivy."

"I saw Ivy earlier and she didn't say anything about it."

"She said you ran past her and she 'certainly wasn't going to go chasing you down the hall.' I told her I'd give it to you."

"What is it?"

"It's in my office. Follow me." He stuck his head into the hall, looked both ways, and scurried out of the Middle Chapel toward the business office.

"Who was this friend?" I asked, trotting after him. "Did he leave a name?"

"It was a woman. According to Miss Ivy she blew through here like a bat out of h-e-l-l," he spelled, and I wondered if, like me, Manny feared the karmic consequences of cursing in the presence of the dead.

I followed him through the empty reception area and down the corridor to his no-frills office. A black rolling suitcase, the kind favored by flight attendants and frequent fliers, leaned against one wall.

"You don't know who left it?" I asked.

"I didn't see her. You can ask Miss Ivy in the morning. Listen, I've got to go. I'm on the board of the Rotary Club, and we're meeting at Inn Kensington in ten minutes."

"Manny, did Miss Ivy say if the woman told her *any-thing*? Left a note, maybe?"

"Nope. I assumed you were expecting it. I thought maybe it was an artist thing."

"An artist thing?"

"I'm a CPA, Annie. What do I know from artistic temperament?" Manny shrugged his well-padded shoulders, locked up his files, and left me alone with the mysterious black suitcase.

Chapter 7

I often think that the night is more alive and more richly colored than the day.

—Vincent van Gogh (1853–1890), Dutch painter

Van Gogh had a unique talent. And, apparently, unique vision.

—Georges LeFleur

I stared at the ordinary suitcase from across the small room as though it were a poisonous snake. Had a resentful Dr. Gossen spent the afternoon thumbing through his tattered copy of *The Anarchist's Cookbook*? Would a tug on the zipper rocket me into the fourth dimension? *This'll teach an artist to mess with an anthropologist,* I imagined him cackling as he stuffed fertilizer and diesel fuel into the bag and rigged it with a timer.

Get a grip, I scolded myself. Dr. Gossen was a respectable college professor.

This line of thinking failed to reassure me. My father was also a respectable college professor, and some of his colleagues were downright certifiable.

Was that a ticking sound I heard?

Okay, Annie, calm down. Manny said a woman left the

suitcase. It couldn't have been Mary; Miss Ivy would have recognized her. Maybe Evangeline dropped off a few things for the night in the cemetery. But surely she would have called first to tell me. I pulled my cell phone out of my overalls pocket. Recently I had made a vow to keep the gadget charged and on my person, figuring that as a communications device it might work better that way than when it had a dead battery and was stuffed in my sock drawer.

It was fully charged. There were no messages.

The only other woman who might associate me with the columbarium was Cindy Tanaka. With a sense of urgency I crossed the room, knelt, and held my breath as I unzipped the suitcase.

No bang, no explosion, no homemade bomb. Only a leather camera bag and a bundle wrapped in a bright orange towel with Garfield the Cat's grinning face. Inside the camera bag was the dismantled camera Cindy had used the other night along with several murky snapshots of *La Fornarina*.

Sitting back on my heels, I listened for the sound of anyone lingering outside Manny's office. All was quiet. Slowly I unwrapped the Garfield bundle. Inside was the metal box from Louis Spencer's sepulcher. The old lock was in place and looked untouched.

I checked the suitcase's side pockets for a note or a letter—anything that would provide a hint as to what was going on here. I knew that suicidal people often made a point of tying up loose ends before making their final departure, and Cindy had struck me as the type to get her affairs in order. But why would she leave all this for me? Why hadn't she turned in the metal box to the cemetery office, as we had agreed? Did she want me to take care of it?

Another wave of sadness washed over me, and I struggled to push aside the memory of finding Cindy's body.

Minutes passed as I debated my next step. I repacked the

suitcase, zipped it shut, and eased Manny's door open. All was quiet, so I pulled the black bag, its plastic wheels clacking loudly, out of the office, along the hallways, and up and down the short flights of stairs to the Chapel of the Madonna. Mary was on the scaffolding, touching up the paint of the blue sky as she grooved to her iPod.

"Swear to God, Annie," she said, peeved. Evangeline had left a message this morning that Mary was in a rotten mood because she had chickened out of last night's graveyard slumber party. Tonight they were set to try again. "That Roy dude? Hung out trying to talk to me, like, for-*ever.* If you leave me alone here one more time, I'm gonna . . ." She glanced down at me. "You okay?"

"Sure," I said. "Just a little tired." Not wanting to relive this afternoon's gruesome discovery, I decided not to mention it to Mary.

"What's with the suitcase?"

"I need to hide it."

"Where?"

One of the many things I loved about Mary was that when I showed up trailing a suitcase to hide, she asked "where" rather than "why."

"Somewhere in the columbarium. I don't want to be seen leaving with it," I said, thinking of Russell, the observant cemetery savant. I had no idea why Cindy had left the suitcase for me, but she must have had a reason. The least I could do for her was to find out what it was.

"Do you need to hide the whole thing?" Mary asked, clambering down from the squeaky scaffolding. "Or can we unpack it? It'd be easier to hide smaller objects."

"Good point." Ex-drug-user teenage runaways made by far the best assistants when it came to skullduggery. I unzipped the suitcase and removed the camera bag and the towel-shrouded box.

"Can we lose Garfield?"

"Sure," I replied, unwrapping the metal container.

"What's in the box?" Mary said, grabbing and shaking it.

"Hey!" I said, snatching it back. "Be careful with that."

"Why? Is it gonna explode?"

"Hard to say."

"What's in it?"

"I don't know."

"Then how do you know you need to hide it?"

"I'd just feel better if it disappeared for a while. Long story."

"Sure you don't want to see what's inside? I can never wait to open packages. One Christmas my kid sister and I opened all our presents in the middle of the night. It was a real drag on Christmas morning, though."

"It's . . . private."

"Whatever you say, boss." Mary shrugged. "It's so old and cruddy it should fit right in around here. Why don't we put it in one of the niches?"

I investigated the nearest glass-fronted compartment. "It's locked. Can you open it?"

"These old locks are tougher than they look," Mary said, examining the lock. She rattled it, banged on it, and shook her head. "I could probably pick it, but my tools are in the City."

"You have lock-picking tools? You never told me that."

"I didn't want to worry you. Remember my ex, Paul, the locksmith? Locksmiths have great tools."

"So says the bumper sticker."

"Don't you think it's weird that all locksmiths aren't burglars? I mean, it'd be easy, right?"

"I guess most folks are honest. Rich people give us the keys and security codes to their houses all the time so we can do our work. But we don't steal from them."

"Hmm . . ."

"Mary, don't even think it."

"Oh, all right. I still say it's weird, though. Anyway, there must be a master key that opens all these boxes. We could search the office."

I tried to imagine riffling through Miss Ivy's desk, and conjured instead a visual of a cop shining his flashlight through the window and catching us red-handed, which I was fairly sure would get us bounced from the columbarium.

"I think we need an alternate plan," I said.

"We could bury it in one of the courtyard gardens."

"The gardeners are always fussing over those. One of them would probably dig it up."

"There was an interment in the mausoleum yesterday. We could unseal the stone and put it in there."

"There's a fresh body in there, Mare."

"Eeewww."

What to do, what to do . . . I recalled learning in my sophomore-year evolutionary biology class that humans rarely looked up because our ancient ancestors had almost never been attacked from above. Artists and architects, though, often located the most interesting details up high, out of harm's way. Craning my neck upward, I scanned the alcove's curved ceiling. The subtle up-lighting illuminating the room emanated from behind the wide cornice molding.

The molding. Of course.

But not here, I thought. The box would be safer in another alcove.

"Help me move the scaffolding."

We unlocked the wheels and dragged the creaky contraption out of the Chapel of the Madonna, down the hall past two alcoves, and into the Chapel of the Lullabies. Locking the scaffolding in place, I climbed up and peered over the edge of the cornice. A thick rope light snaked its way through the space behind the molding, but there was just enough room for the metal box.

Mary handed me the box and I set it in carefully. "How does that look?"

"It casts a shadow," Mary replied. "A rectangular shadow. It's kind of obvious."

"Hold on." Standing on tiptoe, I rearranged the rope light so that it went around the box rather than beneath it. "Better?"

"It'll do."

I hopped down and checked for myself. The light was irregular in that one spot, but from the floor the difference wasn't very noticeable.

We pushed the scaffolding back to the job site, where I unpacked the camera while Mary snagged a scraping tool and started fiddling with one of the niches. She hooted in triumph when the glass door swung open, and I tucked the camera pieces behind the funeral urn inside. I sent a silent apology to the niche's resident, Mr. Salvatore DeFazio, hoping he didn't mind the illegal sublet.

"What the heck are these supposed to be?" Mary demanded, fanning the air with the photographs.

"Let me see." We squinted at the photos.

"Is that Fornie?" Mary asked. "Whoever took these is a lousy photographer."

It was always difficult to study paintings thirdhand, through photos, but this much was obvious: the painting in the photo was not the cheap computer reproduction I had seen in the Chapel of the Allegories. The frame was different and the gloss was duller than the highly varnished copy. Whether or not it was a genuine Raphael was impossible to tell from the shadowy snapshot.

I put the photos in a brown paper bag left over from the other night's takeout, rolled the top closed, and placed it in the red plastic tub of art supplies. Mary and I returned the empty suitcase and camera bag to Manny's office and settled in to restore the lunettes.

After tonight's touch-up painting, we would let everything dry for a week before applying a nonyellowing polyurethane sealant. The last step could be completed using a ladder, so tomorrow the maintenance crew would disassemble the cumbersome scaffolding. The week of drying time might also allow me to figure out what the hell was going on with *La Fornarina* and to decide what to do with the metal box from Louis Spencer's crypt. I would retrieve the box when we returned to seal the painting.

Quiet reigned, and I lost myself in the sensuous pleasure of touching supple brush to creamy paint, of melding the hues of the wet pigments to create new tones. Oil paints allowed the underpaint to shine through, which was why the work of lazy forgers, who only painted the topmost layers, was so easy to spot.

"I wonder what's in that box," Mary mused as we floated clouds in the still-wet azure sky. Last week I had taught her how to feather the whites, grays, and violets into the pliable blue paint so that the clouds appeared ethereal rather than cottony. "I saw a movie once, where this guy? He found a mysterious box that turned out to contain the mummified hand of his lover, complete with diamond engagement ring."

"I'm pretty sure this box doesn't have a mummified hand inside."

We painted in silence for a while.

"I saw this other movie?" Mary continued. "Where a fortune was hidden in a box like that. Only it wasn't regular money, it was Confederate money, like from the Civil War?"

"Confederate bills aren't valuable, are they?"

"No. I mean, I guess collectors want them but I don't think they're worth much. But the bad guy didn't know that, so he killed a lot of people trying to get it."

"What a moron."

"Yeah. He was pretty cute, though."

"You watch a lot of crappy movies, Mary."

Mary snorted. "Like you don't?"

"At least they don't involve mummified hands or adorable psychopaths."

"Maybe you should get out more. And why are you in such a bad mood?"

"Sorry, Mare." I still couldn't bring myself to talk about Cindy. "Things have been a little nuts."

She nodded and painted some more. "I also read this story one time . . ."

By the time midnight rolled around, I was ready to risk a curse from beyond and break into the metal box myself just to put a halt to Mary's speculation on its contents and endless plot summaries. I ushered my assistant out of the columbarium, wishing her luck facing her fears in the graveyard tonight and instructing her to call if anything went wrong. Then I locked the door and returned to put the finishing touches on the angels' wings. My arms and shoulders felt the strain of working overhead on the wobbly scaffolding, but I was determined to complete this phase of the restoration.

Suddenly I heard a noise. I could not be sure of its origin because of the incessant creaking of the scaffolding, so I held still for a minute.

Nothing.

I resumed painting, my hands busy but my mind free to wander. Why did Cindy leave the suitcase with me? Why hadn't she turned the box over to the cemetery? Was I supposed to return it to Louis' crypt? Had she been so absorbed in her own misery that—

I heard it again: something between a bump and a scrape. Heart pounding, I glanced around. Nothing. The noise had seemed far away, but it was impossible to judge sound accurately in this place. Could it be Michael? Generally I didn't hear him until he wanted me to.

I set my palette on the scaffolding's wood planks, dropped my brush in the jar of mineral spirits, and climbed down. Padding softly to the alcove's arched opening, I stood stock-still and strained to listen.

Silence.

Probably my imagination running amok. It tended to do that. Still . . . I riffled through my tote bag until I found the travel-sized can of aerosol hair spray that an SFPD homicide investigator—who used to be my friend until the drug trafficking incident last fall—suggested I carry in lieu of mace. It was cheap, she had told me, legal, and effective when sprayed in an attacker's eyes. Unable to stand the suspense and emboldened by the thought that any miscreant would receive a snootful of Lady Clairol Extra-Firm Hold, I decided to investigate the source of the noise.

I stuck my head out the Gothic arch and peered up and down the hall. I saw only long banks of glass-fronted compartments holding bronze urns and boxes. No lovesick Roy Cogswell, no after-hours cleaning personnel. Nothing out of the ordinary.

My old sneakers were silent as I crept down the main hallway, through the Chapels of Peace and Rest, veering off through the Gardens of Prayer and Supplication and through the Chapels of Mercy and Resignation until I stumbled upon the Chapel of the Allegories, where the Raphael copy hung. *La Fornarina* seemed to smirk at my overactive imagination. Hussy.

I must have taken a wrong turn. The Chapel of the Allegories was a dead end.

There was the sound again, closer this time, and rhythmic. Footsteps. Heading my way.

I was trapped.

I considered hunkering down and praying that whoever was approaching would walk past, but given the sins of my youth I thought it unwise to rely on the power of prayer alone. The Chapel's floor was made of stone, the walls were solid metal-and-glass compartments. Unless I was struck by lightning and reduced to a smoking pile of ash I didn't have a chance of joining the current residents.

That left the ceiling.

I glanced up. The compartments stopped about twelve inches from the nine-foot arched ceiling, creating a narrow shelf along three sides of the alcove. I might be able to squeeze myself in and hang on long enough for whoever was approaching to leave, as long as they didn't think to look over their heads.

Now all I had to do was get up there.

I scanned the wall for a foothold. The compartment doors were set flush with each other with no toehold between them. A better bet seemed to be the projecting metal prongs that studded the walls to the left of each compartment, a few of which held cone-shaped vases, their flowers drooping. I grasped the prongs of an empty vase holder with my right hand, and reached up to grab another with my left. My right foot stepped gingerly on one about a foot from the floor. I steadied myself, tried not to fall backward, and lifted my left foot, hoping to scale the wall like Spider-Man.

I was about three feet off the floor when the metal hoops began to bend under my weight. My fingers and toes scrambled for purchase, but the pesky law of gravity tugged me backward. I made one last effort, pushing hard against the prongs beneath my feet to boost myself within reach of the next row of vase holders.

The sound of my not-inconsiderable derriere landing with a thud on the hard stone floor reverberated through the alcove. The approaching footsteps halted for a moment, then sped up. Adrenaline shot through me, my butt smarted fiercely, and my breathing was labored. I tried to breathe through my nose, but the snorting was even noisier than the panting. I leapt to my feet and flattened myself against the wall to the left of the arched alcove doorway, the can of hair spray in my right hand. Checking to be sure the can's nozzle was pointed in the proper direction so that I didn't inadvertently blind myself, I held my breath and waited.

A figure rushed through the doorway. I screamed, leapt out, and unleashed a barrage of Lady Clairol at a ghoulish green face. The masked figure yelled, and gloved hands flew to its eyes. Adrenaline pumping through me, I lowered my head and drove my shoulder into its solar plexus, ramming the figure against a bank of niches. It yelped as the vase prongs dug into its back. My knee slammed into the ghoul's groin, and he collapsed on the floor. The ghoul clutched at my legs as I darted toward the doorway, but I kicked out, hard, and shook him off.

Down the hallway I sprinted, past row upon row of alcoves, up the stairs, down another hallway, and up yet another set of stairs. I heard swearing and grunting from somewhere behind me, and the sound of footsteps slapping on the floor as the ghoul took up the chase.

Skittering around a corner into the Chapel of the Beatitudes, I saw a green Halloween mask lying on the floor. It was not the warty one my attacker had been wearing, nor was it the elongated one the grave robber had worn the other night with Cindy. What—was there a costume wholesaler down the street? And was I dealing with one guy with a mask fetish, or could there be a whole club of graveyard lunatics running around in Halloween disguises?

And where the *hell* was the exit?

Calm down, Annie. Now was not the time to panic.

Cursing my lamentable navigation skills, I crouched behind a winged sculpture in the Garden of Peace to try to get my bearings. Out of the corner of my eye I saw the flash of a tall figure and took off again, darting into the newer mausoleum wing, with its soaring cathedral ceilings and shiny pink marble crypts. Stars winked through the atrium high overhead, but the sound of footsteps spurred me on. I dashed back across the balcony connecting the new addition to the older part of the columbarium, hoping to lose my pursuer in the maze of short hallways and dark alcoves. Skidding to a halt in the Alcove of Repose, I squatted behind a baroque fountain flanked by two white stone benches.

Taking care not to make any noise, I inched Cindy Tanaka's map out of my bib pocket. From the Alcove of Repose it was a quick jaunt down the hall, past the bathroom, over to the stairs to the Main Cloister and the exit. I memorized the route, shoved the map back into my pocket, and listened for my pursuer.

All was quiet.

I crept toward the alcove doorway, looked about, and darted down the hall. I had reached the small bathroom when something hit my back, shoving me violently through the door, where I fell to the hard tile floor. The door slammed behind me, and in the pitch-black I thought I heard the jangle of keys and the sound of metal scraping and clicking. I threw myself against the door, but it was locked from the outside.

Trapped like a rat in the bathroom of a columbarium. It lacked dignity.

On the plus side, I was alive and only slightly worse for wear. My labored breathing echoed in the absolute darkness. I swung my arms blindly in the air until my fingertips found the string pull for the overhead light. I switched it on and, sight restored, spied a window behind the toilet. Climbing onto the toilet seat, I examined the small colored glass window of quatrefoil design that overlooked the Main Cloister at least twenty feet below. Generations of sloppy paint jobs had sealed it shut and I had no tools with which to pry it open. And even if I shattered the beautiful glass, I would break a leg—or more likely my neck—if I jumped to the hard tile floor below.

The window was out. The bathroom's floor was cement, the walls sturdy plaster. No help there. I always carried my keys in my overall pocket, but the master was of no use on the exterior lock.

My cell phone! I was becoming a true convert to technology. For the second time that day I dialed 911 and waited for the operator to answer and send the troops to my rescue.

And waited. I glanced at the readout: *No Signal.* I moved to another spot and I tried again. Still no go. I held it high, held it low. Cutting-edge cellular technology had been foiled by old-fashioned plaster walls, vast tile floors, and banks of metal compartments.

I pressed an ear against the bathroom door, but heard nothing. Maybe the ghoul had left and I could curl up in the corner and sleep until the cleaning crew showed up in the morning and let me out.

Or maybe the ghoul was summoning reinforcements to draw and quarter me. Did I really want to hang around and find out what a man who liked to wear Halloween masks at night—while running around graveyards and columbaria no less—was capable of?

There must be a way out of here. I looked up. The ceiling was composed of cracked glass tiles, similar in size and shape to acoustic tiles. A dim light illuminated the translucent ceiling from behind, suggesting open space beyond. It seemed a bit dicey, but what other options did I have? On the bright side, if I fell it would be a quick trip to the crematorium.

I stepped onto the toilet seat, took a deep breath, and hoisted myself onto the sturdy porcelain sink. I steadied myself with one hand on the tulip-shaped light fixture over the sink and slowly lifted my right knee onto the old-fashioned towel dispenser, the kind made of steel that housed a cloth towel on an endless loop. Balancing myself gingerly, I brought my left knee up to join the right. The towel dispenser groaned. Good thing I'd held off on that third slice of pizza.

From this precarious perch I was able to reach up to the glass tiles overhead. Pressing the fingertips of one hand against one of the larger tiles, I pushed it up and to the side. I poked my head through the hole and saw a large, open space formed by the columbarium's roof above and the glass ceilings of the alcoves below. A foot-wide metal beam separated the ceiling tiles of one room from those of its neighbor, and provided access to the overhead lights.

If I were careful I could crawl along the beam, remove a glass ceiling tile from another room, drop down through the hole, and escape.

If I weren't careful, I would crash through the glass ceiling tiles and die on the hard stone floor. Or be shredded by the broken glass, horribly disfigured, and forced to wear a Halloween mask for the rest of my life.

Reaching my arms and shoulders through the opening, I placed my hands, palms down, on the metal beam, lifted my left foot onto the tulip light above the sink, and hoisted myself up. My actions dislodged the glass lamp shade, which shattered loudly on the concrete floor. I slid the glass tile back into place and began to crawl.

The string of lights that illuminated the glass ceilings of the chapels below guided me along the beam. I moved swiftly, exhilarated at my acrobatic escape but uncertain where I was heading. As far as I could tell, I was somewhere in the vicinity of the Chapel of the Allegories when I heard voices. I peered over the edge of the beam and saw two human-sized shapes in the room below. The beautiful pastel-colored glass ceiling tiles obscured their masked faces, and try as I might I could not make out what they were saying. Fearful of attracting attention, I remained frozen, hoping they would soon leave.

Twenty minutes later, they were still there. *What are they waiting for?* I wondered. My knees started to ache, so I rested my weight on my elbows, my rear in the air.

My cell phone shrilled.

Aw, geez! The figures below looked about. I pulled the phone from my pocket and threw it as far as I could. The vivid beats of Oakland's own Mistah F.A.B. bounced off the glass tiles and echoed through the empty space. The figures in the room below ran off in search of the sound.

Crawling as rapidly as I dared, I came upon a small ventilation window. I shoved it open and spied a flat roof about five feet below.

It was now or never.

Rolling onto my stomach, I backed out the window, feet-first, maneuvered my hips over the ledge, and lowered myself as far as I could to close the distance to the rooftop. Taking a deep breath, I let go, landing on the first-story roof. I stumbled a little, but remained upright, feeling absurdly pleased with myself. I was never any good at PE in school, but give me the proper motivation and I was Wonder Woman.

When the adrenaline dissipated, I realized that I might be less than Wondrous. I had escaped the columbarium but was now stuck on a roof with a sizable drop to the alley below. I psyched myself up and tried to ignore a sudden visual of my landing butt-first on the asphalt. Even *I* didn't have enough padding in my backside to prevent a broken tailbone. Maybe I *should* have had that third slice of pizza.

One thing was clear: I couldn't stay here. I lay down on my stomach, let my legs drop over the edge, and started to inch my hips and rear into space. Easing over the side, I held on to the rim with a death grip and hung by my hands.

Strong arms grabbed my legs from below and tried to pull me the rest of the way off the roof. I thrashed and kicked and, locating my hair spray in my pocket, reached behind me and spewed Lady Clairol for all I was worth.

"Aaargh!" my assailant yelled. He let go of me and we both fell backward, he on the hard concrete, I on top of him. I jumped to my feet, spraying my mace substitute with one hand and flailing with the other, kicking out and trying to land a blow to the groin but instead connecting with his thigh as he rolled into the fetal position at my feet. I couldn't help but notice that he wore no ghoulish mask.

"Goddammit, Annie, knock it off!"

Michael.

Chapter 8

Art is much less important than life, but what a poor life without it.

—Robert Motherwell (1915–1991), American painter

I admire the idealism of the American abstract expressionists. I especially enjoy how easy it is to forge their work.

—Georges LeFleur

I punched him as hard as I could, but only made contact with his bicep. Protecting his head with his arms, Michael looked up at me, his eyes streaming tears. "Annie! It's me!"

"I *know* who it is! You scared the *crap* out of me!"

I kicked at him again, but he grabbed my leg so that I was forced to hop on one foot.

"*Knock it off!*" Michael scrambled to his feet and hoisted me over his shoulder, carrying me down the alleyway to the street. His shoulder dug into my stomach as he jogged, each jarring step forcing the air out of me. My attempts to inflict bodily injury gave way to the pressing need for oxygen, something that seemed to happen with disturbing frequency whenever I was around Michael, though usually for different reasons.

He opened his truck door, dumped me in, shoved himself in next to me, fired up the engine, and screeched away from the curb.

"You good-for-nothing, two-timing, son of a—"

"Calm down, Annie."

"What the *hell* do you think—"

"I said *calm down!*"

Michael's voice was sharp and his countenance so grim that I was shocked into silence. In the sporadic illumination of the passing streetlights I noticed his eyes were red and swollen, his elbows were bloodied, and he was breathing as hard as I was. The palms of my hands smarted, I had scraped one knee, and my butt felt bruised.

The ringside judges awarded me this round by a split decision.

Michael sped through a maze of quiet residential streets and into the hills of nearby Piedmont. Glancing frequently in the rearview mirror, he finally came to a stop in a pool of light near a pair of closed iron gates that hinted at a large estate beyond. His damp, red eyes scanned the length of the silent street before he turned off the engine and turned on me.

"What in the *hell* is going on at that place?" Michael demanded, draping one long arm on the steering wheel.

"*You* tell *me,* Mr. Art Thief."

"I told you I wasn't in the business anymore."

"Then what were you doing at the columbarium?"

"I was *trying* to do a good deed. Mary called and said she was worried about you working there all by yourself. She asked me to make sure you got home."

"How did she get your phone number?" I didn't know Michael's number; why did Mary?

"I gave it to her the other day, for emergencies." Michael leaned his head back against the headrest. "She said you'd gotten yourself involved in a bit of a mystery. Something about a metal box."

"And you raced to my rescue, is that right?"

"As a matter of fact, yes. I was afraid you were in danger."

"Well, I'm not."

"Oh, really? Do you always leave the building by jumping off the roof?"

I glared at him.

"I suppose Mary might have been matchmaking again," Michael mused. "She's not wild about this Josh person."

"Don't call him that," I snapped, annoyed because what he said was true. Mary thought Josh's earnest approach to life was at odds with my suspicious take on the world. "What were you doing in the alley?"

"Looking for you, what do you think?" he groused. "I tried your cell phone but the first call didn't go through, and you didn't answer the second. I was looking for a way to break in when I saw two men in masks running around inside, and then all of a sudden you were climbing out the ventilation window. I was trying to *help* you, Annie. Is that so hard to believe?"

"I guess not," I sighed. Michael X. Johnson had complicated my life on many occasions, but had also saved my neck a time or two at no small risk to his own. "Thank you."

"You're welcome." He fixed me with a steady look. "I don't know what's going on here, and I have a sense you're not about to tell me. May I suggest that you at least consider finishing your work at the columbarium during the day, when people who don't wear masks are around?"

"I need you to do something for me," I said, changing the subject.

"You want a *favor*? After you sprayed me with toxic chemicals?"

"It was just hair spray."

"And then you *kicked* me! In a rather private place, too. And don't tell me you didn't know what you were doing."

"I kicked your thigh. That's not private."

He snorted.

"I'm sorry if I hurt you. Now, will you do something for me?"

"Why should I?"

"I need your help."

Curiosity got the better of him, as I suspected it would. "With what?"

"I want you to find Raphael's *La Fornarina*."

"It's in Rome. I forget which museum—maybe the National Gallery? There, all done. Happy to help."

"I think it might be here somewhere."

"Impossible."

"I wouldn't be so sure."

"If you know so much, what do you need me for?"

"I want you to steal it."

Michael gaped at me, his mouth opening and closing wordlessly. He shook his head and started up the truck, his expression grim. "You're certifiable, you know that? I don't know why I even try."

"I'm serious, Michael."

"I'm sure you are," he said as we headed down the posh winding streets of Piedmont. "That's what scares me."

"If the painting's at the columbarium it would be a cinch for you to abscond with it," I pointed out.

"What about the guard dogs and the silent alarms you told me about?"

"I made those up."

"No! You mean there *isn't* a pack of vicious hounds waiting to rip my throat out?"

"Sarcasm doesn't suit you, Michael," I lied. "Besides, that was when I thought you were going to steal something."

"And now you *want* me to steal something?"

I nodded. "Now that I know you're not after it."

Michael took a deep breath and let it out forcefully. "Before I agree to anything I want you to tell me who those guys in the masks were, and why you felt compelled to leave the columbarium by way of the roof."

We halted at the stoplight in front of the Grand Lake Theater. The venerable old movie house featured an enormous 1920s neon sign with a marquee that listed the films showing on one side, and political statements on the other.

"I don't know," I said, distracted by this week's posting exhorting the citizenry to rise up and demand paper-ballot voting. Paper ballots seemed like a good idea, I thought. It worked for the French. I yawned, suddenly tired.

"Annie?" Michael prompted.

"It might have something to do with a box that one of those ghouls stole from a crypt . . ." I trailed off.

As we skirted Lake Merritt I realized Michael was taking me home. My truck was at the columbarium, I had not packed up my painting supplies, and I had told management to dismantle the scaffolding in the morning. "Hey! I can't go home! I have to go back!"

"Sorry, sweetie. That train has left the station."

"How am I supposed to get to work tomorrow?"

"Walk. The exercise'll do you good." Michael pulled into the gravel parking area behind my apartment. "Wait until the office opens, gather your stuff while others are around, and *don't go back.*"

I gave him a mock salute as I climbed out of the truck.

"Keep yourself safe, Annie," he said, his voice gentle. "No painting is worth your neck."

"But what if *La Fornarina* really is there somewhere?" I mumbled, then slammed the truck door. I hated it when men got all reasonable and mature when I was still in the peevish stage of a relationship.

I marched to the front door, let myself in, and locked the solid oak door behind me. Gravel spurted as Michael drove away.

I spent a restless night, falling asleep at around three in the morning, and slapping at the snooze button when the alarm shrilled at eight. I took a shower and pulled on a clean pair of paint-stained overalls and a long-sleeved T-shirt, then caught my damp hair up in a covered hair band. One great thing about being an artist is that paint doesn't care how I dress, and most people cut me a lot of slack. Then again, if I didn't watch out I'd wind up looking like Einstein. People had cut him a lot of slack, too.

Much as I hated to admit it, Michael was right. I had gotten caught up in something that resulted in me scuttling through the columbarium's light well and jumping from roofs, and I didn't even know whether the ghouls were after Louis' box or an alleged masterpiece. Plus, a young woman was dead. Time to reevaluate the choices I was making. So what if the fate of one of the world's art treasures lay in my hands? Who did I think I was, a paint-splattered Joan of Arc? What I was *supposed* to be doing was finishing curtain rods for the Design Center and putting together drawings for a new mural for a mortgage broker's office in Alameda. Today I would return to the columbarium, retrieve the box, turn it over to the police, and let Frank's contacts at the FBI worry about whether a priceless piece of Italian cultural heritage was hidden in an Oakland columbarium amidst men who got their kicks wearing Halloween masks.

I emerged from my apartment to find the skies gray and chilly and smelling of rain. I hoped it would hold off until I got to my truck—I owned several umbrellas, but could never locate one when I needed it.

The unseasonable weather matched my mood as I started trudging the two miles to the columbarium. Last night's acrobatics had left me with a scraped knee, a sore butt, and assorted strained muscles, each of which complained vociferously as I walked along streets lined with charming houses and chunky apartment complexes. The older apartment buildings featured bay windows and elaborate marble entry halls, but the newer ones had been erected during the real estate boom of the 1970s, when aesthetics gave way to slapdash construction. The names of these flat-roofed, multistory, gravel-encrusted monstrosities, such as Mira Vista Manor and Royal Palms Courtyard, were so inappropriate that I wondered if the developers had been indulging in irony.

As I climbed the rolling hills, my thoughts turned toward last night. Apart from a few heavy objets d'art, the columbarium didn't contain much of commercial value. It seemed unlikely that the masked intruders had broken in to deposit a loved one's cremains. If they were after the metal box, why hadn't they grabbed me and demanded I turn it over instead of locking me in the toilet? Had they been planning on coming back for me, when I made my daring escape? And how did they know I had the box in the first place?

Michael wasn't off the hook in my mind, either. His sudden appearance at the columbarium—not once but twice in the past few days—was a big part of the reason I was even considering the wild idea that the columbarium unknowingly possessed a Raphael masterpiece. So perhaps the ghouls hadn't been after me or Louis' box at all, but were searching for *La Fornarina*.

I tripped on a crack in the sidewalk, my teeth clacked, and I swore a blue streak in French. That reminded me of my grandfather, and I realized I'd forgotten to ask Michael what he knew about the Italian fake buster, Donato Sandino. I made a mental note to get Michael's number from Mary.

On Piedmont Avenue, a charming street fronted by quaint stores, boutiques, and restaurants, I dodged a mother with tots in tow headed for a bagel shop and veered into Peet's Coffee for a caffeine boost. Pausing in front of the small Piedmont Theater, I sipped my strong French roast and gazed at a cheap apartment building that had recently been converted to an expensive retirement community. In front of the 1950s-era building of blocky beige concrete and sliding aluminum windows was a large wooden sign stating EVER-GREEN PINES—ASSISTED LIVING FACILITY.

Manny had mentioned yesterday that this place was home to Mrs. Henderson, the columbarium's retired secretary extraordinaire. I thought of how Miss Ivy stuck her nose into everything, and realized that secretaries were like chambermaids: they knew where the dirt was. Perhaps Mrs. Henderson could allay my fears about *La Fornarina,* and I could get back to work with a clear conscience.

The glass double doors whooshed open as I approached, and my senses were assaulted by the pervasive smell of disinfectant and overcooked cafeteria food. But the foyer was pleasant, with cheerful art on the walls and tall green potted plants in the corners.

I approached a blue-haired woman seated at a tall reception desk and asked for Mrs. Henderson.

"I'm afraid you're too late," she replied, her wrinkled face a study in concern. "She's gone."

"Gone?" My heart sank. Half a century in service to the columbarium, and then she passes away within two years of retirement. *Let that be a lesson to you, Annie.* "I'm sorry to hear it. Do you know if there will be a service?"

"Beg pardon?"

"A memorial? I'd like to let her old friends know."

"Oh, my dear, you misunderstood me. Mrs. Henderson's not *dead.* Good gracious."

"Oh." I felt like an idiot. I must have death on the brain. "Well, I'm glad to hear that."

"No, no, not *dead.*" The receptionist giggled, and I wished she would stop. "She had a hair appointment this morning."

"Do you know when she'll be back?"

Blue Hair glanced at the large round clock on the wall behind her. "Should be any time now. Are you a family friend?"

"One might say that." Then again, one might not.

"Would you like to wait? She shouldn't be long."

"Thank you." I took a seat on a slippery vinyl sofa and tried to ignore the receptionist, who was recounting my faux pas to a tiny woman with skin the color of tobacco. The two women shook their heads and laughed, and repeated the story to an old man in a plaid shirt who pulled up in an electric wheelchair.

Looked like I was to be the butt of many a joke at Evergreen Pines. Cancel my donation to the AARP.

I reached for my cell phone, patting my pockets until I remembered that the device was languishing somewhere in the dropped-glass ceiling of the columbarium. It dawned on me that I had no clue how to retrieve my cell phone voice mail from any other phone. Still, the person I most wanted to hear from was Cindy Tanaka. Yesterday's events came back to me with a wave of sadness. . . . Cindy would never call me or anyone else. All night I had been pushing an idea to the back of my mind, trying to ignore it. What if Cindy hadn't killed herself? What if there was something in that box worth killing for?

"The van's returned from the beauty parlor," Blue Hair called out.

Lost in thought, I jumped at the sound of her voice.

"Goodness gracious, you're a nervous Nellie," she laughed again. "You may go see Mrs. Henderson now, if you'd like. Take the elevator to the third floor, follow the green line to the end, then follow the red line. Suite 327 will be on your left."

I exited the elevator and, feeling like Dorothy on the road to Oz, followed the line of green linoleum tiles that snaked along a dim interior corridor. The décor was Early Hospital Utilitarian: beige Formica surfaces abounded, and heavy railings were screwed into the walls to assist those with unsteady gaits. Nurses and nurses' assistants in bright pastel smocks and white pants padded about on crepe-soled shoes, filling out forms, counting pills into trays of white paper cups, and murmuring amongst themselves. An old man slumped in a wheelchair rolled himself along with one sneaker-clad foot, his whiskered chin resting on his chest. No one paid the slightest attention to me, and I was surprised that a stranger would be permitted to wander about unchallenged.

I had always envisioned my own old age spent in a quaint village in the south of France, or on some sunny beach in Mexico. I vowed to start saving money, soon. Too bad I was scarcely able to pay my bills. It made it tough to build a retirement portfolio.

The green line at last dead-ended. A red line branched off to the left, and a blue line branched off to the right. I turned left to find a pair of double wooden doors, above which a sign announced the entrance to THE REDWOOD WING. The doors opened onto a tasteful hallway painted a soft rose and decorated with glass sconces, the floor covered in Italian ceramic tile. Several oak doors were propped open, allowing the frenzied excitement of game shows to drift into the hall, though there were no other signs of life. By the time I found suite 327, I was a bit unnerved by the whole scene.

A brass plate on the wall to the left of the door was in-scribed MRS. HENDERSON. PLEASE KNOCK. I knocked.

"Come in!" a hearty voice replied, and I entered a large space laid out more like an apartment than a nursing home. On the right was an oversized door leading to a spacious bathroom, its white tiles gleaming. Straight ahead of me a wall of windows offered a view of misty rain clouds hang-ing over the hills of Bayview Cemetery. Near the windows a blue-and-white-striped love seat and a rosy brocade arm-chair were arranged around a low coffee table. Against the left wall a hospital bed was draped by an exquisite blue-and-white wedding ring quilt and matching pillow shams. The nightstand held a brass reading lamp and numerous pre-scription bottles mixed in with a forest of cheerful greeting cards. The floor was carpeted in a creamy Berber, and the pale yellow walls were hung with framed photographs of beaming, gap-toothed children as well as colorful crayon pictures drawn by childish hands. A silver bowl of potpourri on the oak bookshelf helped to mask the antiseptic smell from the hallway.

What drew my attention, though, was the framed and matted poster of *La Fornarina* above an antique writing desk. On the desk was a vase overflowing with daffodils and a faded eight-by-ten photograph of a couple. The woman looked like a middle-aged Mrs. Henderson; the man was gray-haired and leaned upon an elaborate silver cane.

"And who might you be, young lady?"

Mrs. Henderson had bone-white, tightly curled hair, and wore a high-necked lace blouse and gray wool skirt. A cro-cheted rainbow-colored shawl hugged her thin shoulders. Large, naturally misshapen pearl earrings hung from her earlobes, and a matching string of pearls encircled her throat. The backs of her clasped hands were dotted with liver spots, and her long, graceful fingers were manicured. A plain gold wedding band adorned her left ring finger. Mrs. Henderson appeared to be in her seventies and, except for the wheelchair she sat in, radiated good health and humor. Cloudy brown eyes sized me up.

"I'm Annie Kincaid," I said, hovering in the tiled entry. "I'm sorry to drop in on you unannounced."

"You aren't planning to steal from me, are you? Kidnap me? Do evil deeds?"

"I, uh . . ."

She smiled. "Come in, come in, Ms. Kincaid. You have an honest face."

So much for the saying "with age comes wisdom."

She waved me into a chair at a café table graced by a hand-tatted doily and an Italian fruit bowl with two shiny Macintosh apples. On the wall next to the table a curio cabinet displayed a collection of ornate silver. I felt like a scruffy scullery maid encountering the lady of the manor.

"Tell me about yourself, Ms. Kincaid," Mrs. Henderson said.

"I'm a faux finisher. I have a studio in San Francisco."

"Ah, a businesswoman! Are you here to sell me something?"

"Uh, no. I'm an artist, and—"

"An artist . . . Young women these days have opportunities of which the women of my generation could scarcely dream. How I envy you, my dear."

"It has its ups and downs"—boy, did it ever!—"but on the whole I wouldn't change a thing."

"That's the spirit! Well, Ms. Kincaid, since you're not here to pick my pocket nor to decorate my humble abode, to what do I owe the honor of this visit?"

I smiled and started to loosen up. Mrs. Henderson's old-fashioned manners put me at ease. That is what ladies of the manor do when scullery maids come a-calling.

"I'm working on a project at the Chapel of the Chimes. I understand you were the director's secretary for fifty years."

"I was the director's secretary for *fifty-one* years," she sniffed. "I tell the girls I've seen more dead bodies than *this* place ever will, and believe you me—that's saying something."

"Would you mind if I asked a few questions?"

"Fire away." She cocked her head and looked at me expectantly.

"What can you tell me about *La Fornarina* hanging in the Chapel of the Allegories? I see you have a poster of it here, as well."

Mrs. Henderson grew still. "They say it's a copy. A nineteenth-century copy by Crispin Engels."

"Yes, that's what I was told, as well."

We stared at each other.

"Have you ever been to Rome, my dear, to the Barberini Palace Museum?"

"A long time ago, as a child."

She gazed out the window. "I always loved *La Fornarina*. After twenty years of service, I asked to hang it in my office, and Mr. Cogswell agreed. For the next thirty years the little baker girl looked over my shoulder as I worked."

"Is that right?"

"Thirty years. Thirty *years*. Longer than you've been alive, am I right?"

"Close enough."

"Then one summer my husband was felled by a heart attack—high cholesterol, you know—and we had no children. Never been blessed . . ."

I was starting to get impatient, and wondered if Mrs. Henderson was as mentally alert as she had at first appeared. Where was she going with this?

"When my dear Charles died, I was at my wits' end. I

spent weeks in a dark room, wondering what to do with my-self. We'd planned to travel the world when we retired, and I felt cheated by fate. I was angry, of course—angry at Charles, angry at God. Furious, to be honest.

"I realized I had two choices. I could sit around in my widow's weeds and mourn what would never be, or I could embrace the gift of life and fulfill my dreams. So I took a leave of absence from Chapel of the Chimes and went to Europe. I spent several days in the National Gallery of Art in London, looking at its Raphael collection, then went to the Prado in Madrid, to the Louvre, and finally to Palazzo Pitti in Florence. I spent nearly a month doing nothing but drinking in Raphael's talent."

"It sounds wonderful," I said.

"The last stop was Rome. For an entire week I sat on a bench in the National Gallery at the Barberini, just gazing at *La Fornarina*. I was there when the museum opened first thing in the morning, and had to be shooed out at the end of the day. The guards took to calling me *Signore Fornarina*."

"Is that so?" I said, wondering how soon I could excuse myself and leave. Mrs. Henderson was a nice old lady, and I admired her taste in art—it seemed unlikely she'd been the one responsible for the Tim O'Neill painting in the cemetery office, for example—but it didn't seem that she could tell me anything of interest. The thought of Cindy churned in my gut, and I felt the urge to go paint something.

"My dear, I am not losing my faculties." Her eyes twinkled, and I blushed that she had read my thoughts. "There is a point to this story. Something was wrong with the painting."

"With *La Fornarina*?"

"The very one."

"What was wrong with it?"

"Unlike you, I'm not an artist, so I don't know how to ex-plain what I saw. Something about it was just—off. It seemed, I don't know . . . *modern* somehow. And I wasn't the only one who thought so."

Now she had my attention. It was hard to describe the feeling I got when I saw a top-notch forgery, except to say that it was a gut-level certainty that something was "off." Did Mrs. Henderson share this rare talent?

"What do you mean you weren't the only one?"

"There was a fellow, an Italian fellow." Her eyes took on a faraway look. "Anyway, it was all for naught. He went on his way, and I returned to Oakland. Still, I insisted we have the columbarium's painting assessed a few years ago. It was determined to be a nineteenth-century copy, and the provenance was in order."

"Do you remember who did the authentication?"

She waved a hand. "The name escapes me at the moment. It's in the file at the columbarium."

"The file seems to be missing. You wouldn't happen to know where it could be?"

"It should be right there, in the main file cabinet, as always. Let me see . . . the name started with a P. Powers? Phillips? No, Pitts—something Pitts. Dreadful little man, but he came highly recommended."

My heart sank. Trained at London's esteemed Remington Museum, Dr. Sebastian Pitts had a long list of scholarly publications, each more pompous than the one before. Several years ago he had relocated to San Francisco's Brock Museum and become the City's reigning art expert. When Pitts spoke, the art world listened.

Too bad he was an idiot.

"Do you know if Dr. Pitts ran any tests on the painting?"

A timid knock on the door preceded the entrance of a petite housekeeper carrying a stack of towels; she quickly disappeared into the bathroom.

"I don't want to talk about the little baker girl anymore,"

Mrs. Henderson said with a bluntness borne of age. Silence reigned until the housekeeper departed. "What else can I help you with?"

"Are you familiar with Louis Spencer's crypt?"

"Of course. Poor little thing died long before I started working there, but I remember his pyramid very well. Louis was Mr. Cogswell's cousin."

"Mr. Cogswell? You mean Roy Cogswell?" I was math-challenged, to be sure, but the dates seemed wrong.

"Good gracious, no. Bernard Cogswell, Roy's father. He was the director of Chapel of the Chimes for decades, long before Roy took over. Bernard and Louis Spencer were inseparable as children, I was told." She rolled her wheelchair over to the window, where colorful pots of winter flowers bloomed, and began inspecting their leaves. "Both boys were from local Piedmont families. The way I heard it, they were playing in the cemetery one day when Louis fell in the pond and drowned, right before Bernard's eyes. I always thought that was why Bernard pursued a career in the death business."

"The death business? Is that what you call it?"

"I spent fifty-one years being circumspect, my dear. Do you know how many ways I know of *not* saying 'dead'? The day I retired I swore, as God was my witness, never to use a euphemism again." She pinched off a faded azalea bloom. "Death is a business like any other. Those of us who work in the industry learn to accept that—or we find another job."

"I can imagine. Mrs. Henderson, did you ever hear anything about valuables in Louis Spencer's crypt?"

"Oh, sure, Bernard used to say there was a fortune in those crypts, and he said he knew because of the things buried with Louis. But I think he was all talk. Just because something's old doesn't mean it's valuable—just look at me." She laughed at her joke. "Still, if you ask me, Bernard was drawn to the business in a way that wasn't healthy. He was a very religious man, but he seemed, shall we say, *enthralled* by the business of laying the dead to rest. It fairly consumed his life. I wasn't afraid to tell him so, either. Years of faithful service provide one with a degree of latitude."

"I'll bet he wasn't happy to hear that."

"Oh, he didn't pay much attention. In those days mere secretaries—especially female secretaries—weren't accorded much status, no matter that it was I who actually ran the place. What bothered me most, though, was what Bernard did to his boy."

"What do you mean?"

"After his wife died, Bernard moved with his son into the caretaker's cottage. I never understood why. It's not as if he couldn't afford a real home. That was no place to raise an impressionable motherless child, surrounded by graves, grief, and the rituals of death. Roy grew up to be as morbid as his father." Mrs. Henderson rolled herself over to the bathroom and emerged with a long-spouted watering can. "As for me, I like flowers."

"You have quite a green thumb. May I help you with that?"

"Sit, sit." She waved me off and started to water the plants. "The secret to healthy flowers is to give them water that's just slightly warm. Try it, you'll see. I planted the gardens in the columbarium."

"There's a full-time gardener now."

"Don't I know it. I used to tend the gardens, keep the books, answer the phones, console the grieving . . . everything. It took a dozen employees to replace me."

"Your life sounds fascinating," I said. "You should write your memoirs."

"Actually, I—"

A loud knock announced the arrival of a portly, middle-aged nurse. Dressed in squeaky white athletic shoes and a tunic printed with somersaulting bears, she carried a plastic pail brimming with bottles and cloths. "Mrs. Henderson, how are we today? Time to check our insulin before our massage!"

"Going to join me, are you, Nurse Hamilton?" Mrs. Henderson replied tartly. The nurse pursed her lips and glanced at her watch. "And I was so enjoying our little chat, Ms. Kincaid."

"I should go anyway," I said, getting up. "I've got to get to work. It's been wonderful meeting you, Mrs. Henderson."

"Anytime, my dear, anytime. I do so look forward to company. Perhaps we could go for a stroll one fine sunny day."

"Would that be all right?" I asked, looking at the attendant.

"She's not a prisoner," Nurse Hamilton said as she began unloading her supplies and rolling up her sleeves. "You just have to check her insulin and keep her from sweets."

"I keep *myself* from sweets, thank you very much," snapped Mrs. Henderson.

"It's a date," I said. "Soon, I promise." Handing Mrs. Henderson one of my business cards, I left the women to continue what had the earmarks of a familiar debate. I hurried along the red line, through the double doors to the green line, down the elevator, and out of Evergreen Pines, taking great gulps of the rain-fresh breeze to clear the cloying mixture of potpourri and disinfectant from my lungs.

The rain started coming down harder, and I hurried through the drops as I headed toward the columbarium, reviewing my conversation with Mrs. Henderson in my mind. If the suspicions of a graduate student and a retired secretary were to be believed, Raphael's sixteenth-century masterpiece had until recently been hanging in Chapel of the Chimes, labeled a nineteenth-century copy. Presumably, it had then been switched with the cheap digital reproduction. Of course, neither woman was an unimpeachable source. Cindy Tanaka's reasons for believing the painting was genuine, whatever they were, had gone with her to the grave. Mrs. Henderson seemed sharp as a tack, but by her own admission had no formal training in art. I supposed it was possible that she had an innate flair for recognizing fakes, but that alone would not be sufficient to make a credible accusation. My natural talent had been honed by years of tutelage at the knee of my grandfather, an acknowledged art expert. Authentication was a tricky business, and forgers made fools of even those with years of training and experience.

And speaking of fools . . . I made a mental note to look up Sebastian Pitts, who might have stumbled across something pertinent without realizing it. Then I made a mental note to remember my mental notes.

I picked up the pace and at last reached the carved stone arches of Chapel of the Chimes Columbarium.

Two police cars were parked in the circular drive.

Rats.

Chapter 9

I think that if you shake the tree, you ought to be around when the fruit falls to pick it up.

—Mary Cassatt (1844–1926), American painter

The best fruit is plucked from the branches without delay.   —Georges LeFleur

Only an hour ago I had vowed to go to the police with the metal box from Louis Spencer's grave. Now that the police had obligingly come to me, I found my heart pounding and fought the urge to flee. Childhood habits die hard, and my adult interactions with the authorities had not laid those fears to rest.

Calm down, Annie, I scolded myself. *You're not the center of the universe.* The cops could be here for any number of reasons.

I entered the Hall of Tranquility but veered into the office when I spied the officers speaking with Roy Cogswell in the Gregorian Garden. Miss Ivy's lip curled as she gave me the once-over, and I had the distinct impression she did not approve of my rain-soaked artistic attire. I didn't think much of her outfit, either: she wore a short skirt with a black-and-white Holstein cow pattern, a wide patent leather belt, and a tight red sweater cut low enough to display much of her bony, freckled chest.

"Why are the police here?" I asked, wiping the rain from my face with my sleeve.

"There was a break-in last night."

"No kidding? Is anything, uh, missing?"

"Not that we've discovered, but we're still checking. Did you hear or see anything?"

"No, but I left early."

"The police want to speak with you," she said, sucking on her teeth. "I've been calling you at home."

"I'll talk to them. Listen, did the woman who left the suitcase for me the other day say anything?"

Miss Ivy's lips were pressed together so tightly that it looked as if she had to pry them apart through sheer force of will. "I am not a storage locker attendant."

"I know, I'm sorry. I had no idea she would be bringing it in," I replied in the soothing tone I used with crying infants and snarling dogs. "Did she mention her name?"

"No."

"Do you remember what she looked like?"

The secretary gave me an odd look. "Isn't she a friend of yours?"

"Yes, but I'm just not sure *which* friend, if you see what I mean."

"Pretty girl. Asian. Petite. Seemed in a hurry."

Cindy Tanaka.

"And did she say anything?" I asked, trying not to sound eager.

She shook her head.

"Anything at all?" I persisted. "It's important."

Miss Ivy crossed her thin arms over her flat chest. "This whole thing is odd. Very odd. I think—"

I followed her gaze over my shoulder, where a cop stood

next to Roy. Whatever I did, it would not be wise to mention
Michael, in case he had returned to the columbarium last
night as I'd asked. I should also keep mum about the metal
box and *La Fornarina,* at least until I had a chance to speak
with Sebastian Pitts. And if I told them about being chased
through the columbarium last night they might well wonder
why I had failed to report it.

So I fell back on a familiar response and danced around
the cop's questions. Without out-and-out lying I managed to
leave the young, inexperienced police officer with the impression that I had seen and heard nothing. After fifteen
minutes of this the officer seemed satisfied with my apparent cluelessness and thanked me for my help. I wondered if
he was being sarcastic.

I hurried upstairs to the Chapel of the Madonna to find
my red plastic storage tub upended, and the paints, brushes,
and other supplies scattered across the floor. The brown
paper bag containing Cindy's photographs was gone, but a
quick inventory of my shoulder bag revealed that my wallet
and valuables were still there—all five dollars and thirty-
eight cents of it. I packed my things into the bin and cleaned
up the spilled mineral spirits, wondering if I could retrieve
the metal box from behind the ceiling molding without attracting attention. It might be hard to be inconspicuous
while pushing squeaky scaffolding down the hall.

"Why did you lie to the police?" Manny demanded.

I jumped in surprise, hugged the red plastic bin to my
chest, and sloshed mineral spirits on my shirt.

"Manny, you scared me to death!" I put down the bin,
grabbed a paper towel, and dabbed ineffectually at the solvent. No decent lie came to mind, so I channeled Georges.
*When in doubt, chérie, remember ze three magic words.
Deny, deny, deny.* "I don't know what you're talking about."

"I overheard you saying you didn't know what a thief might be after. Did you forget the miniatures collection?"

"Was it taken?"

"No."

"Then what—"

"There are plenty of things a thief might want, such as the artifacts you were asking me about yesterday. It seems strange that you didn't mention any of that."

Manny looked at me with suspicion, and I realized his loyalty to the columbarium might be stronger than our two-week friendship. Had the samosas meant nothing to him?

"I just didn't . . ."

Suddenly the faint but distinct sound of Mistah F.A.B. rang out, singing "Super Sic Wit It." Sure, years of letting my cell phone battery run down and the one time I wanted it to die a quick death, it was alive and chirping from somewhere in the ceiling of the columbarium. The hip-hop tune seemed to go on forever, echoing through the chambers.

Manny gazed up at the ceiling, then back at me. "I think you should get your things together and go," he said softly.

"Manny, please, I assure you—" He pivoted on his heel and marched down the hall with me hot on his heels. "Manny, wait. Is the suitcase still in your office?"

"I thought you took it yesterday."

"I put it back."

"It's not there now. Guess that's one more thing you forgot to mention to the police."

He walked away.

It was after eleven, and I needed to get those faux-finished curtain rods to the Design Center. After lugging my tub of painting supplies to the truck, I drove into the City, pulled into the parking lot of the DeBenton Building, and parked next to Frank's shiny Jaguar.

As I started up the stairs, my landlord was coming down, a sheaf of yellow legal-sized papers in one hand and a large black umbrella in the other. Despite the wind and rain, his hair was perfect. He halted on the step above me.

"Hiya, Frank."

"Annie." He smiled.

Zing.

Dammit!

He stepped aside as an architect started up the stairs. "Come to my office for a minute. I want to talk to you."

"No time, Frank. I'm late."

"You want to hear this."

"I do?"

"Trust me."

I had paid this month's rent, hadn't dented anyone's car or set off the fire alarm. So why did I feel as if I were ten years old and had been busted for painting the caricature of Principal Eisenstein on the fence of Asco Elementary? I had been so proud of the likeness until I realized its very artistry had fingered me. Talent was a two-way street.

I tagged along to Frank's office, whose door was emblazoned with the roaring lion of DeBenton Enterprises. The emblem was on his stationery as well as his fleet of armored cars, but not on the two unmarked trucks in the corner of the parking lot. It was better that people assume the nondescript trucks were hauling sacks of potatoes or plastic lawn furniture than valuable artwork.

"A cargo plane's taking a valuable painting to LAX at two o'clock," Frank said as he hitched one hip on the side of the desk. "I want you on it."

"What for? I'm not a security guard, Frank, remember? Isn't that why you hired Bubba?" I gestured at an imposing man chatting with a woman near one of the unmarked trucks, visible through the large front window.

Frank smiled. "I'm not asking you to strap on an Uzi, Annie. The Getty Foundation is developing a program to train law enforcement personnel to spot forgeries, and several members of the FBI art squad will be there. You should meet them."

"But I have work to do!" I shuddered at the thought of what my grandfather would do to me if he learned I'd been training fake busters. Evisceration without benefit of anesthetic would be only the first step.

Frank laughed. "This is worth a lot of goodwill for you, Annie. You never know when a contact in the FBI might come in handy."

His gaze spoke volumes. I supposed it wouldn't hurt to get some intel on what the FBI's new art squad was up to.

"We'll be back tonight," Frank said. "It's just a quick in-and-out."

"We?"

"I'm personally escorting a valuable piece. I'll be the one strapping on the Uzi."

"All right. When do we leave?"

"Be downstairs in an hour. Oh, and, Annie? It wouldn't hurt to dress more, shall we say, professionally?"

"See you in an hour. With bells on."

As I charged upstairs to my studio I ran through today's To Do list. First, call Grandfather and beseech him to lie low. Second, call the Design Center and reschedule the delivery of the curtain rods. Third, e-mail Josh a status report on the Garner renovation. Fourth, dump Josh. . . .

I left a message for Grandfather at Gallerie des Beaux Arts de Paris. Monsieur Luc Olivier, the director of the gallery, was a snotty little man in a city famous for its snottiness. But I'd known Olivier since I was a tot and was not buffaloed when he tried to pull that attitude with me. After some mutual sniping, he agreed to get word to Georges, as I knew he would. Olivier needed Grandfather much more than Grandfather needed Olivier.

My second call was to the people at the Design Center who—surprise, surprise—weren't ready for the curtain rods anyway. I arranged to bring them in next week. I e-mailed Josh an update on the Garner job but said nothing about breaking up. I wasn't looking forward to a heart-to-heart chat with him but he deserved better than a Dear Josh e-mail.

I scrubbed my hands and face in the kitchen sink and rummaged through the old oak armoire for a change of clothes. I tried to keep a spare outfit or two in the studio for those occasions when paint-spattered overalls and smelly running shoes just weren't "right." I skipped over a short green skirt and low-cut cream sweater (too revealing), an assortment of Mary's favorite things (too Goth), and a tight red cocktail dress (too flirty). That exhausted the options. Frustrated, I poked around some more. At the bottom of the armoire I spied a plastic bag from The Gap, a store I never shopped at. What was that doing here? Was Mary leading a secret yuppie life?

Then I remembered: a few months ago I'd been painting a mural of Pompeii in a client's master bathroom. While I waited for the lava from Mount Vesuvius to dry I amused myself with a copy of *Dress for Success!* I had noticed on the bedside table. Inspired by the thought of "improving my financial outlook," I stopped at The Gap on the way home and bought a pair of sharp khaki pants, a crisp white oxford shirt, a navy blue cardigan sweater, and brown leather loafers. When I got back to the studio I came to my senses. Khakis and cardigans were not what my clients expected from their artist. I had a reputation to uphold. I'd tossed the bag into the armoire with the intention of returning the clothes and getting my money back but had, predictably enough, forgotten about it. I slipped the clothes on now, twisted my damp hair into a knot on top of my head, and applied a little makeup with a light hand.

I looked at myself in the mirror. All I needed was a gold FBI crest on the sweater to pass as Special Agent Annie Kincaid. J. Edgar Hoover would be proud.

I ran downstairs and met Frank under the overhang in front of his office.

"Why, Annie," he said, his eyes lighting up. "You look very nice."

"I'm in disguise. Don't get used to it."

He laughed, and when he leaned over to pick up his briefcase I realized he hadn't been kidding earlier: he was packing a pistol in a shoulder strap under his jacket. We hopped into the cab of a truck with Bubba the security guard—he didn't offer his name and I was too intimidated to ask—and drove to Mayfield's Auction House to pick up a remarkable Goya. I watched, intrigued, as Frank explained the packing process that would protect the painting during transit.

The Goya had been acclimated to a perfect fifty-five percent humidity and placed in a box within a box, the first lined with Tyvek—a moisture barrier used in home construction—the second with acid-free foam. Bubba snapped photographs of each step while Frank supervised. Once the painting was crated, the workers loaded it into the unmarked truck and strapped it to a wall. It looked as if we were in Boxcar Willie's living room.

"Why don't you use one of your armored cars?" I asked.

"It's better to keep a low profile," Frank said. "I have an unmarked follow car with two ex-cops waiting outside. They'll tag along to the airport for backup. But theft is not my top concern. Damage to the painting—from rapid environmental changes, clumsiness, that sort of thing—is a much bigger risk. It's not going to happen on my watch."

After an uneventful trip to the San Francisco Airport south of the City, I watched Frank process paperwork and chat with the warehouse workers. Wincing as a forklift operator headed for the crate with more speed than skill, Frank intervened and insisted the warehouse manager take the controls. The workers laughed at something he said, and I noticed that despite Frank's expensive suit and shiny shoes, he fit right in.

Trotting back to my side, Frank sighed. "Those forklift drivers make me crazy," he muttered. "They've got too much to do, and too little time. And they're used to loading bananas, not art. I'm always afraid they'll skewer a priceless canvas."

Half an hour later, Frank and I were strapped into the jump seats of a cargo plane with an excellent view of the crated painting alongside boxes of sourdough bread, strawberries, and tomatoes. Riding in a jump seat had sounded like fun. The reality was cold, loud, and really, really, boring. There was more legroom than on a passenger plane, but there wasn't so much as a window to look out, much less peanuts or a crappy in-flight movie.

My landlord's thigh kept touching mine as we rumbled through the air. I tried to ignore it, but the more I tried, the more I thought about it. I glanced at Frank, but he didn't seem to notice anything except the BlackBerry device that he typed into furiously, using his thumbs.

"What are you doing?" I shouted over the roar of the engines.

"Working."

"On what?"

"You wouldn't be interested."

He kept typing. I looked at the strawberries. According to the crates, they were FARM FRESH FROM MILPITAS! I hadn't realized food still grew in the South Bay. I thought it was all semiconductors and Starbucks.

There wasn't anything else to see. I was bored and worried about what I would find in Los Angeles—or what would find me. The combination made me chatty.

"You enjoy your work, don't you?" I yelled over the roar of the engines.

"Love it."

"Tell me something exciting."

Frank's thumbs ceased their frenetic hopscotch over the BlackBerry's tiny keypad. "You mean this thrill ride isn't exciting enough?"

"It's pretty exhilarating," I shouted. "But tell me something juicy about the art security business."

"I'm actually pretty excited about a new global tracking system developed in the Netherlands. It meets international air regulations, *and* has total GPS and satellite line-of-sight signal penetration. The best part is we can get global coverage with a remote-monitored base station. All we need to do is adapt it for mobility and we're good to go."

The engine roared and I waited.

"That's *it*? That's the juiciest thing you could come up with?" I asked finally. Give me the rank odors of turpentine and horsehide glue any day. So long as the phrase "satellite line-of-sight signal penetration" never came up in my work, I would die happy.

"I'm pretty excited about it," he said, and I could have sworn I heard a petulant note in his voice.

"Frank, you transport art and valuables. What about intrigue, adventure, the good stuff?"

"It's not exactly *The Thomas Crown Affair,* Annie. Other than the rare instances I'm around you, I rely more on technology and intelligence than guns and bravado."

"Sounds boring."

"Sounds safe."

"Why are you so concerned with safety?"

"Most people are." Frank gave up on the BlackBerry and slipped it into his pocket. I smiled in triumph.

"Have you always been so focused on safety?"

He chuckled.

"What?"

"Want to know a secret?"

"Yes!" I loved secrets. I would have been a fabulous gossip if I could ever remember any of them.

"I was hell on wheels as a kid," Frank said, crossing his arms over his chest. "I never knew my father, and Mom died when I was young. Her parents did their best but I didn't make it easy. By the time I was a teenager I'd been sent to juvie so many times it felt more like home than my grandparents'."

"You're kidding me."

"Afraid not. At seventeen I was busted for grand theft auto. The judge gave me one last chance to stay out of prison if I agreed to go into the military. Turns out I thrived under the discipline. I did some Special Forces work, infiltration, that sort of thing. After the military I went back to college on the G.I. Bill, majored in finance, and opened a business in the field I knew best—security."

"Damn. I never would have thought it."

"Why not?"

"Well, you seem so . . . so . . ."

"So what?"

"Straight."

"What's wrong with that? I've worked my entire adult life to be legitimate. I would think you'd understand, Ms. Art Forger Felon."

"Hey! Unlike *some* people, I was never convicted of anything, remember?"

"Let's keep it that way." He smiled and his leg pressed into mine, on purpose this time. Our eyes held for a moment, and then the copilot announced we were starting our descent into Los Angeles. I craned my neck to see out the cockpit window, but glimpsed only a thick blanket of beige smog.

For the next hour we waited on the tarmac as the strawberries and tomatoes were unloaded before the crated painting was finally transferred to an unmarked truck. We inched along the 405, and up into the winding hills to the museum. I had been to the Getty before, but in general I didn't "do" L.A. Though I was born in Paris I had thrown my lot in with the Bay Area crowd a long time ago. Except for the obligatory childhood pilgrimage to Disneyland, Northern Californians didn't mix with the folks in SoCal. We thought differently, ate differently, and were not nearly as blond or fit.

The Getty Center was the nation's wealthiest museum but its design reminded me of an upscale shopping mall. Separate buildings housed its phenomenal art collections, and boasted cafés and strolling musicians. I preferred the "old" Getty Villa in Malibu, which housed the Etruscan, Greek, and Roman antiquities. The Getty Foundation was in the midst of a protracted dispute with the Italian government over the origins of some of its art and artifacts. This was a sticky issue because long ago many premiere museums had acquired artwork from a combination of government-sanctioned plundering, smuggling, and outright theft.

The Getty Center was run like a business, selecting as its director an MBA with experience turning profits rather than an MFA with an appreciation for art. The center had cost a cool one billion dollars to build, but extended its largess to the public: it did not charge an admission fee, and was open to all. The Friday afternoon crowd enjoyed the view of downtown L.A. from the terraced gardens as our truck pulled around to the back of the museum. We passed through two sets of locked gates and were met at the loading dock by armed security guards.

A stylish woman in a severe charcoal suit greeted Frank with a kiss on both cheeks, in the French style. They started talking business, and Frank seemed to have forgotten me. I cleared my throat.

"Sorry, Annie," he said. "I need to attend to a few things with Pauline. Miranda will show you around."

An elegant young woman led the way to a windowless private gallery, asked me to wait, and closed the door. In the center of the large room was a table with a light board, a microscope, bottles of chemicals, glass bowls, and a stack of reference books and journal articles. Clear plastic bins held tweezers, cotton balls, steel wool, and other paraphernalia used by art conservators—and art forgers. The gallery's white walls were studded with beautiful paintings, each a stunning forgery. I recognized my grandfather's work as well as several by Georges' protégé, Anton Woznikowicz, and a handful of fakes by Marie Bertolini, whom I'd met at Grandfather's atelier in Paris. There were also several fine works by forgers whose signatures I did not recognize.

Three canvases were of markedly lesser quality and I presumed these were by Jazz Hart. I examined them dismissively. The forgeries lacked the depth of a decent oil painting, and would not pass even a cursory inspection by yours truly. As Georges often said, forgers who couldn't paint should stick to the abstract expressionists.

My grandfather's work dominated the collection, and my breath caught in my throat as I studied each one. Not for the first time, I was struck by Georges' singular ability to replicate so many different artists. There was an Albrecht Dürer watercolor in the style of the meticulous German Renaissance, rendered so perfectly that each hair on the rabbit was distinguishable; a Bronzino oil portrait of a child, her face shining with the smooth, luminescent paleness sought after

by sixteenth-century Italians; a Mary Cassatt painting of two
women taking tea, the frothy lace of their gowns and the
gleaming silver dishes exquisitely slapdash, as befit the Im-
pressionist obsession with the interplay of light and color.
Never had I seen so many of my grandfather's works hanging side by side on the walls of a museum, and my heart
surged as I thought of how proud Georges would be. Of
course, they were in a private workroom, not on public display, but still.

My eyes lingered on Grandfather's version of *La Fornarina*. Relieved to see the painting here—rather than, say, in
the Barberini Palace Museum—I studied her provocative
smile, her laughing eyes. She gazed at me, sultry and sexy,
tempting sane men—and, no doubt, quite a few women—to
stray. It was easy to see why this painting had launched my
grandfather's career as a forger.

"Another time, another place, he might have been a great
artist," said a voice behind me.

I spun around and saw a balding man leaning on a silver
cane. He looked to be in his late seventies, hands gnarled
and face wrinkled, and intelligence glowed in his deep hawk
eyes.

His accent sounded Italian.

"You are Annie Kincaid?"

"Yes."

"So, you admire your grandfather's work."

I pasted a blank look on my face and said nothing.

"It was Georges LeFleur's great misfortune to come of
age at a time when technical talent was less important than
revolutionary philosophy," the stooped man said as he
peered up at *La Fornarina*. He sighed. "Had your grandfather painted a red triangle on a field of black, he might be
hanging in this very museum—in the permanent collection."

As I suspected the man knew, my grandfather *was* hang-

ing in the Getty's permanent collection, as well as many of
the world's other great institutions of art and culture. Just
not under his own name.

"Most artists become bitter when they are spurned by the
art world. But not Georges LeFleur. He and I worked side by
side in Firenze during the floods. He was a gifted art conser-
vator before he began using his talents to create, rather than
to restore, rare masterpieces. But to this day he embraces art
with a joie de vivre that one cannot fault. He is a genius."
The man chuckled and turned his intense gaze on me. "But,
Ms. Kincaid, he must be stopped."

"Who are you?"

"Donato Sandino, at your service, *Signorina*."

"*Signor Sandino*." I held out my hand, though I really
wanted to mow the little fellow down and run for the airport.
"It's an honor. I've heard a great deal about you."

"And I, you," he said, shaking my hand. "Please tell me
that I am correct, and that this is indeed your grandfather's
marvelous copy of *La Fornarina*."

I remained mute. No way in hell was I going to drop a
dime on Georges, not even if Donato Sandino tied me down
and stuck a muralist's pounce stick up my nose.

"It doesn't matter." He waved his hand, as though to swat
a mosquito. "Tell me, *Signorina*, are you familiar with the
saying about the French realist Jean-Baptiste Corot?"

Indeed I was. It was one of Georges' favorites. "They say
that Corot painted two thousand canvases, five thousand of
which are in America."

Sandino chuckled again.

"But Corot was an altruist," I pointed out. "He allowed
poor artists to sign his name in order to sell their paintings."

"There are many reasons for fraud, *Signorina*," Sandino
said as he hobbled toward the worktable. "But it is a crime
nonetheless. Have you seen the list I have compiled of the

most-forged artists?" He picked up a laminated sheet and handed it to me.

The list was in alphabetical order and included Corot, Dalí, van Gogh, Modigliani, Remington, and Utrillo. I was surprised that neither Reubens nor Rembrandt was on it, for both had worked with numerous apprentices and had been generous with their signatures. Sandino's list apparently distinguished between the Old Masters who lent their fame to lesser artists, and the modern forgers who were out-and-out copyists.

"Your grandfather seldom forges the obvious works," Sandino continued. "I admire him for that. He is a man of unusual aesthetic sensibility."

I remained mute.

"As in so many things, the United States has become the biggest consumer of stolen and forged art. It may interest you to know that I am planning to move my laboratory here. Sending items to and from Europe has become . . . how do I say? Not workable. Not feasible."

Made sense. Europe was the bastion of Western art, but the American market was red-hot these days, as dealers and auction houses cashed in on the virtually unregulated industry.

"So, here I am, in the City of Angels, teaching your FBI how to spot the obvious signs of forgery so that they may call upon my services in the future. You may imagine how pleased I was to hear that the granddaughter of Georges LeFleur was inquiring after *La Fornarina*."

"I'm afraid you've been misinformed."

"You may speak freely, *Signorina*. I have no interest in your career, and I have more than enough evidence to convict your grandfather many times over. It does not follow, however, that I wish to send him to prison. Who better to understand the plight of an old man than another old man, eh?"

I was fond of Italians in general, but this man's steely determination repelled and frightened me. "I'm not sure what you're getting at."

"The FBI, even Interpol, does not have the expertise to track your grandfather. They must rely upon me. But my memory is not as it used to be. At times I am forgetful. If I were, say, to have a reason to forget, well . . ."

"What are you saying?"

Sandino smiled. "I believe that you understand me, Ms. Kincaid. Raphael's little baker girl is quite special. I became intrigued with her when I discovered your grandfather's forgery in 1966. Although his forgery was in my possession, my interest was piqued, and I began to doubt the authenticity of *La Fornarina* in the Galleria Nazionale. I brought my concerns to the museum administration, but I was laughed at. At the time, I was not sure of my own skills. I began to fear my opinion had been swayed by a romantic attachment to a charming American woman. I am Italian, after all," he said, and placed his hand over his heart. "*Romantico.*"

"Mrs. Henderson."

He looked surprised. "You know more than you admit, *Signorina.*"

"Lucky guess."

"*L'amore e cieco,* eh? Love is blind." He smiled and ducked his head. "I was engaged to another woman at the time, so it was very complicated. Still, I wanted to see the painting that Margaret—Mrs. Henderson—believed to be genuine, but I had difficulty gaining a visa to the United States. As the months wore on my colleagues convinced me that I was being foolish. I was offered a position in Germany, and I made my reputation there.

"But when I learned the granddaughter of the incomparable Georges LeFleur was asking about *La Fornarina,* my old suspicions were rekindled. I spent a great deal of time at the

Barberini, studying their painting. I am now convinced I was right all along. Bring the masterpiece to me, Ms. Kincaid, and I will make your grandfather's troubles go away. He will spend his days painting in peace, no longer sought by Donato Sandino. There are many noble families in England alone who would wish to employ him."

"And if I can't bring you *La Fornarina*?"

He gave a very Italian shrug. "As you can see, Georges LeFleur's work dominates this room. I flatter myself that I can recognize his forger's signature as easily as his talented granddaughter can. He is too well known, *Signorina*, especially since he published his memoirs."

I swore under my breath. I had *begged* Georges not to publish his memoirs, but he'd ignored me, delighted with the project and convinced of his invincibility. For once I hated the thought of being able to tell him "I told you so."

"Georges LeFleur will be found, and he will be charged. For a man his age, it might well be a death sentence. But perhaps you can save him, eh?"

Chapter 10

The artist must try to raise the level of taste of the masses, not debase himself to the level of the un-formed and impoverished taste.

—Diego Rivera (1886–1957), Mexican painter

True art expresses the soul of its creator, nothing more. It need only be sincere.

—Georges LeFleur

I had paid off my credit card bill in full last month, for the first time in five years. I ran it right back up again making my escape from L.A.

After fleeing the sinister Donato Sandino, I took a wildly expensive cab ride to the airport, where I hopped a Southwest flight to Oakland. From there I took the shuttle to BART, BART to the City, another taxi to my studio, picked up my truck, drove back to Oakland, holed up in my apartment, turned off the phone, and opened a bottle of wine.

I didn't want to deal with Frank. I didn't know if he was working with Sandino, the FBI, or both. All I knew was that Grandfather was in trouble, Donato Sandino had given me an ultimatum, and I was no closer to finding *La Fornarina* than I had been a few days ago. In brief, I was clueless, frustrated, and scared. I comforted myself with Chinese takeout and Merlot, watched a mindless reality TV show, and drifted off to sleep.

Saturday morning I sat at the kitchen table and paged halfheartedly through the *Oakland Tribune*. I never used to subscribe to the newspaper, but I'd grown weary of friends nagging me to keep up to date. I now had half-read newspapers stacked in piles throughout the apartment, creating a mazelike atmosphere reminiscent of library archives before the advent of microfiche. The mess was annoying, though my biggest worry was that if I choked to death on a chicken wing one night the authorities would think I was one of those sad, lonely hoarders.

I glanced at the headlines, decided to read the articles later—chaos, politics, and destruction were too much to deal with first thing in the morning—and turned to the local section, where I spied a follow-up story on Cindy Tanaka. I sat up straight and read:

> *Brianna Nguyen, a chemistry graduate student who shared the apartment with Ms. Tanaka, said she was shocked to realize how despondent her friend was. "She was always so driven. Maybe she just couldn't cope." The medical examiner has ruled the death a suicide.*

I dropped the paper, dug through my backpack, and found Detective Hucles' business card and phone number.

"Hucles," he answered on the first ring.

"Detective, this is Annie Kincaid. I found Cindy Tanaka's body, remember?"

"Yes, Ms. Kincaid. How can I help you?"

"I read in the paper this morning that her death has been declared a suicide."

"That's correct."

"But are you sure? I saw Cindy just a couple of days before and she seemed fine."

"That's not uncommon, Ms. Kincaid. Often suicides find an inner peace once they've made the decision to kill themselves."

"Did you know that someone had been stalking her?"

"Her professor, a Dr. Randall Gossen, mentioned it, as did her roommate. But there was no evidence to suggest foul play by that particular individual or any other."

"But who—"

"I appreciate your concern, Ms. Kincaid. If you think of anything pertinent, give me a call."

I hung up, dissatisfied but unsure what to do. This was when a person could really use a friend in the police department. In my case such a friendship seemed as likely as convincing my hair to behave on a regular basis.

I couldn't shake the feeling that Cindy's untimely death was connected to the Raphael, and/or the grave robbery. After yesterday's lovely little chat with Donato Sandino, I felt like I should be tracking down a masterpiece. I glanced at the clock. *Oops.* No time for such things now. I had to head into the City to teach the faux-finishing class at the Home Improv. I threw on some clothes and rushed out to the truck. Traffic was light and I got creative with the speed limit. Twenty minutes later I exited at Bayshore, careened across Home Improv's pitted parking lot, and raced through the cavernous warehouse store to the paint department, a mere seven minutes late.

Waiting for me were two men wearing the bright red Home Improv apron and buttons reading ASK ME! One was a fortyish, short man in a Burpee cap, the other a pimply-faced, elongated teenager. They'd cleared off two large tables and brought out the prepainted boards, paint samples, and before-and-after photographs I'd dropped off a couple of days ago. Next to these were the mounds of faux-finishing supplies the store hoped to peddle to the class: brushes and paints, glazes and rags, solvent and overpriced "faux-finishing liquid." When the store manager offered me the job he'd made it clear that he expected to sell plenty of the premixed quarts to my students even though they could mix their own, and achieve a better effect, at one-tenth the cost. I'd held my tongue and agreed to his quid pro quo. The guy had to make a living, I supposed, though it got my goat that art supplies were so expensive. The art supply house near me sold "artists' mineral spirits" in cute little six-ounce jars for the same price as a gallon of the stuff at the no-frills hardware store down the street.

"The great thing about faux-finishing is there's no 'wrong' way to do it," I lectured to the little crowd of eager stipplers. "It's all about experimentation and having a good time. Remember my personal mantra. 'You can always paint over it.' So let your inner artist come out and play!"

I felt a little silly talking like this, but my enthusiasm was genuine. No two ways about it, faux-finishing was a hoot.

As the class oohed and aahed over my sample boards and before-and-after photos there was one more tardy arrival: a tall, muscular African-American man dressed in perfectly faded jeans, work boots, and a white linen shirt. He looked like a glamorous Hollywood version of a contractor.

"Bryan!" I hadn't seen my old friend Bryan Boissevain in ages. We hugged. "What are you doing here?"

"You *know* I've been wanting to faux-finish the down-stairs bathroom, baby doll, but your rates are too pricey for me. Besides, I never get to see you anymore, so here I am!"

I set him up at the table, turned back to the group, and launched into an explanation of how to apply a tinted, transparent glaze to the prepared surface area, and then manipulate the glaze with rags, plastic bags, dry brushes, combs, or a combination of all four.

"We're using oil-based products today," I continued. "A common mistake is to use water-based faux-finishing products. They may seem more user-friendly, but the water-based products dry too fast for beginners and are best left to experienced hands. Slower-drying oil-based products keep the surface 'open' longer, allowing you to start over if you make a mistake. And remember, if you haven't made a mistake, then you haven't faux-finished!"

Everyone grabbed a prepainted sample board, chose paint colors, and began mixing their glazes. I was so busy answering questions and intervening in tinting disasters that I didn't notice someone else had joined the group. Leaving Latisha mixing a burnt sienna glaze, I whipped around and bumped into Curly Top Russell—literally.

"Russell! What a surprise," I said. Seeing the cemetery employee in a real world setting was as jarring as the time I'd run into my dentist at a bowling alley, rolling a gutter ball and guzzling cheap beer.

"You mentioned the class and it sounded interesting." He smiled but his heavy-lidded eyes were expressionless. "I own an old Victorian, not far from here. In Hunters' Point."

"Um, great," I said. Hunters' Point was full of fine old houses, but had a reputation as a rough neighborhood. It was hard to imagine this anemic cemetery fan living there. "Welcome."

I set Russell up with sample boards, glaze, and paint at the far end of one of the tables, and tried to ignore him as his pale eyes continued to track me.

". . . so I said to myself, *why* have you never been to Coit Tower?" Bryan was regaling his tablemates with a long-winded tale of his latest passion: experiencing the tourist's San Francisco. He punctuated his comments with a glaze-filled brush, flinging drops of solution in the air. I grabbed his hand and repositioned it over the sample board.

I took a spin around the other table, where Katy had gotten so distracted gossiping with Latisha about Selena's good-for-nothing husband that her glaze had developed a hard edge.

"It doesn't look right," Katy complained. "There's something wrong with the glaze."

"It's drying before you're done," I replied and handed her more sample boards. "Here, try again. And this time, concentrate. Selena's husband is no-good trash, but that's not helping you learn to faux-finish." Katy sighed like a martyr and started over.

"My color looks flat," Latisha said.

"You're wiping off most of the topcoat." I had her stir in more pigment. "If you take off too much you won't get the proper color saturation."

"I dropped my brush," Warren cried, staring at the floor. "It made a mess."

What was this, kindergarten? Teaching was clearly not a profession for the patience-impaired.

"Accidents happen!" I chirped with a gaiety I did not feel as I handed him a paper towel. "Pick up the brush, wash it off in the mineral spirits, and get right back to it!"

I went to assist a sweet, overweight man named Rick who tackled his sample boards with more determination than talent. Wrinkling his forehead and biting his lower lip, he dabbed on the paint with trepidation.

"Put a little more oomph into it," I suggested.

"For crying out loud, Bry, I said to myself," I heard Bryan nattering on. "You've never even been on a *cable car*! Have you ever tried Rice-A-Roni? No! Why, that doesn't even half make sense." His tablemates nodded in agreement.

Margaret, a fifty-something homemaker, had brought her

teenage daughter Rochelle, who wanted to faux-finish her bedroom "from top to bottom." Their color choices made me cringe, but who was I to dissuade the duo from lilac and turquoise harlequin-patterned walls?

I checked in on Russell, even though every molecule in my body screamed to avoid him. "Lookin' good, Russell." He patted at his sample boards listlessly.

"So then my friend Annette asks me, have I ever been on the Mexican Bus?" Bryan was telling his neighbor, Katrina. "And I said—"

"Annette?" I interjected, my paintbrush pausing in midair over Rochelle's turquoise patch. "Annette who?"

"Annette Crawford," Bryan said. "You remember her."

"Of course I do. She stopped taking my calls."

Annette Crawford was a no-nonsense, supersmart, ultra-cool homicide inspector for the San Francisco Police Department. A decade my senior, she was the type of woman who could dress up in a satin ball gown and four-inch heels, size up a bloody murder scene, and attend an awards dinner with the mayor without skipping a beat. Last year, we had begun a tentative friendship based on a mutual respect for each other's ability to lie (in my case) and to ferret out said lies (in her case).

"You can hardly blame her, Annie, after the drug bust."

Several heads whipped around to stare at me. I corrected Rochelle's board and then edged over to Bryan, hoping for discretion.

"You and Annette talk? About Rice-A-Roni?"

"Don't be silly. She's a hush puppy fan, and I like to tell you I knocked her on her fine ass with my dirty rice and jambalaya," Bryan said, his Louisiana bayou accent thickening as he spoke of the food of his childhood. He glanced over at Rick. "Don't look now, buddy, but you've sprung a leak."

"Help!" Rick called out as he mopped up his board. I

reached over and rectified the situation without blinking an eye. After my years in the business, glaze drips were a piece of cake.

"I mean, you and Annette are still friends?" I clarified.

"After the Chagall fiasco, we started talking. She's a local history buff, did you know that?" Bryan gushed. "We took the Mexican Bus last night and went through tequila and limes like there was no tomorrow!"

A few months ago I had hopped the brightly painted bus named "Lulu" with Mary and Samantha. For the cost of a ticket, the Mexican Bus drove the boisterous crowd from one salsa club to the next, ushering us inside to drink and dance, then loading us back on the bus to head to the next stop. As soon as the door closed, the booze, limes, and salt-shaker emerged, the driver cranked up the music, and the bus swayed as its tequila-soaked passengers sang and danced through the streets of San Francisco.

That night my wallet had been stolen while I was mamboing at Rock-a-Pulco, and Mary and I had had to break into the studio through the window, nearly setting off the burglar alarm. We awoke the next day with pounding heads, queasy stomachs, and vague memories of having had way too good a time.

"How come you didn't ask me to go?" I said, hurt.

Bryan looked guilty. "Honey pie, you *know* how much I love you, but Annette needed to let her hair down—she's been working so hard—and you two aren't exactly on good terms, so, well . . ."

"That's okay, I understand." I felt a rush of self-pity. It was like getting stuck at the loser table at an otherwise raucous wedding.

After another hour of questions about color choices and texture options, I sent my students home armed with buckets of glaze, pots of paint, and bags of paintbrushes, rags, and sponges. Home Improv associates rang up sales in the hundreds of dollars, and the store manager beamed at me.

As Bryan and I made our way across the parking lot, he looped a heavy arm around my shoulders and announced he was taking me to lunch at Fisherman's Wharf.

"No one but tourists eat at Fisherman's Wharf," I protested. "I haven't been there since I was a kid."

"That's my point, baby doll. I haven't been in *years,* since I was fresh off the boat from Louisiana. But tourists come from all over the world to see the sights we locals don't take time for. Aren't you the least bit curious?"

"Anything else on your list?"

"All sorts of *fabulous* things." He fished a piece of paper from his pocket. "Fisherman's Wharf is right at the top. Ooh! Maybe we could take a cable car there, and kill two birds with one stone!"

"If you're buying, I'll go to the Wharf. But we're *not* waiting in line forty-five minutes for a cable car. I'll drive."

Despite Bryan's desire for what he called the "T.T.E.—Total Tourist Experience," I nixed his suggestion to park in one of the high-fee garages near the Wharf and instead spent fifteen minutes searching the neighborhood for a metered space. As we walked the long city blocks to Fisherman's Wharf, Bryan read aloud from a tour book.

"Did you know that Fisherman's Wharf is the *third* most visited sight in America? Guess what's first and second!"

"The Frick Museum in New York City. I love that place."

Bryan snorted. "Disney *World* and Disney*land.* Isn't that something?"

"You bet." The ocean breeze flung my hair into my mouth and I spat it out.

"Let's see . . . did you know that a man named Henry Meiggs built Fisherman's Wharf to ship lumber? Doesn't that mean it should be called Lumberman's Wharf?"

"Lumberman's Wharf sounds awkward."

"True. Hmm, it says here that Meiggs was run out of town by a mob bent on revenge. Now, *that's* interesting." He paged through the book. "Dang it all. It doesn't say what he did. Don't you hate that?"

"Probably slept with somebody's wife," I suggested as we neared the tourist area, its sidewalks overrun with displays of T-shirts, sweatshirts, key chains, sunglasses, and disposable cameras from the cramped souvenir shops. The wharf was not yet in sight but the caws of the seagulls and the smell of sea air said we were close.

"Or many men's wives. It was a big crowd. Then there were the Chinese immigrants who sold food from 'junks,' and of course the Italian fishermen," Bryan read on, undaunted, weaving through the crowds that streamed out into the street. "It says when the Ghirardelli Chocolate Factory was opened to the public, the area became more of a tourist destination and less of a working dock."

"Oh yeah?" I said, listening with half an ear.

"Listen to this. Domingo Ghirardelli, originally from Italy by way of Peru, discovered that cocoa butter drips off bags of ground cacao beans. This technique continues to be the most common method for making chocolate. Huh. Who knew?"

Bryan's reference to the Ghirardellis turned my thoughts to Bayview Cemetery, where the chocolate mogul had built a beautiful crypt near the Locklear Memorial, and I imagined Domingo Ghirardelli watching the crowds in the square that bore his name from his eternal perch on the Oakland hillside. That thought reminded me of the masked ghoul at Louis Spencer's crypt, and once again I wondered what was going on in that place.

But as we walked along, I started to relax. The sights and sounds and smells—especially the smells—of Fisherman's

Wharf brought back visceral memories of childhood outings to the City, and I started to relax. I remembered one trip when Georges had insisted on going to the Wax Museum, where he chortled to himself for the entire tour. My older sister, Bonnie, got the willies and went to stand by the exit, but Grandfather and I had lingered, laughed, and critiqued the gruesome displays. Some of those wax artists are quite talented.

The area had been built up in the intervening years, but there were still huge steaming vats of water for the crabs, and street vendors selling shrimp cocktails and loaves of fresh-baked sourdough bread. Several of the Italian seafood eateries that dated to the 1950s had been converted to up-scale seafood restaurants. A few of the docks were reserved for working fishermen, but many now offered tours of the bay and rides to Sausalito, while others had been ceded to the raucous sea lions, who lolled in the sun and bellowed at the tourists. Every so often someone tried to get the City to relocate the sea lions, but visitors loved them and so they remained. Besides, those sea lions were *mean.*

Bryan dropped a dollar into the hat of a man covered from head to toe in silver paint; the man did a convincing imitation of a robot. We then took a few minutes to watch a long-haired young man spin cans of spray paint to create colorful drawings of the solar system. The throng clapped to show its appreciation.

Consulting his tourist manual once more, Bryan suggested lunch at an unpretentious diner with red vinyl booths and a view of the sea lions. We ordered the house special and iced tea, and broke open a warm boule of sourdough, slathering chunks of the fragrant bread with fresh butter.

"Looks like you have an admirer," Bryan said, arching an eyebrow as he sweetened his tea with two scoops of snowy white sugar.

"Who?"

"That fellow in class who followed you from the cemetery."

"Curly Top?" I said, aghast.

"That's his name?"

"His name's Russell. I just can't get past the hair."

"Okay, he's not what one would order on the Internet, but it's good to have admirers. *Heterosexual* admirers, in your case," Bryan clarified.

"I have heterosexual admirers. What about Josh?"

"Hmm."

"What's that supposed to mean?"

"To tell the truth, I've been wanting to talk to you about him."

"What's wrong with Josh? He's gorgeous, and sweet, and—"

"Yes, he is. That's the problem, girlfriend—he's *too* sweet. We think you need someone stronger."

"Who's the 'we' who thinks all this?"

"Your friends, Annie."

The red vinyl creaked as I sat back in a huff. "And you're suggesting I hook up with *Curly Top?*"

"Course not, girl, simmer down. I'm just saying, is all."

"Bryan, you're something else. You're on my case for months to get some, and when I find a perfectly respectable boyfriend you say he's not good enough."

The waitress gave me a knowing look as she delivered two hollowed-out loaves of sourdough bread filled with creamy clam chowder. The taste of the salty clams and the velvety potatoes made it official: I was on a trip down memory lane.

"Good?" Bryan asked, blowing delicately on a spoonful of soup.

"Great."

We enjoyed the meal and chatted, Bryan bringing me up

to date on his life. As he signaled to the waitress to bring the check, I gazed out the diner's picture window upon the bustling crowd of tourists. Bryan was right: we locals should take advantage of our charming tourist attractions. There were strolling lovers, excited children dashing between the arcade and the carousel, a cluster of Japanese tourists, tattooed bikers, strutting teenagers, Billy Mudd, and Randy Gossen . . .

Mudd and Gossen?

"Anyway, enough about me. Getting back to you. Annette thinks you're using Josh."

"What?" I asked, twisting in my seat for a better view. Had Billy Mudd just walked by with Cindy's thesis adviser?

"To avoid getting involved with your landlord."

Must have been my imagination. How would those two even know each other?

I turned back to Bryan. "Let me get this straight. Annette won't talk to *me,* but she's happy to discuss my love life with *you?*"

Bryan shrugged, his dark, espresso-colored eyes radiating innocence. "She hasn't exactly met him, but from what she's heard, she's not so sure about this Josh person."

"Bryan, I'm sorry but I've got to go," I said, leaping up. "We'll finish this discussion later."

Chapter 11

The public history of modern art is the story of conventional people not knowing what they are dealing with.

—Robert Motherwell (1915–1991), American painter

The public history of modern artists is the story of mostly conventional people attempting to be unconventional. —Georges LeFleur

The moment I stepped into the street I was swallowed up by the surging crowd. I hopped up and down and stood on tiptoe, and at one point thought I spied Billy's platinum-blond head, but by the time I had pushed through the throng and climbed onto a bench for a better view he was nowhere to be seen.

"Annie!" Bryan caught up with me. "I had no *idea* you were so sensitive, baby doll. Not another word about Josh, I promise."

"It's not that. I thought I saw someone I knew."

"Everything okay, sugar?"

"Yeah. I think so. Everything's fine, but I've really got to go."

I left Bryan chatting up a family from Dubuque as they waited in the queue at the turn-of-the-century carousel on

Pier Thirty-nine. My enthusiasm for the tourist's San Francisco did not include blaring calliope music, and besides, I had a masterpiece to track down.

First, though, I decided to drop in on an old acquaintance. I got the number from Directory Assistance, and his receptionist assured me he would be in the office until four o'clock. Firing up the truck, I headed to the office of Dr. Sebastian Pitts, art authenticator to the stars.

Years ago Pitts had unwittingly certified as genuine several of my teenage forgeries, and for this service earned my grandfather's eternal scorn. Georges besmirched Pitts' career at London's Remington Museum by writing an article documenting Pitts' numerous professional errors, and Pitts returned the favor a few years later by engineering my dismissal from an internship at the Brock Museum, derailing my bid to become a legitimate art restorer. Since then he and I had butted heads on more than a few occasions, and we both walked away with headaches.

I braked at the corner of Taylor and Washington and waited for a packed cable car to clear the intersection. Passengers hung from the sides of the car, snapping photographs and shouting the Rice-A-Roni jingle. It was corny, but it made me laugh. Maybe Bryan was on to something with his tourist's view of San Francisco. Maybe I should have joined him on the carousel instead of dropping in on someone who had caused me so much grief.

Sebastian Pitts had left the Brock Museum's employ to open his own art authentication business on Geary, off Union Square. Fortunately for the supercilious British sycophant, art was a wide-open business in which the "experts" incurred little or no penalty for giving bad advice. It was legal to sell some sucker a three-dollar, garage sale painting as a four-hundred-thousand-dollar Paul Klee as long as the expert could reasonably claim to have believed it to be genuine. As Frank DeBenton once told me, when it came to purchasing a van Gogh on eBay—or anywhere else—the law of the land was caveat emptor.

I left my truck at the Ellis-O'Farrell Garage, walked three blocks to Pitts' office building, and took the stairs to the fourth floor, hoping to mitigate the effects of yesterday's samosas and today's sourdough extravanganza. Panting, I paused at the landing to admire the hallway's travertine marble floor and barrel-vaulted ceiling and the French plaster finish in a sublime shade of bisque. I had used the technique on half a dozen living rooms in chichi homes in the Berkeley hills and had charged through the nose for each one, in part because the process was so time-consuming to apply, but also because my grandfather had taught me long ago that rich people don't value anything unless it costs them dearly.

The rents in this building must be astronomical, I thought. Pitts was moving up in the world.

Just beyond the men's room I spied WINDSOR ART APPRAISALS—DR. SEBASTIAN PITTS, PHD, ESQUIRE stenciled in gold on the frosted glass of a closed office door. A woman in her twenties rested her pen on her cherry-wood desk and smiled at me as I entered.

"Good afternoon, ma'am," she said, her blinding white teeth framed by ruby-red lips. Her straight brown hair was parted on the side and swept her shoulders in a fashionable flip. She must have emptied an entire can of hair spray on it this morning because not a single hair was out of place, and when she moved her head the flip swung in a coordinated fashion. I watched, fascinated. Those of us with naturally curly hair found stick-straight hair intriguing. "How may I help you?"

"I'm Annie Kincaid. I'm here to see Sebastian Pitts, if he's free."

"Certainly, ma'am." She picked up the phone. "Dr. Pitts, an Annie Kincaid is here to see you." She turned away from me, ducked her head, and lowered her voice. "No, I'm not kidding. Yes, I'm positive. She said 'Annie Kincaid.' "

The receptionist set the phone down and gave me a curious look. "Dr. Pitts will be right with you, ma'am. May I get you something? Tea? Gingersnaps?"

"No, thank you."

"I just brewed a pot of excellent Earl Grey. It's wonderful with fresh organic milk."

Yuck. "I'm fine, thanks."

I settled into a soft ecru leather sofa, picked up a copy of *Burke's Peerage* from a side table, and skimmed lists of the Queen of England's third cousins twice removed. *What's the deal with the anglophilia?* I wondered. San Franciscans, like other Americans, were not immune to the appeal of a British accent, but in general we were rabid antimonarchists.

The receptionist's telephone buzzed. "Dr. Pitts will see you now, ma'am. It's down the hall and to the right."

Feeling as if I were about to have blood drawn, I shuffled along a Persian wool floor runner to a closed office door. When I touched the brass handle I received a small shock. It seemed a fitting metaphor.

"Why, Annie Kincaid," Sebastian Pitts oozed as he rose from his oversized leather desk chair. Five feet six inches tall, Pitts was round and pasty, with muddy brown hair, shaggy eyebrows, and crooked yellow teeth. He was dressed in an exquisitely tailored three-piece gray suit, but he still reminded me of the snake-oil salesmen of yore. "I could scarcely credit it when my girl told me you were waiting."

"Nice digs you've got here, Sebastian. I see you're doing well."

"Indeed. Indeed, I am. Please, won't you have a seat?"

Pitts' affability tweaked my antenna. Our interactions had never been even remotely civil. What was he up to?

I took a seat in a wingback chair and faced Pitts across the broad expanse of his antique walnut partners desk.

"I don't understand the name, though. Why *Windsor Art Appraisals*?"

Pitts smiled. "An old family name."

Not *his* family name, I thought, but it beat *Pitts' Art Appraisals,* hands down.

"I was surprised to learn you'd left the Brock Museum," I said.

"It was not an easy decision, no, not easy at all, but one must follow one's destiny, mustn't one? I approached Mrs. Brock late last year with the idea of striking out on my own. She was most encouraging, of course. Such a dear, dear woman. I am proud to count her among my closest friends and supporters. She agreed that what this city needs is a really top-flight art expert, someone to encourage the development of private art collections in the homes of our finest citizens."

"Can't argue with you there." *Too bad the city doesn't have one yet.*

"As I was saying to the governor just the other day, the chief obstacle to the creation of a respectable amateur art collection by private citizens such as yourself, my dear, is a dearth of knowledge on rarified topics," he continued with what I suspected was his scripted sales pitch. If the name-dropping fool thought to sell me something, he was plumb out of luck. Even if I had money to invest in art, why would I? If I wanted to hang a masterpiece in my apartment, I would just forge one.

"As I said to my close, personal friend the mayor, we in Northern California are blessed with an abundance of natural and man-made wealth," he droned on, "and we owe it to ourselves—indeed, we owe it to future generations—to grow it."

"Grow what?"

"The wealth."

"What about art?"

"That, too."

"Sebastian—you don't mind if I call you Sebastian, do you?—I hope this doesn't sound rude, but I haven't the foggiest idea what you're talking about."

Pitts leaned back in his chair and smiled like the Cheshire cat. "I am simply saying, Annie, that in my new venture I perform a public service by assisting clients in cultivating a love of beauty. And despite what you and your grandfather may think, I do have a trained artistic eye. Oh, perhaps I am not as gifted as others—never let it be said that Dr. Sebastian Pitts, Esquire, is not a modest man—but I like to think I've learned a little something over the years. Not the least through my various run-ins with those of your ilk."

"I have an ilk?"

Pitts winked and I repressed a shudder.

"You know of whom I speak, Annie. Your grandfather is an amazing man."

"We agree at last."

His smile faltered for a moment; then, having decided I was joking, he chortled. "Ah. Aha! Still the same old Annie. Quick with the quips."

"My ilk's like that. We're the quicker quipper uppers."

"Just so," he said, looking confused. He leaned forward. "May I confess something, Annie?"

"Sure, why not? My good friend the archbishop says confession's good for the soul."

"Over the years we've had our little, er, 'professional disagreements,' shall we say? But because of you, I'll never look at Old Master drawings the same way. 'Credit where credit is due' has always been my motto."

Dr. Sebastian Pitts, once my sworn enemy, was acknowledging not only my talent but my grandfather's as well? Was this some sort of trap? Was Pitts wearing a wire?

Calm down, Annie, I scolded myself. No FBI agent in his right mind would recruit Pitts. Maybe he had mellowed. Maybe, in his new line of work, he'd realized I was no threat to him. Maybe he'd contracted a brain-eating virus. I decided to accept his olive branch, but to keep my eyes open.

"I, uh, thank you, Sebastian. That's very kind of you to say."

"You're welcome. So. Annie Kincaid. What brings you here today?"

"Do you recall assessing a painting for Oakland's Chapel of the Chimes a few years ago?"

He nodded. "I did it as a favor to Mrs. Brock. She asked me to help out a friend of hers, the wealthy philanthropist Aaron Garner."

As world-famous cities went, San Francisco was not large, so I was not surprised that Aaron Garner ran in the same circles as Agnes Brock. After all, Frank DeBenton knew the same people through his business ventures and charity balls and such. Still, it was disconcerting to realize that so many of my patrons—and enemies—were connected. It reminded me that I might have to change my name and relocate one day.

"Do you remember your findings?" I asked.

"It was what it claimed to be—a copy of *La Fornarina* by a minor English painter. Can't remember the name right off."

"Crispin Engels."

"That's it. I saw immediately the painting was a charming, albeit maladroit effort." He fixed me with a piercing stare. "Please don't tell me your grandfather painted it."

"Certainly not," I sniffed. "Did you conduct a fiber or paint flake analysis?"

He shook his head.

"X-ray diffraction, or fluorescence, maybe?"

"They weren't necessary. It was clearly labeled a copy, and the provenance was in order. The only mystery was why the columbarium bothered having it assessed in the first place. I had the sense the old woman pushed for it."

"You mean Mrs. Brock?"

Now he looked offended. "Don't be absurd. I am referring to some secretary at the columbarium. Why Roy Cogswell listened to *her* is beyond me. She was a pushy old broad."

So much for Pitts' mellowing.

"Not like the lovely Helena . . ." He trailed off, a faraway look in his eyes.

"Helena the cemetery docent? You know her?"

"We met that day, and our paths have since crossed from time to time. A magnificent woman. Tortured, alas. She lost her only child in an automobile accident, you know. Tragic. Simply tragic. I wonder, have you heard if she ever got her house with a view of her son's grave and the bay?"

"I have no idea."

"Money wasn't a problem, that's for sure. Mr. Garner could afford the best."

"Why would Aaron Garner buy Helena a house?"

He looked surprised. "It is customary for a husband to provide a home for his wife."

"But she's married to Dick Somebody. He's a doctor."

"She remarried after she and Garner split. You didn't know? Helena was Garner's first wife. It was their son who died. I was able to mitigate her maternal grief somewhat by acquiring for her the rarest of treasures, an *original* Tim O'Neill landscape of cottages nestled in a verdant valley. Perhaps you've seen it? Helena hung it in the cemetery offices. How typical of her to wish to share such beauty with others."

"*You* bought her the O'Neill?"

"Oh-ho! I'm afraid my pockets are not that deep. Aaron Garner paid for it, but I *arranged* for the extremely rare purchase of an original. O'Neill is a close, personal acquaintance of mine."

"But, Sebastian, Tim O'Neill mass-produces posters that he calls paintings," I protested.

"He's one of our most successful modern artists," Pitts pointed out. "Let's please refrain from the old debate about what is art and what is illustration. Why, even the great Norman Rockwell—"

"But O'Neill signs his work with ink mixed with drops of his *blood*! He hires artists to dab 'highlights' on posters and charges *thousands* of dollars! He—"

Noting the disapproving look in Pitts' eyes, I caught myself. "But as you say, they sure are pretty," I added lamely.

A grandfather clock chimed. I needed a drink.

"Allow me to take you out for a cocktail, my dear," Pitts gushed as he stood up and came around the desk, and I wondered if Pitts and I were on the same wavelength. Had the earth tilted on its axis? "We'll toast our new friendship and let bygones be bygones. Have you ever considered going into the business of art authentication? Why, with your unique, er, talents and my client list, we could do very well. Very well indeed."

"I don't know, Sebastian," I said, rising from my chair. "I usually talk people *out* of buying things."

"There's a good deal more money to be made in selling art than in rejecting art, Annie. Why don't you think about it? Come, let's talk over spirits."

Looping his pudgy arm through mine, Sebastian Pitts escorted me downstairs and over two blocks to Wolfgang Puck's Postrio Restaurant. There we enjoyed a drink called an Agnes Road made of ice-cold vodka, lime juice, and cranberry juice, shaken like a martini. By the time we were on our third, I was considering taking Pitts up on his business offer. As my grandfather always said, *Work smart, not hard, chérie.*

Georges said this as part of his campaign to convince me to follow in his felonious forging footsteps. All things considered, I preferred an occupation that didn't include the risk of spending one's golden years as a guest of the state.

Chapter 12

This painting, this work that you mourn for, is the cause of many griefs and troubles.

—Berthe Morissot (1841–1895), French painter

Art is but a soap opera rendered in pigment.

—Georges LeFleur

"When's the last time you spent a sunny Sunday in Golden Gate Park?" Bryan demanded over the phone too early the next morning.

I groaned, snuggled deeper under the covers, and regretted not turning the damned contraption off last night.

"None of that, now," Bryan chastised. "Up and at 'em!"

"Bite me."

"Aren't we Miss Grumpy Pants in the morning? Rise and shine!"

"I need my beauty sleep."

"Ain't nothin' wrong with you that a dose of fresh air won't cure, baby doll. Besides . . ." Bryan paused dramatically. "Annette will be there. It's the perfect chance for you two to make up."

I opened my eyes. "It's against my principles to sell out to the Man," I grumbled.

"Don't be absurd."

"Okay, it's against my principles to sell out to the Woman."

Bryan snorted. "You *know* you want to, sweet cheeks. Don't even try to tell me you haven't missed her. You and I both know you need all the friends you can get in law enforcement."

I hesitated, tempted.

"C'mon, it's a beautiful day in the neighborhood!" Bryan sang. "We'll picnic on the grass and frolic in the sunshine."

"Annette agreed to picnic and frolic?" Annette struck me more as the champagne-brunch-at-Chez-Panisse type.

"Get your carcass out of bed, missy, and meet us at the concession stand at Stow Lake. Elevenish. I've packed the food and wine, so you don't need to worry about a *thing*."

I sighed. "All right. But if Annette is mean to me, I'll make you pay."

"Honey pie, if anybody's mean to you, they'll have to answer to me."

Smiling, I lounged for a few more minutes, gazing at the bright green mulberry leaves dancing in the breeze outside my bedroom window. The clouds had parted, and brilliant sunshine poured in. I was due at Pete's mother's house for dinner tonight at six, but until then I'd planned on sleeping in, and then trying to track down a certain masterpiece. If Sebastian Pitts' assessment could be trusted—a big if—it meant the nineteenth-century Engels had been at the columbarium a few years ago but at some point had been replaced by a digital copy. Sandino thought the Barberini's *La Fornarina* was "off," so the whereabouts of the genuine Raphael remained an open question. What if the columbarium had had the original all along? I wouldn't put it past Pitts to fail to recognize an original masterpiece, especially since he hadn't bothered to run any scientific tests.

I had considered going back to search the columbarium,

but it was Sunday and there were services in the chapel. And Bryan had a point: a day of sun and fresh air would be good for me. If I spent any more time cooped up in the columbarium I'd end up as sallow-faced as Roy Cogswell or Curly Top Russell. And short of getting arrested again, when would I have another chance to see Annette? Maybe she'd be willing to look into Cindy's death for me.

I threw back the covers and shuffled down the hall to the kitchen, where I put water on to boil, then climbed into the bathroom's claw-footed iron tub for the world's shortest shower. My subconscious had heard my neighbors running the water all morning, which meant it would be hours before hot water was available from the old Victorian's ancient boiler, which I half suspected was still fueled by whale oil. Over the years I had learned to live with the inconvenience because the alternative was to pay more rent. I gritted my teeth to keep from howling as needles of icy water pierced my flesh. *Do it for the whales,* I told myself.

Through the splatter of the shower I heard the telephone ring and hesitated, shampoo dripping down my face. If I fled the cold water to answer the phone I'd never find the strength to get back in, and I could hardly spend the day with suds in my hair.

Besides, it was probably Josh. He had a knack for calling at the worst possible moments. Josh called every day. Sometimes twice.

It was starting to annoy me.

Annie, I chided myself, *Josh is a sweetheart. You really don't deserve him.*

Soap-free at last, I cranked off the water, toweled briskly to get my circulation moving again, and slipped into a terry cloth robe. The kettle was whistling when I hurried into the kitchen and poured boiling water over freshly ground Peet's coffee. It would be good to join my friends in the park. I'd been brooding too much lately. My grandfather was in trouble; Raphael's great masterpiece might be in the wrong hands; and a young, vibrant graduate student was dead.

And my friends didn't like my boyfriend.

I had gone through a long dry spell before Josh, and had gotten to the point where it was easier to sublimate with chocolate or alcohol than to date men I had no interest in. Josh was a wonderful person, but the truth was that my attraction to him was mostly physical. The more time we spent together the more I found my mind wandering, wondering about two other men in my life, both of whom scared the you-know-what out of me, emotionwise.

I was brooding again. Time to get a move on.

As I dressed I listened to my phone messages. One was from Josh, but the other was Michael saying that he had searched the "place" for the "item" but found nothing. Huh. So Michael couldn't find anything in the columbarium. I trusted his searching skills far more than my own, so I could scratch that item off my list.

What really confounded me was that Michael did something I asked him to. What should I make of that?

In deference to what promised to be a warm spring day I dressed in cutoff denim shorts, a fuchsia T-shirt with a Bahamas logo, and a bright blue hooded sweatshirt. As I searched for my car keys I thought about someone else who might enjoy a picnic. I made a phone call and headed over to Evergreen Pines.

Mrs. Henderson was waiting in the foyer, chatting with the blue-haired receptionist. Dressed in a pale yellow polyester pantsuit and a black-and-orange Giants baseball cap, Mrs. Henderson clutched a straw bag decorated with blue and yellow raffia flowers, and smelled of suntan lotion and lilacs. I helped her into the passenger's seat, folded up the wheelchair, and slung it into the truck bed.

"And how are you this fine fair morning?" she asked as we pulled away from the curb. "I was so pleased when you called!"

"I'm sorry about the last-minute invitation, but I only just heard about the picnic," I apologized. "I've been looking forward to seeing you again. I'm glad you're free today."

"Child, I'm free most days. That's the advantage to being old," she explained as we sat in the usual weekend traffic jam queuing up for the toll plaza. "Time is the one thing there's plenty of. Until you die, of course."

"I suppose so," I said.

"There are worse things than death, you know," she replied. "A life of missed opportunities, for example."

I smiled at her.

"Lord knows I've made some questionable choices in my life. I suppose everyone has. But when I look back, I find it's not what I did that I regret. It's what I *didn't* do."

"You remind me of my grandfather," I said, for the old reprobate often expressed similar sentiments. Given Georges' many felonies, though, I could only imagine the nature of the opportunities he'd decided to pass up.

We spoke about *La Fornarina* as we crossed the bridge and headed toward Golden Gate Park, but Henderson clammed up and got misty-eyed when I mentioned Donato Sandino. I wondered whether he was one of those items she regretted.

When we arrived at Stow Lake I left the truck in a fire lane, blinkers flashing, unloaded my passenger and her wheelchair, then rolled her over to the concession stand.

"Yoo-hoo, Annie! Over here!" Bryan called.

Dressed in tight shorts and a muscle shirt, lean and handsome and perfectly groomed, Bryan was the embodiment of the gay male stereotype. His partner, Ron, was the opposite. A Stanford MBA with a PhD in economics from Yale, Ron was a name partner in a downtown investment firm. When in business mode, Ron favored custom-tailored British suits, crisp oxford shirts, and sober silk ties, but in his free time preferred ratty T-shirts and Levi's with holes in the knees. He snacked on Cheetos while cheering on his beloved Green Bay Packers, drank cheap beer, and gave Bryan's interior decorating schemes a wide berth.

He and Bryan had been together for years, and I had been honored to stand up as their best woman during San Francisco's brief flirtation with marrying same-sex couples. When the state courts nullified the marriages a few months later, City Hall refunded their license fee. Bryan framed the refund check and hung it in their bathroom.

"Baby doll!" Bryan called out. "You came! I knew you would."

I made the introductions, and left Mrs. Henderson conversing with my friends while I hurried to move the truck to a legal parking space.

Rats. A chartreuse parking ticket adorned my windshield, flapping like a flag in the breeze. Apparently my emergency blinkers had not fooled the parking cops. When it came to hunting down evildoers, the CIA had nothing on San Francisco's meter corps.

I drove around for several minutes before pulling off an impressive feat of parallel parking, squeezing into a spot sandwiched between two monstrous SUVs. I was tempted to bang into the shiny painted bumper of the space hog behind me when I remembered a lesson my grandfather had taught me when I was eight years old. We'd been riding the crowded Paris Metro when an old woman boarded the car and shoved me aside. I was about to push her back when I felt my grandfather's hand on my arm.

"*Non,* Annie. You must not."

"But, Grandpapa," I'd protested with the faultless logic of an outraged child. "She pushed me first!"

"*Oui, chérie,* she did. But that does not give you permission to respond in kind."

"Why not?" In an eight-year-old's tit-for-tat world, there was no room for generosity of spirit.

"Because we must strive always to be civilized, *ma petite,* especially when others are not. Otherwise society will plunge into an abyss of chaos and destruction from which humankind will never escape."

I'd fallen silent, impressed by Georges' depth of character. Years later, I realized he had cribbed this bit of philosophy from *Star Trek*'s Captain Kirk, but decided it had merit nonetheless.

It was an idyllic day for a picnic in the park. Birds twittered and swooped across the water, a dog barked happily, urging his person to throw a stick, and families arranged their moveable feasts on the verdant lawns that stretched along the banks of the duck-filled lake. Willow trees fluttered in the breeze, their sinewy branches caressing the surface of the water with languid grace. Young lovers and laughing children in colorful paddleboats circled the island in the middle of Stow Lake. A small group of pierced and tattooed young men and women, dressed in black, waited in line at the refreshment stand to buy corn dogs and soda. An elderly couple conversed in a guttural Eastern European language as they strolled along the shore, he leaning upon a cane, she leaning upon him.

Parking ticket or no parking ticket, life was good.

I made it to the picnic table just as Mary, Evangeline, and Pete arrived carrying a basket of oatmeal chocolate-chip cookies. Annette joined us a few minutes later with a bottle of wine, looking relaxed in jeans and a starched red blouse. Accompanying her was a fluffy toylike white dog who greeted me with unrestrained canine love and adoration. *At least Miss Mopsy's glad to see me,* I thought. The dog and I had met last year, when I was sort of breaking and entering while searching for a missing Caravaggio. Miss Mopsy had been abandoned by her people, and Annette wound up adopting her. Annette nodded pleasantly at me, but I noticed she took a seat at the opposite end of the picnic table.

Ron poured wine and Orangina, and we helped ourselves to sesame crackers, three kinds of cheese, fresh organic veggies with a creamy herbed dip, and wheat-berry and potato salads. There was cold grilled Cajun-spiced chicken, individual pots of soufflé, and my personal picnic and holiday favorite: clam dip with salty Ruffles potato chips. I love Ruffles because they have ridges.

I was pleased with myself for thinking to invite Mrs. Henderson, and watched as she turned her smiling face, flowerlike, to the sun. She ate little, and declined the offer of cookies and soda.

"Are you diuretic?" Pete asked.

"Diabetic, my dear," she answered. "Yes, I am. I took my insulin before we left, so I should be fine. But one can never be too careful."

"I'll bet you saw some interesting things working at a cemetery," Ron said.

"Why, as a matter of fact . . ." Mrs. Henderson replied, and regaled us with a tale about orchestrating the funeral of a carnival dancer. "Lesson learned—never, ever trust the word of a bearded woman."

"Words to live by," Bryan said, and Pete nodded solemnly.

There was a lull in the conversation as the sun and digestion combined to make us lazy.

"Hey! I want to go out in a paddleboat!" said Mary. "Who's with me? Annie?"

I surveyed the table and saw the chips and dip were still plentiful. "Maybe in a little while," I said, pulling the basket toward me. "You go ahead."

"It looks dangerous," said Pete. "Anything could happen. Look at that water."

The water was murky and green—icky, but hardly dangerous, I thought. "I think the water's only a few feet deep, Pete. It's a man-made lake, after all."

Mary turned to Annette. "Whaddaya say, Inspector? Ron?"

"I think I'll take a pass," Annette replied.

"I'm not budging an inch," Ron chimed in. "I'm going to sit right here and do nothing."

Mary turned to Bryan, who cuddled Miss Mopsy in his brawny arms. "Bryan?"

"Honey pie, I am *so* not into paddleboats."

"I'll go," Evangeline said and belched loudly.

"Good appetite," Mrs. Henderson murmured.

"Pardon my French," Evangeline said. "S'go."

Pete rose to accompany them.

"Hold my cell phone so it doesn't get wet, okay, Annie? If Dante calls, answer it, but if it's from A.J., don't answer it. If it's from—"

"I'm not answering your phone, Mare," I said and dropped it in my shoulder bag.

Mary, Pete, and Evangeline arrived at the boat rental kiosk just ahead of a dozen or so pierced and tattooed Goths. Unnaturally pale and clothed in black, a few of the Goths wore splashes of pink and some of the women shaded their ashen complexions with crepe-festooned black parasols.

"Annie," Annette said. "It's good to see you again. I'm sorry to hear about your recent trauma."

Bryan avoided my eyes. Big mouth.

I shrugged, not wanting to spoil the beautiful day with thoughts of death. Mrs. Henderson raised an eyebrow but was too well bred to ask.

"Someone I knew died," I told her, "and I discovered her body. I didn't know her well, but it was still a shock. The police say it was suicide, but she didn't seem like someone who would do such a thing."

"I'm sorry, dear," said the elderly woman, resting a soft hand with skin as thin as crepe paper over mine. I returned her squeeze.

"I can't shake the feeling that there's more to it," I said to Annette. "Maybe you could check into it? I know it's not San Francisco's case but . . ."

"No offense, Annie," Annette said, "but there could be all kinds of reasons she'd want to kill herself, reasons you would know nothing about."

"But—"

"You do tend to jump to conclusions. Remember last fall, when you thought that sculptor had killed Evangeline because she didn't show up for work?"

"And that time you thought my downstairs neighbor was a mobster because he wore a diamond pinkie ring?" added the ever-helpful Bryan.

"I still say he's not to be trusted," I muttered.

"And we won't mention how you managed to get arrested for smuggling drugs," Annette said.

"You were smuggling drugs?" Mrs. Henderson asked. "Oh my."

"I wasn't smuggling drugs," I assured her. "I was accidentally transporting drugs."

My friends rolled their eyes.

"Hey! It *was* an accident!"

Ron patted my hand. "I believe you, Annie."

"Thanks, Ron." I glared at Bryan and Annette, who looked as if they were stifling guffaws. "Need I remind you two Doubting Thomases that, other than the part about killing Evangeline, I was right about the sculptor?"

"True enough," Annette said. "But what on earth made you think it was a good idea to steal the evidence?"

"I was bringing it to the police!"

"You're not supposed to take evidence from a crime scene!" Annette snapped. "You're supposed to leave it alone and call the cops!"

"I know, but—"

"Ooh, look! There's Mary and Evangeline! Hellooooo!" Bryan waved as the pair chugged past in their bright blue paddleboat. They waved back. "And just *look* at the baby ducks. Ducklings are the cutest!"

Ron started laughing at Bryan's transparent attempt to lighten the mood, and Annette joined in.

"You're right, Annette," I conceded. "I got in over my head that time, and my first call should have been to you. I won't do that again, I promise. I'm sorry, truly."

"I know you meant well, Annie. Apology accepted," Annette said, and I relaxed. "But why do I get the feeling that this is the calm before another storm?"

"Beats me."

"Are you psychic, my dear?" Mrs. Henderson asked Annette.

"I sure hope not. Not when you consider my line of work."

"Wouldn't being psychic help you solve crimes?" Bryan asked.

"I deal with enough unpleasantness as it is," Annette said, and accepted the chilled bottle of Sierra Nevada Pale Ale that Ron handed her. "No way do I need to see a murder happen."

"Maybe being psychic would help you win the lottery," Bryan suggested.

"Maybe so. Except for one thing—I'm not psychic."

"Getting back to my friend . . ." My crowd's conversational style veered toward the circuitous.

"Maybe it was a love affair gone sour," offered Bryan. "That happens all the time."

"Seems kind of drastic," Ron said. "Why not just break up with him?"

"Perhaps she was involved with a married man," Mrs. Henderson piped up, snacking on a sesame cracker. "I know someone who's involved with a married man."

"She might have been pregnant and couldn't stand the shame!" suggested Bryan.

"This isn't the fifties, Bry. More likely she cracked under the pressure of graduate school," Ron said. "I came close to dropping out and backpacking through Europe a couple of times when I was at Stanford."

"That was before he met me," Bryan said, beaming at Ron.

As Annette reached across the table for a slice of cheese-cake, I noticed she wore a gold chain with a medallion of a cross with a rose at the center.

"Pretty necklace, " I said. "I saw a cross like that at a cemetery recently."

"My auntie gave it to me," she said, fingering it. "I had dinner with her last night so I made a point to wear it. I'm not much of one for jewelry, but I like it."

"Is it a special design?"

"It's Rosicrucian."

"It's what?"

"Rosicrucian. The cross with the sign of the rose is the emblem of the church. Don't you know the museum down in San José?"

"I've heard of it, but never been."

"I grew up in east San José, used to visit the Rosicrucian Museum all the time. They've got this recreated Egyptian tomb, with mummies and all, used to scare the you-know-what out of me. But I whined until my mom took me, of course. My aunt's a member of the church."

"Why would a church be so interested in Egypt?"

"Supposedly there was a pharaoh who started part of the

belief system . . . but then it's a Christian church, too. I never quite figured that part out. It's a bit mystical. The guy who founded the church and museum down in San José, H. Spenser Lewis, went on a whole bunch of Egyptian expeditions and digs in the twenties."

"Spenser Lewis?" I repeated. "That was his name?"

"Yeah, why?"

"The other day I witnessed a grave robbery from the tomb of a Louis Spencer. And in his tomb there's a stained glass window with the same design as your necklace. And Egyptian paintings and a saying, 'may the roses bloom . . . something . . .'"

"'May the roses bloom upon your cross,'" Annette finished with a nod. "It's what they say, like a greeting or a benediction. Roses are symbolic of life, the cross is a sign of the human body. But what grave robbery are you referring to, exactly?"

"I just happened to be in the wrong place at the wrong time—"

"No surprise there," Annette muttered.

"—and someone was robbing Louis' grave. I was with the woman we were just talking about, the grad student from Berkeley who died."

Bryan and Annette exchanged Significant Glances.

"I know a graduate student at Cal," Mrs. Henderson said, already catching on to the plan to change the subject whenever the tension at the table rose. "Oh! Look at Pete run!"

We all turned to watch as Pete loped along the shoreline and across the bridge to the island, trying to keep abreast of Mary and Evangeline.

"Why won't they let him in the boat?" Annette asked.

"He's afraid of the water," I said.

"That poor man. He's besotted," said Annette, shaking her head.

Mrs. Henderson nodded. "With that large lesbian."

"What lesbian?" I asked.

"The one in the motorcycle jacket." Despite the warmth of the day, Evangeline wore her riding leathers. Mary's ripped black gauze tunic, in comparison, seemed more appropriate to the occasion.

"Evangeline's not a lesbian." At least, I didn't think so.

"She isn't?" Mrs. Henderson said. "I just assumed . . ."

"We all did, honey," Bryan said. "Just goes to show."

I noticed more Goths gathering by the lake and trooping across the footbridge to the island. A few held sock monkeys and flags aloft as they shouted to others ensconced in paddleboats on the water. The Goth fleet seemed to be swelling, the boaters clutching fluorescent green, blue, and pink plastic water cannons that contrasted sharply with their funereal attire.

As I turned back to the clam dip, a war whoop split the air. I looked up to see the Goth fleet dividing and engaging, the boaters' legs pumping furiously as they splashed toward one another, bellowing taunts and insults.

"Arrrrgggghh!" the Goths yelled as they slurped up lake water in the plastic water cannons and stood, paddleboats rocking wildly, took aim at one another, and let loose great streams of the brackish water. A shaggy-haired woman armed with a water cannon half as tall as she was hollered a riposte and fired a stream of water that struck a bald, tattooed man in the chest, sending him tumbling backward into the murky lake. In one final act of heroism, he lobbed his water cannon to his boat mates before standing up in the four-foot-deep water and wading to shore in defeat. The shaggy-haired woman's boat crew threw their hands in the air and cheered lustily before their attention was drawn to a boatload of Goths clad mostly in pink.

"Arrrgggghhh, beware the wrath of the Pinks!" the new arrivals cried, water spewing in great arcs toward the shaggy-haired woman's crew. Shrieks and shouts of vengeance issued from the beleaguered boat. From the safety of our picnic table, Miss Mopsy yapped furiously.

"My word," breathed Mrs. Henderson.

"What in the world's going on?" I asked.

"Gommmphhtt," Annette mumbled around a mouthful of cheesecake.

"Golf what?" Bryan asked.

She swallowed, took a sip of beer, and hushed the dog. "Goth naval battle. I assumed that was why we came today. Don't tell me you've never heard of it. It's a tradition."

"Goths have traditions?" Ron asked.

Just then Mary and Evangeline rounded the bend of the island. Pete, taking in the scene from the top of the bridge, began to shout, "*Stop!* Evangeline, Mary! Stop!"

It was too late. With a bloodcurdling yell, the pirate crew descended upon our friends, soaking them with a water barrage. I heard Evangeline howl in outrage, and feared the consequences.

Pete ran down the bridge and waded into the soupy water. "*Evangeline!*" he called. "*Mary!*"

Bellowing defiance, Evangeline dove into the lake and swam to a nearby boat. Shooting out of the water like a killer whale, she seized a blond woman by the arm and tossed her into the lake, then grabbed the edge of the boat and flipped it over, sending its occupants to their soggy reward. Grabbing a water cannon from a sputtering Goth, Evangeline righted the overturned paddleboat and boarded her spoils of war. She maneuvered the paddleboat into position and took out the head Goth with a well-placed shot in the schnozz. Mary, still in her own boat, leapt to her feet and swore a blue streak, threatening all Goth pirates with lifelong vengeance.

"Aren't you going to *do* something?" I asked the representative of civil authority at our picnic table.

Annette looked at me as if I had grown horns. "Like what?"

"Like stop it."

"On what grounds?"

"Well, because . . . surely they're breaking some law."

"I'm eating cheesecake. Anyway, this is San Francisco, girlfriend." Annette shrugged. "Goth naval battles are the least of our worries. And look—they're not involving the innocent," she said, gesturing to a pair of cuddling lovers who paddled past the melee, unscathed.

"They involved Mary and Evangeline!"

"Bad day to go boating in black."

I heard the roar of a hideous beast and saw Pete had climbed into Evangeline's boat, and the two of them were dunking all attackers. Standing back to back, Pete and Evangeline strafed anyone who dared come near. Mary paddled over and joined them in the boat, nearly tipping it over. She then provided the leg power as the trio made their way toward the shore, where a knot of irate pirates informed them that they had broken the rules of Goth naval engagement. Evangeline, unrepentant, flipped them the bird.

Our three friends sloshed over to the picnic table, dripping wet and spitting mad.

"Did you *see* those guys!" Evangeline bellowed. "What kind of place is this!"

"The attack was entirely unprevaricated!" Pete seconded. "They are maniacs, these Golfs! Miscreants! Misnomers!"

"You've got to hand it to them, though, they've got courage," Mary said and slogged over to a patch of sunny lawn, where she lay down spread-eagled to dry. "Pink is the new black, you know. I wish I had the guts to wear it, but I'm not worthy."

"What do you mean?" Ron asked, amused. "How worthy does one have to be to wear pink?"

"When you're a Goth, it means a lot. It's a matter of principle. I can't in good conscience wear pink until I spend at least one night in that damned cemetery."

"You shouldn't be in a cemetery at night," said Mrs. Henderson, frowning. "There are strange goings-on there."

"Lions, and tigers, and bears . . ." Ron chanted.

"Oh my!" Mrs. Henderson finished.

It sounded as though Mrs. Henderson was slurring her words a bit, though I knew she hadn't been drinking anything stronger than iced tea.

"Tonight's the charm, though, I can feel it," Mary said, ignoring the warnings. "Right, Evangeline?"

Evangeline shook her soaked leather jacket and scowled. "I gotta take a shower. That lake smelled funky."

"Nothing like a good old-fashioned Goth naval battle to top off a Sunday picnic, wouldn't you say?" Bryan said cheerfully, putting the food away. Miss Mopsy was on cleanup duty.

After helping to pack up, I wheeled Mrs. Henderson to the truck. Her head lolled a bit. "Are you feeling okay, Mrs. Henderson?"

"Fine and dandy, sweet as candy. Oh, look at the birdies!"

We zipped across the bridge to Oakland, and I pulled into the loading zone in front of Evergreen Pines. All the way back Mrs. Henderson had been singing "The Way You Wear Your Hat," though most of the lyrics made little sense. I unloaded and unfolded her wheelchair, guided her into it, and whizzed her up the elevator and down the hall to her room.

". . . oh no, you can't take that away from me . . . !" she crooned as I helped her onto the bed.

"Are you sure you're feeling all right?" I asked, worried now. I didn't know Mrs. Henderson well, so maybe she always went loony tunes after witnessing a Goth naval battle. Still, it seemed wise to check. "Why don't I get a nurse?"

"Nun-sense!" she said, and chortled. "Did you hear what I said? And I'm not even Catholic!"

"Yes, but—"

"I can check it myself, young lady. My insulin, I mean. I just need this glu . . . gluck . . . this thing." She pointed at a machine marked GLUCOMETER.

"Sure you don't need help?" I persisted.

"I can do it!" Mrs. Henderson said in a tone I imagined she had perfected during fifty-one years of running a large staff. "It's a brand-new thingie, just got it this morning."

"I'm just going to, um, get something to drink. Be right back." I ducked out of the room and made a beeline for the nurses' station.

A Filipina woman looked up from some charts. "Yes?"

"Mrs. Henderson needs some assistance checking her insulin levels. And . . . she's acting a little loopy."

"More than normal?" asked the nurse. "She saw the doctor just this morning. Do you know if she was drinking or eating sugar?"

"I think she was pretty careful."

"I'll check her glucometer." She headed briskly into room 327. "Good afternoon, Mrs. Henderson. Can I help you with that?"

"I've got it!" Mrs. Henderson said crankily.

The nurse smiled but did not budge.

"There. See? Perfect." Mrs. Henderson fell back against her pillows as the nurse checked the reading. I looked at the reading, too, though I had no idea what was acceptable and what should send me scurrying to call 911.

"How do you feel?" the nurse asked.

"I'm a little peaked is all," Mrs. Henderson said. "I think I'll just lie down for a few minutes. Then I'll be fine. Right as rain. Raindrops keep fallin' on my head . . ."

I drew a crocheted afghan over her legs. "Thank you for coming to the picnic."

"Thank you, dear. I had a lovely time."

"Goths and all?" I asked.

"Golfs and all." She smiled, and closed her eyes.

Chapter 13

I paint self-portraits because I am so often alone, because I am the person I know best.

—Frida Kahlo (1910–1954), Mexican painter

I have painted numerous self-portraits. In each one, I look remarkably like Rembrandt.

—Georges LeFleur

Mrs. Henderson wasn't the only one feeling a mite peaked. I made it home by three and enjoyed the rare luxury of lolling on the couch with the latest novel Oprah told me to read. My horizontal posture amplified the aftereffects of wine and potato chips, so my reading session soon morphed into a long nap. It was nearly six o'clock by the time I changed into a flowing Indian skirt and embroidered peasant blouse, put my hair up with a couple of chopsticks, drank my afternoon cup of coffee, sprang for a bottle of wine, and screeched to a stop in front of a modest ranch-style stucco house on a quiet suburban neighborhood in Hayward.

The house looked circa 1960, and its façade mimicked every other house on the street. Over the years homeowners had sought to ameliorate the monotony by painting their homes in the hues one more happily saw adorning Spanish bungalows, whimsical Victorians, or Florida cabanas: brilliant blues, soft lilacs, bright yellows, and shrieking pinks. Pete's mother's house was a particularly virulent shade of rose with muddy brown trim.

Before I could extricate myself from the seat belt's embrace, Pete emerged from the house and waved. Two short, stout, older women flanked him, their resemblance to Pete apparent in their sparkling brown eyes and broad faces. All three wore grins from ear to ear.

"Welcome! Welcome, Anna! Welcome!" they called out as I walked up the cracked concrete path to the front porch, where I was enveloped in lavender-scented hugs as the women greeted me in a mixture of broken English and Bosnian. Pete attempted simultaneous translation while he introduced me to his mother and maternal aunt.

"I brought you some wine," I said, offering the bottle.

"You no need! No need wine! We thank you," Pete's aunt exclaimed, and rushed the bottle, carried aloft like a great prize, into the kitchen.

We followed her into the house, where the aroma of exotic spices filled the air and family members milled about. There were old, toothless, scarred men; plump, smiling women with polite but guarded gazes; children of all ages, yelling and chasing a curly-haired dog that barked playfully; and several Americanized couples, whom I assumed were the parents of the children. The interior looked like most homes of its era, filled with worn but comfortable upholstered furniture, a few adorned with colorful slipcovers; simple wood tables and chairs that had been polished with lemon oil to a high sheen; a battered leatherette recliner smack in front of the television set; an old, upright piano that played host to a forest of family photos spanning numerous generations.

A frail-looking, elderly man approached us. He held out a small shot glass, and Pete began the introductions.

"Anna, this is my uncle Sidran. Sidran, this is my friend Anna Kincaid."

Uncle Sidran gave me a gap-toothed smile and handed me the glass, filled to the brim with a clear liquid. "Libation for you. Anna! You drink. Is good!"

I held the glass to my lips and my smile froze. The stuff smelled foul. Uncle Sidran was beaming, so I took a sip. It didn't taste bad, but my lips and tongue went numb.

"Is good?" he asked.

"Yeth. Ith gweat."

Uncle Sidran slapped me on the back and roared with laughter, while Pete hurriedly exchanged whatever the old man had given me with *loza,* a grape brandy similar to grappa. It was a wicked drink, but at least it didn't turn anything numb.

Uncle Sidran winked, and I winked back. He and Grandfather would have gotten along famously.

Pete's mother came over and Pete introduced her as Bosanska or Businski Bajezdagic; I didn't quite catch the name. "You call me Mama," she said, settling the issue. Funny how languages had different words for father, but mothers were "mama" the world over.

A good-looking man introduced himself as cousin Catiz, flung an arm around my shoulders, and escorted me to the fireplace, whose simple white-painted mantel was crowded with votive candles and flower vases. Above the mantel hung the painting I had restored, festooned with ribbons. Family members gathered around and heaped me with praise. If I always received this kind of adulation at the end of a good day's work, I almost wouldn't need to get paid.

After introductions too numerous and multisyllabic to remember, I was offered the seat of honor at the far end of the long table in the cramped dining room. The table was covered in a snowy linen cloth, and sparkled with china and crystal. Three long-necked, vaselike ceramic pots contained a regional specialty called *bosanski lonac,* a kind of hot-pot stew. Pete's aunt ladled out generous bowls of the slow-roasted delicacy, which was heavy on the meat and light on the vegetables. I'd made my way through about half my portion, enjoying the food as well as the family's boisterous conversation, when Mama swung through the room carrying a platter of sausages called *cevapcici* that looked remarkably like feces. Confident that Mama was not the sort of woman who would countenance such a thing in her kitchen, I took two. Next came a platter of little patties Pete referred to as *pljeskavica,* which looked like tiny cow pies. I tried two of those, as well.

"You married, Anna?" asked one of the younger women from down the table. I couldn't for the life of me dredge up her name.

"No, I'm not," I said, shaking my head.

"Ah . . ." said a chorus of knowing relatives.

I shot a look at Pete, who was blushing.

"You wan' get marry, Anna?" asked one of the older, bolder women. I couldn't remember her name, either.

"No, not really," I said, hoping to nip this discussion in the bud.

"Ah . . ." the chorus repeated delightedly.

Uh-oh. Maybe it was customary for respectable young Bosnian women hell-bent on marriage to deny that they wanted any such thing. Maybe I should have said "Yup, you betcha. Gonna land me a sucker." Maybe then they would shake their heads at my lack of femininity and drop it.

Time to change the subject.

"So, Pete tells me you all may have ancestors in Bayview Cemetery."

Silence blanketed the room. Even the seven children at the kiddie table looked somber.

"What did I say?" I whispered to Pete.

"Mama say our family, they are buried in the Potter Field," Pete replied. "They have no grave markers. This is very distressing."

"The location of their graves would have been noted somewhere, wouldn't it?"

"The land is not sacred. She may be sold," Catiz explained. "The bodies would be disemburied."

"Such talk no good. Is happy time," Mama Pete interjected, and I got the feeling that despite her motherly smile Mama ruled her realm with an iron fist. "Anna, you like my dolmas?"

"They're delicious," I said. Dolmas were balls of meat and vegetables, wrapped in grape leaves and kale and seasoned with complex spices. Bosnian cuisine seemed to be heavy on ground lamb and beef. Everything was savory and delicious, but I was unaccustomed to so much meat, especially since I'd been dating Josh the Vegan. In my case semi-vegetarianism stemmed from a lack of funds and cooking skill, rather than from principle.

Just when I thought I couldn't eat another morsel, Pete served me a meat-filled pita called a *burek*. I asked if *burek* referred to the whole dish or to the meat inside, and the men started chanting something that Pete translated as "All pitas are *pitice*, only *burek* is *pitac*!"

Well, of course.

I looked around for clarification, but every question I asked was met with shouted laughter. By then the *loza* had kicked in, so I laughed too.

"Anna! You sing!" someone called out from down the table, and the others joined in. "Sing, Anna!"

I'd never been much of a singer, probably because I

couldn't sing for squat, but at the moment I didn't think it mattered. So I stood, held my glass high, and launched into the only song that came into my mind, "John Jacob Jingleheimer Smith." The children had learned the song at school or in the Scouts, and chimed in, delighted to show off for their parents. Their high, angelic voices were charming, and the adults beat a rhythm on the tablecloth with their hands, or just watched, eyes glowing, as their children sang. "Ta da da da da da da da!" we shouted in unison, and I took my seat to thunderous applause. Nobody requested an encore, though.

After hours of dinner, it was time for dessert. Pete's mother and aunts circulated large platters piled high with honey-sweetened, layered pastries, some of which I recognized as baklava. Accompanying these was salep, or tea, and kava, a strong, espressolike Turkish coffee. Now I knew why Pete was such a wonder with the studio's espresso machine. Good coffee was in his blood.

The men and I lingered at the table, lighting cigars and cigarettes and pouring shots of a dangerous-looking, clear liquid. Probably the stuff that made my lips numb. Either that or lighter fluid.

Uncle Sidran took a seat next to me, elbowed me in the ribs, and gestured with his cigar toward Pete. "Pete. You like?"

I smiled. "Yes, I like Pete."

Uncle Sidran roared. "All girls like! All girls like Pete!"

The men roared in approval, chugged the liquor, and slammed the glasses on the table.

"Anna!" cousin Catiz called out. "You toast now, yes?"

I was toasted all right, so I followed the men's example and held my glass aloft. "All girls like Pete!" I shouted, chugged the drink, and slammed the glass on the table. The fiery liquid tore down my throat and exploded like a bomb in my stomach. My eyes filled with tears, and for a scary second or two I thought I was going to hurl my dinner back onto the table. I gasped for breath, and let loose a thunderous belch. The men looked impressed.

Sidran poured another round. "Pete big man. Big, strong man! Make big strong babies!"

The men roared again, and I didn't have the heart to squelch their assumption that Pete and I would be making babies. It was kind of sweet, in a misguided and thoroughly outrageous way.

So I held up my glass. "To Pete and hith big, thtwong babieth!"

The women had emerged from the kitchen and were standing around, drying their hands on dish towels and clucking amongst themselves. I realized I had been spending all my time with the men, and imposed myself on the females, tipsy though I was. My timing was impeccable: the kitchen was spotless.

I noticed a Tim O'Neill calendar hanging near the refrigerator. The man's floral infatuations were haunting me.

"I speak with docent Helena yesterday, Anna," said Mama Pete. "Tomorrow I begin to work there."

"What will you be doing?"

"The souls of the Potter's Field must be organized. Perhaps we can find where everyone is, Helena says. And we will clean up. Wednesday and Thursday Pete and the other boys will come and help with shovels and pick-axes."

"That's great," I said, smiling at the image of a bevy of Bosnians on the job, under Mama's watchful eye.

"I will run the community service program. Naughty young people will help to set things right, maybe they learn respect for the dead. Anna, did you see Helena loves Tim O'Neill too! Helena says one day we live in a world like O'Neill painting. You see I have calendar! How lovely she is, the painting in the office! You could paint like that, Anna, if you tried."

I gritted my teeth and smiled. "I don't think I have it in me, Mama Pete."

Around midnight I crashed. I was too drunk to walk, much less to drive, so I was assigned the upper berth of a bunk bed in Mama's cramped guest room. I was awakened sometime later by the ringing of a cell phone. It took me several moments to realize the annoying mechanical tune was emanating from my purse—I'd forgotten to give Mary back her cell phone. By the time I located it, the ringing had stopped. The display said *Number not available.*

I heard a strange noise from somewhere below me, and peered cautiously over the edge of the bunk. The lower berth was occupied by a stout, snoring woman in her fifties, her face covered by a mop of gray fur. I blinked, trying to get my eyes to focus. Either her wig was askew or she'd fused with a swamp rat sometime in the night.

With exaggerated care, I climbed down from my perch and made my way down the dark hallway to the bathroom, nearly jumping at my reflection in the mirror. My hair was snarled, my mascara had smudged, and the enameled chopsticks in my hair stuck straight up like a pair of antennae. I looked like a Martian raccoon. I'd left my twenty-first birthday behind more than a decade ago, and the evening's overindulgence showed on my face.

As I ran cold water to wash my face, the cell phone rang again. At this hour I imagined it was probably one of Mary's bandmates looking for her.

"Bosnian hotline," I answered, chuckling to myself. That *loza* was good stuff. "How may I direct your call?"

"Annie?" Mary's voice sounded tinny, not like herself.

"Mare? What's wrong?"

There was a scuffling sound, and a mechanically distorted voice came on the line. *"Tell us where the box is, and we'll let her out of the crypt."*

"What? What crypt?"

"The . . . it's a really nasty crypt. If you don't tell us, we'll hurt—I mean, we'll kill her." In the background I heard the muffled sound of someone coaching the caller.

"Put Mary back on," I demanded, anger overcoming my fear.

"She's locked in the crypt, and it's a really nasty one, too. Tell us where the box is. And don't call the police. If you do, we'll know."

"How will you know?"

"Hold on." I heard more murmuring and the caller returned. *"We tapped your phone."*

"I'll use another phone."

"Also, we have an informer. . . ."

More shuffling sounds, and a different voice came on the line. This one whispered, *"If you call the cops, don't expect to see your friend in the same light again. It's a shame: she's a real pretty girl."*

My heart raced. Unlike the other clown, this guy sounded like he meant business. "Okay, okay. I won't call the cops. But we have to do this in person. When you release Mary, I'll tell you where the box is. Not before."

More muffled discussion, and the first voice came back. *"You have ten minutes."*

"I'm in Hayward. I need more time."

"Twenty, then."

"Maybe half an hour."

"Okay—"

It sounded as though the phone was wrenched away. The whisperer got back on. *"Get your ass over to Bayview Cemetery, now, before we're forced to get really ugly. I mean, make her ugly."*

He hung up.

I ran.

Chapter 14

I found one had to do some work every day, even at midnight, because either you're a professional or you're not.

— Dame Barbara Hepworth (1903–1975),
British sculptor

I often paint late at night. The peace and quiet are soothing, and one may more readily hear the gendarmes approaching. — Georges LeFleur

I was picking my way across the sleeping forms littering the living room floor when a hand grabbed my ankle. I bit my tongue to keep from screaming, and looked down into the smiling face of cousin Catiz.

"Where's Pete?" I whispered.

"He is next door, at our uncle's house," Catiz said. "But I am here."

I hesitated. The men on the phone had not sounded like pros, though I supposed I was not the best judge of criminal expertise. Besides, Michael had once told me that amateurs could be more dangerous than seasoned professionals. Should I bring someone along to help rescue Mary? Someone, say, like a big, strapping Bosnian?

"Catiz, I was wondering . . ." I stopped, recalling how, not so long ago, Pete had been injured trying to help me. I'd vowed then never to endanger my friends again. Not intentionally, anyway. "Would you tell Pete that I had to run? Thank everyone for me?"

"Of course," he said, crawling out of his improvised bedroll. "Do you need help?"

"No, thanks," I said, appreciating his gallantry and muscled chest. "It's just girl stuff."

He nodded, kissed my hand, and watched as I hurried out to the truck. I swore as I realized that it had started drizzling again. Just perfect for racing to a crypt in the middle of the night.

As I drove, I pondered acting like a sane citizen and calling the police. But I couldn't help thinking that a bunch of squad cars, sirens blaring, bearing down upon the cemetery in the middle of the night would worsen our cause. The voices on the phone seemed to be after Louis' box, and I was ready to hand it over. Perhaps it was just that simple. Transforming a straightforward exchange into a hostage situation made my already *loza*-challenged stomach clench. I couldn't let anything happen to Mary.

Ignoring the speed limit and the rain, I made it to the cemetery in less than fifteen minutes. The gates were shut, so I parked at the curb and unlocked the pedestrian access gate. Now what?

"*Keep walking,*" a short man in a goblin mask whispered as he materialized at my side and grabbed my arm. I jumped, swallowed hard, and remained silent. The man searched my bag, confiscated Mary's cell phone, and shoved something hard into my right side. I couldn't tell if it was a gun, a finger, or a toilet bowl brush, but figured it was best to assume the worst.

A second, taller masked man materialized at my left as we hurried along the curved access road. I shivered as we skirted the pond where Louis Spencer had drowned, so many years ago. In the distance I glimpsed his crypt. We headed up and over the hill, passing one of the cemetery's older sections. I wasn't familiar with this area, but in the misty, silvery light of the graveyard I spied a marker inscribed with the name Frederic Olmos Blood. How appropriate.

I tripped on a tree root, splashed in a puddle, and the taller ghoul steadied me with a hand on my elbow. "*Step carefully,*" he whispered, his voice low and surprisingly polite.

"*Shut up,*" whispered the other one.

Eucalyptus trees rustled in the wind, and wet grass clung to our shoes. The three of us were soaked by the time we halted in front of an old square crypt made of gray stone blocks streaked with black moss. The stones were crumbling from years of neglect, and the dank air of the crypt was redolent with mold and decay. The iron door had a small barred opening, as if the crypt's inhabitants needed a peephole to check out visitors, and a shiny new padlock winked in the moonlight.

"Mare?" I called through the bars.

"Annie?"

"Are you all right?"

"I'm *locked* in a *crypt!*"

"She's fine," whispered the short man. "And you will be too, if you tell us where the box is. Otherwise I'll just leave you two in there indefinitely, bound so you can't call for help."

"Annie!" Mary cried. "I'm totally freaking out here!"

"Maybe I'll go ahead and shoot you before I leave you," added the ghoul with a laugh. "The rats would like that."

"It's in the columbarium," I said in a rush. I drew the line at bullet holes and rats. "In the Chapel of the Beatitudes. Now let her out."

"*Where* in the chapel?" He shoved the gun under my chin.

"Near the ceiling, in the crown molding. There's an inconsistency in the light. You'll see when you get there."

"Very good. Did you open it?"

"Are you kidding? I don't need a curse from beyond the grave," I said. "Haven't you heard what happened to the folks who opened King Tut's tomb?"

"Hey, I saw that show—" the tall ghoul whispered.

"Shut up, idiot!" the shorter goblin hissed. "You'd better be telling the truth, lady. For your sake, and for hers."

He opened the heavy Master Lock, shoved me hard, and I stumbled into the crypt, knocking over Mary. Before we could scramble to our feet the iron door clanged shut and the padlock was snapped and locked. I shook the door anyway, watching through the peephole as the masked ghouls disappeared over the hill.

Trapped in a crypt. I tried to decide if this was better than being locked in a toilet and figured it was a draw.

"Annie?" Mary said in a thready voice from the shadows. "I don't suppose you brought my cell phone?"

"They took it."

"A flashlight? Tools, maybe? *Some* way to get us out of this hellhole?"

"I'm afraid not."

"You didn't bring *anything*? Some heroine you are."

"Listen, Mare, it's nearly three in the morning! I wasn't thinking very clearly." Considering I'd been drinking unidentifiable liquids with Uncle Sidran all evening, it was amazing I'd been coherent enough to answer the phone.

As my eyes adjusted to the dim light I realized my assistant's hands were bound behind her. "Turn around and let me untie you."

"Did you at least tell anyone where you were going?" Mary asked over her shoulder.

"They warned me not to," I protested, struggling with the thick rope and trying not to dwell on the obvious: I should have left word with someone as to my destination. I wondered how much I could blame on the fuzzy aftereffects of *loza*.

"Shit, Annie! You of all people should be carrying a damned gun by now!"

"So says Ms. Gun Control. If I'd brought a gun—something I don't want and can't afford—they would have just taken that, too. Maybe even used it against us. And need I point out that if *you* hadn't insisted on spending the night in a cemetery, none of this would be happening?"

"It's not my fault!"

"I didn't say—wait a minute. Where's Evangeline?"

"Cops busted her for trespassing a couple of hours ago. I hid behind some trees so I could bail her out. But after the cops left those masked creeps blindsided me. What's taking you so long?"

"Hold still, this rope's putting up a fight." Whoever tied her up must have been a sailor or an Eagle Scout or a psychopath, because he sure knew what he was doing.

I finally managed to pry the stiff binding off her wrists. As Mary rubbed her skin, I searched for a way out, cringing as my fingertips encountered dust and cobwebs and the dried-out husks of things I didn't want to think about.

"You drove your old truck here, didn't you?" Mary asked, sounding tired.

"No, I brought the Porsche. It seemed like a special occasion."

Mary snorted.

"Of course I drove the truck. Why?"

"Because if you had a nice, normal car, you could point your thingy at it and set off the car alarm. You know, attract someone's attention."

"My truck doesn't even have power windows," I said. A spider—or something with a disturbing number of ticklish legs—darted across the back of my hand and I did the Icky Bug Dance, stomping my feet and shaking my hands.

"What are you doing?" Mary asked.

"Spider. I think."

"Ha. Just be glad it's not a cockroach. You should've seen the one I found yesterday in my apartment. It must've been six inches long—"

"Mary, swear to God, if you say one more word I'm going to choke you." I hated cockroaches with a passion bordering on insanity.

"Figures," she muttered.

"That's enough!" I snapped, impatient with her uncharacteristic whining. "I came here in the middle of the night to rescue you. A little gratitude would be appreciated. Now help me find a way out of here."

"I already looked," she grumbled. "There isn't one."

I kept searching—there wasn't anything else to do—and for a few minutes all was silent.

"I am *so* creeped out right now," Mary said.

"I know, Mare. But two's company, right?"

I thought she nodded, but it was hard to tell in the shadowy crypt. The three small windows were covered with iron bars, so even if we managed to break the glass without slicing our wrists open and inadvertently committing suicide, the bars would prevent our escape. The crypt's floor, ceiling, and walls were cold, hard stone. I tried not to think about the bodies that inhabited the six sepulchers lining the walls.

After several more minutes of fruitless searching I gave up and sat, wet and shivering, on the grimy floor next to Mary. *Think, Annie, think.* No cell phone, no one knew where we were, no nothing. On the plus side, we weren't in any immediate danger and the ghouls had seemed more intent upon retrieving the hidden box than hurting us.

"Hey, it's not so bad," I said, draping an arm around her. She leaned against my soggy shoulder. "It'll be morning in a few hours. And at least we're out of the rain. All we have to do is keep our spirits up—so to speak—until the gardeners show up. They come to work early, right?"

Mary didn't say anything.

"Mare?"

"The thing is . . ."

"What?"

"I sort of took the box. Temporarily."

"You *what*?" I dropped my arm and glared at her.

"I was going to put it back!"

"Mary, that's not the point! Why did you do something like that?"

"I couldn't stand the suspense. I *had* to know what was in it."

"You realize this means those ghouls will be back?"

"Not necessarily."

"Why not?"

"I switched it with another box. You know, in case you checked to see if it was still there. It kind of depends on whether or not the ghouls open it, and figure it out."

"What did you put in the box?"

No response.

"Mare?"

"Mr. DeFazio."

"Mr. De—you mean his ashes?"

She nodded.

I covered my head with my arms and curled into the fetal position, icky things be damned.

"I mean, it's not like he's gonna care, right? Guy's dead, right?"

"Where's the original box?"

"Evangeline and I buried it. That's how come we got caught by the cops."

"Why would you bury it?"

"Just till tomorrow. I was gonna ask Dante to come back for it. I couldn't get back in the columbarium 'cause the staff locked up when they left, and then Evangeline was freaking out, said I couldn't carry it on the motorcycle with us. Besides, the new guitar player at my apartment keeps going through my things. Can you believe the nerve of that guy? Just because I borrowed some of his indigo eye makeup—"

"Where did you bury the box, Mare?" I asked, trying to keep her on track.

"Under the redwood trees."

"In Potter's Field?"

"Annie! I wouldn't desecrate a grave."

"You desecrated a niche!"

"I didn't think of that. That's kind of creepy, isn't it?"

"Yes. Yes, it is."

"But we buried the box under the trees, where there are no graves."

"Yes there are, they just aren't marked. That's Potter's Field."

"You mean, like Artie the Pothead Potter?"

Artie belonged to the pottery co-op at the DeBenton Building. He was the only tenant besides me who set off the alarm, and he had the excuse of habitual drug use.

"A potter's field is an area set aside for people who don't have the money to buy a plot. I have no idea where the name comes from."

"It's from the New Testament, the Book of Matthew," Mary said in a defeated tone of voice. "After Judas returned the thirty pieces of silver he'd been paid to betray Jesus, the priests used the money to purchase a field to bury foreigners. They bought land that was no good for farming, where artisans dug clay for pottery."

Because of her current take on life, it was easy to forget that Mary had been brought up in a Pentecostal church. One of her party tricks was to name all the books of the Bible, in order. When she was really drunk she would reel off the "begats" in a single breath.

"The band Anthrax sang a song about it. Tom Waits did, too," she added. "I can't believe I buried the box where there are bodies. Do these potter people have coffins, at least?"

"I guess so. It's not a mass grave, or anything. They're just buried closer together and without headstones. And they don't own the land."

I thought of the vagrants and friendless folk who had ended up buried in Potter's Field, and wondered if it mattered to them. Did their souls linger, unable to shuffle off this mortal coil until they were reunited with home and loved ones? What if they had no home or loved ones? What about professional vagabonds, like my grandfather? Then again, Georges claimed Paris as his spiritual home. He'd probably want to be buried in Père Lachaise, the final resting place of such immortals as Mozart, Chopin, and our very own Jim Morrison.

I shifted, trying to get comfortable. The marble sepulcher was cold against my back, the stone tiles hard beneath my rear.

"So what was in the box?" I asked. If the ghouls were going to murder us over it, I wanted to know what the hell was in there.

"A couple of photographs. Some little metal toys, an old

pocket watch, a few cards and letters. It looked like junk, frankly. I didn't get to go through it 'cause Evangeline was all freaked out, she wouldn't even look. She was standing guard near the road, which was why she got busted and I didn't. Good thing I buried it, huh, or the cops would have taken it."

"It would have been better if they had," I pointed out. "I should have turned it over to them the minute I laid my hands on it."

"Why didn't you?"

"I thought it might have something to do with *La Fornarina*."

"And 'cause you're stubborn as a mule."

"There is that."

"How come you had the box in the first place?"

I gave her a quick rundown on my encounter with Cindy Tanaka at Louis Spencer's crypt.

"Do you think the box is connected to her death?" Mary asked, her voice troubled.

"I don't know. It seems awfully coincidental, but the police are convinced it was suicide. Maybe they'll investigate more when we tell them what happened tonight."

"Um, I don't think that's such a good idea."

"Why not?"

"I'm kinda in trouble already. I didn't want to tell you 'cause I knew you'd worry."

Oh Lord. "What did you do this time?"

"Hey! You should talk."

"Sorry. What happened?"

"There was a little dustup at the club last week, and I'm kinda on probation. That's also why I hid when the cops came. Think Evangeline will understand?"

"Oh, sure. It's a matter of sisterly solidarity."

"That's what I figured, too. That's why we can't tell the

cops what happened tonight. They might start wondering what I was doing here."

"But if those ghouls return—"

"I bet we could take them. They only got the upper hand 'cause they surprised me, and I freaked out a little bit when I saw those masks. I mean, I was all alone and it *is* a graveyard."

"Don't blame yourself," I said.

She leaned her head on my shoulder. Despite spending hours in this crypt she smelled of shampoo and baby powder. I felt a surge of protectiveness and rested my head back against the sepulcher.

I awakened to the sounds of rain and a distant car engine. Blinking at the dim light that fought its way through barred windows and cobwebs, I extricated my arm from beneath Mary's head, wincing at the needle pricks that signaled the resumption of circulation, and struggled to my feet. Through the little window in the door I spied Helena walking near the access road, sheltering herself with an umbrella decorated with Monet's *Water Lilies*. With her were Pete's mother and aunt, huddled together under a plain black umbrella, listening as the docent pointed to various markers and chattered nonstop.

"Is someone there?" Mary croaked from behind me. "Yell!"

I hesitated. I wasn't sure why I was hiding from the head docent, except that I didn't like her and she obviously didn't like me. Plus, I suspected Helena's first instinct would be to call the cops. Better to try our luck with a kindly gardener.

The women headed down the path. Pressing my face against the door to scope out the scene, I felt it move. All of a sudden the door swung open, and I stumbled out.

"Annie!" Mary scrambled after me. "What did you do?"

"Nothing," I said, pointing to the padlock, which hung open on the metal hinge.

Mary and I gaped at each other; then I closed the door and we scurried across the cemetery as fast as we could, brushing dust and cobwebs and all manner of crypt detritus from our clothing and hair but getting soaked as we ran through the rain. As we skirted Potter's Field, I noticed a section of the border fence had been recently repaired and at the edge of a much older section of cemetery stood a shiny new monument to the memory of Chad Garner.

Aaron Garner's son. I had painted his portrait what seemed like ages ago, long before getting involved with his grieving mother.

Mary and I detoured around the brick cottage housing the cemetery's offices and headed for the main gates. Glancing over my shoulder, I saw Curly Top at the leaded glass window, watching us with flat, expressionless eyes.

Back at my apartment, Mary ducked into the shower while I checked my messages. Two, both from Josh. I sighed. I had to do something about that relationship, and soon. Josh deserved someone who would value him for his many virtues, and I deserved someone who would value me despite my lack of same.

The bathroom door opened and a cloud of steam escaped.

"It's all yours!" Mary called out. She'd been in a great mood since she realized her night in the cemetery meant she'd achieved a Goth Personal Best. "There may not be much hot water, though."

I stood under the frigid spray long enough to scrub myself raw in an effort to rid my pores of dank, stale, moldy crypt air.

I made coffee and sourdough toast, and my assistant and I sat at my pine kitchen table, sipping, munching, and avoiding one another's eyes. I was dressed in a fresh white T-shirt and comfortable old jeans. Mary was too tall for my pants, so I lent her a short black skirt and a Grateful Dead T-shirt that had hitched a ride home from the Laundromat last week.

The arms of my Krazy Kat kitchen clock read nine thirty. I cleared my throat. "About Evangeline . . ."

Mary nodded. "I've got fifty bucks in the toe of a boot in my apartment. Think her bail will be more than that?"

"I've got a better idea. Let me call Elena." Elena was my friend Pedro Schumacher's girlfriend who had left the Oakland Public Defender's Office a few months ago to open her own shop. I had always wanted a friend with a criminal defense practice, and could not have been happier had the pope commissioned me to paint his portrait.

Elena agreed to meet us at the city jail, and Mary and I piled into the truck, popped in an old White Stripes tape, and sang as we headed for Seventh Avenue. On the way we passed a metal sculpture of letters spelling out THERE.

"What's *that* supposed to mean?" Mary sounded peeved. I often had that reaction to modern art, myself.

"It refers to the Gertrude Stein quote about Oakland. You know the one, 'There is no there, there.' "

"What's *that* supposed to mean?" Mary repeated.

"It's a popular misconception that Stein was referring to Oakland being boring—she grew up here—but she was actually talking about the fact that her childhood home had been torn down. It's one of the world's most misunderstood quotes."

Oakland was a great, historic, and really interesting city. It was the home of the Black Panthers, the founding chapter of the Hell's Angels, and the silver-and-black attack of the Raiders football team. Gorgeous examples of art deco architecture lined Broadway, the waterfront offered ample views of the cities across the bay, and serene Lake Merritt hosted flocks of migratory birds as well as Italian gondolas. There was a bustling Chinatown, a vibrant Latino quarter, and shops stocking African, Caribbean, and Ethiopian goods. It was also one of the nation's most ethnically diverse and integrated cities. Unfortunately, there was no denying that it suffered from a serious inferiority complex living in the shadow of stunning San Francisco and notorious Berkeley.

"It's not even funny," Mary said.

"It's not supposed to be, Mare. It's supposed to be deep."

"You know, Annie, you're kind of weird."

"I'm not weird, I'm educated."

"Same thing sometimes."

We parked at a meter and joined the mélange in the police station. Weaving through the throng, I heard numerous languages spoken in tones ranging from the stoic to the hysterical. Elena and Pedro greeted us warmly, and after waiting an hour, filling out pages of forms, and a mad dash to the cash machine, we bailed Evangeline out. Elena told us Evangeline would likely get a stern lecture on trespassing and a stint in community service when she returned for her hearing. I treated everyone to a leisurely lunch at Tamarindo's, then dropped Mary and Evangeline on Piedmont Avenue to pick up Evangeline's BMW motorcycle.

I checked the clock on my dashboard and decided upon today's agenda. All I wanted to do was to stretch out on my futon sofa at home and take a nice, long nap. The gray, rainy day seemed to second the notion. But it was almost two in the afternoon on a Monday, and I was supposed to be checking on Aaron Garner's house construction. I opted for a large Peet's coffee and headed for the City.

The renovation was progressing well, and I thought Garner would be pleased when he returned. The men digging in the garden had unearthed more headstones and lined them up along the side of the house so that the little alley resembled a narrow graveyard.

Today Norm was wearing a ripped and stained navy blue

T-shirt that read I'M THE ONLY HELL MY MAMA EVER RAISED.
A roll of blueprints stamped ETHAN MAYALL, ESQUIRE was
shoved under one beefy arm. Norm gave me his version of a
smile as he stood at the top of the back stairs and watched
me approach.

"I got a new joke. Wanna hear it?"

"Not if it involves private parts or bodily functions."

He shrugged and went on to the next subject as we
walked around the house to check the trim details. I handed
him a copy of the paint schedule, which I had sent to the
housepainters, and promised to follow up with the "smart
house" technician who was wiring the place for computers.

"Ethan's been bustin' my balls again," Norm complained.
"Keep that dick-wad away from me, will ya?"

"He's the architect, Norm. He's supposed to have some
say in the project."

"He's an asshole."

"Maybe so, but he's an asshole with blueprints." I flicked
the roll under his arm. In this business He Who Held the
Blueprints reigned supreme, for without them the City
would not issue construction permits.

"Garner called this morning. He's comin' home tomorrow."

I nodded. Josh had mentioned this in his messages.

"I told him about those grave markers. He sounded pretty
excited and said something 'bout doin' some kinda cemetery
exhibit. Says he wants to talk to you about it."

"Why me?"

"How should I know? I ain't your damned secretary,
a'ight?"

"Hey, Norm, how do you get approval to develop a subdivision?"

"It's a pain in the ass. In the City you have to apply for
permits and variances, then start the environmental review.
Takes years."

"Is it the same in Oakland?"

"Dunno. Ask Garner. He's the subdivision king."

"The what?"

"How'd you think he made his money? He builds upscale communities in Danville and Blackhawk. Made a shitload kowtowin' to yuppies who wanna impress their friends."

"I thought Garner was a history buff."

"He is. But there's a huge market in bulldozing orchards and puttin' up high-class spit n' cardboard miniestates. Strictly bidness."

"I'm surprised."

"Why? It's in his blood. His great-grandfather, whatzahoozits, made his money developin' subdivisions. When San Francisco was the wild Barbary Coast, full o' gold miners and whores, Garner started buyin' up land and promotin' Oakland as a safe place to raise your kids while you took the ferry to your office in the City."

"Oakland was the safe alternative?"

"That was back when there was nothing in the East Bay but oak trees and whatever Indians and Mexicans the Europeans hadn't killed or run off."

"You should volunteer with a local history association, Norm. You know an awful lot about this area."

He snorted. "My dad was the one. Never shut up about this stuff. Well, time to get to work."

"One more thing," I said. "Do you know Aaron Garner's ex-wife?"

"Which one? There's a whole bunch."

"Helena."

"Sure, I know 'er. She was two wives ago. Lives down the street," he added, jerking a muddy thumb in the direction.

"Down *this* street?"

"Yup. The big brownstone."

"Wasn't that a Designers' Showcase house?"

Once a year a bevy of interior designers descended upon one of the City's nicer homes to showcase the latest trends in furniture and interior design. As soon as the house had been pimped, the place was opened to the hoi polloi, who paid a hefty fee to tromp through the palaces of the wealthy and gawk at how the other one percent lived.

This particular home stuck in my mind because, at the behest of a designer I was then wooing, I had agreed to paint a guest bathroom with an absurd mural that made the occupant feel like a bird in a cage. The wraparound mural had a claustrophobic effect, and was a blatant rip-off of a famous Calistoga muralist, but I had been new in the business. It took me a few years of owning my own studio before I said no to anything short of out-and-out forgery. I remembered the home's windowless basement had been transformed into a mirror-lined, chandeliered ballroom, and an attic room had been labeled "the artist's atelier," though there was so little natural light no working artist would ever have used it. All in all, it was a rambling, somewhat monstrous, mansion.

Norm shrugged and lit a Marlboro.

"Does anything about Helena strike you as, you know, odd?"

"She lost her kid a while back, so I guess she's had it kinda hard," he said, blowing out a cloud of tobacco smoke. "Tell you one thing. I wouldn't touch that broad with a ten-foot pole. High-maintenance, society type. Me, I like girls that drink beer from the bottle."

"I'll keep that in mind."

"If the interrogation's over," Norm said, "I gotta go."

I finished up with the tile layers, consulted with the painters, and went out to deposit my paperwork in the cab of my truck. It was still raining, the anemic sort of drizzle that often passes for rain in the Bay Area. After a day of this I was already getting seasonal affective disorder. As I turned around, Curly Top Russell was standing behind me, holding an umbrella over our heads.

"Hey, Annie."

"Russell!" I took a step back. The cemetery employee had not mastered the concept of personal space. "What are you doing here?"

"Mr. Garner asked me to look at those headstones you found," he said, a spark in his pale eyes. "Could you show them to me?"

"I'm late for an, uh, appointment a few doors down. The headstones are in the alley at the side of the house."

"Oh. Want me to walk you?"

"No, thanks, I'm good," I said.

He didn't move.

"Let me know what you think. Bye." I brushed past him and hurried down the flower-edged sidewalk to a massive brownstone structure from the late nineteenth century. I climbed the curved marble steps to the carved mahogany doors and pushed the old-fashioned doorbell.

As I waited I peeked back down the street.

Russell stood in the driveway in the rain, watching me.

Chapter 15

A picture is something which requires as much knavery, trickery and deceit as the perpetration of a crime. —Edgar Degas (1834–1917),
French painter and sculptor

I have never been interested in ballerinas. Not in painting them, that is. —Georges LeFleur

"Yes?" squawked a male voice through the intercom.

"Um, Dr. . . . Dick?" I stammered. Intercoms made me nervous.

"Yes?"

"It's Annie Kincaid. We met the other day at Bayview Cemetery?"

"Of course! What a surprise. Come on in."

The door buzzed and I pushed it open, pausing in the foyer to allow my eyes to adjust to the dim light. Many of the sumptuous multimillion-dollar homes of Pacific Heights and Cow Hollow were jammed so close together that little sunshine could penetrate their palatial interiors. I took in the entry hall's sweeping staircase and rich mahogany paneling, and realized everything was exactly as I remembered it:

same fussy wallpaper, same massive gilded mirror, same tacky knockoffs of Renoir's floral masterpieces.

"To what do I owe this pleasure?" Dick called out as he descended the plush carpeted stairs.

"I hope you don't mind my dropping in like this," I said. "I thought I'd take a chance on catching Helena."

"Oh, I'm sorry. She's out. I'm not sure when she'll be back. . . ."

"It was a long shot, but since I was in the neighborhood—"

"Do you live around here?"

"Ha! I mean, I wish. It's a gorgeous area."

"We like it," Dr. Dick said with a casual shrug.

"I'll bet. No, I'm working down the street, on Aaron Garner's house renovation."

Dr. Dick's soft brown eyes flashed. "Ah. The infamous Mr. Garner."

"I take it you're not a fan?" I had wondered how Helena's new husband, the guts n' butts man, felt about having her ex living close by. My parents insisted on inviting my ex-fiancé to Kincaid family holidays, and that was enough to make me choke on my cranberry sauce.

Dick smiled sadly. "Nothing we all can't cope with. I just wish he'd chosen to live elsewhere, that's all. Let me fix you a drink," he said, escorting me into the next room. "Do you like scotch?"

"Love it," I said as we passed through a shadowy dining room with deep red lacquer walls. My step faltered when I noticed my portrait of Chad Garner hanging over the carved stone fireplace. It was a good painting, if I did say so myself. I had been able to capture the intensity and volatility of the teenage spirit, while portraying the gentleness and hope in the boy's dark eyes. When Aaron Garner commissioned the painting he handed me several photographs of Chad, saying only that his son was "unavailable." It was not uncommon for artists to work from high-quality photographs rather than sittings; these days, few people who could afford to have their portrait painted could take the time to pose for hours, and squirmy young people were the most difficult subjects. Garner had given me no clue that I was painting a memorial to a dead child.

I wondered if my host realized I had painted the boy's portrait. I'd signed it, of course, but unless they were hoping to cash in on a piece, few art lovers took notice of the artist's signature. Dick seemed friendly enough but his wife Helena might not appreciate knowing of my role in creating this remembrance of her lost son.

"Single malt?" Dr. Dick offered, holding up a bottle of eighteen-year-old McCallan.

I shook my head. "I hate to say it—I *really* hate to say it—but I'd better pass. I've got a lot of work to do."

"How about coffee, then?"

"Coffee would be great, if it's not too much trouble. Are you sure I'm not interrupting anything?"

"Not in the least," he assured me, leading the way to the kitchen. "I was writing up charts. As luck would have it, you happened upon me on my paperwork day. I relish the break. I went into medicine to heal people, not to push paper!"

I smiled. Silly me, I would have thought paperwork would be a nice break from sticking things up patients' butts.

I took a seat on a swivel stool at the dark granite kitchen counter and watched Dr. Dick putter about. The cabinets were a polished cherry, the gleaming six-burner chrome stove was professional-grade, and a stained glass cupola above our heads filled the room with sparkles of dancing color. It was a pleasant but overblown room, more impressive than cozy. Framed photographs lined one wall, and in a few I thought I recognized a teenage Helena, though her companion had been cut out of the photographs.

"You know, I've been here before," I said. "When it was the Designer Showcase."

"Ah yes. I believe half of San Francisco took the tour. You should have seen the carpet!"

"I can imagine. But I'm afraid I did worse than that. I painted the birdcage room."

"You painted that?"

"I apologize. It was done under duress."

"How so?"

"They paid me."

He chuckled. "Some people love it, and when they don't the room's good for a laugh. We bought this place as a temporary abode, anyway. That's why we never bothered to change anything. It even came furnished."

Dr. Dick and I lived in different worlds. When I needed a "temporary abode," I slept in my truck.

He set a steaming mug in front of me along with little Italian painted pots of sugar and cream. I savored the rich taste of well-brewed coffee for a blissful moment. "So, are you building a new house?"

"Helena has her heart set on something in particular, but we're not sure if it will happen," he said, pouring a finger of scotch into a Steuben crystal tumbler. "I don't much care where I am as long as my lovely wife is at my side."

I smiled. It was nice to know that there were still men who found their stout, middle-aged wives worthy of such love and devotion. Dr. Dick seemed like a keeper.

"Dick, did Helena say anything about a problem at the cemetery?"

"Apparently there was a trespasser last night," he said. "She ran out of here, irate, when she got the call. She hates it when kids mess around in there."

"Did she say anything about a recent grave robbery? I witnessed someone trying to take a metal box out of a crypt

a few days ago. The person I was with was supposed to report it and turn the box in, but didn't. And then she—well,
she was the one who had just killed herself when I saw you
at the cemetery the other day."

"I'm so sorry," he said. "Was she a troubled person?"

"I met her only once. But before she died she left the box
with me, and I meant to take it back to the cemetery office,
but to make a long story short, two goons came after me and
my assistant trying to get the box."

"Are you all right?" he gasped. "When did this happen?"

"Last night. I wondered if Helena might have any idea
about what was going on."

"It sounds to me as though you should be careful in that
place. I already told Helena I don't want her there after dark
unless I'm with her."

I glanced at the clock. It was almost four. "Thank you for
the coffee. I'd better get back to work."

"Thank *you* for interrupting my paperwork," he said as he
escorted me to the front door, this time passing through a
high-ceilinged sitting room. A Tim O'Neill original hung on
the wall above a celadon silk couch.

I looked at it, then at Dick.

"Atrocious, isn't it?" He laughed.

"You don't like it?"

"*Hate* it. Looks like it should be adorning the cover of a
frothy romance. I like Edward Hopper. Wayne Thiebaud.
Real painters. What do you think?"

"I, uh . . ." Long ago my grandfather had taught me to
never, ever criticize a host's home or taste, no matter the
provocation. *You never know, chérie,* Georges had said in as
stern a voice as he was able to muster with me. *The rich
have an inconvenient way of being well connected. It is one
of the reasons they are so rich. Today's fool is tomorrow's
senator.*

"It's, um, pretty."

"And you, my dear, are diplomatic." He shook his head. "Never understood Helena's taste in art, but she says it reminds her of her time with her son."

"I heard he passed away. I'm sorry."

"It was years ago, but it still haunts her. I suppose it always will."

I said nothing. I could only imagine the pain of losing a child.

"Listen," Dick said, changing the subject. "Helena bought a painting at an art show last week. It's still in one of those cardboard tubes. It seems to me it must be bad for an oil painting to be stored like that. Since you're here, why don't I show it to you and see what you think?"

He opened the hall closet door and began rummaging through a bundle of cardboard tubes, the kind architects used for blueprints and Haight-Ashbury head shops used for Day-Glo posters. "Aha! Here it is." He struggled with the plastic plug on one end.

"Need a hand?" I asked, trying to pry the end off as he held the tube.

"What is going on here?" Helena's outraged voice called from the doorway. "You! Dick!"

For a split second I thought she was calling me a dick, and despite my grandfather's tutoring I nearly responded in kind.

"Give that to me," she demanded, holding out one hand. Dick surrendered the tube. She tucked it under her arm, and turned on me. "What are *you* doing here? Why are you going through my things?"

"I was just—"

"She's working at Aaron's place, darling. When she learned we lived nearby she stopped in to say hello."

"And you decided to entertain her in my absence?" Helena glared at her husband, who squirmed.

"I'd best be going," I said, inching toward the door. "Thanks again for the coffee and conversation."

Neither Dick nor Helena said anything as I crossed the shadowy foyer and slipped out the front door. Hurrying down the steps and along the wet sidewalk, I wondered about their relationship. Nothing in Helena's attitude indicated the least bit of warmth, much less respect, for her husband. I could only speculate what it was about this unpleasant woman that made Dick so smitten.

Curly Top was nowhere to be seen, so I fired up the truck and started across town. I wished I could have seen the painting Dick was trying to show me. Surely it couldn't be an original Raphael that Helena had squirreled away in a cardboard tube. She didn't need the money, her worship of Tim O'Neill suggested she had no taste, and it would be an awfully risky thing to do. Still, I didn't trust her.

I pulled into the parking lot of my studio building and parked next to Frank's shiny Jaguar. As I climbed the stairs I ran through today's To Do list but couldn't remember what was on it. That was the problem with mental To Do lists.

I flung open the door to find Mary sitting on the wood plank floor, Louis' metal box in her lap and its contents scattered around her.

"I don't see what they were so excited about," Mary said as she helped herself to a blue Peeps marshmallow chick from a package she'd bought for half off at the after-Easter sale at Long's Drugstore. "It's just junk."

"You went back and dug it up, after what happened the other night?"

"Dante did it for me. Got back this morning and boy, was he pissed about me going without him and almost getting arrested!" Mary smiled. "He said he just dug it right up, 'cause he blended in with a bunch of Bosnians."

I jumped at the sound of the espresso maker spitting. Speaking of Bosnians . . . "Is that you, Pete?"

"It's Evangeline," Mary said. "She's scared to look at this stuff. Says it's unnatural."

"I ain't takin' no chances," Evangeline called out. "I'll jes' stay back here."

"Sounds like you've got the espresso machine working," I said. The only other person who was able to manage it was Pete. The two might well be a match made in heaven.

I sank to the floor, helped myself to a Peeps, and sat cross-legged next to Mary. My assistant was right: the contents of the metal box were something of a letdown. There were a couple of lead soldiers, an old pocket watch, a lock of hair tied with a blue silk ribbon, and a couple of dingy letters. I skimmed them. They appeared to be from Louis Spencer's relatives. Sad, but hardly enough to justify chasing a person around a columbarium, much less killing a young graduate student. "That's it?"

"Some crappy baseball cards," Mary said, pulling an envelope from the bottom of the box.

"Baseball cards?" I said. They would have to be from the 1920s and '30s at the latest. "That has possibilities. The last time my nephews visited we went to Collectors' Corner to buy Pokemon cards. The baseball cards in their display case were worth hundreds of dollars."

"Serious?" Mary said, popping another Peeps in her mouth and shrugging. "Maybe there's a Babe Ruth card. Babe Ruth's a good candy bar, but I like Abba Zabba better."

I nodded. "I like Three Musketeers."

"What, are you's two kiddin' me?" Evangeline's face was a picture of indignation as she poked her head around the kitchenette partition. "Is it mint?"

"You mean the flavor?" Mary said.

"You mean the color?" I said.

Evangeline made a production of rolling her light blue eyes and letting out an exasperated sigh. "Like, 'mint condition'? Duh." She fixed me with a look. "I thought you was Ms. Smarty-Pants."

I didn't recall applying for the position. In fact, depending on if I'd had enough sleep and when I'd last eaten, I was sometimes Ms. Dopey-Pants.

"Evangeline, how much would a mint-condition Babe Ruth baseball card be worth?"

"Dunno. Hundreds of thousands, pro'ly. Maybe more."

"Serious?" Mary said again.

"Is there a Honus Wagner?" Evangeline asked, relenting and coming over to check out the stack. "That's the Mona Lisa of baseball cards. One sold for more than a million bucks on eBay. They're rare on account o' they put his card in tobacco pouches, but he was against using tobacco, so they had to pull it."

A million bucks? Now, that was a treasure worth killing for.

Mary reached for the cards, but Evangeline intervened. "Gimme that. Your fingers are blue. Look at 'em."

We looked. Her fingers were a bright Peeps blue.

Evangeline sorted the cards but found no Honus Wagner. No Babe Ruth either. And none were "mint," having gotten moldy and brittle after decades in a dank tomb. Nonetheless, I asked Evangeline to show the cards to a dealer. Couldn't hurt to have all the facts.

"What's this?" Mary asked, as she pulled something from beneath the silk lining.

It was an exquisite miniature portrait on an ivory oval that looked as if it might be by Rosalba Carriera herself. Could this be what all the fuss was about?

My studio neighbor and friend Samantha poked her head in the door. "Knock, knock."

"Sam!" we said in unison.

"The three of you look like naughty children," Sam said in her soft Jamaican lilt as she sank gracefully onto the Victorian sofa. "What you got there?"

"It's a miniature portrait. Isn't it lovely?"

"It's beautiful."

"How late is Mayfield's Auction House open?"

"It's almost closing time, but it's not far. Should I give Rachel a call?"

Rachel agreed to spare us a few minutes if we hurried over. Despite the rain, Mary and Evangeline took off on the motorcycle to investigate the worth of the baseball cards, while Sam and I piled into my truck. We pulled up to the warehouse near the San Francisco Design Center, snagging a rare parking space right in front.

Samantha's former assistant Rachel had learned a lot in her two years at the auction house. She wore her honey-colored hair in a neat coil at the back of her neck and a fine gray wool skirt in place of her old jeans. Pulling on a pair of clean white cotton gloves, she spread a velvet cloth on a worktable and switched on a gooseneck lamp. She examined the miniature with a magnifying glass and returned to her desk to search for comparable sales on the computer.

"This is older and higher quality than the others at the columbarium. Much higher quality."

"Is it a Rosalba Carriera?"

"Could be. Could very well be. Assuming it's genuine and the provenance can be established, it should fetch a pretty penny. A pretty penny indeed."

Sam and I shared a smile at Rachel's tendency to say everything twice.

"How much?" I asked.

"Brace yourselves," she said, looking up at us with a bright smile. "Up to twenty-five thousand dollars."

Chapter 16

*What was a masterpiece a hundred years ago is no
longer so today.*

—Alberto Giacometti (1901–1966),
Swiss painter and sculptor

*A faddish canvas might be hidden in a closet be-
hind the galoshes. A sculpture, at best, might be
moved to the garden and used to feed the wildlife.*

—Georges LeFleur

I remembered when twenty-five thousand dollars seemed like
a fortune. True, it was a lot of money for a tiny piece of painted
ivory, but it hardly seemed sufficient to justify kidnapping
Mary and me and threatening us with bullets and rats. On the
other hand, I had read that the average bank robbery nets only
three thousand dollars, so perhaps it was all relative.

I dropped Sam at her Chinatown apartment, crossed the
bridge into Oakland, and trudged up to my apartment, where
I made a dinner of a pear and gorgonzola cheese. I ate in
bed, wearing the oversized T-shirt that served as my night-
gown, and was falling asleep when Evangeline and Mary
called to report that Collectors' Corner had offered nearly
ten thousand dollars for the baseball cards.

The contents of the metal box now totaled thirty-five thousand dollars. Had I missed anything else of value? Perhaps the toy soldiers were worth something to a collector, or the letters and photos to a museum. It wasn't a bad night's work, but it wasn't Blackbeard's treasure chest.

The phone rang again and I jumped on it, hoping it was Grandfather. Instead, it was our old pal Donato Sandino, checking on my progress—or lack of progress, I thought to myself—with *La Fornarina*. The Italian reminded me of what was at stake: my grandfather's freedom. I spent another restless night.

The next morning, in deference to a break in the rain and because I wasn't planning on climbing scaffolding, I dressed in a flowered skirt, a bright blue tank top, and sandals. I would be catching up on paperwork and finishing the pirate drawings at the studio, so I should manage to remain presentable. I hoped the out-of-character attire would lift my mood. Cindy's death still bothered me, I wondered about Donato Sandino's plans for Grandfather, and I worried that Helena might have rolled up Raphael's masterpiece like a cheap poster. I could almost hear the centuries-old varnish crackling.

Since I had a little extra time this morning, I decided to visit Mrs. Henderson and ask about Helena and about the legend of treasure in Louis Spencer's crypt. The retirement community looked and smelled as it had the other day. When I approached the front desk, the same blue-haired receptionist was chatting on the phone. She looked up with a smile, but the smile shook when she recognized me. She hung up.

"Hello," I said. "I'm here to see Mrs. Henderson."

"Oh dear," the woman said. "She's gone."

"Hairdresser's again?"

"Oh, goodness, no," she said, avoiding my eyes. "She's . . ."

"What?" I urged, starting to worry.

"I'm so sorry, dear, she . . ."

A nurse who had been smoking outside walked up to the counter. "Are you family?"

"I'm her niece," I lied.

"She was taken to Summit Medical Center in a diabetic coma."

"A what? She was fine . . ."

"These things can come on quickly. She came back from an outing on Sunday—"

"Yes, I know. We went on a picnic."

The woman's lips formed a straight line of disapproval. "You should have watched what she ate. She loves sweets."

"She seemed very careful, and when we got back she checked her blood sugar. The machine said everything was fine."

"You must have read it wrong," said the nurse. "I'm sorry."

She hustled down the hallway, her ample hips chugging from one side to another.

"There, there, dear," clucked the blue-haired woman. "Nurse Ratchett has a rather blunt way of putting things. She means well. It wasn't your fault."

An elderly woman with a strawberry-blond rinse accompanied by a stooped man with a hearing aid joined us. "What wasn't whose fault?"

"Mrs. Henderson," the receptionist replied in a loud voice.

"Shame," the man croaked. "She was so happy about writing her autobiography, too."

The two women nodded.

"Was someone helping her?" I asked.

"Pardon?" The man reached up and fiddled with his hearing aid.

"Was someone helping her?" the receptionist repeated loudly.

"Chinese girl. Pretty as a China doll."

"She wasn't Chinese, Ned. Not every Asian is Chinese, for heaven's sakes," said the strawberry blonde with a fond but exasperated smile.

"Korean, then," Ned said.

"Did she have an accent?" I asked him.

"What's that?"

"An accent," I shouted. "Did she have one?"

"Nope. Mrs. Henderson was as all-American as apple pie."

"No," I said loudly, "the girl. The Asian girl."

"Don't suppose she did, come to think of it."

"Could she have been Japanese-American?"

"A Japanese porcelain doll. I was stationed over there during Korea, you know."

"We know, Ned, we know," the receptionist said, winking at me. I was starting to like Blue Hair.

"Was her name Cindy?" I asked the group. "Was she a graduate student at Berkeley?"

"That sounds right," the strawberry blonde said. "My grandson went to Cal."

"Good school," Ned said. "Go, Bears."

"*I* graduated from Stanford," the strawberry blonde said. "Go, Indians!"

"Bears!"

"Indians!"

"They're called the Cardinals now," Blue Hair interjected.

And I thought *my* crowd's conversational style was linearly challenged.

"Come to think of it," the receptionist added before the Cross-bay Big Game rivalry flared up anew, "she hasn't been around in a few days. Not since Wednesday, at least. She used to come every other day."

"What about Mrs. Henderson's autobiography? Was there a manuscript?" I asked.

"Nope, she was a widow woman," Ned replied.

"Ned, hush," the strawberry blonde said. "No, dear, I don't think they'd gotten that far. The girl used a tape recorder, tiniest little thing you've ever seen. Amazing what they can do with technology these days."

"So how come they can't fix this d-a-m-n hearing aid of mine?" Ned barked.

Blue Hair rolled her eyes.

I thanked the folks for their help and rushed out to my truck. At Summit Medical Center, I found Mrs. Henderson still unconscious, her sister and a handful of nieces and nephews surrounding her bedside. She was in serious condition, they reported, but the doctors were optimistic.

"I don't understand it," I said. "We checked her blood sugar the minute we returned from the picnic. The nurse even checked it. The machine said she was fine."

"Did you notice anything odd about her behavior?" asked Mrs. Henderson's nephew, Abe, a physician's assistant.

"She seemed a little, well—inebriated. But I know for a fact that she wasn't drinking."

"That's a common insulin reaction," Abe said. "We see it in the ER all the time. It's easy to confuse an insulin reaction with intoxication."

"But the test strips were normal. The nurse said so."

"It can come on suddenly," Abe said, and his wife placed a comforting hand on my shoulder. I was glad to know that Mrs. Henderson had such a loving family. "Diabetes is unpredictable, and at her age it's a delicate balance. You can't blame yourself."

I went out to my truck and sat for a long time, thinking. The "Japanese doll" was dead and the columbarium's long-term secretary was in the hospital. Suicide and diabetic comas, my ass.

There was a killer on the loose.

I headed north, to UC Berkeley. This time there was no Pink Man to lead me to the Chemistry Department, but a clutch of anxious-looking students pointed me in the right direction. A bored-looking work-study student sent me to the TA office when I asked for Brianna Nguyen.

I wouldn't have pegged this young woman as a graduate student, much less a chemist. She looked about twelve years old, and was dressed in tight jeans and a bright pink blouse. Her arms were covered with sheaths of material, but her shoulders were bare. Either the sleeves had been ripped off her blouse or something had chewed off the fingers of her gloves, I couldn't decide which. She sat hunched over a large three-ring binder, two composition books, and a stack of loose papers, a Star Wars pencil bag jammed with fluorescent highlighters beside her on the Formica-covered table.

Brianna did not seem surprised when I asked about Cindy, and reviewed a stack of cramped, neatly written lecture notes while she spoke.

"Omigod, I was so shocked. Omigod. I'm, like, so grossed out right now?"

Highlight in blue, highlight in green.

"Anyway, omigod," she said. "I am, like, *so* glad I didn't go to med school like my folks wanted? Sweartogod, I would've barfed every day. I nearly barfed when I saw Cindy. I had to, like, identify her? It was terrible. Omigod."

She exchanged the green highlighter for a bright purple one.

"I saw Cindy a couple of nights before it happened," I said. "She seemed fine then. Can you think of anything that was bothering her?"

She highlighted an entire paragraph in purple. "Maybe the painting deal. And some jerk-off was harassing her. Plus, she was seeing this guy? And he was, sort of like, married? But only sort of."

"Sort of?"

"Separated, I guess. Anyway, they seemed really happy."

Her highlighter squeaked and my skin crawled.

"What was his name? You knew him?"

"Met him once. He was kind of old, but well preserved."
She giggled. "I mean, not crotchety or anything. White guy.
Blond hair, pretty buff."

"How old? Forties? Fifties?"

"Forties maybe. Dunno."

"What about his name?"

She shook her head. "If I knew I woulda told the cops.
They searched her room for clues to his identity, ya know,
like on all those shows? Cindy and I used to watch *CSI*. The
shows never say what a mess the forensic guys make, though.
There's, like, fingerprint powder *everywhere*. Cindy'd be
pissed if she could see it."

"I'll bet. What did you mean by the 'painting deal'?"

"She was doing a project with this old lady? And the old
lady thought there was this total masterpiece at the cemetery
place where Cindy was working. I guess she tried a coupla
times to get experts to look at it, but they didn't believe it
was real. She was afraid someone would take it. I guess it's
worth a lot of money or whatever."

"Did she take any notes? What about the tapes?"

"Tapes?"

"She was taping interviews."

"Oh. That's weird." Highlight in pink.

"What's weird?"

"There were some of those minicassettes in some car-
tons? And the tape was pulled out of the cartridges. Like she
was despondent, least that's what the police said. But it
wasn't like her. She was real neat and tidy."

"Could I see her room?"

"Nothing to see," Brianna said, highlighting in green.

"Cindy's family came by yesterday and went through everything. They didn't want any of her, like, books or notes or anything. Just took it all to the Dumpster. It was pretty sad. I mean, my folks would rather I go to med school, but at least they're *interested* in what I'm doing." For the first time since I'd entered the room, Brianna stopped highlighting and met my eyes. "Why are you asking? Who are you again?"

"I met Cindy the other night, and she asked me about the painting, which made me wonder. You said someone was harassing her?"

"Yeah." The chemist turned to her notebooks. "She didn't say much, just not to tell anybody where she was. I was, like, whatever. I told the police but I couldn't tell them anything, ya know, concrete."

"Do you know if it was a man or a woman?"

She shrugged. "Mostly she was worried about the painting deal. She brought in some pieces for me to analyze. That's not my specialty? But I, like, ran a couple of tests for her."

My heart sped up. "Pieces of the painting?"

Brianna nodded.

"What did the tests show?"

"That it was pretty old. I found lead in the white paint, and it, like, breaks down with age? So I calibrated the breakdown. It was a few hundred years old."

By itself, the test didn't prove anything. A forger could fool the chemical dating process by mixing new pigments with scrapings from an old lead lantern. But it did rule out the more innocuous explanations. Crispin Engels wouldn't have bothered with lead scrapings because he never claimed his copy was an original.

"There was something else. . . ." Brianna scratched her nose with her highlighter, leaving a fluorescent orange streak. "Something about the linen was off."

"The linen fibers from the canvas?"

"Yeah. I think the linen dated like from the Renaissance."

Crispin Engels also would not have used a Renaissance-era canvas. But Raphael—or an ambitious forger—would have.

"Brianna, could I get a copy of the report?"

"What report?"

"The report on the tests you ran."

"There wasn't, like, an official report. It was just a print-out. I gave it to her professor."

"Dr. Gossen?"

"Uh-huh. He said he'd give it to Cindy 'cause I was on my way out of town."

"When was this?"

"Must've been last Tuesday. Wait—Wednesday. I guess."

I thanked her and left her to her frenzied highlighting. Dr. Gossen was not in his office and the administrative assistant had a few choice words for people who lied to hardworking secretaries. I decided not to ask her for Gossen's home address.

Heading back to Oakland, I followed Martin Luther King Boulevard under the BART tracks, got caught at a red light, and noticed the sign for Lois' Pie Shop. I liked the idea of a shop dedicated to pies even though I wasn't much of a pie fan. I liked chocolate. Leave the fruit out of dessert, was my motto. It occurred to me that Billy Mudd's office was nearby—I had been there once during the Save the Fox Theater campaign. I drove around until I spotted the small sign for Precision Builders. It was located down a long driveway, behind another single-story office structure, in a utilitarian cinder-block building.

White Chevy trucks sat in the driveway and men bustled back and forth loading lumber onto the truck racks. I nodded as I passed them and went through the metal doors into the shop, which was fragrant with the aroma of freshly milled wood. The shop was a single huge room jammed with woodworking equipment, stacks of lumber, and unfinished wood trim, cabinets, and furniture. Wood shavings littered the concrete floor, and in one corner a Latino man pushed two-by-fours through a table saw.

A place like this is Josh's dream, I thought. Too bad Billy Mudd was such a pig. They might have been good friends.

A corner of the space had been sectioned off into an office, where I found Billy pacing like a caged lion and screaming into the phone. He rolled his eyes when I walked in but ignored me until he'd vented his rage at the unfortunate soul on the other end of the line and slammed down the phone. "What the hell do you want?"

"Good to see you, too, Billy. I have a few questions."

"Why would I answer any of your questions?" The phone rang again and Billy snatched up the receiver. "*What!*"

While he bellowed at this new intrusion, I snooped. There were a handful of photos on his desk, which I assumed to be his ex-cheerleader wife and their two adorable towheaded children. The bookshelves held binders of building codes, relics of the historic buildings he had razed—a section of a carved wooden banister, a stone corbel from a fireplace—and numerous cardboard blueprints tubes. I recognized the fleur-de-lis insignia of Ethan Mayall's architectural firm on one, and pulled it out.

"Put that down," Billy said and snatched the cardboard tube from my grasp.

"I'm working with Ethan on a job in the City."

"Bully for you," he said, tossing the tube into a box on the floor. He returned to his desk and threw himself into his desk chair. Mudd's eyes were rimmed in red, and he looked haggard beneath his tan.

"What are you working on with him?"

"None of your goddamned business."

"Just wondering. Seems like a coincidence. By the way, I thought I saw you at Fisherman's Wharf the other day. How do you know Professor Gossen?"

"Annie, you're a pain in the butt. Always have been. Your mouth's too goddamned big and your nose is just as long."

What could I say? I didn't like the man, but he was not altogether lacking in judgment.

"You came here to ask me about the architects I work with?"

"No. I came to ask if you were planning to build a development on cemetery land."

"Why would I do that?"

"Wouldn't you have to buy the land first?"

He stared at me, and his phone rang again.

"You're a busy boy, Billy."

"No shit, Sherlock. So you'll understand when I tell you I don't have time to chat. I'm not endangering any historical buildings, I'm just going about my business making a living. Maybe you should do the same and leave me alone."

"Did you know Cindy Tanaka?"

"Get the fuck out of here," he hissed, a sound more threatening than his bellow. He grabbed me by the elbow and dragged me toward the door. The Latino man stopped sawing, but made no move to intervene. "I'm a happily married man. Now stay out of my goddamned business."

I blinked in the sunshine. "How 'bout you guys?" I called out to the workmen loading the truck. "Any of you like to contribute to a fund-raiser for women's equality in the trades?"

No one spoke. I took that as a no.

Back on the road, I realized Billy had not denied knowing Cindy Tanaka, only that he had done anything wrong.

Since Billy described himself as a "happily married man," it seemed doubtful he was planning to dump Mrs. Mudd and the mini-Muddites to run off with a graduate student. Billy made my stomach heave but I imagined he seemed masculine and confident compared to the pasty academics Cindy spent most of her time with. Otherwise intelligent young women fell for married sleazoids every day. So perhaps the suicide scenario was plausible.

But suppose Cindy had mentioned to Billy her conversations with Mrs. Henderson and her suspicions about *La Fornarina*? It had been my experience that older men don't pay much attention to what young women said, but what if he had put two and two together and realized that if the columbarium possessed a genuine masterpiece, they would be fully independent and have no need of possible real estate deals? Would he have been ruthless enough to kill Cindy in order to ensure her silence? Could he have tricked Mrs. Henderson into eating a Twinkie?

I found myself heading for Cindy's apartment, wondering if the garbage had been picked up.

The building looked exactly as it had the other day. It was unsettling to think that the death of a young woman had so little effect on everything around her. I circled to the rear of the duplex. A large green Dumpster smelled like sour milk, rotting vegetables, and day-old Pampers.

Shawna pulled up on her bike just as I was standing on tiptoe, peering over the metal side into the abyss. Behind her was another girl, this one with white-blond hair astride a bright pink Barbie bike.

Every neighborhood should have such a ten-year-old squad on patrol.

"Hey," I said.

"Hey." Shawna's solemn eyes watched me. "This is my best friend, Hannah. Whatcha doin'?"

"I think something valuable might have been thrown away by accident."

"You goin' in there?" Hannah asked, a frown worrying her pale forehead.

Not if I could help it. "I'll pay you a dollar to go in for me."

"No way," Hannah laughed.

Shawna looked disapproving. "You crazy, lady."

"Five dollars?"

"Mama said not to take money from strangers," Shawna said with the air of an outraged ethics professor. "Plus, it's stinky in there."

She was right. It ranked pretty high on the noxious fumes quotient.

Two teenage boys ambled over. They wore jeans that hung loose and low, and huge T-shirts that fell to their knees. Their hands were shoved deep in their pockets in what I could only assume was an effort to keep their pants from falling down around their ankles.

"'S'up?" They lifted their chins at Shawna and Hannah, who returned the greeting.

"What's she gonna do, go in there?" the taller boy asked.

"This is Kareem and Anthony," Shawna said, the neighborhood's Welcome Wagon.

"Hi," I said. "I'm Annie."

"'S'up?" they answered. "You gonna go in there?"

"How much money would it take to get you to go in there for me?" I asked, ever hopeful.

"More'n you got," mumbled Kareem.

"Nuh-uh. These are new Nikes," explained Anthony.

Since when had young people become so fastidious? When I was their age I would have happily gone into a Dumpster for cash. Then again, maybe that said more about *me* than about the youth of today.

"All right, fine. Great." I marched back to my truck, unearthed a pair of latex gloves that I use for faux-finishing, and returned to the Dumpster. "Anybody know where I can get a ladder?"

My audience shook their heads, so I looked around and spied a crate by the back fence. I brought it over to the Dumpster and climbed on it, but still needed some serious athletic prowess to lift myself up and over.

What a day to wear a skirt.

Snapping on the gloves, I managed to hoist myself onto the side, but couldn't get my rear end far enough onto the ledge. Moved by a spirit of gallantry—or fearing embarrassment if I fell backward with my skirt flying over my head—Anthony of the bright white Nikes stepped onto the crate, placed two broad hands on my waist, and lifted me onto the side as if I weighed no more than Shawna.

With a smile of thanks I swung my legs over the side, closed my eyes, and let go. One sandal-shod foot sank into something soggy, while the other plunged straight to the bottom of the Dumpster, burying my right leg up to my thigh. I forced my thoughts away from what I was standing in, and started searching.

The Dumpster must have served more than just Cindy's duplex, because there was a whole lot of refuse in there, much of which was in flagrant defiance of Oakland's green recycling program. I pushed aside moldy coffee grounds and blackening banana skins, mounds of potato peels, and an open container of gloppy yogurt. Numerous plastic bags had ominously squishy contents, and I could have sworn one was moving. A paper grocery bag contained used Kleenexes, about a mile of dental floss, and an old tube of toothpaste. I poked around a bit and finally unearthed a plastic garbage bag neatly sealed with a plastic twist-tie. That looked promising. Using the back of my wrist to push my hair out of my eyes, I managed to leave a smear of something I didn't want to know about on my upper cheek.

Hearing muffled giggles, I glanced up to see Shawna and Hannah, no doubt held aloft by their teenage accomplices. But it would take more than the ridicule of little girls to daunt me. I'd grown up with an artistic soul in a small provincial Central Valley town; I had been inured to derision and mockery at a young age.

I gave them a bright smile as though to prove how much fun I was having. Hell, it worked for Tom Sawyer. "Sure you don't want to join me?"

This sent them into peals of laughter.

I turned back to my search. Opening the garbage bag, I found several tiny cassettes, but the metallic tape had been torn out and creased, and I doubted they could be salvaged. A stack of notes beneath them seemed like a better bet. I started sorting through them, tossing aside seminar notes and discussions of research materials. At last I uncovered a composition book, which fell open to a page of notes on Rosicrucianism. A sketch of a cross with a flower in the center was titled MAY THE ROSES BLOOM UPON YOUR CROSS. Flipping through the book, I saw Louis Spencer's name and a discussion of the pyramid structure of his crypt. Tucked between the pages was a receipt for a digital copy of *La Fornarina,* by Raphael.

Aha!

"Found something!" I sang out.

No response.

"Guys?" I called. "Hello?"

Nothing.

I had registered the clicking of Shawna's bike a few minutes ago, but was so caught up in the discovery of Cindy's notebook that I hadn't paid attention. With a sinking feeling I realized I had no plan for getting out of this reeking hellhole. I reached up and latched on to the side of the Dumpster, searching for a foothold. I upended a plastic diaper bucket and stood on it so that I could peer over the side.

A car sat in the alley. A dark sedan. The kind detectives drove.

I dropped back down, muttering to myself about young hoodlums who didn't have the courtesy to warn a person to cheese-it when the cops showed. What to do, what to do . . . In all of my years of training at Grandfather's knee, not once had he offered a lesson on Dumpster diving.

On the plus side, my olfactory sense seemed to have given up the ghost, and the little delinquents were unlikely to tattle to the authorities. As long as I hunkered down in the trash, I would be safe. No way would anyone think to look in the—

"Fancy meeting you here," Detective Hucles said as he squinted down at me.

"Detective." I nodded, casual as one could be while standing thigh-deep in lumpy yogurt and soiled diapers. Hucles looked tired, his eyes red and lined, his tie loose at the collar.

"You look terrible," I blurted out.

"This from the woman in a Dumpster. What's that on your cheek?"

"I'm trying not to think about it."

"I don't blame you. Ms. Kincaid—"

"Call me Annie," I replied. No point in standing on ceremony.

"Annie. Are you going to tell me what you're doing in there surrounded by garbage? And not just any garbage, but Cindy Tanaka's garbage?"

I drew a complete and total blank.

"The Oakland PD doesn't look fondly on citizens interfering in an ongoing investigation, Annie."

"I thought you were convinced it was a suicide," I said. "Does this mean you've changed your mind?"

I heard a police radio crackle. It sounded as if reinforcements had arrived. Hucles held my gaze a moment longer, but he had hard-to-read cop's eyes. Was he about to ticket me? Arrest me? Burst out laughing?

"Find anything?" he asked.

"I think so. Cindy's notes."

"A suicide note?"

"No—research notes."

He held out his hand, and I reluctantly surrendered the composition book. He flipped through it and handed it to someone I couldn't see.

"What's with the gloves?" he asked.

"Have you *seen* what's in here?"

"I can only imagine. You always carry latex gloves with you?"

"Usually. I—" Wait a minute. Did the detective think I was trying to avoid leaving fingerprints? *Try acting innocent for a change,* I scolded myself. *Especially since this time you are.* "I'm a faux finisher. I use these gloves for work, and I was just trying to stay clean. This place is disgusting."

"Which begs the question, what are you doing in the Dumpster?"

Something wet and slimy fell against my bare knee. I couldn't bring myself to look.

"Um, Detective? Do you think we could have this discussion some place else?" At this point, being taken downtown to an interrogation room could only be an improvement.

Hucles disappeared from view, and two young officers popped up. What followed was not one of my better moments. The cops grabbed my arms and pulled, but between my lack of upper body strength and their lack of coordination, I wound up banging against the front wall of the

Dumpster, twice, and falling on my butt in someone's dis-
carded pizza. By the time I was hauled unceremoniously
over the side I was smeared and slimed and bruised in places
I didn't know could be bruised.

I collapsed on the crate, peeled off my gloves, and tossed
them into the Dumpster.

Hucles was waiting, his arms crossed over his chest.
"Better?"

I hesitated before answering. "Hard to say."

"Where were you on the night of the twelfth?"

"I worked late at Chapel of the Chimes Columbarium,
where I'm restoring some murals. My assistant was with me."

"Name?"

I offered Mary's name and phone number.

He flipped through his notebook. "A Ms. Sally Granger,
administrative assistant in the anthropology department at
UC Berkeley, told me you lied to her to get Cindy's address."

"Um . . . that's true."

"Care to elaborate?"

"Gossen wouldn't give it to me. And I was worried about
her."

"Why? You said you hardly knew the woman."

I fessed up and told him about the masked grave robber
stealing Louis' box, and the possibility of a Raphael at the
columbarium. "And on Sunday, a woman who was secretary
at the columbarium for fifty-one years went into a suspicious diabetic coma."

"Why didn't you go to the police right away with this information?"

"At first I thought Cindy or the cemetery management
would call. And then it just all seemed pretty far-fetched, especially the bit about the Raphael. In the end . . . I was just
stupid, I guess."

"Professor Gossen spoke about test results from a valuable painting. That's the one you're talking about?"

"Yes, I think so."

Detective Hucles took a deep breath and flipped through his notebook. He wrote down Mrs. Henderson's information, read some more, then fixed me with a steady gaze. "I'm choosing to believe your version of events, for now. If I have any reason to doubt you, we're going to have problems. Do I make myself clear?"

I nodded. "Crystal."

"That's it, then. You can go."

"I . . . er . . . Cindy's notebook? Could I take a look . . . ?"

"That's the problem with these darned homicide investigations, Ms. Kincaid," Hucles said with a shake of his head. "Everything's potential evidence. Forensics is on their way, and they'll have to try to figure out what might be significant and what might be the result of a faux finisher falling on her butt in the evidence."

I deserved that. Hucles seemed okay for a cop. And he hadn't arrested me, so he was a good egg in my book.

The detective accompanied me to my truck, where I reached in back of the seat and extracted Louis' box.

"Oh, Kincaid," he called as I started up the motor. "Don't make any travel plans."

Civilian detective or no, I thought as I climbed into my truck, trying to ignore the items drying on my skin, I still wanted to talk with Roy Cogswell. I was in desperate need of a shower, but I'd been meaning to talk to the columbarium director for days, and it was almost quitting time. I made a U-turn and headed north to the columbarium, pulled up to the curb, and started searching for a quarter for the parking meter. I was rifling through the door pockets—usually a mother lode of loose change—when a knock sounded on the passenger window.

It was Helena, in a neat cream pantsuit and a robin's-egg-blue paisley scarf. I leaned across the bench seat and opened the door. She climbed into the passenger's seat, folded her hands in her lap, and stared straight ahead. I thought I noticed her nostrils flaring, but she didn't mention anything about my appearance or aroma.

"Helena? Something I can do for you?"

"Hands off my husband."

"Dr. Dick?"

"His name's Richard!"

"Fine, Richard. I'm not even remotely—"

"Don't bother denying it. I saw how he reacted to you," she said, pursing her lips. "I've had experience with this kind of thing."

"You mean Aaron—"

"I have no intention of discussing my personal life with you, young lady."

It had been my experience that people who suspect their spouses of cheating aren't famous for their logic. "You started it," I muttered.

"She's a senile old bat, you know."

"Who?"

"Henderson. She had a thing for my husband, too. Don't think she didn't."

"Helena, I swear to you that I have no romantic interest in your Dick—your husband—whatever. And even if I did it wouldn't do me any good. He's nuts about you. We talked about you, mostly."

"Do you expect me to believe that?"

"Yes, I do. It's the truth."

She looked at me, her hazel eyes limpid and yearning. Helena was a rhymes-with-witch-on-wheels, but some men loved the idea of rescuing an unhappy, demanding woman. It was a twisted version of the Prince Charming fantasy.

"Honest. He told me he'd live anywhere 'as long as his lovely wife was at his side.'"

She looked as if she were choking back tears.

"You're a lucky woman, Helena."

"He's such a dear man," she sighed. "I'm sorry I said those things to you."

"I'm just glad we got that straightened out."

Now that we'd built a little sisterly camaraderie, I thought I'd take it out for a spin. "Why didn't you want me to see the painting in the tube?"

"I've seen how you sneer at the Tim O'Neill in the office." She sniffed and lifted her chin. "You are rude and sarcastic."

"I'm sorry. You have every right to enjoy whatever art you please."

"I wish the whole world were like an O'Neill painting," she sighed.

I glanced out the windshield and saw Curly Top Russell walking up to an old beat-up Cadillac a few meters ahead of us.

Helena looked at her delicate platinum-and-ruby watch and frowned. "Is it time to leave already? Where *does* the time go?"

Russell climbed into the car, pulled the door closed, and started swinging his arms in the air, as if punching the roof.

"What's he doing?" Helena asked. "Dancing? Boxing?"

"Maybe stretching?" *What a geek Russell is,* I thought. "You were saying about the O'Neill painting?"

"I wish I could follow one of his garden paths, enter a warmly lit cottage, and sit by the fire with a cup of tea. Do you remember the scene in *Mary Poppins* where the children and Bert the chimney sweep jump into a sidewalk chalk painting?"

I smiled. "It's my favorite part."

Russell was now bobbing back and forth, though not to any discernible beat.

"My son died, you know," Helena whispered.

"I know. I'm so sorry."

We sat in silence. The truck's small cab started getting stuffy—and fragrant of eau de Dumpster—so I rolled down the window. I heard the muffled sound of someone crying for help. In the car up ahead, Russell's movements had slowed.

Something was wrong.

I leapt out of the truck and ran over to the Cadillac. Russell's body jerked and his face pressed up against the driver's window.

His eyes were full of terror.

Chapter 17

Nudity, of course, is a problem for Americans. It disrupts our social exchange.

—Eric Fischl (1948–   ), American painter and sculptor

I do not understand those who are offended by the sight of a nude body. Perhaps they have too many mirrors in their bathrooms.   —Georges LeFleur

"Unlock the door!" I yelled, jerking on the handle and banging on the window. "Russell, unlock the door!"

The driver's door wouldn't budge, so I tried the rear door, then ran around to the passenger's side. All locked. I pounded on the windows and yelled, but there was no response. Russell was no longer moving, though his eyes were wide open.

Helena stood on the sidewalk, wringing her hands.

"Do you have a cell phone?" I demanded.

She shook her head. I pushed her in the direction of the cemetery office. "Go get help! Call 911! *Now!*"

She stumbled off. My shouting had attracted the attention of one of the cemetery gardeners, a white-haired man who headed this way, pruning shears in hand. I looked around for something to break the glass with, saw nothing, and ran to my truck. Flinging my seat forward, I fumbled in the mess for the metal bar that formed the handle of the tire jack. I ran back to the Caddy and swung it against the passenger's-side window, hard. The heavy metal bar bounced off the safety glass. *Shit!*

I took a deep breath and tried again, using all my strength, and this time the glass cracked and bent inward. Another swing shattered it into a thousand tiny pebbles. The gardener knocked away the remaining shards with his gloved hands and unlocked the door. I climbed in and felt something stab me in the hip.

"Russell! Can you hear me?"

Curly Top's face was red and swollen, and he was wheezing. I grabbed him by the shoulders and together the gardener and I dragged him across the seat. I knelt on the curb, holding Curly Top half in, half out of the car. The gardener took off his hat and swatted at the air while I loosened Russell's tie and started talking. I don't know what I said, but I was still nattering on when the paramedics arrived. The gardener drew me away and the paramedics laid Russell on the ground and began barking orders. I heard something that sounded like "epi push," and the echo of sirens rang in my ears.

A young man with a sleek black ponytail instructed me to sit on the curb while he treated several small cuts on my hands, an abrasion on my brow, and scrapes on my knees. The paramedic's voice was low and soothing.

"Is Russell all right?" I asked.

"He's alive. Much longer and he wouldn't have been."

"Was it a heart attack?"

"Looks like anaphylaxis. His medic alert bracelet says he's allergic to bee stings."

"A bee sting did all that?"

"Lethal things can come in small packages."

The police arrived as the paramedics loaded Curly Top

into the ambulance and raced away toward Summit Medical Center. I described what had happened, and Helena and the gardener confirmed my story.

"He was stung repeatedly," said a gray-faced cop in a wrinkled uniform. "Could be a bee got trapped. A paper wasp, now—they'll mess you up good if you're allergic. It may have been building its nest and got pissed off when the engine started."

"I think you should call Detective Hucles," I said. "This might be related to another case he's working on."

"Hucles?" the cop asked. "He's been workin' twenty-four hours straight. We're a little shorthanded down at the station."

"I just saw him a little bit ago. Really, I think he'd want to hear about this."

The cop shrugged and walked off.

I sat in the cab of my truck, stunned and so weary I didn't care what I looked and smelled like. I hadn't seen Manny since our last less-than-friendly interaction, but he came over, offered me a Coke, and asked if I needed anything else. His gentle eyes were shadowed with worry. I thanked him, told him I was fine, then drifted off to sleep.

"Is this some kind of elaborate plan to spend time with me?" Hucles said, startling me awake.

"What? I . . . uh . . ." I surreptitiously wiped a little drool off the side of my mouth and pretended I hadn't been asleep.

He started asking questions. How did I know the victim? Did I know he was allergic to bees? Was I sure the car doors were locked when I arrived? How did I happen to be here?

"I don't understand how this could have happened," I murmured.

"Sometimes bees try to nest under the hood of a car, then come in through the heating vents."

"That's what the other guy said," I replied, remembered something buzzing past me. "But Russell must have driven to work this morning, so the car had only been parked there for a day. And why didn't he just jump out?"

Hucles looked away. "The locks seem to be malfunctioning. It happens sometimes on older cars. He probably panicked. They found his Epi-pen under the seat. He must have dropped it when he was trying to use it."

"Detective, this seems awfully coincidental. Could it have been on purpose?" I asked, hearing my voice waver. "Could someone have tried to kill Russell?"

"Here's an idea. Why don't you leave the detective work to me? It was good you called me in on this. I'll look into any connection between the incidents."

I nodded.

"You can go for now, but I'm sure I'll have more questions for you. Here's my card again, just in case you think of anything else," he said, and then his voice gentled. "Listen, is there anyone you want me to call to come get you?"

I shook my head. All I wanted to do was go home, have a stiff drink or ten, and crawl into bed.

The sun was setting by the time I pulled into the tiny lot behind my apartment building and squeezed into a space between my neighbors' nicer cars. Today had been the kind of day that made my third-floor location seem like a ridiculous assumption of health and well-being. I slogged slowly up the steps, pulling myself up by the sturdy oak banister. I unlocked my door, grateful to be home, tossed my keys in the little bowl on the hall table, and froze.

My apartment had been ransacked.

The futon mattress had been tossed on the floor, my bookshelves were emptied of books, and the area rug was heaped in a corner.

Fear, even anger, was muted. Mostly I felt numb.

I snatched up my keys and thundered down the stairs. If someone was still there, they could help themselves to my crappy TV, half a loaf of moldy bread, and a four-year-old tube of mascara. I would *not* risk another confrontation with a ghoul in a Halloween mask, and I couldn't bring myself to go through an interrogation with Hucles for the third time in the same day. There was nothing in that damned metal box worth any of this.

I hopped in my truck and sped to San Francisco, putting the bridge and the bay between me and the goings-on at the cemetery. The numbness wore off and I started fuming. I'd had it up to here with ghouls in masks and the mysterious secrets of the columbarium. I stopped by my studio, but it was quiet this evening. On the plus side, no one had tossed the place. On the downside, no one was around, not even Frank. Usually I relished the peace of my studio after-hours, but tonight I did not want to be alone. Still, I strapped on my apron, put in an old Pretenders CD, and tried to lose myself in painting. Art always relaxed me, but tonight I jumped at every sound, real or imagined.

I left by ten and drove around aimlessly, trying to decide where to go. I could join the gang at the club where Mary's band was playing, but I quailed at the thought of a raucous crowd and pounding music. Funny thing, somehow I wound up right down the street from my landlord's apartment. I didn't want to analyze it too closely, but Frank's place seemed synonymous with safety and security.

On the other hand, suppose he was entertaining A-list clients with an elegant catered dinner party? I imagined the clink of silver against fine china, the murmur of refined conversation, the glug-glug-glug of seventy-dollar wine being poured into crystal goblets. Frank would preside at one end of the table, handsome as ever in black tie. At the other end, his girlfriend, Ingrid, would be smiling, the consummate hostess. If I showed up in my disheveled state—my skirt was dirty, my blouse was torn, I was adorned with garbage drippings, and my hair was, as always, wild—I might not make the best of impressions.

While I debated, a car pulled out of a space at the curb. That decided it. If that wasn't divine intervention, I didn't know what was.

In case Frank was home alone, I should bring a peace offering. There was a great pizza place down the street and I couldn't remember the last time I had eaten, which just went to show how abnormal things had been lately. I ordered an extra-large thin crust with green peppers, mushrooms, and pepperoni, and used their tiny, dimly lit bathroom to wash up as best I could. I would smell like the cheapest institutional soap, but that was better than dirty Pampers.

The only other time I'd been to Frank's apartment we had entered from the parking garage, and he had used a key to access the elevator. This time I would have to deal with a doorman. On my own. Late at night. Looking a fright.

Remember, chérie, I heard my grandfather whisper, *you are a LeFleur. LeFleurs have been guests in the world's finest homes. Never apologize for who you are.*

I strode into the lobby, pizza box in hand. The fellow sitting behind the desk was of below-average height and above-average weight. His shiny brass name tag indicated his name was Darryl.

"Good evening, Darryl," I said in an oh-so-refined tone. "Mr. Frank DeBenton, please."

"Aah . . . Mr. DeBenton?" Darryl's thin hair was tucked under his cap, and he wore a red jacket that reminded me of Sergeant Pepper. "Aah . . . was he expecting you?"

"Certainly. I brought pizza."

Darryl looked skeptical.

Do not be intimidated, chérie, my grandfather continued. Hauteur *will succeed where* politesse *may fail.*

"I'm in a hurry, Darryl."

"Are you, uh, a friend?"

"Mr. DeBenton will not be amused to learn of your interest in his, shall we say, affairs."

"Oh, aaah—" Darryl's rheumy blue eyes gave me the once-over, while he was apparently trying to reconcile my appearance with my attitude.

Do not give up, ma petite. *Never be the first to blink.*

"Darryl?" I said peremptorily.

Darryl picked up the phone and after a brief exchange said, "This way, ma'am," and escorted me to the elevator, where he pressed the button for the tenth floor. "Have a good evening, ma'am."

"Thank you, Darryl." I smiled to myself as the doors closed but stopped when I caught a glimpse of my reflection in the gilt mirror some misanthrope had hung on the elevator's side wall. It was much larger than the one in the dim pizza parlor restroom, and despite my earlier efforts my hair looked totally out of control, my mascara was smudged, and my lipstick had smeared. My blouse was torn at the shoulder, and my black bra strap played peekaboo. My skirt was stained and one button had popped off. I looked like a hooker who'd been caught holding out on her pimp.

No wonder Darryl had been so worried. Doubtless I'd already triggered some new talk on the doorman gossip mill about J. Frank DeBenton's interesting taste in ladies of the evening. The world being what it was, I thought, his reputation would only be enhanced.

I did the best I could to fix the mascara and smooth my hair, but gave up by the time the elevator opened with a soft *ping.* I stepped into the hallway and noticed an open door at the end of the corridor. I walked toward it cautiously, balancing the pizza box on one hand.

I tapped on the door as I stepped into the foyer. "Frank?"

There was no reply. I felt a shiver of anticipation. What if

Frank wasn't home? What if the masked ghouls had somehow tracked me here and were lying in wait? What if Frank lay in the bedroom in a puddle of blood? What if—

Frank stood next to the fireplace where flames were burning low. One hand rested on the mantelpiece, the other held a tumbler of amber liquid. He wore charcoal-gray wool pants and a pearly gray silk shirt, unbuttoned at the collar. It was a scene right out of *Vanity Fair.*

"There you are. You okay, Frank?"

He watched me for a long moment before nodding.

"I hope you don't mind that I showed up like this. I mean, I know it's late but I brought pizza. . . ." I felt foolish, and my annoyance grew. *Gee, Frank, don't go out of your way to make me feel welcome.* "Why don't I just close the door?"

When I limped back into the living room, he looked me over, pausing at my bloody knee. The paramedic's bandage had already fallen off. Frank nodded again and drained his glass.

"You can take the couch," he said, and walked out of the room.

"Frank?" I called after him. No response. I put the pizza on the counter and sat on the couch, confused.

After a moment Frank returned with a first-aid kit. Stocking a first-aid kit was one of the many things on my To Do list; all I had in my apartment was an empty tube of Neosporin and an ancient box of Band-Aids. I almost said as much, but Frank wasn't in a chatty mood, and as he squatted in front of me, I caught a whiff of alcohol. Only he could do drunk this straight, I thought to myself, and smiled. The smile was wiped off my face the next moment, as Frank slapped wet gauze on my knee.

"Ow!"

Frank's dark eyes met mine, and he pressed a little harder. I flinched, but held my tongue. "Is this a bad time?"

"Why do you ask?" he said without inflection, smearing antibiotic cream on my knee and applying a bandage.

"You're acting strange."

"*I'm* acting strange?"

"Yes, you're acting strange."

"*I* am?"

"See, now, Frank, we could go round and round with this or you could just tell me what's on your mind."

Frank sat back on his heels. "Let's run through it, shall we?"

I was kind of sorry I'd asked.

"First, you run out on me in L.A. without saying a word. I spent three hours searching the galleries for you and had to make up an excuse for the FBI team and Sandino. Second, you show up with a pizza, unannounced, in the middle of the night. And C, you're injured, your clothing is torn, and your hair's a mess." He gestured grandly and for a moment lost his balance. "I think I've proved my point."

"Um . . ." I replied. My hair really did look awful, though it was in poor form for him to say so.

He stood up, dumped everything into the first-aid kit, and weaved out of the room.

"Frank—" I hobbled after him. Before I got halfway across the room, he returned with sheets, blankets, a towel, and a pillow, and dropped them on the couch.

"Aren't you going to ask me what happened?" I asked.

"You want me to ask you what happened?"

"Isn't that customary in these situations?"

He shoved his hands in his pockets and rocked on his heels. "Who do you think I am, your father?"

"What? No, I—"

"That's what you think, isn't it?" he demanded belligerently. "*I'm* the one who scolds you for running around in the middle of the night with art thieves, aren't I? *I'm* the one

who gets upset when you put yourself in danger, don't I? *I'm*
the one who acts like a goddamned fool when you show up
in the middle of the night dressed like a three-dollar whore,
aren't I? Good ol' stuffed-shirt Frank!"

"Take it easy, big guy," I said, holding up my hands in
mock surrender. "Let's not say anything we'll regret when
we're sober, okay?"

"You think I'm drunk, is that it?"

"Well, you have to admit you're—"

"I may have had a drink," he said. "Or two."

"Maybe so," I said in a soothing tone.

"But I'm a far sight from not knowing what I'm saying."

In fact, he seemed to be having no trouble at all finding
the right words, whereas I was acting as if I were still under
the influence of Uncle Sidran's Mystery Tonic.

"What the hell are you doing here, Annie?" Frank took a
step closer, bringing him much too close to me.

"Um, I had a hard day and . . . I wanted . . . I needed . . ."
I stammered. I licked my lips, and tried hard to think. "I had
a *really* hard day."

"Screw this," Frank said, grabbing me by the upper arms
and kissing me, hard.

I was so shocked that I stiffened, but then the juices
started flowing and I was swept up in the whole thing. By
the time Frank deepened the kiss, settling one hand on my
waist and moving the other up toward my breast, I forgot
about the hair situation and started wondering whether
Frank still carried a condom in his pocket. By the time he
started nibbling at my neck, I had pretty much abandoned all
logical thought. And when Frank shoved my shredded
blouse to the side and took down my bra strap, then began
kissing his way along my breast, I was ready to forfeit san-
ity altogether.

The phone rang.

Personally, I never answered the phone when I was too busy, and this moment seemed to qualify. More than most, in fact. But Frank went very still upon hearing the first ring, then lifted his head and looked at me with the second ring. By the third he had removed his hands from my nether parts and headed for the phone located on a small table near the couch. He faced away from me, toward the fire, as he picked up the receiver.

"DeBenton," he said, as if expecting a late-night business call. "Yes, she is. Yes, I understand. I'll let her know."

Frank gazed at me as if he'd never seen me before.

Uh-oh.

"That was your friend Michael Johnson. He says you should call him tomorrow."

"Oh. Thanks. How did he know I was here?"

"How should I know?" Frank seemed equal parts disappointed and furious. It made me remember how much I disliked his stuffy, disapproving way of going about life. *Damn,* though, he was a good kisser.

"I'm going to sleep," he said as he strode across the room.

"Yeah, me too," I said to his back. "Awfully big day tomorrow, no time and energy for wild sex."

He stopped, hung his head as if debating something, then turned and met my eyes. "Is that an invitation, or a challenge, or are you just speaking without thinking?"

"I, um . . ." It was much easier to be a smart-ass when Frank wasn't looking at me.

"That's what I thought. Good night, Annie. We'll talk in the morning." He disappeared down the hall.

I plopped back down on the couch and reviewed my options. I could go down the hall and force myself on him. Judging from his earlier behavior, I was guessing I could turn the tide without working too hard. Frank's kiss had gotten me pretty wound up, and after months of trying to ignore the heat between us all my molecules were yelling *Yes! Yes! Yes!*

On the other hand, sleeping with my landlord seemed like a Really Bad Plan, especially since he wasn't the kind of guy who would be willing to back off on the rent in order to keep me in his bed. Not that I approved of that sort of thing, but still. I could just see his uptight expression in my mind, and hear him saying something along the lines of, *"It would cheapen the both of us, Ms. Kincaid, were we to blur our contractual obligations,"* even as we were in the middle of doing the nasty.

Then there was the way he answered the phone in the middle of the night, "DeBenton," as though he were still in the military. And the way he dressed, for heaven's sake, as if he were going to a business meeting at all hours of the day and night. The man wore creased jeans.

Oh yeah. Also, Josh and I were an item. Geez, I kept forgetting. That man better get home soon or fit me with a chastity belt.

Slipping into the bathroom down the hall, I took a hot shower and scrubbed myself raw. I had to put my dirty clothes back on afterward, but it was better than nothing. I covered the couch with the soft cotton sheets, spread out the blanket, and lay down. The pillow was soft and smelled like Frank, and I snuggled into it. It was much better this way, I told myself as I closed my eyes. But goodness, could that boy kiss.

The next thing I knew soft light was streaming through the large living room windows and the clock on the mantel read 6:17. A host of heretofore unheard-from muscles made known their existence, and when I rolled over my knee barked at me. Walking gingerly around the living room loosened it up, but it still grumbled.

Last night Frank said he wanted to Talk. But Talking led

to Languaging, and no matter how long I lived near New Age Berkeley, I would never be any good at it. That threat alone was enough to scare me out of bed at the crack of dawn. I wrapped some pizza slices in a paper towel and tiptoed out of the apartment.

I pressed the elevator button, and after a moment the doors slid open to reveal a fiftyish woman in a fur coat, wearing too much perfume and holding a yappy dog. I limped onto the elevator and smiled, but she wouldn't stop staring.

"Rough night," I said, taking a big bite of pizza and watching the numbers flash as we zoomed down ten floors. "But he pays well."

Chapter 18

Iron rusts from disuse, stagnant water loses its purity, and in cold weather becomes frozen; even so does inaction sap the vigors of the mind.

—Leonardo da Vinci (1452–1519),
Italian painter and inventor

Use it or lose it. —Georges LeFleur

I stopped at a café on Chestnut, washed up in the bathroom, ordered a coffee with a shot of espresso, and nursed it for an hour while I perused the local rags. The "Advice from the Sexpert" column was conducting a lively debate on whether or not men could be lesbians. I read both sides and considered the issue. In true Bay Area fashion, the consensus was that men had the *right* to be lesbians even though they couldn't *be* lesbians.

I ordered another coffee to go, stopped at a doughnut shop to pick out a couple of dozen, and ate an old-fashioned on the way to Aaron Garner's house renovation. It wasn't yet eight in the morning and the job site was in full swing. Construction workers were early risers, and say what one might about Norm, the man knew how to run a crew.

I found Norm arguing with Ethan Mayall at the soon-to-be kitchen counter. The architect wore a lamb's-wool sweater, pressed khakis, and brown penny loafers while Norm's ripped jeans were just this side of indecent and his T-shirt read NO, I DON'T HAVE A MOOD DISORDER. I JUST HATE THIS *&%$(#* RAIN! The air between the two men crackled with tension.

"Doughnuts!" I called out. If carbs, fat, and sugar couldn't defuse a situation, nothing could.

"What the hell happened to you?" Norm growled, cramming a glazed doughnut into his mouth and masticating vigorously.

"You're supposed to ignore my appearance, like Ethan here."

"Wasn't some guy, was it? 'Cause I don't hold with that sort of thing."

"Nothing like that, just clumsy." I reminded myself to call the hospital and check on Curly Top. "Doughnut, Ethan?"

"I'm watching my weight," he said and patted his concave stomach. "I gained half a pound last weekend at the Napa Valley Wine Festival."

Norm and I glared at him until he took a doughnut.

"Are you working with Billy Mudd on a development near Bayview Cemetery?" I asked.

Ethan choked on a chocolate candy sprinkle. "That's confidential."

"Listen, shit-for-brains." Norm loomed over him. "The lady asked nicely, so either you tell her what she wants to know or you're gonna need a court order to get my size-fourteen work boot outta your ass."

I stared at Norm. He shrugged.

Ethan crumbled. "I, uh, yes, I am. Working with Billy Mudd, I mean."

"What's the big secret?" I asked.

"Aaron Garner said to keep it confidential. And Billy Mudd threatened to beat me up."

"Nice," Norm said without a trace of irony.

"But why would Aaron—"

"Why don't you ask me yourself?" Aaron Garner appeared behind us, his elaborate comb-over undulating in the breeze from the open window. Ethan, Norm, and I tried not to stare.

"I didn't realize you were back, Aaron," I said. "How was your trip?"

"Splendid, just splendid. Josh is staying a few more days to be sure the project gets off to a good start. Now, if you'll excuse us, gentlemen, I'd like a word with Annie." He ushered me down the back stairs to the garden. "Norm tells me you found some fantastic old headstones."

"Ricardo and his crew dug them up."

"What a find. I'm thinking of funding an institute on the history of Bay Area cemeteries. Does that sound too gruesome?"

"Not at all," I said, wishing my hero Norm were with us. I led the way into the narrow alley lined with old marble gravestones.

"You've been a busy girl," Aaron said softly from behind me. "Seems you've discovered my little secret. I hired Ethan to design a housing development inspired by the art of Tim O'Neill."

I turned to face him. "Where?"

"Near Bayview Cemetery."

"Near or on?"

"On unused cemetery land."

"Are you referring to Potter's Field?"

"Annie, those graves have been abandoned for decades, a century even."

"But, Aaron, the cemetery is part of Oakland's history."

"Don't be a naïf, Annie. Need I remind you that the San

Francisco Bay Area is the most expensive housing market in the nation? That land isn't being used and the cemetery needs the money. If I don't develop it, someone who cares less about historical preservation will."

"Then why is it a secret?"

"Because as soon as the word gets out, the history buffs and tree huggers will launch their protests. Listen, Annie, I'm offering to fund a historical project. Perhaps it could even be a part of Chapel of the Chimes. I'd put you in charge, pay you a generous wage."

"I don't know the first thing about cemeteries, Aaron. If you're serious about the project you should consider hiring Russell, he's the expert."

"Who?"

"Russell, from Bayview Cemetery? He was here looking at the headstones?"

"Oh, right. Helena recommended him. To tell you the truth, I find her fascination with that cemetery rather morbid. She hasn't been the same since our boy, Chad, died."

"I'm sorry. That must have been awful."

"It was my fault. Chad and I argued, and he stormed out. He drove too fast, and . . ." Garner shook his head. "Helena blamed me, too, and our marriage never recovered. All she wants is a home overlooking her son's grave. Is that too much to ask?"

"It is if it means destroying other peoples' graves. There *are* loved ones in Potter's Field, Aaron."

"No one *cares* about them! My son *died* there. Crashed through the fence at the top of the hill!" His face reddened in anger. "If his grieving mother wants a house there, *by God* she'll get one!"

"Whatever you say, Aaron. Good to see you again." I pivoted and hurried down the narrow, gravestone-lined alley.

*   *   *

"Frank."

His shoulders twitched as he stood with his back to me, searching through the top drawer of his office filing cabinet.

"How are you feeling today?"

"Mmmpht."

"Glad to hear it. I'm doing much better, myself."

"Mmmm."

"Cat got your tongue? Or was it a hair of the dog?"

Frank turned to face me. "What, not even a hello this morning?"

"No time for that."

"For a hello?"

"For a Talk. No time for Talking or Languaging."

"I don't understand."

"My point exactly. Do you know Aaron Garner?"

"Who do you think recommended you for the job that's kept you solvent lately?"

"What are you talking about? I knew Garner from the Save the Fox Theater campaign. I even recommended he hire Josh."

"I know. And Aaron asked if I'd vouch for you both."

"He *did*?"

"I was happy to do it. You're an excellent artist, and Josh seems like a good man, even though—never mind."

"Never mind what? Out with it."

"He's not the right man for you." Frank's dark eyes held mine for a beat too long, and I flashed on the memory of his mouth on mine. I took a deep breath and looked away.

"Is Garner a good person?" I asked.

"He's a sharp businessman, and on the whole I'd say he's decent as long as you're not married to him. Why?"

"When you say 'as long as you're not married to him' do you mean in the sense that he cheats on his wives, or in the sense that he kills people and buries the bodies in the basement?"

Frank slammed the file drawer shut. "What in the world are you talking about?"

"There are some odd goings-on at Bayview Cemetery. And I've just learned that Garner's planning to develop the portion of the cemetery known as Potter's Field because those residents don't own their land."

"What residents?"

"Bodies, whatever. It's what they're called."

"That's odd."

"Tell me about it. Anyway, a graduate student I met there died, a cemetery employee is in the hospital, and the columbarium's retired secretary is in a diabetic coma."

"And you think one of the City's most illustrious citizens had something to do with all that? Annie, I wouldn't want Aaron Garner to marry my sister, but I rather doubt he's murdered anyone or engineered a diabetic coma. I don't think he'd even know how."

"All right, different subject. You know Sandino believes me about the Raphael."

Frank crossed his arms. "If he does, he's the only one."

"Have your art squad friends turned up anything on a forgery of *La Fornarina*?"

"Not so far. Are you suggesting the painting is connected to these other events?"

"I don't know. But Cindy Tanaka—"

"Who?"

"The Berkeley grad student who died. Cindy had just sent paint flakes and threads from the columbarium's copy of *La Fornarina* to a lab to be analyzed. The results fit the painting's sixteenth-century origin."

"Really?" He cocked his head and looked intrigued. "Who did the analysis?"

"Dr., uh, Brianna Something."

"Dr. Brianna Something?"

"The last name escapes me."

"What lab does Dr. Brianna Something work at?"

Busted. "Okay, she's a chemistry graduate student. But these tests aren't rocket science."

Frank ran a hand through his hair. "You'd damned well better be sure of what you're saying if you expect me to bring it to Interpol."

"Look, Frank, about last night—"

"Don't you dare bring last night into this discussion," Frank barked. "Either we're talking about art crime or we're talking about the two of us taking this relationship to another level. We are not mixing those two topics. *Ever.*"

"Frank," I said quietly. "You know who my grandfather is."

After a moment Frank let out a rueful chuckle and shook his head. "Don't I just? All right, get me the test results from your Dr. Brianna Something and I'll take it to the authorities."

"Will do!"

"But, Annie, a favor? Make sure your grandfather and I never meet."

"I think that would be best," I said, gave him a smile, and turned to leave.

"Oh, and one more thing," Frank said, grasping my arm and turning me to face him. He cupped the back of my head in one hand and gripped my waist with the other. His kiss was slow and thorough and very, very sexy.

After a long moment Frank lifted his head and ran his thumb across my bottom lip.

I tried to remember how to breathe.

"Just wanted to make sure last night wasn't a fluke. You'd better have a talk with Josh. Tell him it's over."

Somehow I made it up the stairs to my studio, where I found a note from Mary indicating that she wouldn't be in today due to some Goth event. Having spent a night in the cemetery, Mary was now pink-worthy, and she thanked the gang effusively:

> I am really touched, you guys, and not in a touched-by-a-perv-on-BART kind of way. You're such effin' angels to support me in my time of need!! I l*o*v*e you guys!!!

I added the note to the collection of Maryisms tacked to the bulletin board.

This was good, I thought. I could use some time alone. Since yesterday two people I knew had landed in the hospital, I had found semi-sort-of proof that a sixteenth-century masterpiece was floating around somewhere, and my handsome, by-the-book landlord had kissed me. Twice.

I called Summit Medical Center and received the welcome news that Mrs. Henderson had rebounded and was doing well. When I asked about Russell I realized I couldn't remember his last name, and figured "Curly Top" wouldn't be much help. The candy striper I spoke with was unable or unwilling to help, so I crossed my fingers for Russell's speedy recovery and decided to check on his status later with the grand pooh-bah of gossip, Miss Ivy.

As I reached for my apron, I realized I was still wearing the torn blouse and skirt, which were not improved by having been slept in. My trusty painting overalls were still clammy from yesterday's downpour, and I'd neglected to replenish the clothes in the armoire. Since Samantha never arrived at her studio before ten, I called and asked her to bring me something to wear.

At last I settled in to put the finishing touches to the Design Center curtain rods. I cleaned off stray gold and silver leaf, checked to be sure the glazes had been applied evenly, softened the antiquing effect by buffing lightly with steel wool, and started inspecting each and every one of the five hundred wooden curtain rings.

Samantha showed up an hour later with a colorful muumuu concoction that looked regal on her but downright silly on me. She insisted the outfit was an old one and that I should feel free to splatter it with paint. As I slipped it on, I caught a subtle whiff of patchouli, a scent I associated with Sam and warm friendship, and it lifted my spirits.

I returned a few phone calls, updated my calendar, and wrote Josh an e-mail on the progress of Aaron Garner's house renovation. As I finished the business report I hesitated, my fingers hovering over the keyboard. Should I tell Josh what had been going on at the cemetery and columbarium? Should I break up with him? Should I chuck it all and join my grandfather in his game of international hide-and-seek with Interpol?

I typed *Hugs, Annie,* and signed off.

Wrapped in my floaty muumuu cocoon, I shuffled over to the velvet couch and took a nap, woke up forty minutes later groggy and combative, took advantage of a pause in the rain to walk to a deli for a turkey-and-Napa-mustard sandwich, ate half of it, and spent the rest of the afternoon sketching drawings for a mural that would transform a mortgage broker's office into a scene from *Pirates of the Caribbean.* Why a mortgage broker wanted to remind his clients that they were being robbed by high interest rates was beyond me, but I had to hand it to him—there weren't a lot of brokers with such imagination.

At seven, I ate the other half of my sandwich while mulling over the *New York Times* crossword puzzle and listening to an NPR report on mud slides in the Santa Cruz Mountains, and avoided thinking about Frank. By nine I had caught up on my paperwork—a rare occurrence—inventoried the painting supplies, and straightened up the studio. I had even cleaned the innards of the espresso machine with a vinegar-and-water solution, the way you're supposed to but I never had.

By nine thirty my desk was clear, the drawings were finished, and the studio sparkled. Only one thing remained: admit that I was afraid to go home. I was scared in a different way to drop in on Frank again, and I wasn't up for a serious discussion with Samantha or for dealing with Bryan's boundless enthusiasm. Coping with Mary's Goth-and-musician-filled apartment was never an option. So I took a fleece blanket out of the steamer chest. It wouldn't be the first time I'd spent the night in the studio.

But it was the first time I'd awakened with a hand over my mouth.

Chapter 19

The buildings will be my legacy. They will speak for me long after I'm gone. . . .

—Julia Morgan (1872–1957), American architect

An artist creates something from nothing, nurtures it lovingly, and when it is complete sets it free to follow its destiny. I have tried many times to explain this to the FBI. —Georges LeFleur

I bit it.

"Ow! Not nice, sweetheart."

"Michael, what the hell is *wrong* with you?" I demanded and sat up. "What are you *doing*?"

"I just didn't want you to scream," he said, shaking his injured hand. "Why are you sleeping in your studio?"

"Because."

"Because why?"

"I felt like it."

"Afraid to go home, huh?"

"Why would you think that?"

Michael shrugged. "Why aren't you at your boyfriend's?"

"Josh is out of town."

"I was referring to Frank DeBenton. What's going on between you two?"

"How did you know I was at Frank's last night? Are you *spying* on me?"

"It's my job to know such things."

"You don't *have* a job."

"Come on. You're coming to my place."

"No, I'm not."

"Yes, you are."

"Not to *your* place, I'm not. You'll take me to someone else's place."

"God save me from women with good memories." He grabbed my shoulder bag. "What's that you're wearing? You look like a reject from a luau. And you smell a little funky, pardon me for noticing."

"Turn around while I change."

"I've seen you in your undergarments before, remember? And a very pretty sight it was, too."

"Michael, if you don't turn around this minute, I swear I'll—"

"You'll what?"

"Tell my grandfather you've been a cad."

Michael turned his back with a put-upon sigh. I scrambled into my decrepit overalls and running shoes, which were, thankfully, dry.

"Let's go."

The night air was chilly and wet and smelled of the brine of the bay. Jazz played softly on the CD player in Michael's truck as we drove across town to North Beach.

"Where are we going?" I asked.

"A little place I stay when I'm in the City."

He pulled over and expertly maneuvered the large truck into a minuscule parking space on Green Street, just a block off Columbus. It was nearly two in the morning, and with the bars about to close raucous partiers streamed onto the sidewalks shouting jovially at the top of their lungs.

"Lively neighborhood," I said.

"I like it."

Michael nodded toward a stucco duplex, and we climbed a flight of interior stairs carpeted with an ornate oriental runner. At the top of the stairs he unlocked a glossy, deep red door, which opened onto a decent-sized room lined with bookcases groaning under the weight of art tomes and artifacts. The rosy wood floors and creamy walls glowed in the warmth of the light cast by old-fashioned brass floor lamps with fringed shades. A faded brocade love seat and two soft burgundy leather chairs sat before a huge window with floor-sweeping burgundy velvet curtains that framed a view of the lights of Columbus Avenue. To the left of the living room, a black-and-white-tiled kitchen sported a stainless steel refrigerator-freezer and a Wolfe range, and gourmet copper cookware hung from an iron pot rack. White wood cabinets with glass doors revealed a collection of charming French crockery and crystal stemware. A tall wood wine rack made up one wall of a cozy breakfast nook outfitted with a café table and black wrought-iron chairs. Somebody—Michael?—had spent a lot of time and money to make this a home.

"Wow. Nice place," I said. "Whose is it?"

"You've got trust issues, Annie," Michael said, tossing his keys into a Moroccan brass bowl on the kitchen's cobalt-blue Italian mosaic counter.

"I can't imagine why. Now tell me what's going on with Grandfather."

"Let's have a drink first. This is a fine Bordeaux that I've been saving for a special occasion. I think you'll like it." He poured the deep red wine into crystal water glasses, in the manner of Italians. "To the future."

One could hardly refuse a toast to the future. We clinked glasses.

"The Galleria Nazionale in Rome has confirmed that its *La Fornarina* is a fake."

I spewed my wine on Michael's white shirt. "Are you *serious*? Where did you hear that?"

"No more wine for you." Michael crossed to the kitchen sink and dabbed at his shirt with a washcloth. "It's official, but the Ministry of Culture is keeping it under wraps for the time being."

"Please tell me it's not Georges' work."

"You're the best person to determine that, but Georges swore up and down he only painted the one that Donato Sandino showed you at the Getty. No, it looks as if it might have been an innocent mix-up. During World War One a top-notch copy of *La Fornarina* was stored at the same facility as Raphael's original."

"And this 'top-notch copy' was so brilliant that the romantic symbols in the background had been painted over just like the original?"

"That remains to be seen."

"I suppose Crispin Engels, the British painter, might have done so as a tribute to the legend of Raphael and his mistress," I mused.

"Maybe so." Michael gave up on his shirt and leaned against the sink. The wet fabric clung to his flat stomach and muscular chest.

I averted my eyes. "It really was an honest mix-up?"

"I was skeptical, myself. But from what I've been able to piece together, it seems Julia Morgan went to Europe after World War One to buy art and artifacts for the newly built Chapel of the Chimes Columbarium. Among her purchases was a nineteenth-century copy of *La Fornarina* by Crispin Engels. Apparently what she brought home was not the copy, but Raphael's original. Both paintings have authentic provenances, but they were applied to the wrong pieces."

"Who's your source at the Barberini?"

"Ask your buddy Frank."

"*My* Frank? Frank DeBenton?"

"As you say." He cocked his head. "*Your* Frank."

"But—"

"He's running this op. With his pals at the FBI and Interpol, of course."

"How did you get involved?"

"Two separate inquiries about *La Fornarina* came in to my Web site over the past few weeks. I became curious and contacted DeBenton."

"Why didn't he say anything to me?"

"I believe he's trying to protect you. He's the gallant type, isn't he?"

"I can't believe him," I snapped, anger at Frank's patronizing ways surging through me.

"You're in over your head with DeBenton, Annie. If you're not careful he'll bust you one of these days."

"Frank can't bust me, because I haven't done anything wrong." This was my mantra, which I recited whenever I needed to be reassured about my precarious perch on the path of righteousness. It usually didn't work.

"Ah, but you will," Michael said, reaching out and tucking an errant curl behind my ear. His large hand lingered on my face, caressing it gently.

I swallowed hard. "Listen, Michael, I can't have you putting the moves on me tonight."

"Why not? We're all one big, happy family, aren't we? You're sleeping with Frank while Josh is out of town, Frank's sleeping with you while Ingrid's out of town. . . ."

"First of all, I'm not convinced Ingrid even exists," I said, swatting his hand away. "I think Samantha said she met her just to win the bet."

"Oh, no doubt. Sam sounds like the type to lie about such things."

"*Second*," I said, ignoring him because he was, of course, right. Sam's perch on the straight and narrow was as solid as a rock. The wonder was that she still associated with me. "I did not sleep with Frank. I slept over. Big difference."

"Josh appreciates such distinctions, does he?"

My stomach fluttered. It would be best not to mention to Josh where I'd spent last night. Or where I was spending tonight, for that matter. Aw, geez. Josh and I had better have The Talk before *I* started refusing to consort with the likes of me.

"You know, Annie," Michael said as he refilled his glass of wine and, after a slight hesitation, poured a dollop into my glass. "If you were mine, the distinction wouldn't matter. You spend the night with another man and somebody's head is going to roll."

My mouth opened and closed, guppylike. *If you were mine?*

Michael smiled his devastating smile, the one that made his eyes crinkle and my knees wobble. "Relax. I brought you here tonight for two reasons. Number one, to keep you safe. Number two, to talk business."

"Number one, thank you. Number two, what business?"

"As you know, I've gone legit."

I snorted.

"Don't be so cynical. It was your idea in the first place. Last fall you suggested I steal artwork from thieves and return the pieces to their rightful owners, remember?"

I did. But I'd been mocking him.

"So I looked into it. Do you know what the reward is for the Vermeer stolen from the Isabella Stuart Gardner Museum?"

"A lot?"

"More than it's worth on the black market, that's for sure. And no unpleasant encounters with the authorities. I'm getting too old to run from the cops."

"How old are you?"

"None of your beeswax."

I smiled and took a sip of excellent Bordeaux. "I inspired your change of heart, eh?"

"You and my probation officer."

"You're on probation?"

"The FBI nabbed me at Anthony Brazil's gallery, remember? We worked out a mutually beneficial arrangement. Seems the FBI was looking for a missing Monet that I happened to have access to."

"That was fortunate."

"Always good to have a chip in the game."

I thought about *La Fornarina,* the chip I needed to ensure that Grandfather remained safe from the clutches of Donato Sandino.

Michael continued. "So I set up the Web site to locate more stolen art. I must say, these amateur art thieves are none too bright. You wouldn't believe how gullible many of them are. Makes me ashamed to call myself a thief."

"Well, every profession's got a few bad apples."

"Their lack of sophistication is my gain, however. I've found a valuable Remington and a set of Piranesi drawings, and I'm hot on the trail of some Iraqi antiquities."

"How does it work, exactly?"

"Thieves contact the Web site to get an estimate on the artwork's market value. I compare the description and photograph they send me against the registries of stolen art, and if something turns up I notify the FBI. I collect the reward money, the FBI returns the art to its owners and prosecutes the crooks. It's a win-win situation. Meanwhile, I spread the word through other channels that I'm an art authenticator willing to turn a blind eye to the occasional shady deal. As you know, fencing art for a decent price can be more difficult than stealing it."

"What if the art's not stolen?"

"Then I give them an estimate of how much it's worth and cash their check."

"Clever."

"Except I have to be careful not to ruin my reputation in the art underworld. If anyone suspects what I'm up to, I'm out of business."

"You could continue with legitimate art authentication."

"Where's the fun in that?"

Good point. For lifelong felons such as Michael or my grandfather, the thrill was in the chase.

Michael leaned back against the counter and crossed his legs. "No, a straight-up business arrangement has never been my cup of tea. I prefer to profit from hunting stolen art. At the moment the only people who know what I'm really doing are some insurance adjusters, a handful of FBI agents, and you. Which brings me to my next question."

Uh-oh. "Yes?"

"I don't know jack-all about authenticating art."

"True."

"I need a front person to evaluate the paintings."

"Don't look at me."

"Why not? You're Georges LeFleur's granddaughter. That means something in this world, whether you like it or not."

Don't I know it? I thought. "I've worked for years to be accepted as a legitimate artist, Michael. Can you imagine what would happen if I set up shop with a known art thief?"

"But, Annie, I've got the FBI's stamp of approval. Frank DeBenton, your personal pillar of rectitude, didn't hesitate to call on me when he needed help."

"He's not my 'personal pillar of rectitude.' "

"Frank has proprietary feelings for you. He didn't tell you what I said on the phone last night, did he?"

"What are you talking about?"

Michael sipped his wine and gazed out the kitchen window. "I asked Frank to tell you that Italy's Ministry of Culture had conceded the Raphael forgery, and your deal with Sandino was on."

"*What?*" Frank knew the forgery had been confirmed *and* that I had a deal with Donato Sandino—and hadn't said anything to me? Had his kisses been an attempt to distract me? If so, the ploy had worked.

"Still sure you have nothing to worry about from De-Benton?"

"The man's dead to me."

"So will you think about our working together?"

"You're a liar and a thief."

"I've never lied about being a thief. At least you know what you're dealing with."

"Not to mention my grandfather will keep you in line."

Michael chuckled and glanced at his watch. "It's three in the morning, Annie. Nothing good ever happens at three in the morning. Except in bed, of course. Why don't you see how you feel after a good night's rest? My room's down the hall," he said, standing and stretching. His muscles rippled, and I couldn't help sneaking a peek. "You, my dear, may sleep anywhere you choose."

"Is that an invitation?"

"It would be," he said. "But I suspect that if you came to me now it would be to spite DeBenton, and I'd rather he not be in bed with us. I've never been into threesomes."

Our eyes held for a long moment. Sleeping with Michael would clarify my relationship with Frank, no two ways about it, but would complicate just about everything else and probably not in a good way. Still, my libido was running high and Michael was sexiness on a stick.

Then I remembered Josh. Good ol' Josh. We *had* to talk before anything, with anyone, went any further. I owed him—and myself—that much. "I'll take the couch, thanks."

"As you wish."

"You know, Michael, in your own twisted way, you're an ethical man."

"Is that a challenge?" he said silkily, his green eyes intense.

"Just a comment."

"Don't tempt me. I'm still new to the ethics biz," he said, and switched off the lights. "Night, sweetheart."

"Good night." I felt like giving Michael a hug, but instead went into the living room and lay down on the couch. I pulled a soft quilt over me and drifted off to sleep.

When I awoke it took a moment to remember where I was. Raindrops splattered against the living room window, and I thought I heard the rumble of thunder in the distance. More rain. It was abnormal. If I'd wanted Seattle weather I would have moved there years ago. Yawning and stretching, I looked around the pleasant room and studied the titles on the crowded bookshelves. Victor Hugo's *Les Contemplations* sat alongside *Les Misérables,* and Diderot's *Encyclopédie* slouched against Baudelaire's *Les Fleurs du Mal* and Rimbaud's *Le Bateau Ivre.* I smiled at the sight of a well-thumbed, unabridged Larousse French-English dictionary. I knew Michael spoke French, but hadn't realized he had such a literary bent. The taller bottom shelves were crammed with oversized art books similar to the ones I kept in my studio for research. Michael was apparently devoted to his new avocation. Maybe a leopard *could* change its spots.

My eyes came to rest on a corner of a gold gilt picture

frame peeking out from behind a walnut corner cabinet. Was Michael still absconding with stolen paintings? Or was this one to be returned to its owner? Surely Michael knew how to hide art more cleverly than that.

I pulled the painting from its hiding place. It was a charming and surprisingly good rendering of the Mona Lisa signed *Annie Jane Kincaid, Age 10.* Years ago I had given it to my grandfather for his birthday, and his eyes had grown misty at this evidence of burgeoning criminality. I'd last seen the painting in Paris, hanging in Grandfather's atelier in the Place des Vosges. How had Michael gotten his hands on it?

I looked around again. The apartment was too cozy, too individual. Michael held his cards so close to his chest that I had imagined his home would be more impersonal. Unless . . .

I stormed down the hall and threw open the bedroom door, snatched a hairbrush from the top of the bureau, and flung it as hard as I could at Michael's sleeping form. He sprang out of bed wearing only black silk boxers, and landed on the floor in a jujitsu stance. If I hadn't been so angry I would have laughed.

"*Jesus,* Annie! What the hell's wrong with you?"

"Why is my Mona Lisa here?"

"Your *what*?"

"Don't play coy. It doesn't suit you."

"I have no idea what you're talking about."

"My forgery of Mona Lisa. It won an award when I was ten and I gave it to Georges."

"Ah, that one." Michael crawled back into bed, folded one arm behind his head, and scratched his flat stomach. "He asked me to hold it for safekeeping."

"Liar!"

"Annie, please. You're screeching."

"This is Grandfather's apartment, isn't it?"

"Don't be absurd."

"Liar!"

"Well, my pants do seem to be on fire." He winked and patted the covers. "I'm regretting my self-control last night. Come here."

I grabbed a fingernail clipper from the bureau and hurled it at him. He swatted it away. "Hey! Be careful! For someone who's not very athletic you've got a hell of a pitching arm."

"You brought me to *Grandfather's* apartment? Georges has an *apartment*? I've been spending the night on friends' couches and all along he had this place in North Beach?"

Michael ran a hand through his tousled hair and yawned, making a squeaking sound. Furious, I looked around for possible projectiles.

"Annie, are you pissed because I said it was my apartment, or because Georges didn't tell you he had a pied-à-terre?"

I launched a stick of deodorant at him, but my aim was off and it bounced off a forgery of Velasquez' *The Water Seller of Seville* and landed in the laundry hamper. "You and Georges were made for each other! You can *both* go to hell!"

Grabbing my shoulder bag, I stomped out of the apartment and into the pouring rain. I hurried down the street to Café Trieste, ordered a double espresso and a chocolate croissant, gazed at the dreary weather, and pondered my equally dreary state of affairs.

At the moment I loathed Frank, Michael, *and* my grandfather. In fact, at the moment the only man in my life whom I did not loathe was the one I was planning to break up with.

That did it. I was swearing off men for the foreseeable future. I would sublimate with chocolate, I thought with a bite of warm croissant.

A gust of wind rattled the café's front window and jolted me from my reverie. *Okay, Annie, focus. Forget Michael and his lying, thieving, sexy ways. You've got bigger fish to fry.*

Aaron Garner and Billy Mudd were planning to develop a
Tim O'Neill–inspired subdivision on Bayview Cemetery's
Potter's Field, and Helena was champing at the bit to build
a home with a view of her son's grave. The cemetery didn't
have the money to fight the development unless it came up
with some big bucks. I'd shot down Roy Cogswell's hope of
cashing in on the miniature portraits collection. What else
might there be of value?

I drummed my fingers on the tabletop, annoying the elderly man at the next table, who stalked out in a huff. Let's
see, cemeteries had bodies, and lots of them. And gravestones. And monuments. And crypts. Louis Spencer's crypt
had contained more than a bowing stained glass window.
The metal box Cindy Tanaka and I had found held objects
worth thirty-five thousand dollars. Might other crypts have
hidden wealth? I remembered Mrs. Henderson telling me
that Roy Cogswell grew up in the cemetery, which meant
he'd had plenty of time to explore the crypts. Roy was also
tall. And lanky. I closed my eyes and imagined him in a cape
and a green mask.

Well, duh.

I raced out of the café, flagged down a taxi, picked up my
truck at the studio, and headed across the bridge to the
columbarium. Miss Ivy wrinkled her nose when I swept in.

"Where's Roy?" I demanded.

"You look like a drowned rat," she sniffed.

"Thanks. Where's Roy?"

"He left not long ago with a professor from Cal. They
went over to the cemetery office. What do you—"

Darting through the raindrops and splashing through the
puddles, I reached the former caretaker's cottage and barged
in, prepared to confront Roy and demand an explanation.

The words died on my lips when I saw the gun.

Chapter 20

. . . Art is a habit-forming drug. That's all it is, for the artist, for the collector, for anybody connected with it. Art has absolutely no existence as veracity, as truth.

—Marcel Duchamp (1887–1968), French painter

If art is a drug, then I must be the head of a drug cartel, which sounds very dreary.

—Georges LeFleur

Staring down the barrel of a deadly weapon is a terrifying experience. Even when the man holding the gun looks like he's ready to keel over.

"Get in here," Roy hissed and slammed the door behind me. On the brown Naugahyde couch sat Dr. Gossen and Helena, pale and wary, like children waiting to be shown into the principal's office. Over the stone fireplace, Tim O'Neill's floral version of domestic heaven seemed to mock our little party.

"Hey, Roy," I said, trying to sound calm. "What's going on?"

"Sit on the couch with them," Roy said, gesturing with the gun.

"The gun's not necessary, is it?" I asked, moving toward the others.

Roy shook his head, as though he were trying to rid himself of thoughts. "I don't know what to do. This is terrible."

"I have to say I'm surprised, Roy," I said. "You're the last person in the world I would expect to be brandishing a weapon, much less robbing graves."

"You think I wanted to desecrate Louis' crypt? I had no choice!" He sank into an upholstered chair but kept his weapon trained on us. "I needed money, and I needed it fast. My father always said there was treasure buried in Louis Spencer's crypt. I never used to believe it, but Russell convinced me to look. And then Cindy showed up, of all the nights! I was scared witless."

"And you needed the money to fight off the land development?" I asked.

He nodded. "Garner found a loophole in the land deeds. Under the law, the Potter's Field residents can be removed and the land sold provided the developer agrees to relocate and rebury the remains. Do you know what that would have done to my father, to the good name of Cogswell?"

"Really, Roy, you're overreacting," Helena piped up. "The bodies in Potter's Field don't care where they are. Why waste that beautiful view on a bunch of . . . those kinds of people?"

"You stupid bitch!" Roy yelled, swinging the gun in her direction. "You're the cause of all this!"

Clearly Helena had not caught on to my calm-down-the-psycho-with-the-gun game plan. I shot her a *will you shut up, you fool?* look, and she crossed her arms and sat back with a huff.

"You felt pressured to accept Garner's offer, is that it?" I said gently.

Roy's eyes looked tired and unfocused as they turned toward me. "Annie, you don't understand. Our financial situation was my fault, all my fault. I gambled the endowment funds on the green burial movement, but it hasn't done well. Garner made a generous cash offer, and the board's fiduciary responsibilities require it to accept the offer unless I could find another way to pay off the debt and finance the earthquake retrofit. When the buried treasure angle didn't pan out, I hoped the painting would be our salvation. And he"—Roy gestured at Dr. Gossen—"said it was valuable."

"I don't know anything," Dr. Gossen babbled, holding his hands up. "I was gobsmacked by the whole thing. *Cindy* said the painting was worth a lot. I only just got around to reading a prospectus she had written up about the whole affair. But then her boyfriend told me to keep my 'nosy nose' out of it, and Cindy killed herself, and then her roommate brought me the results of some tests . . . I was only trying to help."

"How did Cindy get involved with all of this?"

"She was doing some research in the cemetery," Roy said. "I gave her a key to the place and suggested she speak with Mrs. Henderson. I guess Cindy decided to write up her biography, which of course included Henderson's lifelong obsession with that damned painting."

"*La Fornarina*?" I clarified.

"We took it to an expert a while ago," Roy said with a nod, "but he confirmed it was a copy from the eighteen hundreds. I looked over the file again, and the authenticator had no doubt. But Cindy insisted, and then with those test results . . ."

"That girl got what she deserved," Helena muttered from the couch.

My stomach clenched in anger, but I ignored her. I could only deal with one crazy at a time, so I thought it wise to focus on the one with the gun. The rain pounded on the roof, and the wind rattled the eaves. Although it was not yet noon, the sky outside the window was dark, lending a surreal quality to our bizarre discussion.

"Roy, none of this explains why you're holding us all at gunpoint."

"I lost control of everything! First Cindy, then Russell—someone's *killing* people over this! I wouldn't have hurt you, you know," Roy mumbled, and the revolver drooped in his pale hand. "But Russell was furious that you sprayed him with mace."

"It wasn't mace, it was Lady Clairol. Extra-firm hold."

Roy ran his hand through his hair, leaving a tuft sticking out from his scalp at a forty-five-degree angle. He could use a spritz of Lady Clairol himself at the moment.

"Poor Russell!" he lamented. "I knew he had allergies, but to die like that . . ."

"Russell's dead?" I gasped, recalling with a pang the helpless look in his eyes as I pounded on the Cadillac's windows.

"No. No, it looks like he'll pull through. But he *almost* died. Russell was just trying to help me save the cemetery. He loves this place as much as I do. But he wouldn't stop, even after what happened to Cindy. If we had found a fortune in Louis' crypt we wouldn't have to sell the land. But that stupid metal box was full of ashes! When I went to the crypt today to put it back I found—"

"I told you a long time ago there was nothing worth stealing in that crypt," Helena snapped, her coral lips twisted in an ugly frown. "Just accept the situation, Roy. The housing development will be beautiful, inspired by Tim O'Neill's wonderful paintings, no less."

"You found the Raphael in Louis' pyramid, didn't you?" I asked Roy, ignoring the head docent.

Roy looked at me, surprised, and nodded. "It was in the

sepulcher. Someone put it right where the metal box had been. How did you know?"

If only I'd figured it out sooner. I imagined I would never know what happened to Cindy Tanaka after we parted ways the night we met—did her late-night assignation with her "sort of" married lover turn into a nightmare with Billy demanding she tell him about the painting? Threatening her? Cindy must have come back the next morning, switched the original with the digital copy, moved *La Fornarina* somewhere that felt safe—Louis Spencer's already robbed crypt—and then left the suitcase with the box for me at the columbarium. Had she wanted me to replace the metal box in the crypt, and thereby find the little baker girl?

"Who would break into a crypt?" Helena frowned. "Some people have no respect for the dead."

"Listen to me, Roy," I said. "If you've got the original painting, I can broker a deal for you with the Italians. I know some folks, officials at the National Gallery in Rome. You'll have plenty of funds to take care of this place." I paused and held out my hand. "Just give me the gun."

"How do I know you won't shoot me?" he whined, swinging the gun toward me. I cringed. A whiner with a weapon was not a comforting combination.

"I promise," I said. "I'm not a violent person."

"*She'll* shoot me," Roy said, nodding at Helena, who looked as if she was plotting that very thing.

"No, she won't," I insisted. "I'll hold the gun."

"It's not even loaded," he sighed, defeated, and handed it to me.

"Glad to hear it." I checked the weapon for bullets; it was empty. My grandfather had long ago taught me the care and feeding of small sidearms—"just in case"—though I refused to own one because I didn't think I had the guts to shoot anybody except by accident. I slipped the ugly thing into a pocket in my overalls. "You know what they say—guns don't kill people, bullets kill people."

Roy, Dr. Gossen, and Helena looked confused.

"It's a *joke*, folks. Let's all lighten up a little and see if we can figure out what's going on."

A crack of lightning made us all jump and illuminated the stained glass window behind the counter.

"Is that a Rosicrucian cross?" I asked to keep the conversation going until I could figure out what to do. We could be here awhile because at the moment I was clueless. "I noticed a similar one at your house, Helena."

"That's an heirloom from Dick's side of the family," she said.

"The whole family's Rosicrucian," Roy explained. "In fact, Louis Spencer was named for Spenser Lewis, who founded the church in San José. But we kept quiet about it. Father was afraid it would hurt business."

"You're related to Dr. Dick?"

"My grandfather and his grandmother were brother and sister. What does that make us?"

"Beats me," I said, my genealogy-chart-making skills failing once more.

"Second cousins," said the anthropology professor.

"Did you all know the stories of treasure in the crypts?" I asked Roy.

"Sure. Aaron, Dick, Helena, and I all grew up here, went to Piedmont High together. Dick was in love with Helena even then, I think." He looked at Helena. "When you married Garner it nearly killed him."

Helena smiled in satisfaction, and again I wondered what it was about this woman that caused men to lust after her so. It had to be something unnatural.

"Let me get this straight, Roy," I said. "If you found something valuable enough you could persuade the board not to sell Potter's Field to Aaron Garner and Billy Mudd, is that right?"

"Why do you think I've acted like such an idiot?"

"But then someone was trying to stop you and Russell. And Cindy." And if Garner and Mudd didn't acquire the land, Helena wouldn't get her house with a view of her son's grave. How far would Aaron Garner be willing to go to ensure his ex-wife's happiness? Could he be putting those headstones from his yard to good use?

"Where's the painting you found in the sepulcher?" I said.

Roy stood, reached around the counter, and brought out a long cardboard tube. "Take it, it's yours. I can't do this anymore."

I uncapped the tube and slid the painting out. For all I knew I would find Crispin Engels' copy, or even the cheap digital one. But the merest glance revealed the canvas was old, very old. I took the painting to Russell's desk and slowly unfurled it. Everything receded as Raphael's beautiful baker girl, his lover and perhaps his wife, gazed at me with utter self-assurance across the distance of five centuries.

I reminded myself to breathe, so exhilarated and frightened was I to touch Raphael's great masterpiece. I had to get it to the authorities, and fast. I had to—

The door flew open. It was Dr. Dick. With a gun. And, I presumed, bullets.

"*There* you are," he said to Helena, who smiled coquettishly.

I reached into my pocket and pulled out Roy's weapon.

"Don't even think about it, Dr. Dick," I said, channeling Clint Eastwood.

He paused.

"Her gun's not loaded, darling," Helena said, and Dick smirked.

I *knew* I didn't like that woman.

"Give me the gun, Annie," Dr. Dick said. "Go on, now. Or I'll shoot Roy."

I handed it over. Dick stuck it in my face, and pulled the trigger.

I knew for a fact the gun was empty, but the good doctor didn't. My heart leapt into my throat, and my bladder threatened to explode. Note to self: *in the future, avoid psychopathic physicians willing to shoot you in the head at point-blank range.*

"Empty it is," he said in a conversational tone. "Why would you threaten me with an empty gun?"

"It was worth a shot. So to speak." I thought my voice wavered but it was hard to tell over the sound of my pounding heart.

Dr. Dick spotted the painting. "Lovely, just lovely. And it is the original?"

"Hard to say," I hedged.

He shrugged. "The box, please."

"What box?"

"The one from Louis Spencer's pyramid. Time to tie up the loose ends. As if it's not bad enough being forced to work with Garner on this housing development, I had to take care of all of these fortune-hunting idiots who were trying to stand in our way. The past few days have been very difficult. You have no *idea* what stress does to the gastrointestinal tract."

At the moment, I thought I just might.

"Darling, Roy says the box only held worthless ashes," Helena told him.

"I'm not about to take his word for it, pet," Dick said with a smile for his wife. "I want to put everything back where it belongs, make sure nothing incriminating is floating around." He held his gun to my head. "*Where's* the box?"

"If I tell you, what's to keep you from killing us?"

"Tell you what. Either you tell me if the painting is real and where the box is, or . . ."

Silence hung over the room like a thundercloud.

". . . I'll destroy the painting." Dr. Dick reached into his jacket pocket and pulled out a small vial of clear liquid. "This is concentrated sulfuric acid. Are you familiar with it?"

"Chemistry's not my strong suit," I said.

"Never would have made it through medical school, then! Sulfuric acid is a combination of hydrogen, sulfur, and oxygen. It's highly corrosive. We used to sing a little ditty about it in organic chem class.

> 'Little Johnny took a drink,
> but he shall drink no more,
> for what he thought was H_2O was H_2SO_4.'"

Helena laughed and clapped her hands.

Good Lord, she's as nutty as he is, I thought. Dr. Dick was right. They were made for each other.

"If I pour this acid on the painting, the resulting exothermic reaction will eat right through the canvas," he continued.

"You can't do that!" I protested.

"My dear, I assure you, I can. And I will." He uncapped the vial. "Two little questions. Is the painting real? Where's the box?"

"But—"

"Is. It. Real?" Dick repeated, tilting the vial over *La Fornarina.*

"*Yes.* Don't. *Please.*"

"That wasn't so hard, was it?" He recapped the vial and dropped it in his pocket. "Now, where's the box?"

"It's hidden."

"Roy said he put it back in Louis' crypt," the ever-helpful Helena offered.

"That was a decoy," I said. If I told Dick I'd given the box to the police, what was to keep him from murdering us right here? I'd take my chances outside. "I know where the real one is."

"Where?"

"In a crypt."

"But not Louis' crypt?" He looked suspicious.

"No, another one, up on the ridge." I met his eyes, hoping I sounded sincere. "Near the Locklear Memorial."

"All righty." He grabbed the Raphael with one hand. "Helena, pet, stay here. I don't want you getting your footies damp and catching a cold. The rest of you, come with me."

I took a step toward him. "Please, Dr. Dick. Leave the painting." The centuries-old paint and varnish would be able to withstand a little rain, but not much.

"I'm afraid I can't do that."

"At least let me put it in the cardboard tube to protect it."

"I never could resist a request from a pretty girl," he sighed. "Go ahead, but hurry up."

I carefully rolled *La Fornarina*, whose steady gaze seemed to reassure me, slipped it in the tube, and popped on the plastic cap.

"What are you doing here, Professor?" Dick looked over at Gossen. "You were so stubborn about not giving me Cindy's personal information, I assumed you were smart enough to stay out of it."

"I was gobsmacked by the whole thing—" Gossen stammered.

"Never mind," Dr. Dick interrupted him. "Wrong place, wrong time, eh? Come along now."

Ever the genial host, Dr. Dick ushered Roy, Dr. Gossen, and me outside, where we huddled in the shelter of the cottage's portico. "All the way up there?" he asked with a twinge of annoyance, as though I had suggested we park in the farthest corner of the Wal-Mart lot. "Not the nicest afternoon for a stroll, is it? Do you know, I think a little murder-suicide in the crypt by a despondent art forger might be just the ticket."

He gestured with his weapon and the four of us started hiking. Within minutes we were soaked, and I tried to ignore the rivulet of water running down my back. I scanned the gray landscape, but though the cemetery was open for business, there wasn't a living soul in sight. Accustomed to bright sunshine as their birthright, Californians are bewildered by bad weather, and tend to hibernate at home watching videos until the sun comes out again.

Dr. Gossen slid on the muddy asphalt path, and Roy Cogswell sniveled and wrung his hands. Neither promised to be much help engineering an escape. If we were going to get out of this alive I would have to take action. I just didn't know what. *Grandfather,* I beseeched, *give me some ideas here. I need your help.*

Run, chérie! Vite! *Hide!*

I can't, Grandfather. He'll destroy the painting.

No painting is worth your life, Annie! Not even one by ze great Raphael. I will paint you another, but run!

He'll shoot me, Grandfather.

Zen talk to 'im, chérie. Let 'im know zat you are a person, not an object to shoot.

"Dr. Dick," I said. "You don't really want to hurt anyone, do you? Why don't you take the painting and go? It's worth a fortune, you know."

"You think I want the painting? I just didn't want my old cousin Roy here to use it to stop our housing project. I'll return it to the Barberini Palace, where it belongs."

"That's very admirable," I said, trying to resurrect the camaraderie we'd enjoyed over coffee and scotch a lifetime ago. "Really."

He gave me a crooked, raffish smile. The rain had plastered his silvering hair to his head, but he was still a good-looking man. Were it not for the fevered glint in his eye, and the fact that he was pointing a gun at me, he might have been a charming escort.

"And if I let you go you'll promise not to say anything, is that it?" He laughed. "You'll keep quiet about Cindy and Henderson and Russell?"

"Of course I will. What . . . what did you do to Mrs. Henderson?"

"The nosy old broad was renewing her questions about *La Fornarina*'s authenticity, and blabbing it to the world in her biography. Cindy told her darling Billy all about what she had learned from the old lady, and Billy mentioned it to me. Henderson urged Cindy to hide the painting, but the girl refused to tell me where, so I gave her a few medications to keep her quiet for good. Then I went to the retirement home, where I blended right in. No one questions a doctor in a white coat. I simply gave Henderson a quick shot of a placebo in place of her insulin, and readjusted the calibration on her glucometer so she went into a diabetic coma. One great thing about knowing how to save lives is that you also learn how easy it is to take them."

"That's horrifying."

He shrugged. "Now do you see why I don't think you'll keep your mouth shut?"

Oops. "Sure I will."

"I've been lied to by plenty of patients, Annie. I know when someone's telling me the truth and you, my dear, are fibbing."

Dr. Dick might be crazy, but he wasn't stupid.

"Were you the one who trashed my apartment?" I asked, hoping to keep him talking.

"I'm surprised you could tell," Dr. Dick said in a disapproving tone. "Really, my dear, you should tidy up more often. Your apartment was a mess."

"I like it that way."

"One of your kind neighbors let your 'uncle' in the building's front door, and then I simply picked the lock. Young women should be more careful. I needed to know what you were up to. You're awfully curious for a faux finisher."

"We're like that."

"It's a pity," he said ominously.

Our soggy foursome slogged its way up the hill. I spied the stack of Civil War cannonballs and flirted with the notion of clonking Dick on the head with one, but couldn't figure out how to distract him long enough to pry one loose from its mortar. I imagined myself kneeling in the mud pawing at the cannonballs while Dr. Dick blew me away.

"Annie, take comfort from the fact that you will go to your heavenly reward knowing a priceless masterpiece has been saved. It will be discovered with your bodies, and repatriated to Italy where it belongs."

What a dick.

As we neared the crest of the hill I thought I saw something move. But the clouds were low and visibility was poor, and try as I might I could make out nothing more inspiring than silent, stone angels.

All of a sudden a large brown head popped up from behind the Gandolfi family monument. *Pete!* My friend gestured incoherently and ducked back down as Dr. Dick whirled around. He eyed me with suspicion and I tried to look defeated. It wasn't much of a stretch.

"Where is it?" Dr. Dick demanded.

"A little farther," I said, remembering that Pete had planned to meet his mother, Evangeline, his cousin Catiz, and assorted Bosnian relatives to work in the cemetery today. If I could stall Dr. Dick for a few more minutes we might get out of this alive.

Over the pouring rain and the rumble of thunder I thought I heard a car approaching. A big white truck emerged from a rain cloud, sped up the hill, crossed a patch of grass, and slid to a halt on the hill above us. Billy Mudd jumped out of the cab.

Dammit! The odds were bad enough before, but with Billy here—

"Dick, you piece of *shit*," Billy snarled.

Dr. Dick aimed the gun at him, and grabbed me by the arm. "Stay out of this, Billy. I've got everything under control."

"Like hell you do. Let these folks go. This has gone far enough."

Well, who knew? The Evil Developer had a conscience after all.

I had hoped Dr. Gossen and Roy would seize the moment to escape, but both men were rooted in place, gawking. One would think they'd never been kidnapped at gunpoint before.

"We're on the same side, Billy," Dick said in a soothing "there, there, Doctor'll make it all better" voice. "Go home and let me take care of this. I'll call you later."

"Dick—"

"We've got a lot of money wrapped up in this project, Billy, and so far your role has been on the up-and-up. It would be a shame for you to be implicated in this."

Billy seemed to hesitate.

"Ask him about Cindy Tanaka, Billy," I said.

"What about her?" Billy replied.

"She didn't kill herself—" A pistol jammed into my side and I fell silent.

"Shut up!" Dr. Dick screamed. "Shut up or I'll—"

A pot of plastic flowers flew past his head, and Dick swung around and started firing wildly at fog-shrouded memorials.

"Take cover!" I yelled, and wrenching my arm from Dr. Dick's grip I dove behind Billy's truck. Dr. Gossen and Roy scrambled to join me, Billy jumped behind a headstone shaped like a weeping willow, and Dr. Dick staggered under a barrage of stones, sticks, dead flower arrangements, a pair of pruning shears, a broken rake, several sprinkler heads, a Mr. Igloo cooler, and at least three pairs of athletic shoes. I could have sworn a Civil War–era cannonball or two sailed past. Only the fact that none of my Bosnian friends had grown up playing America's favorite pastime saved Dr. Dick from severe head trauma.

I heard a rumbling sound, and in the blink of an eye part of the path and hillside gave way with a great *whoosh*. Billy's truck creaked and groaned before rolling onto its side, wiping out several small headstones and clipping Billy, who clutched at the grass briefly until the truck started sliding downhill, dragging him with it. I heard Dr. Dick laughing until the ground collapsed beneath him and he too was carried along as the mud slide picked up momentum. For a split second I thought Dr. Gossen, Roy, and I would be spared, but a sudden jolt beneath us had us slipping and sliding, groping and grasping. As we tumbled down the hill I grabbed for something solid, digging my nails into a man's skinny leg and getting clocked in the mouth by someone's elbow. We slid ten, twenty, thirty feet. Everything was dark and wet, so slippery that it was impossible to gain purchase as rocks and stumps, branches and headstones plunged down the steep hillside, creating a solid wall of mud. I felt myself doing somersaults and couldn't tell which end was up, so I concentrated on holding my breath and trying not to panic. As they said in the '70s, *go with the flow*.

After what seemed like an eternity the slide slowed and finally stopped. I scraped the mud from my eyes, spat out a mouthful of muck, and took a deep breath. We had been deposited at the bottom of the hill, near the main cemetery gates. Flailing around and trying to stand up, I felt a mass of sludge settle in the rear of my overalls and tried not to think of the graveyard effluvia that encased me. The clinging mud made it hard to move, so I rested for a moment and took in the scene. Billy's truck was lodged at the base of a large oak tree, and on the edge of the slide zone I saw Helena run out of the cottage and take a swing at Mama Pete, who ducked and started walloping the docent about the head and shoulders with a muddy bouquet of plastic daisies. I heard Pete and Evangeline calling my name, but hesitated to reply in case Dr. Dick was near, prepared to shoot me for the sheer joy of it.

Ah, chérie! You are fine, non?

Yes, Grandfather. For the moment, anyway.

Quel soulagement! *And ze Raphael?*

Merde! I plunged my arms into the lake of mud, searching for the cardboard tube containing the precious painting. A few yards away Dr. Gossen sat shaking his head and looking befuddled. Rain had washed the mud from the professor's face, and the paleness shone in the dim light.

"Are you hurt?" I called out.

He shook his mud-caked head.

"Help me, then! We need to find the tube with the painting!"

We crawled around the slide zone, feeling for the tube.

"I found something!" he shouted.

I slithered toward him and together we excavated it. It wasn't the cardboard tube. It was an arm.

I did a quick head count. Billy Mudd was resting near his truck, Roy Cogswell was being assaulted by an outraged Bosnian mother, and Dr. Gossen was with me. The arm belonged either to a disinterred body or to Dr. Dick.

"Annie!"

"Pete! Over here!" I called. He, Evangeline, and Catiz slogged through the muck and helped us dig out the body.

"You hokay, Annie?" Evangeline asked, her mild blue eyes worried.

"I'm fine, thanks. I'm so glad you guys were here."

"No kiddin'. We was about to leave 'cause of the rain, but we thought we'd wait and see if it cleared up. Whoa! This guy's a goner, ya ask me."

"Dick!" I heard Helena scream. "My darling Dick!"

"Did you call 911?" I shouted, but she ignored me and ran full-throttle toward us, fell to her knees, and started pawing through the mud.

"We need something to dig with," I said to Pete.

"We will get." Pete spoke rapidly to Catiz, who sent a hovering cousin to fetch the tools the Bosnians had brought to clean up Potter's Field. With the aid of shovels and trowels we unearthed Dr. Dick. Helena threw herself on him, sobbing, and I pushed her aside to see if he was alive. I thought I felt a thready pulse but he was unconscious.

"Get help!" I said, and as Pete bounded off toward the cemetery office I turned on Helena. "*Now* don't you wish you'd called 911?" It was a cheap shot, but considering her beloved husband had intended to murder me—with her endorsement—I thought I was entitled.

"Everyone! Listen up! This is extremely important. We're looking for a cardboard tube, the kind posters come in. It's got to be around here somewhere."

Leaving Dr. Dick to the ministrations of his beloved Helena, the rest of us fanned out across the slide zone to search for the missing Raphael. I felt a tightening in my chest, which meant either I'd inhaled a lot of mud or I was starting to panic. Even if we found the painting, the odds of being able to restore the damage wrought by tons of mud and graveyard debris seemed overwhelming.

"I've got it!" Billy yelled, holding up a muddy tube. "It landed in the cab of my truck."

Bien fait, *chérie,* my grandfather whispered. *Ze great Raphael would zank you eef 'e could.*

"Jeee-sus, wouldja get a look at my truck?" Billy muttered as we sat on a bench outside the columbarium.

After giving my statement to a bone-weary Detective Hucles, I had called Frank from the office. He arrived in an armored car and whisked *La Fornarina* away, promising to take it straight to Donato Sandino at the Getty Museum. The Italian fake buster would unleash the battery of restoration skills he'd mastered during the Arno River flood to repair any damage Raphael's masterpiece may have sustained.

I watched Pete, Mama Pete, Evangeline, Catiz, and several other cousins gesticulating energetically as they gave their statements, and wondered if the cops would be able to figure it all out. An ambulance escorted by a squad car had taken Dr. Dick and Helena away. Dr. Dick was alive but just barely, and I'd heard the EMTs puzzling over the terrible third-degree burn on his thigh. The vial of sulfuric acid must have been crushed during the mud slide. *Let that be a lesson to you, Dr. Dick,* I thought. Nobody messes with the little baker girl.

Miss Ivy, who'd had the presence of mind to call the fire and rescue squads when she heard the hillside give way, was distributing warm blankets and mugs of steaming coffee. It wasn't Peet's, but at the moment it was manna from heaven.

It was still raining, but at this point clean water could only help the situation. The straps and bib of my overalls sagged, and the mud-filled pants rode low on my hips. I'd been trying to scoop the muck out of them, but this proved hard to do and still remain a lady.

A flatbed truck rolled by, hauling the contorted mess that used to be Billy's pickup.

"I'll bet your insurance covers it," I said. "You know, mud slides, acts of God . . ."

Mudd glared at me with a baleful expression.

"I have to confess that I was surprised when you came to our rescue, Billy. Don't take this the wrong way, but I never pictured you as one of the good guys."

He shook his head. "Cindy and I met here, you know, when she was photographing some of the crypts. I know it's kind of weird, but sometimes I just sit in this cemetery, and enjoy the peace and quiet." He paused and his voice lowered. "I thought Cindy killed herself because of me. Because of *us*. I've got a wife and kids. What the hell was I thinking?"

That Cindy was young and pretty and adoring?

"Never again," Billy said, his chin thrust out. "It's the straight and narrow for me from now on."

I was skeptical, but who was I to say? I'd read that *Fatal Attraction* had driven an entire generation of philanderers into temporary fidelity. If a movie could inspire better behavior in an audience, then perhaps the murder of a young woman could reform Billy's character.

"You couldn't have known what Dr. Dick was up to, Billy," I said. "He fooled all of us."

"Maybe so. But I'll never know, will I? And Cindy paid the price for my mistakes."

There wasn't much to say to that, so we watched the crowd begin to disperse and the squad cars leave. One of the cops signaled that we could go.

"Well," Billy sighed. "If you'll excuse me, I've got an appointment with a marriage counselor."

Now that it was safe to return to my apartment, I was looking forward to a long, hot shower. Assuming hot water was available. At this point, I'd settle for a long, cold shower. Anything to remove this clinging mud.

I was searching my bag for my truck keys when Michael approached, twirling a huge yellow-and-black-striped umbrella on his shoulder. He was dry and gorgeous and smelled as delicious as ever. He lifted one foot onto the bench and leaned on his knee.

"This is probably an inappropriate thing to say, under the circumstances, but that wet T-shirt you're wearing is making me hot."

"You're incorrigible," I said with a reluctant smile. "How did you know I was here?"

"The mud slide's been all over the news. I figured if there was a natural disaster you had to be involved."

"Thanks a lot."

"Plus, Frank called. He asked me to tell you that Sandino's crew is at LAX waiting for him to arrive with the painting. They're as eager as a heart transplant team."

I smiled, relieved. Now that Sandino had the original Raphael, both the painting and my grandfather were safe. For the moment anyway.

"The Italians are offering a nice reward for the relatively safe return of their national treasure. You can afford to go hang out on a beach in Hawaii for a while, see how much trouble you can get into amidst coconut oil and mai tais," Michael said.

"Loitering in the Louvre is more my style," I replied. "But any reward money should go to the columbarium. They were the ones who kept the Raphael secure all these years, and they need the cash to preserve Potter's Field."

"You did good work, Annie," Michael said. "I'll make sure the right people know."

"We were lucky," I said, shuddering at the memory of Raphael's great masterpiece buried beneath tons of mud, degrading by the soggy second. "It was nearly destroyed."

"As your illustrious grandfather is fond of saying, close only counts in horseshoes and hand grenades. If not for your quick thinking, who knows what might have happened."

"Dr. Dick said he was going to give it back to the museum."

"And you're taking the word of a homicidal doctor?"

"I guess you're right."

"Of course I'm right. I'm always right."

"Listen, I've been thinking," I said. "You say there's good money in the art retrieval business?"

Michael looked surprised. "Let's put it this way—you'd have to paint half a lifetime to earn the equivalent of a single reward."

I mulled that over. Working at the columbarium had taught me that life was short. I was thirty-two years old, owned a successful San Francisco faux-finishing business, and still had to work like a dog to make ends meet. When I started True/Faux Studios five years ago I'd known it would never be a gold mine, but I hadn't realized how all-consuming it would be. How much longer would I be willing to sacrifice all the other joys life had to offer—a dog, beach vacations, a mortgage—just to scrape by? Unless I landed a sugar daddy, won the lottery, or joined my grandfather in the family forgery business, I would spend the next thirty years laboring away with little to show for it.

"Would this business involve graveyard mud slides and homicidal physicians?" I asked.

"So far it's pretty much about e-mails."

E-mails sounded good. I could handle e-mails.

"I wouldn't want to give up my studio."

"You wouldn't have to. Just cut back on the jobs you don't want to do anyway."

"And we'd be partners?"

"Absolutely."

"I want sixty percent."

He laughed. "Twenty-five."

"No way."

"Thirty."

I glared at him.

"Forty-five."

"*Fifty*-five, plus business cards engraved 'Kincaid and Johnson.'"

"Johnson and Kincaid."

"It was my idea!"

"Kincaid and Johnson sounds like we sell men's clothing."

"Fine. But I want *genuine* engraving on the business cards, not the cheap printed stuff."

"Your name in raised type, eh?"

"Yup."

"Done."

"And you have to get rid of the *Whistler's Mother* graphics on the Web site."

"Hey! People love the dancing grannies."

"Not me."

"Okay, a fifty-fifty split, engraved business cards, and due respect for Whistler."

Frank was sure to have a hissy fit when he heard. But I had a few choice arguments to counter with, not the least of which was the fact that DeBenton Enterprises had been employing the dreaded Michael X. Johnson of late.

"Let's do it."

He nodded and gave me a crooked grin. "I'll let you in on a little secret, Annie. I don't know that much about art."

"That's supposed to be a secret?"

"So we have a deal?"

"Deal." I held out my hand and we shook.

"One last thing," Michael said, his eyes lingering on my wet, sticky T-shirt. "What's your policy on workplace fraternization?"

"In your dreams."

"Sweetheart, you have no idea."

Author's Note

All the human characters in *Brush with Death* are fictitious, but some of the nonhuman characters are very real, and worthy of special mention.

Chapel of the Chimes. Oakland's Chapel of the Chimes provides services as a crematorium, columbarium, and mausoleum—but its neighbors know it as a historic landmark that welcomes visitors with open arms. Founded in 1909, the columbarium has undergone numerous expansions and changes in response to the evolving needs of the surrounding community.

The illustrious architect Julia Morgan—most famous for her work on Hearst Castle—took over the design of the building in 1926, reworking older areas and adding new sections inspired by the dramatic Romanesque Revival and Gothic styles she loved. Morgan worked with local and Old World artisans skilled in concrete tracery, ironwork, and the decorative arts. Natural elements are echoed in stained glass, mosaic, and murals; complex groin vaults, quatrefoil windows, and Byzantine designs abound. What she couldn't find locally, Morgan unearthed in her travels—sumptuous historic decorations were brought over from Europe and

seamlessly integrated into Chapel of the Chimes' tranquil
maze of intimate, unique chapels and chambers.

The cyclical nature of life and death is reflected in the elements of water, sky, and lush gardens included throughout
the columbarium. Morgan also installed innovative electric
skylights that are still opened on sunny days to invite in the
light and air. Even today canaries are kept to sing near the
fountains, and when the skylights are open wild birds swoop
in to enjoy the gardens.

After Julia Morgan's retirement in 1951, Aaron Green, an
associate of Frank Lloyd Wright, was hired to design an addition to Chapel of the Chimes. Though the new section is
distinct from the old—with majestic, sweeping rooms re-
placing the older, more personal chambers—Green included
many elements from Morgan's decorative designs. Here,
again, the elements of garden, sky, and water are prominent,
and are reflected symbolically throughout the columbarium
and newer mausoleum sections of the building.

Despite yet another expansion in the 1970s and 1980s,
Chapel of the Chimes retains its intimate appeal. Located at
the end of Piedmont Avenue, the columbarium offers con-
certs, recitals, and holiday celebrations, and invites the public to enjoy its history and beauty. Chapel of the Chimes is
not associated in any way with the neighboring cemetery,
and any and all details about financial issues and business
matters are entirely fictional products of the authors' imagi-
nations.

La Fornarina. La Fornarina, by Raphael Sanzio of
Urbino, is a real painting residing in the Palazzo Barberini, at
the Galleria Nazionale d'Arte Antica. Any and all insinuations
that it was replaced with a copy are purely fictitious and were
fabricated for the sake of the story. Otherwise, the painting's
history is accurate as represented within these pages. *La*

Fornarina, or "the little baker girl," is an exquisite painting of a young woman whom Raphael may very well have loved and even secretly married, though there is still a great deal of controversy over this interpretation. The botanical symbols of fertility in the background were indeed unveiled during a recent cleaning, as was a small ring on her finger that is believed to have been painted over posthumously by Raphael's students in an effort to avoid speculation over the lady's identity . . . and her relationship to the artist. Raphael died on his thirty-seventh birthday, shortly after completing *La Fornarina.*

Annie's Guide to Marbling

Try this at home!

"Marbling" was popular in the eighteenth and nineteenth centuries, especially in the European colonies, where wealthy residents hired itinerant artists to mimic expensive marbles and semiprecious stones on trim carved out of cheap, locally available woods. Today's faux-finishing techniques can lend the beauty and formality of stone to any paintable surface, from furniture to fireplace mantels to entire walls . . . even cars!

Standard Beige Veined Marble

Marbling Supplies:

Base Coat: Off-white, beige-gray semigloss alkyd interior house paint

Glazes:

  White glaze: 2 parts white or cream alkyd interior house paint, 1 part glaze medium, 1 part thinner

  Tan glaze: 2 parts tan alkyd interior house paint, 1 part glaze medium, 1 part thinner

Artist's paints: Burnt umber, raw sienna, mars black, and Davy's gray

Note: Paint color choices depend upon the stone you want to mimic! Feel free to experiment with lighter glazes on a black background, for example.

Other Supplies:

Very soft, dry, three-inch paintbrush
Thin "liner" artist brushes for veins
Feathers (Goose are great; any large enough to paint with will do. Don't buy them—I pick them up off the ground.)
Clean cotton rags or cheesecloth
Cotton swabs
Mineral spirits
Glaze medium
Protective gloves
Plastic dishes, shallow bowls, or palettes

Before you start:

Study. Look at real samples of the stone you wish to mimic, and note how the veins run, how mottled the background is, and the variation in color and texture. Many marble and stone distributors have broken tiles or parts of slabs that are free and readily available. Some will even chip off little pieces of slabs of special stones, or offer inexpensive samples.

Decide whether you want a polished finish, which means that the colors are deeper and shiny (as though wet), or a honed finish, which looks matte and almost dusty, and not as colorful.

Prepare the surface. Sand or spackle so that the surface is as smooth as possible if you are going for a "polished" look.

If you are a free spirit (or lazy, like me) simply transform surface imperfections into marble veins, pits, and splotches.

Paint the base coat. Apply base coat and allow it to dry thoroughly according to the manufacturer's directions. Remember, other colors may be used for different effects, such as black for Tinos Green or Red Levanto marble, orangey-red for Rosso Verona, dark beige for travertine limestone. No need to stick to nature, either: your imagination is the only limit. Just remember that the base color will show through and provide your background color.

Marbling:

First of all, protect your hands with gloves!

Create a mottled background texture over base paint. Wad up a cotton rag or cheesecloth and wet it with mineral spirits and a little glaze medium. Dab it into a small amount of white glaze poured onto a palette or plastic dish. Gently roll the wadded cloth onto the surface in a random fashion, creating uneven "drifts" over the entire surface. Step back occasionally and make sure you aren't unconsciously creating patterns or forms that look like worms or circles.

Soften blotches. Using the three-inch paintbrush, *lightly* pass the bristles over the white to soften the effect. If you want to add other colors, now's the time. Let the colors drift into one another, but don't mix them.

Repeat process with the darker tan glaze.

Apply veins. This is the fun part! Using your feather or artist's liner brush, dip it into the tan glaze or thinned artists' paints and apply a series of squiggly lines that come together and then flare apart. Leaving your wrist loose, hold the feather or brush as lightly as possible. Let it flop around, creating a wonderfully chaotic line. Note how veins run in real marble: generally from one side to another, in a nervous, fidgety line, *not* in a criss-cross grid pattern. Follow along the sides of your drifts of color.

Soften. Using the dry three-inch paintbrush, lightly brush over wet veins in both directions, allowing the wet paint to smudge and drift.

Revein. Now go back in and pick out some strong veins where you will reapply paint. Marble usually has faint, deep veins, and a few that are obvious and close to the surface. Pick these out. Use the cotton swabs to push from under and over the veins, thinning them in some areas, while allowing for girth in others. Add splotches of strong white veins in some areas.

Vein with mineral spirits. Wetting an artist's liner brush in mineral spirits, run along some sections of the drying paint to "open" areas. As you apply the solvent, the paint will pull away, allowing the base paint to show.

Protective finish. The surface does not need to be sealed unless it requires extra protection, as on the floor or in the bathroom, or if you wish for a high-gloss polish. Note that light, white or cream marbles will "yellow" if you apply an oil or mineral-based varnish; use a water-soluble one instead. Amber shellac can also be used over surfaces where a mellowing amber is an advantage, such as golden marbles. A "honed" look can be accomplished by adding a little chalky white paint to a matte sealer before application.

Suggestions:

Don't feel constricted to mimicking real stone. Paint offers limitless possibilities—that's the fun of it! Try outlandish color combinations; sprinkle gold or silver metallic powders into topcoats; drift in little flakes of metallic gilding papers.

Cut a potato into crescents and uneven round shapes. Press these into glaze or draw with their edges to create "shells" as found in fossil stones.

Be sure to stay random! This is the hardest thing for beginning faux finishers, who create unconscious patterns in their painted finishes. Step back from your work often and assess it from a distance.

Feel free to add more and more layers of glaze and veining—this will increase the rich, deep sense of stone.

Let veins and drifts of color run off the visible plane—don't end everything at the corner of the wall or side of the panel. Make it look as though the marble was cut from a larger piece of stone.

In vast areas such as entire walls, apply an overall glaze and use newspaper or bunched-up plastic bags to create a less detailed marbleized texture.

Have fun!